THE KILLER MEET

The bird's head separated from its body. A perfect hit. But where was the gunman?

"Von Kelsing." The voice came from behind him.

The industrialist spun around. He knew the voice was neither Reiser's nor Schmidt's. His two companions were, in fact, frozen in their tracks. The voice without a face was bouncing off trees and rocks in every direction. Von Kelsing looked hard at the trees on the edges of the hunting ground. Nothing moved.

Then came a deep laughter, a mocking laughter, bounding off the surfaces of rocks and trees in all directions. The disembodied laughter rose higher in pitch. Von Kelsing found himself out of control, screaming, "Stop! Stop!" Then he heard the high-pitched screech of Bruno Schmidt. Reflexively von Kelsing moved to whirl around a second time; he found to his amazement that he was unable to turn. Another human being, rock hard, straight as a steel girder, stood fast against him. Von Kelsing felt the stranger's breath against the back of his neck. Then, he spoke. The voice was an American voice, an eastern voice, hard and cynical.

"What's your problem, von Kelsing? I made it on time, didn't I?"

"Are you Dartley?" asked von Kelsing.

"Dartley sent me," replied the stranger. "You can call me Savage."

THE CRIME MINISTER

by
Ian Barclay

WARNER BOOKS

A Warner Communications Company

WARNER BOOKS EDITION

Cover design by Gene Light
Cover photo by Dan Wagner

Warner Books, Inc.
666 Fifth Avenue
New York, N.Y. 10103

 A Warner Communications Company

Printed in the United States of America

First Printing: December, 1984

10 9 8 7 6 5 4 3 2 1

Chapter One

The refrigerator was late. Colonel O'Rourke at the PX in Vogelweh had promised an early-afternoon delivery. Now, with only fifteen minutes before the entire von Kelsing entourage was scheduled to leave for midnight mass at the Düsseldorf Cathedral, the only Christmas gift Werner von Kelsing had waiting for his wife Mitzi was his late mother's six-carat pear-shaped diamond. He'd had it reset as a dinner ring, but what was the fun of it? Mitzi didn't even like diamonds. The daughter of a leading Zurich banker and a natural blonde, she preferred gold. She claimed diamonds made her look prematurely old; hence, the refrigerator. All during August at their Berchtesgaden retreat on the Austrian border, she had complained that only the Americans knew how to combine decorator colors with modern technology. What was the point of her redecorating her country kitchen with slate floors and paneled mahogany cupboards, she kept harping, if she was going to be forced to plunk a "hospital white" refrigerator in the middle of "my beautiful, dark, exotic wood?"

A new friend of the von Kelsings was Jennifer McAdams, the Scottish-born wife of the American commander at Vogelweh. Vogelweh, outside of Kaiserslautern near the industrial Saar, was the largest military housing base in western Europe. After two months of listening to Mitzi, Jennifer had finally heard enough about American refrigerators. One day, she handed von Kelsing a Sears catalogue and suggested he buy his wife a refrigerator for Christmas. If it had not been for Jennifer McAdams he never would have thought of it. She had shown him an eighteen-cubic-foot Kenmore frostless with an automatic ice-maker and two crispers listed at $499.99. With all the available discounts, she thought her husband could have it delivered in cocoa brown, von Kelsing's choice of color, for under two fifty. Jennifer had foreseen no problems. When and where did he want it delivered?

The refrigerator was to have been delivered at the tradesmen's entrance by 3:00 P.M. The only delivery had been a basket of fruit. He could not reach Jennifer McAdams. She was in Texas with her husband, en route to a rodeo at the Houston Astrodome.

Perhaps the color had been wrong. Perhaps the driver had been sent back to the PX for another refrigerator.

But who in the entire von Kelsing household had spoken to a driver with a brown refrigerator from Vogelweh? His major domo, Albert Maier, had contracted swine flu and was bedded down under doctor's orders in his apartment over the old stables. His English butler, Edwards, had by previous arrangement been given the entire week off so that he could join his dying sister in Surrey; Herman, the valet, who was the acting butler, insisted that the only delivery, aside from the fruit, had been a last-minute order of garlic sausage from the Decker farm for Christmas breakfast. As for his wife, von Kelsing did not dare question her. Mitzi's perversity was such that she could easily have opened the crate, decided cocoa brown was not mahogany and sent it back. Worse, she might have concluded that "poor Werner" should not be allowed the pleasure of surprising her; he had cruelly allowed her to suffer the absurdity of a white refrigerator all summer long.

No, he was overreacting, von Kelsing decided. On instinct, he called his plant manager. That was it. They had probably delivered the refrigerator to his plant by mistake.

"Herr Bertold, this is von Kelsing."

"Happy Christmas, mein Herr."

"No, no, no, Herr Bertold. Listen to me. There is a refrigerator. I ordered it for my wife from the American PX, the military post exchange in Kaiserslautern. Vogelweh. In actual fact, General McAdams ordered it. It is a Sears, Roebuck product, a Kenmore refrigerator."

"I am writing all this down."

"Yes, a brown refrigerator."

"Brown?"

"Are you having trouble hearing me, Herr Bertold?"

"Nein, mein Herr."

"This refrigerator, brown, cocoa brown, was to have been delivered to my house by three P.M. General McAdams is now on holiday in the United States."

"Perhaps there was an accident."

"You will call the main office, Herr Bertold, the main office for Sears and Roebuck. It is in Philadelphia."

"Ja, mein Herr."

"It is still afternoon in the United States, Herr Bertold. The Sears and Roebuck offices are still open, do you understand?"

"I will find the refrigerator."

"Very good, Herr Bertold."

There was a pause.

"How are things, Herr Bertold?"

"We never stop, mein Herr."

There was another pause. A longer one this time.

"And the absentees?"

"I am waiting for the midnight shift."

"I am not talking about the midnight shift. I am talking about the third shift. The evening shift. How many absentees?"

"Almost ten percent. In the restricted area it is closer to twenty. Even Herr Rosenfeld called in sick."

"Herr Rosenfeld?"

Herr Claude Rosenfeld, a French Jew of German parentage, was the world's leading authority on laser weaponry. Von Kelsing–Schmidt's laser research project, subsidized in part by a secret NATO fund, was under the strictest security. Claude Rosenfeld, to von Kelsing's knowledge, had never been sick, not once. To von Kelsing he was the epitome of the German Jew, the world's most disciplined mind with its most passionate commitment to scientific truth. The Fuhrer had made his most serious mistake in eliminating the German Jew, von Kelsing had often confided to his oldest friends, Bruno Schmidt and Willi Reiser. In his opinion Hitler should have confiscated their wealth and left it at that.

"What is Herr Rosenfeld's sickness?"

"He says he has the influenza."

"And the others?"

"The same."

As he hung up the receiver, von Kelsing smiled a bitter smile. Influenza. What did they take him for? Farmer Decker?

It was the drugs. The thought of Claude Rosenfeld on drugs, too, if that was his problem, made von Kelsing break out into a cold sweat.

In the early seventies the Germans had laughed at the Americans, so recently their military and technological masters. The Yanks had first damaged their economy and then wrecked their national morale with their romantic, idealistic war in Vietnam. Afterward, they seemed to be drowning their sorrows in an ocean of narcotics. Documentary films spoke of two hundred thousand heroin addicts in New York City alone. Germany, of course, was different. It had always been different. Normally, von Kelsing did not dare resurrect the term *master race* except in the company of old cronies from the Third Reich. In any case, there was no need to overstate the obvious; the postwar miracle of modern Germany spoke for itself. Regardless of the Marshall Plan and the International Bank, the Germans, like the Japanese and—although von Kelsing was loath to admit it—the Jews, were a superior race. The national character was self-evident: clean, stubborn, resourceful, hardworking, self-sacrificing. They were a forceful, extroverted people not given to perversity such as chemical addiction. Alcoholics were despised, and why not? Why coddle weaklings? Why glamorize negative images?

By the late seventies the picture had changed. Narcotics were a national epidemic. Pure heroin was available to any German who wanted it. Cocaine addiction, once the privilege of the outmoded aristocracy, was now commonplace among the professional classes. Lesser-known drugs such as "angel dust" and the various amphetamines infected the school-age population, causing outbursts of violence unseen since World War Two. Random murder was no longer unknown.

The drug issue was, at the very least, economic. The Teutonic nation, which attributed its awesome industrial strength to an almost mystical capacity for hard work, could no more survive a pervasive drug culture than could the Imperial Chinese. At the beginning of the twentieth century, whole masses of the Chinese populace wasted away in opium dens; their general stupor contributed to the collapse of a three-thousand-year-old civilization. Eventually, by the early 1950's, Chinese narcotics addiction necessitated the drastic measures of Mao, who brought order out of chaos with execution squads.

In the case of West Germany in 1981, there was no mystery as to cause and effect. If narcotics were responsible for the gradual unraveling of the national will to live, the Turks, by common agreement, were the villains of the piece.

The Turks. At first, they had traveled to the industrial north as seasonal workers. At first, as with part-time employees everywhere in the capitalistic world, there had been advantages for employer and employee alike. The young men from the south, strong but barely literate in either language, had worked for lower wages than their German counterparts. Furthermore, they expected no medical benefits, no pension plans. Best of all, they were in no position to organize into trade unions.

Then reality reared its traditionally ugly head. The fantasy of the hardworking immigrants, however much validated by the industry of the majority of Turkish workers, gave way to a harsher truth. Thousands of illegal aliens had no intention of returning to the slums and oppression of Istanbul; these malcontents formed pockets of squalor in the poorer neighborhoods of Frankfort and Cologne, Munich and Düsseldorf.

Then OPEC, the predominantly Arab oil consortium, doubled the price of crude oil in the late seventies. The American economy, which, like it or not, was the free world's financial bellwether, faltered, gasped and began to run out of breath. Inflation soared to almost 20 percent. Comparisons with the Great Depression of the early 1930's grew louder. In the developing countries such as Argentina and the banana republics of Central America, economic panic found outlets in political oppression, police torture and military seizure of liberal publications. World hunger was at a crisis point. Every day ten thousand people reportedly starved to death.

In the Ruhr Valley of West Germany, once so confident of its technological superiority, the Turks were the labor force first affected by the labor reversal. They were in no position for bank loans. Strong men without formal education in a host country that worshiped schooling, they were at best semiskilled workers. To complicate matters, they were ignorant of *Hochdeutsch*, high German, that most precise of languages. Failing a return home, they had one alternative to despair, the traditional occupation of desperate men—organized crime.

First there were the protection rackets, squeezing their own countrymen who owned and operated small restaurants and *pensions*, mostly bed-and-breakfast places. The West German police, when notified, were unduly unconcerned. The Turks began to grow more aggressive and more confident.

As the eighties began, they began to work in gangs that grew in range and competence. Prostitutes appeared on the streets in growing numbers. At first, the lure was German girls; then girls of mixed ancestry fathered by foreign workers in the early and middle sixties began to make their appearance. Dark-eyed blondes with dusky Mediterranean skin were especially prized. Unfortunately for the Turkish pimps, German prostitution was, by definition, a limited market. Getting laid for free was not that impossible. In the wake of the so-called sexual revolution, the average fraulein was more than willing to experiment with the average herr.

Drugs were the next logical step. Marijuana. Hashish. Cocaine. Morphine. Heroin. Angel dust. The fields of Anatolia in eastern Turkey were bright red with poppies, the natural source of heroin and a traditional cash crop of the Middle East.

There was more. Bulgaria, that most subservient satellite of Mother Russia, was the natural way station between West Germany and Turkey. It served as the perfect haven for the international black market. Arms and ammunition, mainly from Communist countries, could be safely sold to brokers for the Middle East, for Turkey, for the various European terrorists. A stockpile of American and Japanese cigarettes, watches, tape recorders, cameras and electronic toys sat waiting for buyers from the politically explosive lands bordering the eastern Mediterranean. Bulgaria, typically, did little to maintain or support democratic concepts of law and order. Foreign diplomats or narcotics and customs officials raised their objections; the Bulgarian bureaucracy, however sympathetic it pretended to be, was invariably and unavoidably hamstrung. And no wonder. In 1981, Israeli intelligence, for one, asserted publicly to *The New York Times* that 80 percent of the huge hoard of weapons and ammunition that its army captured from the Palestine Liberation Organization in Lebanon had reached there from the Bulgarian port of Varna on the Black Sea.

In international circles, many diplomats did not wish their names to be used for fear of the KGB. They believed that Bulgaria, that most orthodox convert to Soviet Communism, considered anything bad for the West, such as drug addiction among the young, especially the young workers in the aerospace and weapons industries, to be a boon for the Soviet bloc. These diplomats were typically unwilling to take a strong public position against Communist methods for fear of being labeled red-baiters, McCarthyites, Fascists, and anti-Communist fanatics. Privately, they believed that a long history of entrenched western liberalism among the leading intellectuals prevented the Bulgarian problem from being seen for what it was. "It is impossible for the traditional American liberal to believe in the existence of evil. This is why Soviet Communism will eventually devour the West," commented the French attaché in Sofia, M. Rambouillet, to a visiting Pulitzer Prize–winning American journalist.

Turkish authorities estimated that six or seven major Turkish smuggling rings protected by the KGB operated out of Sofia. The currency black market allowed smugglers as much as triple the official rate. Agents and carriers of the drug trade lived cheaply and handsomely at the Vitosha–New Otani off Leningrad Square. That Victorian-Palladian hybrid, granite-gargoyled, gold-carpeted, red-glassed, Venetian-chandeliered monstrosity was jerry-built onto the new revisionist addition, a twenty-story stucco cube with yard-long fluorescent lights glaring in the gray corridors. But at least the plumbing worked. There were hot showers and Johnny Walker Red. The hookers in the casino shaved their armpits and chewed chlorophyll mints. All things considered, the Vitosha–New Otani beat American narcs and the nonexistent Moscow nightlife.

The biggest traffickers never saw or touched the actual heroin. According to official reports, they had other fish to fry. Like arms smuggling, illegal foreign currency and fiscal evasion—avoiding taxes and import-export duties. Some of them even had legitimate businesses.

By the late seventies, a single personality had begun to emerge from the lengthening shadows of West German crime. His name was Ali Ozker. He was the biggest trafficker of them all. On the surface of course, he was the most legitimate businessman. In fact, in the judgment of most experts on both sides of the Atlantic, Ozker laundered almost two billion deutsche marks a year, the proceeds of his heroin dealings in West Germany, through his legitimate businesses there. Nothing about his businesses, mostly cars and electrical appliances, suggested the madness he brought to ordinary people's lives.

Ozker had been born on the Turkish-Iraqi border in 1934, the son of an impoverished watchmaker. By 1980, his history, however vague in spots, was well known to Interpol. For a businessman not yet fifty, his resumé was impressive. So was his appearance. A big-headed, bull-necked man with hooded black eyes and cleft chin, Ozker was all of five feet four, with outsize shoulders and large, muscular hands. He looked like a Mongolian wrestler. A small army of Milanese tailors, world masters of sartorial disguise, were unable to lend him the touch of class he was desperate for. He preferred English jackets, camel hair and Donegal tweed with suede patches at the elbows, to the dark, pin-striped three-piece suits the general public associated with organized crime. He had no intention of looking like a common criminal.

Ozker was a noted womanizer. Rumors placed the number of his illegitimate offspring at seven. His legitimate heirs, a boy, 8, and a girl, 10, were the children of his third wife, a former nightclub singer from Beirut. There were also vague reports of an older boy by a first wife, born in the late fifties and now in medical school.

According to his own accounts, Ozker had left

Turkey at 19 after impregnating the 16-year-old daughter of a small factory owner. He had settled in Munich, where he seemed able to start several import-export businesses with loans from outside the country. In 1970, at the age of 35, he moved to Zurich, Switzerland, where he founded the Opal Watch Company, one of the first manufacturers of digital computer wristwatches. In 1977 Ozker bought a 30-percent share of the Poseidon Shipping Company in Istanbul, claiming he needed to diversify: Japanese watches were seriously cutting into the Swiss watch business. By 1980 he had phased out his other interests and had settled in London. There, with 80-percent ownership, he began his own shipping company, the Konstantine Maritime, which owned and operated four ships ranging from 24,000 to 52,000 tons and which flew the Panamanian flag of convenience. He also owned a twelve-room motel in Jamaica and a thirty-six-unit apartment house, the Ataturk, in Istanbul.

According to Interpol, NATO Intelligence and the CIA, Ozker, beginning around 1977, began to use his various companies for narcotics trafficking and arms smuggling. Swiss Interpol intercepted phone conversations between Ozker and known heroin dealers in Istanbul, especially with Arturo Zaloom, a Syrian, his second cousin. Zaloom had known links with Middle Eastern arms smuggling and with every drug dealer in West Germany.

In the beginning, for industrialist Werner von Kelsing, the rise in employee absenteeism, only 6 percent in 1977, seemed appropriate to the times.

Generally speaking, the foreign workers had saved him money. So, too, von Kelsing understood that West Germany, like most capitalistic nations, was changing. In the past, the small-town folk drank hard liquor only on major holidays, and at funerals and weddings, if then. Now they spent greater and greater amounts of their leisure time mesmerized in front of their television sets drinking vodka, Scotch, American whiskey and Caribbean rum. The muscles formerly spent on soccer fields and in hobbies such as carpentry were now beginning to atrophy. The industrial bosses took some consolation, however, that the minds once preoccupied with trade unions and radical politics were now involved in following the plot lines of American soap operas and situation comedies.

At first, von Kelsing did not believe the statistics about the rising use of cocaine and heroin, even when three alleged pushers, Turks, were arrested and subsequently deported in the spring of '80. But his absenteeism rate was now 12 percent and buttressed by notes from doctors attesting to ailments ranging from arthritis to the flu. None of this "illness" could ever be corroborated in the plant infirmary. Then the inevitable happened. In July of '81, during yearly checkups, fourteen workers, including three engineers, were found with track marks on their arms. During the following summer at different times, several employees, six in all, either went berserk on the job or broke down with uncontrollable weeping and had to be hospitalized overnight.

It was the discovery of his wife's addiction that had turned Werner von Kelsing completely around.

At first, Mitzi's problem, morphine dependence, had escaped him entirely. True, their not infrequent rows had stopped abruptly for no apparent reason. Typically, he took little notice of her outside of their bedroom. There, as of late, beginning in September, he had egotistically assumed that her almost blithering swooning was some kind of sexual breakthrough. He had imagined that he was the occasion for her orgasmic happiness. Still, by the middle of the month he had begun to notice that, when they made love, she never addressed him directly. Mitzi was somewhere else. At the peak of her orgasm, her mind would wander. She'd call out to dead boys she had loved who had been killed in the war. Then, in mid-October, while Mitzi was on a shopping spree in Paris with two of her sisters, her Bavarian maid, Maria, asked von Kelsing to follow her upstairs to his wife's dressing room. There, in a locked drawer behind a stack of Italian *Vogue*s was at least a month's supply of the heroin derivative, in glass vials neatly stacked like artillery shells.

"What are you showing me?" he asked.

"If you don't believe me, mein Herr, take it to a chemist. He'll tell you what it is."

Von Kelsing had hoped against hope that some down-at-the-heels physician was responsible for this turn of events. He had fantasized launching a major media assault on the unscrupulous German medical establishment, with subsidized documentaries on the profit motive in medicine. His own evidence, using a private detective, established clearly that Mitzi had become addicted through her circle of women friends. Her daily companions were mostly upper-middle-class wives with industrialist husbands and their own inherited wealth. Their source of supply was unmistakable: the growing number of drug dealers, mostly foreigners, mostly Turks. All this was happening in the Ruhr Valley where these once devout women had raised their children and worshiped their God with something resembling happiness. At least, that is what Werner von Kelsing chose to believe.

In the background, Mitzi von Kelsing and her two sisters, Ursula and Magda, were helping each other into their magnificent greatcoats. These fitted floor-length coats were black brocade with sweeping sable collars. Black on black. The coats had been a gift from their late mother. By tradition the sisters wore them only once a year, to midnight mass at the Düsseldorf Cathedral on Christmas Eve. Mitzi was staring at her husband with a particularly blank gaze. Von Kelsing wondered if she knew where she was. So far, he had said nothing to her about his discovery. He was, after all, a gentleman of the old school. He had no intention of embarrassing his wife. At the beginning of the month he had embarked on a different route.

He called Herr Bertold again. He had to be

paged: he was obviously looking for the brown refrigerator.

"I will be at the cathedral for midnight mass, Herr Bertold. I expect the matter we spoke about to be resolved when I return."

"Ja, mein Herr. I'm sure I'll find it. In the meantime, happy Christmas."

"We shall see, Herr Bertold, we shall see."

As he hung up the receiver a second time, Mitzi was standing next to him, an odd smile on her lips, her eyes half focused.

"Werner, what are you doing, talking on the phone now?" She giggled. "We're late. Don't you know what it means to be late? Haven't you ever been late?"

He looked at her, wondering about the source of her need. Perhaps it was her religion. After the war, he had converted to Roman Catholicism against his better judgment. It had been a smart move politically, perhaps. Now his only son, Arne, had been thoroughly indoctrinated by the Benedictine monks in Munich. Before leaving for his teaching job in a mission school in Ecuador the previous spring, Arne had explained to his father that he was now a spiritual member of the "Third World," as he called it. He wanted his father to know that he had absolutely no interest whatsoever in taking over the reins of von Kelsing–Schmidt.

"Go to the car," he ordered his wife. "I have one further call to make."

"Schotzie, we don't have time..." his wife began, starting a familiar harangue—except this time her voice kept slipping into a high octave. Her sisters thought this was very funny.

"Go to the car," he repeated. This time his tone was angry. This time his wife obeyed. With the help of Herman, the valet, the three women trudged out into the porte cochere where the Mercedes 600 was waiting in the clear black night.

Von Kelsing's Rolex said eleven forty-five. It was precisely the time he and Willi Reiser had agreed upon two hours before when they had last spoken. This would be their eighth phone call that day. This time, more than a brown refrigerator was unaccounted for.

"Willi?" Von Kelsing's voice was almost inaudible.

"I'm here, Werner."

"Well?"

"They can't find him."

"We should never have paid him so many deutsche marks up front."

"Maybe he's late, Willi."

"Late for what? For Ozker?"

"Ozker is back at the Hotel Vitosha. He arrived in Sofia at four twenty-five on Tuesday on Lufthansa Flight thirty-nine. My sources are absolutely accurate."

"Maybe Mustafa followed him to Sofia."

"Mustafa was to have completed the job by Monday night."

"I'm going to call Bruno."

"Bruno doesn't know any more than I know."

"I still want to speak to Bruno."

"Whatever you say, Willi."

Willi Reiser. Bruno Schmidt. Werner von Kelsing.

The three friends were leading industrialists. They had been in the SS together. Unlike veterans of the other countries, they did not attempt to wax nostalgic about their days in uniform. With respect to the Second World War, they had an unspoken agreement that the best course of action was to get on with their lives. And of course, as before, as always, they never questioned that those lives were inextricably bound up with the destiny of the Fatherland.

Behind the perfect, chiseled features, Werner von Kelsing's computerlike brain was ice cold and as ruthless as a pit viper's. It functioned irrespective of social rituals and the casual behavior occasionally required of a member of the lower aristocracy.

Von Kelsing–Schmidt had been founded by his grandfather, a Prussian soldier turned chemist who perfected smokeless gunpowder in the 1880s. Under his determined grandson, Werner von Kelsing, it grew from western Europe's largest manufacturer of small firearms into a technological conglomerate producing laser weaponry, satellite missiles and the hardware of computerized warfare. The main plant in Düsseldorf, where von Kelsing lived, covered twenty acres. Eleven thousand employees, mostly engineers, worked round the clock at all aspects of research and manufacturing.

Bruno Schmidt, 64, von Kelsing's partner, was the grandson of Ernst Schmidt, a speculator in the

American steel industry; Schmidt had saved von Kelsing in the panic of '94. Afterward, the two names and the two families were inextricably linked. Due to the shelling at the battle of Stalingrad, Schmidt was partially deaf. Still, as with Willi Reiser, his loyalty was absolute, his generosity unfailing. In some ways Bruno Schmidt embodied the German soul. All von Kelsing had to do was ask him, and Schmidt would have handed over his life.

Willi Reiser, 61 like von Kelsing, was the founder and owner of Schiller Pharmaceuticals. He had named his company after the author of *William Tell*. He himself had an aversion to being recognized, possibly because of the disfiguring facial scars he had sustained when his Luftwaffe craft crashed over Leeds in 1943. The son and grandson of chemists, Reiser developed the first tranquilizer in 1948. Ten years later it was the best-selling drug in Europe. By the sixties, after American duplication of his product, he had diversified into cancer drugs. He was the tenth-richest man in West Germany.

After he had discovered the morphine in Mitzi's dressing room, von Kelsing began to meet periodically with his two friends. At first, they met two or three times a month, and then more frequently. They met in his cellar, one flight down from his billiards room. On the other side of an armor-plated door marked "Storage—Keep Out" was an underground shooting gallery. His father had had it constructed during the 1920s. He wanted to perfect his skill as a marksman in the local boar and pheasant hunts. The gun rack was filled with hunting rifles ranging from antique front-loading Schuetzen caplocks with curly brass inlays to a new Remington Model 7 carbine; there was an FG42, a forerunner of the modern assault rifle and an ominous-looking *Maschinenpistol* .38 never designed for killing deer. A Kar 98 taken from his uncle's body at Ypres in 1915 was mounted on a side wall over a small brass plaque explaining its origins. For target practice von Kelsing enjoyed using the pistols he had collected during *his* war, the war Germany would have surely won if the Fuhrer had not gone berserk consulting astrologers and gassing Jews.

"What are we to do?" he had often asked Bruno and Willi elliptically as he blasted the black cardboard cutouts of bears and pigs that moved on a belt across the target area. Reiser and Schmidt would typically mutter, "Who knows? Just shoot, Werner," as if their tension were caused by not enough physical exercise. The three friends knew better. By Oktoberfest they were still meeting in the shooting gallery, except now it was clear to all three of them that they were there to do more than lament the decline of the West. They had to make plans.

Their first objective: to rid the Fatherland of the accursed narcotics trade. Their first target: Ali Ozker. But how? The three men were pushing retirement age and they were celebrities of a sort; their comings and goings attracted attention.

Finally, in the first week of December, a plan

began to take shape. Twenty years previously, when he was in the thrall of his short-lived religious conversion, von Kelsing had taken pity on one of his Turkish workers. The man's 3-year-old son in Ankara was slowly dying from a congenitally defective heart valve. At his own expense von Kelsing had had the boy flown to the De Rossi clinic in Zurich. A team of German and American doctors performed successful open-heart surgery. The Turkish worker in question, a scrawny welder named Cemel Demirel, had literally fallen to his knees and kissed von Kelsing's feet, promising him he would do anything he wanted. According to Mitzi's version of the story, although he himself did not remember it, von Kelsing had helped the teary man to his feet with the prophetic words, "Ah, my friend, who knows in the end which one will need the other more?"

Two decades later, Cemel Demirel was a local crime boss in the Düsseldorf and Hamburg area, a kingpin in numbers, pornography, prostitution and, it was rumored, drugs. In the beginning, Demirel had been deported four times. He had once served eighteen months in Spandau prison for attempting to bribe a cabinet minister and then committing perjury about it on the witness stand. In the end, he was too valuable to too many people.

When the two men, the crime boss and the industrialist, met again after almost eighteen years on the Kaiser soccer field to the west of the city, their respective drivers, each armed with Walther P5's, stayed with the limousines. It was midnight. Demirel was now overweight, with the bulbous nose of a man afflicted with gout and heavy drinking. His black eyes reflected no light. They were as hard and as impenetrable as coal. Finally, von Kelsing spoke.

"I want Ali Ozker dead by Christmas."

Cemel Demirel was too shrewd to play dumb. He listened and said nothing.

"I will pay you twenty-five thousand marks now. If that is too little, say so."

Demirel peered into von Kelsing's face as if he were looking for something. The Prussian's eyes were ice blue and, although cold, absolutely readable. Every emotion registered in the slightest, almost minuscule widening or narrowing of his pupils. Because of this condition, von Kelsing had learned to adopt a squint when he was negotiating. Still, even in the dark December night, the Turk was able to read the pain in the industrialist's face.

"Mein Herr, you are not asking me to kill an ordinary man. You are asking me to kill the king. If I fail, and if Ali Ozker discovers the origin of his assassin, he has the power to kill my family, both here and in Ankara."

By the end of the month, von Kelsing, in remembering his meeting with Demirel, would know that it was at that exact moment, Demirel's split second of self-doubt, that he should have gone elsewhere. He had underestimated the power of ethnic loyalties, particularly among displaced persons in a hostile land. And he had not done his homework. Ozker was Demirel's principal supplier of heroin, and although Demirel looked closer to 60, the two Turks were the same age.

That was not all. The little boy the father had worshiped had grown up into a spoiled ne'er-do-well, a failed musician. He was now living in London with no intention of ever coming home again.

There was a long, uncomfortable pause. Finally, by sheer force of will, von Kelsing broke the ice.

"Besides, with Ozker out of the way, you will be in a position to take over."

There was another pause.

"Mein Herr, I'm afraid my ambitions are somewhat limited."

Yet another pause followed.

"But if this is your request, I am a man of my word. I will do as you ask. Ozker will be dead by Christmas."

Von Kelsing produced an envelope, which Demirel waved away.

"That will not be necessary, mein Herr."

The two men shook hands and walked back to their waiting limousines.

Ten days later, on Thursday, December 18, at 11:00 A.M., a 22-year-old Turk, Mustafa Gürsel, wearing a fake beard and an ill-fitting navy blue Pierre Cardin suit, waited in the crowded lobby of the Vitosha–New Otani. He sat in a faded red velvet armchair staring at the December issue of *Paris Match*, pretending to read an article on Princess Caroline of Monaco. A bulky attaché case sat on his lap; a Heckler & Koch *maschinenpistol* HK53, secure in its shoulder holster, bulged slightly under his suit. Gürsel was waiting for Ali Ozker. The crime boss usually left his room before lunch for a half-hour walk. This information had come from an Ozker bodyguard, a second cousin of his named Raoul. Raoul volunteered information about his boss almost by way of bragging. He never suspected he was part of an assassination plot.

"Do you ever get any exercise?"

"I get exercise."

"You must have to stay indoors all day."

"What do you know about it?"

"I hear Ozker never moves a muscle except when he eats and fucks."

"I wouldn't know."

"I'll bet you wouldn't."

"I'm with him all the time. He takes a walk every day before lunch!"

So that became the plan, to gun down Ozker in the lobby, then to throw a canister of tear gas to confuse the bodyguards. Mustafa's motorbike was propped up outside the side door waiting to take him to the Turkish quarter of Sofia. Within a half hour of the murder, with new identification papers and a disguise, he would be driven to Istanbul. To all intents and purposes he would be the beloved cleaning woman of the Suleiman family returning from her week-long holiday.

A hotel porter, red braid on his black felt jacket, approached Mustafa. He carried a note on a silver tray. Mustafa felt cold sweat trickling under his Dacron shirt.

"You are Mustafa Gürsel?" asked the porter.

"I beg your pardon," answered the Turk, feigning ignorance. Who could know him here?

"I have a note from Demirel. Will you take it?"

The note read, "The job has been canceled. Come upstairs to Room 1756." It was signed "Demirel" in his familiar scrawl.

Without hesitation Mustafa went to the elevator. He still carried his attaché case with the steel canister inside. As he pushed 17, his palms were wet.

Upstairs, two swarthy giants unfamiliar to him flanked 1756. When he approached, one of them confiscated his attaché case, the other his gun. Only then was he allowed to enter the room.

The two-room suite, 1756, had beige walls and brand-new Danish Modern furniture; it looked like a government office. Still, there were differences. The pungent odor of marijuana almost made him choke. Its smoke blurred his view of the men sitting on the far side of the room next to the aluminum-cased windows with the shades pulled down. Popular Turkish music with its ongoing wail issued from a Sony lying on the twin bed nearest to a squat, broad-stomached man. It was Ozker. Who else? The large, heavy-lidded frog eyes and the swollen-looking lips were unmistakable. He sat jacketless, a thick pistol Mustafa could not identify in a shoulder holster strapped over his Buddhalike bulk. There were several bodyguards, Mustafa's cousin among them. He stood in the corner bug-eyed with disbelief.

There was somebody else. A familiar shape. He sat on the end of the bed, his hands folded in his lap, his head slumped down like a politician who has just lost an election. It was Cemel Demirel.

"Come in, Mustafa Gürsel," said Osker in the gravelly tones of a heavy drinker. "Mr. Demirel was just telling us about you. You sound very interesting. I thought we might all take a drive in the country and discuss your future plans."

At the Düsseldorf cathedral, at the Consecration of the Mass, the Cardinal lifted up the von Kelsing chalice. It was encrusted with sapphires and emeralds. Von Kelsing had personally presented it to the prelate when he converted. In the candle-light it was dazzling. The Cardinal intoned, "This is my blood. Take ye and drink." Von Kelsing noticed that Mitzi was nodding off; saliva was drooling from the corner of her mouth.

"Poppa," she called out in a monotone.

Von Kelsing gestured to his wife's sisters. "Let's get out of here."

"Excuse me," he whispered to the couple at the end of the pew. "My wife is ill." It was the von Kelsing pew. Why were strangers sitting in his pew?

The party of four left by a side aisle. Mitzi's head was lolling back and forth like a spastic's. She was smiling broadly, a gurgle of sound playing around her lips. By the time the three black-brocade-enshrouded sisters arrived at the vestibule of the von Kelsing mansion, Mitzi was in tears.

"Forgive me, Werner, I took an overdose—of Valium." And then she giggled. Uncontrollably.

From the front hall, von Kelsing noticed there were strangers in the house. Workmen. He recognized their *Plattsdeutsche* slur. Herr Bertold, his plant manager, was there too. Offering apologies to the women, von Kelsing excused himself. He made for the darkly paneled drawing room; it glowed with twinkling miniature lights. The packing crate for the refrigerator was perfect. Mitzi would never guess the contents.

"Yes, the refrigerator," he affirmed to Herr Bertold.

"Yes, mein Herr, I finally found it in the damaged goods section in Building F. Very strange. Shall we take it out of the packing crate?"

"No, no, no," insisted von Kelsing. "This is a surprise. Just loosen the front part."

"I've already loosened the front part. And see. I made a hole in the bottom for the electrical cord. It is already plugged in."

"Danke schön. That will be all."

"Danke schön, mein Herr."

"Wait, Herr Bertold."

"Is something wrong?"

"No, no, no. Here. Very good. Very good." Von Kelsing handed Bertold and the other workmen what loose bills he had in his wallet.

"Happy Christmas."

"Happy Christmas, mein Herr."

On their way out, the workmen passed Mitzi and her two sisters. By now they had seen the coffin-shaped crate and were eager to inspect its contents.

"Is that for me, Werner?" Mitzi giggled. "Can I guess?"

"Oh guess," ordered Ursula.

"It's the new greenhouse," rejoined Magda.

"Greenhouse?" said Mitzi. "No, Werner is too practical for a greenhouse. This is a cedar chest for my winter clothes. Oh no, wait; there's a humming sound. Ursula, listen."

As the three women leaned forward to listen, the packing case creaked.

"It's a bomb!" joked Ursula. The three women laughed with abandon at their own private humor.

As Mitzi opened the packing case, a panel of iridescent cocoa brown was immediately visible. She knew at once what it was.

"Oh Werner! Magda, look! Look, Ursula! My refrigerator! My refrigerator! For Berchtesgaden. Oh Ursula, look. Frost free. Kenmore. See. The American cocoa brown. Nobody cares about my kitchen but the Americans. Oh Werner, how did you know?"

"Open it, Mitzi."

Giggling, Mitzi von Kelsing opened the refrigerator door.

Her scream was piercing and uncontrollable.

During the war Mitzi had been protected from horror. She and her mother had stayed with her maternal grandparents, who were Swiss, in Lucerne. She had been privately tutored. She had learned to draw with pastels. Every day she had sketched the trumpeter swans.

The bottom shelf of the refrigerator held the severed legs of a man, the black knee socks still on them, the carnage stuffed into the cramped space. The middle shelf was crammed with flesh—a torso and arms, presumably of the same man. The black blood coagulated like blackberry jam. On the top shelf was the head, the dead black eyes staring in front of him. His severed penis protruded from his mouth like the head of a strange, sightless albino snake.

It was Cemel Demirel.

The stench was overpowering.

Quietly, von Kelsing shut the refrigerator door. Leaving the hysterical women behind, he went to call Bruno and Willi.

It was war.

Chapter Two

The choice of an assassin was short and sweet.

The three months preceding that choice were another matter entirely.

The day after Christmas, von Kelsing sent his

wife to the Landau Clinic in Wiesbaden. She was under heavy sedation. Her sisters, Magda and Ursula, went with her. They'd been sedated, too. Although von Kelsing had warned the doctors at the Landau Clinic of his wife's drug dependency, they reacted to that information with indignation.

"That is *your* opinion."

Von Kelsing's agreement with the doctors was that Mitzi would, with the best available medication, "rest." A week later, a Dr. Sauter called him to say that his wife's sisters had been caught smuggling morphine into their sister's suite. Did Herr von Kelsing wish his wife to be released from the hospital? Did he wish the staff to restrain her?

Von Kelsing opted in favor of restraint. As a result, on January 10, Mitzi suffered a complete nervous breakdown. She lost control of her neurological functions; could no longer speak. She drooled like a spastic, moaning and pounding her head against the floor.

Von Kelsing immediately flew by helicopter to Wiesbaden to his wife's side. When he arrived, he found a living corpse. Her vacant, bloodshot eyes stared unknowingly at him. He broke down into sobs at what his life had become. How could he leave her to hire an assassin?

For the first time, nothing made sense to him. He began to blame himself. For Mitzi. For their son. For the Fuhrer, for the defeat of the Fatherland and, most of all, for his own old age. Everywhere, it seemed to him, he had lost control. The longer he stayed at the Landau Clinic, the more he stared into space like his wife. He could not even pray. Who had ever answered his prayers?

With von Kelsing in Wiesbaden, Bruno Schmidt sought his own order. To begin with, he tried to fire every Turk at von Kelsing–Schmidt and replace them with less-qualified German workers. The repercussions were immediate. The editor of *Das Stern,* a personal friend of his, called.

"Bruno, you will hand the country over to the Socialists."

After a long pause, Schmidt thanked his friend. He returned to work in a great depression. Everywhere there was defeat. First the Fuhrer; now the spirit of a great nation was under the control of Communists and foreigners. What could he do? It broke his heart.

In February, Mitzi was recuperating at Berchtesgaden. Von Kelsing had turned the kitchen into a greenhouse and filled it with tubs of flowering shrubs. He built a new kitchen onto the back of the house. It was bright yellow and white, not a trace of brown. It was, by design, a cheerful place. Mitzi would have to get used to it. By the end of the month she refused to go near it. She refused to eat. She spent her days sitting in front of a roaring fire, her eyes glazed over, her mind somewhere else. Among other things, their son Arne had refused to return from Ecuador.

By the middle of March, von Kelsing had begun making phone calls.

THE CRIME MINISTER 33

On March 30, the three friends met once again in the gun room in Düsseldorf.

Von Kelsing made his announcement quietly.

"Gentlemen, this time I let our American friends pick the man."

"What man?"

"I am told he is the best assassin they have. He will come from America with false identification papers. Nothing relating to von Kelsing–Schmidt will be on his person. This is strictly an oral agreement. We write down nothing. He writes down nothing. That way, if our man is caught we will not be implicated."

"Is he expensive?"

"They tell me he's the most expensive there is."

"How much?"

"I don't know exactly how much. I suppose a hundred thousand."

Willie Reiser groaned aloud.

"Willi, you get what you pay for and you pay for what you get," said von Kelsing.

"What's his name?"

"His name is Richard Dartley. I spoke with his assistant, a Mr. Whitney, on his phone service. I arranged a meeting between myself and Mr. Dartley at the Greenmountain Lodge in Greenmountain, West Virginia, on Monday, April twenty-fourth. He said the codeword is 'savage.' The meeting place, South Meadow. Don't ask me what that means. Copy it down if you want. It has probably no bearing on anything."

"What about us?" asked Bruno Schmidt.

"What about you? Don't tell me you want to come, too," said von Kelsing.

"Werner, I never get to travel," whined Reiser.

"Oh Willi," joked his friend, "why would you want to go to Greenmountain Lodge? All the men do there is hunt wild game."

At that, the three men chortled. By common agreement, there was nothing they liked to do better than shoot wild game in the early spring. Werner von Kelsing, his two friends agreed, could be so wonderfully funny, especially in the midst of tragedy. He was the best that the Fatherland had to offer.

There really had been nothing to decide.

Richard Dartley had been recommended, off the record, by some of the most powerful men in Washington.

It would be an adventure, they decided.

They could be boys again. Warriors. Huns. In any event it had been too long, much too long, since any one of them had had a chance to shoot wild game.

Chapter Three

"But Bruno darling, you must take me to the West Virginia. I am mad about the American West!"

"This is not the American West."

"You said *West* Virginia."

"Ilse, this is a hunting trip. Just me and Willi and Werner. We are just going to shoot pheasant. No secretaries allowed."

"But Bruno, you don't understand. My favorite movie star was always John Wayne."

"Oh that feels good! Do that again. Ilse. Oh, Ilse. Oh."

Ilse had to stop speaking. Bruno Schmidt's glans was stretched to capacity. The skin of the head of his sixty-four-year-old cock shone like a ripe plum. She had no time to lose. In recent years he did not maintain his erection long. She lowered her well-practiced lips over his hot sexual knob and ran her wet tongue around the bell-shaped flesh. He loved getting head from her. He hated going to the prostitutes on von Traubelstrasse. He resented paying for sex.

When Ilse de Brock, widow of a general in the

Vichy government, had come to work for him in the spring of '79, she had brought with her other talents besides typing and shorthand. At first, Schmidt had not been able to believe his good fortune. Both his wives had been strict, disciplined women, both daughters of minor officials in the Third Reich. Although neither had been particularly religious, they had both been virgins at the time of their marriages. Their idea of sex was to lie naked in bed under the covers, wait for their husband, Bruno, to spread their legs, insert his sexual member and take his pleasure as quickly as possible. His first wife had died of an ectopic pregnancy in the last days of the war. Schmidt had never heard of such a thing—a fetus growing outside the mother's womb. His search for a competent surgeon had been fruitless. The one doctor available had been a Polish Jew working in the von Kelsing–Schmidt infirmary; he was one of ten thousand Jews, mostly Polish, who had been brought in as slave labor. When the two men, Schmidt and the doctor, had first met, he told Schmidt, in the presence of Frau Schmidt, that he was a brain surgeon. Hearing this, his wife had laughed. "It's like having a dog who can play the piano, isn't it?" she said. A week later, on her deathbed, her ridicule had turned to rage. She wouldn't allow the man to touch her. The infirmary nurse, an Aryan, could do nothing but administer morphine and laudanum and pray to a pitiless God. Finally, after hours of screaming about Jews and Americans, his wife had lapsed into unconsciousness. She died of peritonitis. At her funeral, her pastor had referred to her as "our little saint." Schmidt had one overriding memory of her; it was a negative memory at best: not once in their entire ten years of marriage had he dared suggest to her that she suck him off. Unthinkable.

His second wife, a Bavarian, had at first seemed like the exact opposite of the first. She was a happy peasant with big white thighs and a love of the sensual. Or so he had thought. As it turned out, his second wife's love of the sensual was restricted to Rhine wine, Sacher tortes and Strauss operettas. When it came to the bedroom, the woman suddenly turned serious under the sheets. She acted as if she were in church. When he stroked her, she giggled with nervous embarrassment. He was sorry he had ever penetrated her. Their several bouts of lovemaking had only served to strengthen her divorce case; she claimed there was nothing wrong with their sex life. After ten months of marriage, the judge awarded her five hundred thousand deutsche marks.

When Ilse de Brock applied for the job of his executive assistant, Schmidt was at first unprepared for extracurricular activities. With her lean, athletic frame and fitted suits, Ilse was nothing like the maternal figures he had always sought out for sex. She spoke six languages: English, French, German, Spanish, Italian and her native Polish. The truth was, she spoke eight. And her native language had never been Polish. She had been born Ilse Panov, not Panovski, as it said on her resumé. She had been born in Kiev, not Cracow. Ilse de Brock was not what she seemed.

"You give the best blow jobs, Ilse," grunted Bruno Schmidt as she worked two fistfuls of engorged cockmeat up and down over his steel-hard inner shaft. Her flickering tongue never stopped, not for a second.

What had he done to deserve such an angel in his old age? he had often wondered. Ilse was perfect with the clerical workers, gracious with strangers, diplomatic in the worst crises. What more could a man want? He had hoped for nothing more than a good executive secretary, but there was more. With Ilse there was always more. A lot more. She had been with him only a week, he often recalled, when there had been a major crisis. The incoming Reagan administration had announced cuts in the space program. NATO, von Kelsing–Schmidt's secret patron, had regrettably informed the two industrialists that as of 1983 it was limiting its funds on further research of the laser satellite weaponry program. Both von Kelsing and Schmidt, without hesitation, considered laser satellites the next step in weapons development.

Already, despite outcries from American liberals, the communications satellites had made global military control a reality. The possibility of total world annihilation in the form of laser weaponry was scientifically misleading. True, a space laser could easily pick off deadly Soviet missiles before they reached their western targets. It could also destroy Soviet munition dumps, submarine bases and aircraft factories before the Soviet missiles ever got off the ground. Von Kelsing–Schmidt was interested in further possibilities, specifically the technological tie-in of the laser satellites with limitless solar power. Werner von Kelsing himself was convinced that if the firm concentrated on achieving their long-range goal by the year 2000, the West would be able to control all communications and weapons systems on the planet. In point of fact, von Kelsing–Schmidt had been officially assigned the task of focusing and refining only the firing aspects of the satellite. A nameless American firm was working on its computer core. Other anonymous companies in France and England, known only to the Pentagon, were working on the exterior surface, specifically the problem of how to bond titanium onto aluminum. So far, one-hundred-percent heat-resistant metals were still science fiction.

Unofficially, Bruno Schmidt had been working on every facet of the weapons satellite his mind could envisage. It was part of his German nature, he decided—to be the mastermind. The Americans may have won the Second World War, he reasoned, but its most advanced segment, its scientific and technological community, the tiny group that stood between it and Soviet domination, were 99-percent men of British and northern European stock. Despite the feminist hysteria in America, American women had done practically nothing to advance its standard of living. They were mostly concerned with their own pleasure; mostly, they had contributed to the breakdown of the American family by neglecting their children to embark on careers that provided them more dollars to spend on fashion, cosmetics, cigarettes and alcoholic beverages than the gross national product of all African and South American countries combined. The great masses of the American *schwartzers*—the colored peoples, blacks and Hispanics—were basically a demoralizing, draining force. They provided superior performers in popular music and sports; in their pure form, however, they were unlikely to produce a Beethoven or a Bach for another millenium, if then. As for sports, what superior people had ever made sports the end-all and be-all of their lives? The handful of so-called black inventors were clearly of mixed race and their actual inventions marginal.

Schmidt was convinced that sooner or later America's great masses of half-educated pre-technological people would spell its doom. When that day came, with the new space technology, mastery of the earth would no longer depend on millions of foot soldiers marching in mud and snow. Schmidt's compatriots Werner von Kelsing and Willi Reiser were in complete accord. By common agreement, the three men had no intention of allowing their beloved country to function as a technological colony of the decrepit American empire.

As Bruno Schmidt's climax drew near, Ilse felt his organ swell in her mouth. She mentally prepared herself for the gush of warm sperm. As always, she would swallow his seed with a smile; lick her lips with a look of great satisfaction; and then she would sigh, "Bruno, Bruno, why didn't we meet when we were young?"

In the critical light of early spring, Ilse was awash with gold. She was naked to the waist, her corn-silk blond hair unpinned. Her breasts were flawless. They hung like ripe pears without the least suggestion of blemish or sag. Schmidt loved to reach up and stroke what seemed to him like pale yellow silk. This woman was the best he had ever had. She was more than a mistress, she was also nurse and nun; she attended to his body, she healed his psychic wounds.

He would never forget the first time that Ilse de Brock had awakened his carnal desire. That incident would forever mark the character of their sexual encounters. He had been brooding in his inner office one Saturday afternoon. It was March 1980. An experimental laser gun had backfired, killing his best engineer. The incident had been immediately classified. The engineer's widow was told that a conventional rifle had backfired. The coroner, as was customary in such circumstances, had been paid off. Schmidt had returned to his stark beige and glass office with a heavy heart. He had wanted only to unplug his phone and drink great drafts of Heineken. To him, a failed experiment was like the last days of the Reich. All reason to continue living had turned into black smoke. He remembered how Ilse had unexpectedly redeemed him. He had trudged through his reception rooms with slumped shoulders. When he saw her, he had ordered her to cancel his appointments for the following week. Then he had locked his door, barricaded himself behind his desk, drawn his full-length draperies shut and buried his heavy face in his big red hands. How his secretary managed to enter his inner office, he never could figure out. In retrospect, Bruno decided that, if she had had a key made without his knowledge or permission to her credit, she must have known by instinct the emotional depths to which a man could sink. Certainly, by entering his private sanctum unannounced, she had risked losing her job. By design there had been only two keys to the dead-bolt lock. Schmidt kept one. His lawyer had the other. Each copy had its own serial number; each serial number was registered at the key company's main office in Bonn.

He remembered looking up, startled, when he felt her warm hands massaging the back of his neck. "How did you get in?" he asked. "The door was not completely shut," she answered. He had distinctly remembered pulling the door shut. He distinctly remembered the telltale click. But when he the boss, the industrialist, turned around to confront the insubordinate assistant, the sight of her naked body instantly roused him from his black depression. Her raw beauty hit him smack in the face like a cold iron fist. Her full lips were glistening, her long nipples stiff with arousal, her thatch thick with blond fur. When he thought about it afterward, he realized that it had mostly been the smell of her cunt that woke him up from his bleak vision of the present state of his divided Fatherland. Schmidt could always smell a woman who wanted sex. Any other man, particularly of his class, would have waited for the telltale signs: the lingering gaze, the casual brushing up of cashmere-covered tit or silk-sheathed tummy against his chest or thigh. Not Bruno Schmidt. With him it was always the musk emanating from between a woman's thighs. The best French perfume from Yves St. Laurent or Chanel could not disguise the body heat of a woman who was sexually aroused.

On the spot he had forgiven Ilse everything. He had decided that perhaps in his black depression he had not completely shut the door. Why would she lie to him? Besides, if she had really made a duplicate of his key, she would not have blatantly exposed her illicit activity to him by using the key right in front of his face.

That had been the first time the Nordic goddess stood in front of him and unbuttoned his belt. Then, as now and all the times in between, she had unzippered him and, without saying a word, lowered her wet lips onto his expanding cock. She always seemed to be ravenous for him, grateful for every moment of sexual intimacy, grateful that he had allowed her sexual release.

Ilse had learned everything at Verhonoye, located in the bleak wastelands outside of Kazan where the KGB maintained a camp for "sexual operatives," agents trained in the arts and science of seduction.

She had arrived at Verhonoye two weeks after her sixteenth birthday.

On the first night, the recruits—about sixty girls, mostly in their late teens—were given large tumblers of sweet wine after supper. They were then led to a large gymnasium and ordered to strip. A full-dress staff sergeant at a stage microphone read a statement to the effect that, when they finished their training, they would have no embarrassment about either nudity or sex. Other than that, there had been no instruction whatsoever. After the military speaker finished reading his statement, the side doors to the auditorium opened and over one hundred air force cadets, all buck naked, bounded into the room and took their sexual pleasure. When necessary, they waited in line. That first night, Ilse had been fucked four times in the space of an hour. She had been terrified. She barely lubricated. But she let none of it upset her. Her first love was the revolution. There was a world to be liberated, workers to be freed from lives of drudgery and exploitation.

Six months after she first came to Verhonoye, she was surgically sterilized at the state hospital in Leningrad. By the time she arrived in London for her first assignment the following year, she enjoyed her mastery of the sexual ritual. She particularly enjoyed the demystification of a basic biological function that had led many women into whole lives of misery.

She celebrated her seventeenth birthday in London in bed with a member of the board of directors of Rolls-Royce, whispering into his ear that she'd never seen an engine factory. He found that most endearing. The next night they made love on the floor of the executive boardroom; between orgasms he showed her classified drawings of the latest Rolls jet engine. Her camera in those days was disguised as a box of face powder. She kept it at the bottom of her purse. No man who'd grown up with a mother dared open a box of face powder after the age of two. Ilse sent the engine plans to the Moscow Center through a contact at the Bolshoi.

As it turned out, the Rolls engine incorporated a new valve that solved the problem of loss of pressure in jet engines. The problem had been responsible for power loss in Soviet MIGs over Korea. There the Russians had lost a disproportionate number of their best fighter planes in dogfights. The planes lacked the acceleration of the American B-52's. Because of Ilse's minor coup in obtaining the plans, the Soviets managed to gain an edge in the battle for air supremacy. The Moscow Center was always amused that almost no American girls were sleeping with top executives of Soviet weapons and aerospace industries. It concluded that there were two reasons for this: one, the Americans considered Russian too difficult a language to master; and two, no self-respecting American girl would go to school to learn how to use sex as an intelligence weapon.

By the time she was 20, Ilse was able to seduce any man except for the most recalcitrant homosexuals. There was a different class of sexual agents for them. Within a half hour of meeting the male she had been assigned to, at what usually appeared to be an accidental meeting in, say, a pub, she had commented on how sexy he was, what a great body he had, what an incredibly powerful personality he possessed, and so on. In fifteen years, only one aerospace executive, a Frenchman at Concorde, had successfully resisted her. He was newly married to a Polish dressmaker who was just as persuasive as Ilse de Brock. This man considered himself to be passionately in love. On his own recognizance, he would not so much as look at another woman, certainly not one who wanted to have sexual intercourse within the first hour of meeting.

During the three years she had been Bruno Schmidt's secretary, the Moscow Center had set her up on dates with visiting American engineers and undercover agents, who at worst assumed she was looking for a free meal.

From time to time, in different beds in different Düsseldorf hotels, she was privy to phone calls to department heads at the Pentagon, the White House, Grumman, McDonnell Douglas, Sikorsky. Because of Ilse, the Moscow Center knew about heat-seeking missiles before the American public did.

Bruno Schmidt came in her mouth. Her hot tongue milked every drop of his sperm. With Ilse, and only Ilse, his orgasms engulfed his entire physical being. He convulsed for more than a minute from his toes to the top of his head. Afterward, he felt flushed out. Clean. She always managed to make him forget, if only for a moment, NATO, laser satellites, plastic explosives and the ongoing paranoia of his oldest friend and partner, Werner von Kelsing. What would he do without Ilse?

"Why don't you take a five-minute bath?" she suggested. "I will draw water for our bath. Up. Up. We will send this suit to the cleaners."

The bath and the change of clothes were now ritual. As Schmidt dozed, the tap water gushed into his private bath, a sunken marble tub for two. Besides Ilse, his bathroom was his one escape. Its entrance was hidden behind the grandfather's clock, the door secured by combination lock. Inside was a large chamber paneled in pink Carrara marble. Antique gold fixtures from a whorehouse in Palermo, Sicily, offered just the right touch of decadence. Just a touch. Schmidt didn't believe in wallowing in sex or, for that matter, in music or art. "A place for everything and everything in its place" was his credo. The bathroom's skylight affirmed his sense of reality. It was semi-transparent bulletproof glass.

Ilse usually had five minutes to photograph the contents of his pockets. She quickly removed her shoes and unscrewed the stout wooden heel of the left one. Inside was a miniature flash camera. She had initially used a cigarette-lighter device with a three-inch shutter release she kept stored in the bottom of a fake cigarette. She had thought she had nothing to worry about. Bruno never smoked—that is, until the day, their third time in the bathroom, when he had asked her from the tub to please go out into his outer office and get him another vodka from the bar. When she returned, she was stunned to find him with her fake lighter in one hand and the fake cigarette with its trigger in the other.

"What are you doing with that?" she had asked in her most casual tone. It had taken her six months of training to maintain an unconcerned tone of voice regardless of the circumstances. Now, even attack dogs had no power over her emotions.

"No, my dear," Bruno had commented, "what are *you* doing with a cigarette? You yourself told me they were bad for one's health." With the cigarette between his smirking lips, he was flicking the lighter, unaware that it did not work. "What's wrong with the lighter?" he remarked, inspecting it at closer range than she would have wished. The cigarette in his mouth was not much better. She noticed that the tobacco stuffed into both ends of the cylindrical paper tube was old and dry. His critique was continuing and predictable. "This cigarette is terrible. How can you smoke this?"

She had to act fast. Grabbing both cigarette and lighter from the surprised industrialist, she cracked, "Give me those! The lighter doesn't work and the cigarette's dried out! I took them off my sister in Munich last fall. She was coughing herself to death. Are you trying to kill yourself or something?"

"Munich? You have a sister in Munich?" he had asked.

"No, no," she had continued, realizing her mistake. "We met there for *Oktoberfest*. My sister lives in South America. Argentina. We don't get along. It was a terrible visit. I'm throwing this lighter away for good before you catch lung cancer."

After that she used the heel camera. So far, thank God, Bruno had not felt the urge to inspect her shoes. Over the previous two years Ilse had photographed hundreds of confidential documents he kept in his inside coat pockets: diagrams of experimental weapons, names of NATO connections, tie-ins with the American Department of Defense. Once photographed, she laid them along with his keys, wallet and loose change on the long white marble dressing table on the far side of the room. Whenever Bruno changed the locks or acquired a new key, she unscrewed her other heel, the one on the right shoe. It contained a fistfull of soft modeling wax, which she used to make an imprint. She then carefully placed the imprinted wax in the bottom of her box of tampons. That was the one place Bruno would never dare investigate. He had a phobia about menstrual blood. She then routinely passed the wax imprints on to her contact in maintenance, Greta Polansky, the first thing in the morning, at 8:30 A.M. Bruno never arrived much before ten, if then.

Greta Polansky, the old woman with the cart carrying dusting rags and disinfectant for the bathrooms, was actually Ilse's superior officer. She had been one of the first female members of Lavrenti Beria's foreign intelligence unit. She had one aim now: to make certain that the Moscow Center off Dzerzhinski Square received every shred of classified information from von Kelsing–Schmidt. So far, she had been successful. The KGB had precise information on every advance in rocket fuels and laser technology. In the past, acquiring the latest small-arms data had never been much of a problem. All the Russians had to do was beg, borrow or steal the gun in question and copy it. They didn't even have to smuggle it out of the country in question. Photographs and precise engineering diagrams could be hidden in a microdot. The microdot could then be glued inside a cigarette or a box of candy.

Other methods used by the KGB to obtain western technology included: using third parties to invest in American, British, and West German companies; planting agents in freight-shipping companies and in customs offices to conceal the contents and the destinations of shipments; stealing advanced equipment at trade shows; and above all, buying outright products legally restricted to friendly companies. Indeed, of all the countries in the free world, West Germany had always been the most eager to sell its technology to Russia. Many German businesses that regularly traded with "Silicone Valley, U.S.A." were cleverly disguised fronts for Soviet interests.

Von Kelsing–Schmidt, however, was a major exception. Both men, particularly von Kelsing, were virulently anti-Soviet. For this reason, Gen. Alexander M. Haig, when he was head of NATO, had seen to it that von Kelsing–Schmidt was awarded whatever it needed for its satellite program. Classified information was almost impossible to buy or sell.

Almost but not quite. Greta Polansky, with only an eight-hour workday in her job as head of the nighttime maintenance crew, worked from midnight to 8:00 A.M., after which she had breakfast in the basement cafeteria, usually by herself. She was perceived as haggard and lonely. One of her front teeth was missing. Her face was worn, her baggy smock beyond hope of recognizable style. It was generally believed that she had lost her entire family, her husband and two sons, during the Second World War. That much was true. What well-meaning onlookers did not realize was that after Greta Polansky went home, she put in her false front tooth, applied lipstick and mascara and removed armfuls of shredded documents from the specially designed rubber garment under her smock. With two assistants whom neighbors thought were her nephews she spent another eight hours piecing together the shredded documents. With this simple method, she had restored most of the correspondence between NATO and von Kelsing–Schmidt. Because she had cleaned the office of the company psychiatrist, she knew whatever alcohol, drug or sexual problems existed in the higher echelon of the firm.

She also knew about the brown Kenmore refrigerator from Sears. The bill had come directly to von Kelsing at his office. It had not been shredded. What would have been the point of that? Greta photographed it with the camera she kept hidden in the rubber pouch; it attached to a belt hidden under her dress. It was a flat camera the size of a box of cigarettes. A square of Velcro on the back of the camera attached itself to a corresponding square inside the pouch just below her navel. Perfect.

"Bruno, Bruno, I have never been to West Virginia. I have never been west of Manhattan. How can you go to West Virginia and not take me with you?"

"We're just going to shoot."

"But I like to shoot."

"Ridiculous."

"Why, because I'm a woman?"

"Because you work for me and you do as you're told. Achtung."

Schmidt, awake again, walked into his bathroom retreat and closed the door behind him. His satisfied cock swung in front of him as he walked toward the sunken marble tub. Ilse was up to her nipples in hot, soapy water. Her breasts bobbed in front of her, perfect globes of flawless gold skin. As Schmidt stepped down into his bath, his cock began to lengthen at the sight of her.

"We won't argue anymore, my love," she announced, reaching up for his hand. "I will do whatever you say." Ilse smiled at him like the adoring mother whose son can do no wrong.

She knew she had nothing to worry about. By the time Bruno and his two friends had embarked for the shoot at Greenmountain Lodge in West Virginia, he would have changed his mind about her being there. By then she would be necessary. The two friends, Reiser and von Kelsing, would be furious, but Schmidt would convince them that he needed Ilse to take dictation, and, more important, she was an expert at relieving tension. Besides, she was only a half-educated Polish peasant, wasn't she, and what difference did it make if she came along?

As she soaped his rampant cock underwater, Ilse smiled. Bruno, grateful for her undivided attention, basked in her warmth. He had no way of knowing that her smile concealed her extreme pleasure at yet another job well done. While he had been stretched out on his office couch in his post-coital slumber, she had photographed the contents of his coat pockets. The round-trip air ticket to Wheeling, West Virginia, by way of JFK Airport, New York, New York, was there, along with the expected refuse: dirty handkerchiefs, crumpled gum wrappers and charge-card receipts.

There was something else. A blank 3x5 file card with the single word *Savage* written on it. What did it mean? The English word *savage* came from the French *sauvage*. It meant "wild, untamed." There was nothing untamed about von Kelsing–Schmidt. Surely the word *savage* was a codeword. Surely it had something to do with West Virginia. She was determined to discover its meaning if it was the last thing she did.

Chapter Four

He did not know who he really was. He never had. There were too many layers and not enough time to sort them out. According to his birth certificate, he was born in Washington in 1945 Richard John Woodgate, the son of Richard Woodgate and Martha Dartley Woodgate. When he was 12, much too late, his mother had told him that he was adopted. Ten years later his younger brother George was working for a D.C. judge; George had access to court records on adoption—illegal access but still access. It was then that Dartley learned that there were documents on just about anyone and that they could be had for the right price. Sometimes you didn't even need money, you just needed to know the right secretary in the right office. By the time they were 25, most of the D.C. secretaries, even the married ones, were beyond careers. They took any attention they could get; they'd do anything for a man they got it from.

His real name, his birth name, had been Paul
Savage. His parents had been teenagers, both children of prominent Washington lawyers. The name
Savage was Irish. His parents were Irish and everything else, Heinz 57 American, mostly of British
and Germanic stock. His birth mother's name had
been Whitney. He didn't look like anything in
particular, strictly Middle-American and tough.
Sometimes, because of his high cheekbones and
his love of the wild, he wondered if he had Indian
blood. By the time he was 20, his face was rawboned and square-jawed, with hooded eyes. The
eyes were light gray-green; "the eyes of an Arctic
wolf" was how one female admirer described them.

In 1982 he was thirty-seven and a little thick
through the middle; that, and his thinning black
hair—which he kept cropped in a Marine crew-
cut, fifties-style—told him he'd never see 30 again;
but he didn't care. He was still tough. He could
still jog ten miles a day. He could still stay up all
night and continue working through the next day
if he had to. He could still come three times a
night if the broad in question really dug sex,
something he'd become an expert on. He'd had to
work at that. He'd learned to avoid women looking
for fathers. It took him till he was 33 before he
could identify a woman, almost on sight, who was
desperate for his thick, hot cock up her cooze.

The Woodgates, his adoptive parents, were from
old Colonial stock. They lived in Chevy Chase,
Maryland, in a rambling old Victorian mansion
with a wraparound veranda. His adoptive mother

was the daughter of a Harvard English professor and a free-floating anthropologist mother who had written several short books on the Zuni Indians of New Mexico. She seemed to spend most of her day planning high teas and weekend cocktail parties with a great crowd of highly principled people in the government. The ongoing discussions—all polite—that Dartley remembered in his childhood ranged from the so-called horrors of the red-baiting Sen. Joseph McCarthy to a habitual sidestepping of the race issue with remarks like "I sympathize with their cause, but I don't know how you can talk about rights without responsibility. I'm not sure the Negroes are ready to take on responsibility. Look at how they destroyed all those rose bushes at Roosevelt High School."

In this milieu he grew up, attended Bethesda–Chevy Chase High School, "BCC," where his grades were no better than average and he played no sports. At home, in the family basement, he pumped iron before anyone ever thought of it. His parents were Episcopal, but by the time he was a senior in high school he'd stopped attending church. By then his brain was overflowing with political theories, most of them confused. Every time a new president was elected, his parents and teachers immediately dubbed the man "an idiot," and scoffed at his pronouncements. According to most of the adults in Chevy Chase, Truman was "the idiot who got us into Korea"; Eisenhower, "that idiot who plays too much golf"; Kennedy, "the idiot rich kid, a frustrated movie star"; Johnson, "the psychotic Texas idiot who gave away half the federal budget to the so-called poor people in exchange for votes. Nixon was "an idiot for not burning the White House tapes; Watergate was his own fault." Jerry Ford was "an idiot who couldn't walk a straight line." In Chevy Chase, to call Jimmy Carter an idiot seemed redundant; "his shit-eating grin speaks for itself," was a common remark; Reagan was an idiot "on general principles."

In actual fact, Dartley's father never said what he thought. He just listened to all his friends and relatives complaining and went about his business. Dartley himself was never too clear on what his father's business consisted of. He knew it had something to do with the government. His mother always said the State Department. Once, only once in twenty-odd years, had he heard the word *intelligence* used to describe what his father did. At the time he must have been 13; he thought nothing of it. He thought his father was making a kind of joke, perhaps an ironic comment on what was essentially some kind of paper-shuffling desk job.

Years later, he understood. By then he knew about how the Central Intelligence Agency, the CIA, had evolved out of "Wild Bill" Donovan's OSS, Office of Strategic Services. The OSS was the first professionally organized intlligence agency set up to protect the United States against foreign spies, notably Soviets who were in the dirty business of stealing every available American military and technological secret. In time, the OSS became far more than what it purported to be, mere intelligence. According to some observers, the CIA was a private army at the disposal of the president. To some, this arrangement, if accurately described, violated the separation of powers and turned the executive office into a kind of closet dictatorship. To other analysts, more critical ones, the agency operated independent of any branch of government. It was, in effect, a shadow regime with its own rules, its own objectives, its own code of discipline. To the most alarmed critics, the CIA was a Frankenstein's monster that needed, by definition, to be destroyed. By the late 1970's, scores of former agency officials were writing "tell-all" accounts, in many cases naming names. The most notorious example was Philip Agee, who labored mightily, it seemed, to name every CIA agent in Central and Latin America. The probability that the majority of these were undercover men, some even double agents whose lives were jeopardized by the revelations, did not serve as a deterrent.

Richard Dartley's father, Richard Woodgate, was, amazingly, among those named. In Washington this book caused no commotion. The general public did not rush to buy an embittered man's exposé of what was considered a right-wing institution. By the late sixties and early seventies, huge masses of the population shared a political philosophy that, in terms of the Johnson and Nixon administrations, amounted to a kind of paranoia. After Watergate, attacks on political institutions were almost fashionable. If Jimmy Carter, that most non-presidential of presidents, had decided to sell the White House on the grounds that a president should live in no fancier surroundings than a factory worker, the country would have applauded. In those days, any evident love of power was suspect, a clear sign of degeneracy.

On September 11, 1976, Richard Woodgate was shot to death on a main street of Buenos Aires. As far as his son knew, right up until the end he never knew that his name was on Phillip Agee's list. He was coming out of the American Embassy to a waiting car. He was shot once in the middle of the forehead by a gunman waiting across the street. The weapon used was an AK-47 assault rifle. A crude weapon for a political assassin. Crude but effective. A Russian gun. AK-47's were supplied by the Soviet to any group of terrorists the Communists suspected might be their link to another country it could control. To the Marxists, two generations from provincial serfdom, Communism was evidently the one true faith, and they would brook no heathens and no heretics.

In *The New York Times* obituary, Richard Woodgate was described as "an American security advisor." Dartley remembered his mother's reaction to that. She had assumed her husband was somewhere in Florida. According to her information, he frequently went to Miami, Key West and other southern cities, including San Diego and Galveston, to meet with Immigration and U.S. Customs officials on what was termed "confidential business." He never discussed with her the exact nature of that business. She had always assumed it had something to do with the drug trade or with Cuba. The week of the Bay of Pigs, in 1961, Woodgate had been away on agency business, in Galveston he had said, but she suspected otherwise. When JFK was assassinated in 1963, he had also been away, to Key West, he said. But when he returned, he said nothing and shed no tears. He acted as if there had been no assassination.

Richard Woodgate had never said anything about Robert Kennedy's assassination, either. He had been home when that happened, but it was the same thing as before. No comment. Martha Woodgate knew her husband knew something, but she did not want to know how much he knew. She knew his lack of emotion was not a question of his suppressing his feelings. Her husband was not a cold man. Disciplined was closer to the truth. After his death, what bothered her more than anything was that he had never told her he was fluent in Spanish. She couldn't imagine being married for thirty-five years to a man who, as it turned out, spent most of his professional life in Spanish countries speaking Spanish and she knew nothing about it. He could at least have had an opinion on issues relating to South America. Again, nothing.

At his funeral the son heard his father described as a "courageous warrior" by the vice-president, no less. It turned out his father had been instrumental in the overthrow of Allende in Chile, considered even by liberals to be a Communist puppet posing as a Socialist. It was not until after the funeral, however, when he read a five-part article, in the *Washington Post* about the CIA in Latin America, that he learned his father kept both an apartment and a mistress in Buenos Aires. When Dartley read that, a pivotal switch clicked in his head. On that morning in 1976, his view of the world forever changed. For the first time, he saw the complexity of life, the layering of reality, the juggling of opposing philosophies as necessary tools of the trade of a man who intended to survive. Gone were his naive concepts of neighborhood and family. Gone his boyhood view of liberal America, a vision he'd inherited from one of his grandfathers, who'd fought with Teddy Roosevelt at San Juan Hill. Richard Woodgate, his murdered father, became for him an internal principle moving and breathing within him. The dull, bookish man he had once scorned now represented to his son the outermost limits of disciplined survival. What had passed for blandness now seemed like a laser beam of concentrated fury. For the first time he saw a new kind of warrior, a real possibility for the life he had always dreamed about.

At first Dartley was not clear who the enemy was. Whoever shot his father for a start—simpleminded student Communists more concerned with destroying their parents than with building a strong society. Dartley knew enough even not to worry about the guerrilla fighters and peasant revolutionaries of Latin America. The overthrow of feudal capitalism all over the globe in countries where a few inbred families controlled whole countries was a foregone conclusion. Technology, mostly American, was ushering in changes in communication and education. Masses of starving illiterates were good for nobody's business. In the meantime, as he saw it, the illiterate peasants didn't even know what technology was. In the southern hemisphere, fervent Marxists, mostly under twenty-five, mostly half-educated fanatics themselves, went around preaching out-of-date analyses of social change. These firebrands failed to tell the peasants about the death camps in the Soviet Union. They neglected to mention how after sixty years of their superior political system, Mother Russia still lagged behind the United States of America. In the United States, the so-called scum of the earth, in less than a century had revolutionized every aspect of human existence, questioning and improving, if not transforming, outmoded forms of medicine, transportation, travel, communication, pleasure, even religion. "The huddled masses yearning to breathe free" had invented the assembly line, the minimum wage, freedom of the press, separation of church and state, mass transportation, the electric light, television, the telephone, Xerox, a jury system predicated on the defendant being innocent until proven guilty, civil rights and, above all, the best-dressed, best-educated women in the history of the planet, women who were well on their way to even greater victories.

By 1980, America was the cutting edge of the arts and sciences. It was the world center for dance, painting and the graphic arts. Still, at the center of liberal thought, those who espoused it were labeled conservative, almost Fascist. In America, patriotism was a dirty word. Whole groups of left-wingers, vocal and politically active, were in total support of the peasant revolutions in the south. The more enlightened among them were frequently the enraged grandchildren of Boston Brahmans and southern slaveholders. Their standard of living and their control of the citizenry seemed far less than what their grandparents had enjoyed. The left-wing heirs frequently lived in one-bedroom apartments with roaches and leaking ceilings reading Marx and plotting their revenge on people who drove Cadillacs. In 1976 Dartley did not own a Cadillac. He owned a secondhand Ford. He had not finished college. He had, however, read Karl Marx several times over. He had also pored over Machiavelli's *The Prince*, and Sun Tze's *The Art of War* plus assorted autobiographical essays by Adolf Hitler, Mao Zedong, Ulysses S. Grant. At the time he concluded that Americans were not interested in grand plans for world society; they were more anxious to invent a better mousetrap. He began to realize how much his countrymen would have to pay for their powers of invention.

In the months after his father's murder, his brain burned with a white-hot flame. Gradually he began to change. At the age of 30, using the money his father had left him, he moved out of his mother's house. He took a one-room apartment over a store on K Street in Georgetown. He began to jog daily on the C & O Canal. He changed his eating habits, cutting out sweets and alcohol. In three months he lost twenty-five pounds. He was razor-thin and all muscle. He stopped smoking. Every day he went to the K Street Library and read for several hours at a stretch. In the evenings he stayed by himself in his room, without a phone, radio or television. He stayed still, listening to the sounds of his body, concentrating on directly experiencing his pulse, his heartbeat, every contraction of every muscle, tendon, ligament. He learned that the key to conditioning is mental attitude. He got so good at it he could almost feel the blood in his capillaries. In time, there wasn't a muscle in his body he could not control at will. As for sex, he learned the value of abstinence and the value of release. More important, he learned when each was appropriate.

After six months he left his apartment and moved to his uncle's fifty-acre farm near Frederick, north of Washington. His uncle, Charles Stuart Woodgate, had come out of World War Two at 20 with a severe leg injury sustained at Monte Cassino. He boasted an extensive gun collection: a South African Mamba; a Fydorova Avtomat rifle, the ancestor of present-day assault rifles; a Lewis machine gun, the first light automatic to be used on a large scale in time of war. He showed his nephew how to dismantle, clean and reassemble weapons from every country that had ever manufactured them, beginning in the latter part of the nineteenth century. By then, Dartley went out into the fields by himself and practiced shooting with every conceivable kind of gun and every conceivable kind of target, from hummingbirds to beer cans to garter snakes to specific leaves on trees. After another six months he was a crack shot. "A deadly eye" was how he described himself.

His uncle was also a gunsmith. He made weapons to order, no questions asked, for anyone who had the money and the correct specifications. He made guns that looked like cigarette lighters and fired one bullet. He made guns that could be taken apart and the component parts put together cleverly fitted into specially designed bicycles, tire irons, aluminum crutches. He even made dart guns. He put silencers on just about every weapon that made a noise. He made special bullets, too, that would explode on impact; they could blast apart the brain of a rhinocerous if they had to. His specialty was bullets with poison tips. The hitmen, gunmen, professional assassins who sought out his services did not want their victims to speedily recover like Ronald Reagan and Pope John Paul II. Woodgate's customers wanted dead men. Modern medicine was making it too hard to die. Charley Woodgate was the best antidote to recovery the underworld had ever known.

The older man counseled his nephew, assessing possible career choices, potential contacts, lines of approach. One thing was clear: Richard Woodgate was no ordinary 30-year-old looking for work. He had a mission to drive out demons, all those self-interested vermin who worked at destroying democracy. Communists were first on the list, drug dealers second. Both uncle and nephew decided that the CIA or the Treasury would be an ideal platform for the younger man's talents. If nothing else, he could help train Third World commandos where the governments in question needed help. There was a hitch. Both men had forgotten that the 30-year-old had done no more than eighteen months of college. His grades had been poor. At the time, the late sixties, he had been continuously depressed and into women and booze like there was no tomorrow.

Then there was Vietnam, a personal history he usually left out of his resumé. Since returning stateside he never thought about it, never mentioned it, tried not to think about it. He had left the army with a general discharge after public bouts of rage. Once he fragged a Vietnamese cook. His grenade caused the small-boned oriental to lose an arm. At the sight of the man's arm blowing sky high into the midair, Dartley had laughed. Then there was Min Sing, the almond-eyed beauty he loved. He had asked Min to marry him. Maybe she thought that the marriage proposal, like the cook's grenade, was motivated by drugs. Maybe she didn't believe him. In any case, Min Sing did the unthinkable. She inserted a razor blade into a cork and wedged the insidious contraption into the neck of her vagina. For some reason Dartley had been drunk that night. His erection was nothing to write home about, not that either parent would have wanted to hear about it. Failing grand passion, he began to finger-fuck her and smelled blood. He was sober enough to remember she'd been on the rag the week before. Thinking she'd picked up some mysterious jungle rot, he whispered, "Oh my God, Min, what have they done to you?"

He pulled out his finger to see it cut to the bone and spurting blood. Within the next minute, a minute he could not recall for many years, he bashed in her skull with the heel of his boot. Min Sing, to Dartley's good fortune, turned out to be a full fledged member of the Viet Cong. Still, the incident registered with his superiors. It went on his record. After that, there was no way he'd ever work for the U.S. Government again except in a time of national emergency.

On his uncle's advice, he changed his name from Richard Woodgate to Richard Dartley, his mother's maiden name. This way he could at least begin to believe he had officially achieved a new identity not completely divorced from the past, but not subject to it, either.

The process of beginning his career as an assassin for hire was a little bit more complicated. It took almost a year. Charley Woodgate let it be known gradually by a casual remark here and there over drinks at 1789 or lunch at Duke Ziebert's that if anyone needed an outside man to do a "serious job," he knew of such a man. The man, he said, was one of his long-term clients and the best eye in the business. "Outside men," as they were called, were sometimes needed when the job in question was so risky there was a good chance the assassin might himself be killed or exposed. Exposed was worse. That way, the Marxist press got in on the act. They were in a great position to sow hatred far and wide against American subversives and capitalist pigs. In the meantime, they were busy breeding a whole generation of assassins in their own countries who would soon be heading for the good ol' U.S. of A. and points west. Still, there were advantages. If an "outside man" got caught; if, under torture, he admitted that he was in the hire of the CIA, Treasury, or the American government, where was the proof? The Agency could say, truthfully, it had no record of him except as a troublemaker with severe psychological problems. In Dartley's case, he would be painted as a loner. His history would be brought to light—the fragging incident, the coroner's report on Min Sing. His credibility would be destroyed.

With Dartley, in the beginning at least, there was no evidence he even existed. His name was unknown. He had no resumé as an assassin. How could he? The lone assassin is by definition a special breed. He can't apprentice to another lone assassin. That would be a contradiction in terms. At the start he has to bluff it—exaggerate his war record, lie about the jobs he's done without actually naming the names that never existed in the first place. His salary has to be low but not too low. Otherwise he'd be broadcasting his fear of the whole enterprise, that or publicly announcing his delusions of grandeur. No one wants to hire a psychotic, no matter how lethal. The risks are too great. Secrecy is the name of the game. Otherwise, why not wage all-out war?

It took almost a year. One day Charley Woodgate got a call from an old drinking buddy saying that there would be another call asking for the name of his "friend." The second call came, as announced. A meeting was arranged. Twelve midnight on the jogging path of the C&O. That night as he waited in the dark for his contact, Richard Dartley felt for the first time, the thrill of his own calculating mind.

Almost without his thinking about it, the gears in his head began to move with cold precision. He heard every noise, saw the movement of every leaf in the wind, watched for the unexpected detail and when he saw it, suspected it as possible evil. In that moment the old truths were gone. The social rituals of the British Empire so dear to upper-class Americans like his parents meant nothing, nothing at all. The great American concern for moment-to-moment feelings, "How are you? Are you too cold, too hot, too uncomfortable?" Gone. All of it. His protracted boyhood, that state of innocence that even Nam, even his father's murder had not been able to eradicate, vanished as he waited for his first order to kill. Dartley was now the agent of Death and the instrument of absolute will. He was free of illusion, free of social constraint. He was, at last, exactly where he belonged. He was his father's son.

Yet, when asked for his name as he met the little man with the round face—that anonymous clerk who paid him that first advance, that first ten thousand dollars—he identified himself as "Savage."

Was it to protect Dartley, to throw his employer off guard, to make himself less traceable? He did not know; he didn't have time to think about it. It just came out. When the little man said, "Mr. Dartley, I presume," in his pseudo-sophisticated way, Dartley said, "No, Dartley sent me. I'm Savage."

The little man, of course, hearing the word *savage*, misunderstood. Dartley could tell by the way he blinked that he'd gone from Bogart movies and the Ivy League down to D.C. on full salary the day he finished law school. "My name is Savage," he repeated. "Dartley sent me. I'm the man. What do you want?" The little man was not sure what to do next. He was clearly from an agency. He wouldn't say which one. The advance money he gave Dartley had clearly been collected over a period of weeks. Some of the bills were dog-eared; others were faded. The money was intentionally untraceable. The man the agency wanted killed was an African Marxist, a student leader at Washington's Howard University, a black institution in northeast Washington. The man was radicalizing the "A" students. Some of them were writing articles calling for the overthrow of "pig democracy." Dartley paled when he saw the photograph of his intended victim's ebony face. Washington was already predominantly black. To him, the pure blacks, the blue-blacks, looked like members of the same family. All kidding aside, he could not tell them apart.

"Why don't you have a black man kill him?" he had asked.

"We decided that at this particular time, it would

be too risky to ask a black man to kill another black man. That sounds incongruous, I know. But the chances of four blacks' saying No before we found the fifth who would do it meant that four black men in Washington would know that the radical's death had not been accidental. Somebody would talk, and then he'd have to be killed. It could get very messy."

Dartley got the hint. He really had no choice. Part of him was crying out to be released from a thankless situation. The deeper part wanted the challenge.

The little bureaucrat with the dumpling face repeated his primary demand. "It has to look accidental. And remember, if you're caught, you'll be killed before you have a chance to talk. We have operatives with the D.C. police."

Dartley wanted to ask, "Why don't you have your fucking policemen kill your fucking African radical?" but he knew the police, above all, did not want the murder traced back to themselves.

He had one month to do the job before the African returned home with almost a hundred thousand Afro-American dollars. Dartley studied the man from afar, attended one student meeting wearing a Roman collar; he was the only white person there. He felt he'd blown his cover. The African radical, he discovered, never left black circles. In fact, he was never without an escort of two or three Howard University students. Most of the students in those days wore dashikis, beads and foot-high Afros. At least, Dartley realized, the

African wasn't as anonymous as he looked in the photograph. For one thing, he was five feet six and solid muscle, much shorter and stockier than the average American black student. For another thing, he dressed in olive brown fatigues, in imitation of Fidel Castro, no doubt. He'd also grown a scraggly beard since his ID photos were taken. In person, Dartley began to see his identifying features; he had hooded eyes that were almost oriental and a complexion that was more burnished gold than black. Dartley realized that his long hours of self-imposed training in his K Street apartment and at his uncle's farm had not been for naught. Black people were as different from one another as leaves on a single tree. It was simply a matter of similarities and observing the differences. It was all skill, just like pulling a trigger. The hit itself was another matter. Murder was no big deal only if you didn't mind getting caught.

Finally, with the help of his uncle Charley Woodgate, he figured out a plan. Disguised as an Arab sheik, with false ID and a forged passport, he presented himself to the African at a restaurant called Zanzibar. He knew from simple observation that the Marxist frequently sat in the back holding court with sharecroppers' sons from Georgia and Louisiana. They found themselves in awe of a man who believed in overthrowing whole governments in the name of history. In his disguise, Dartley's face was bronzed, his hair dyed black, his gray-green eyes hidden behind brown contacts and dark glasses. He brought no visible weapon, knowing for certain he would be frisked by the African's bodyguards. He brought with him a forged check from a Swiss bank made out for the amount of twenty-five thousand dollars. It was signed by a hypothetical sheik, Fassad Ibn Saud.

"I cannot be seen with you," he said in an Arabian accent. "This check is from the man who sent me. You do not know him. We are all in sympathy with Yassir Arafat of the Palestine Liberation Organization. Sheik Saud will contact you again."

"You don't look Arab to me," replied the African, staring at the check, turning it upside down several times over, looking at the back of it as he was forcibly removing Dartley's dark glasses.

"My mother, she was English," was Dartley's reply. "In Britain they call me black. I say I am white. They call me black, so I decide I am black."

"Good decision, brother," said one of the bodyguards.

"Keep your mouth shut!" snapped the African, staring at the check, turning it upside down, looking at the back of it. He was as skeptical as Dartley was cold. Finally he found the flaw. "There is no date," he announced. "It just says 1976."

"Oh," replied Dartley, feigning surprise, "I wasn't sure what day I would find you. I told him to leave the date blank. Give it to me. I'll write in the date. I have a new pen." With that, Dartley took out his specially prepared weapon—what looked like an ordinary Parker fountain pen. With a flourish he removed the cap, checked the point to make sure the ink was flowing and carefully wrote in "September 21." While the African scanned the check to make sure it was the right date, Dartley recapped the pen. In recapping he also turned the barrel sixty degrees. A wire-thin needle three quarters of an inch long extended from the end of the pen. Dartley held the pen in his hand like a cigarette while he pretended to look over the African's shoulder. Then he announced that he'd have to leave for another appointment. After what seemed like an hour, the African got up to shake his visitor's hand. What threat could the Arab be to him? The man had no weapons. If the check turned out to be bogus, no harm done. He had lived with disappointment all his life. With his fountain pen still in his hand, almost like an afterthought, almost as if he didn't know it was there, Dartley threw his arms around the African and embraced him. The needle on the end of the Parker went clean through the black man's shirt into his back. In that brief instant, Dartley squeezed the pen; its middle section was pliable vinyl, not hard plastic. The black man felt nothing. He had long ago stopped feeling pain. The two men parted after making a dinner date for the following week. As it so happened, the dinner never came about. Three days after their meeting, the African died in his sleep of an apparent heart attack after being ill with a particularly bad case of the 24-hour flu. Richard Dartley was back on his uncle's farm, five thousand dollars richer. The Arab paraphernalia and the forged papers had all been burned by then. The extraordinary Parker pen had, of course, contained a special compartment filled with ricin.

The next job came a month later. It involved killing a government witness who was all set to testify against a defector from the CIA. The defector had been unlawfully acting as an arms broker for the Communist guerrillas in El Salvador. Someone high up in the agency obviously did not want the defector prosecuted. In the interests of the Free World, it was decided that the general public should not be allowed to think that any help whatsoever could come to the Communists from an informed American citizen. Years later, it was established that the author of this hands-off policy, an undersecretary, was being blackmailed by the defector. The government witness apparently knew about the blackmailing, too. It seems the undersecretary was a closet queen. He regularly left his wife and family in Bethesda and went up to The Continental Baths in New York for a Friday-evening swim and a little non-political activity.

Knowing none of this, only what he was being paid for, Dartley dispatched the government witness by making it look like a gangland killing. He waited until he was alone at night. Then he mugged the guy, forced him into his car, drove him to Great Falls, tied his hands behind his back, shot him in the back of the head with a .38 with a silencer. He left him in the rapids, facedown. The police assumed it was a gangland killing bacause that's what it looked like. When they searched the man's apartment the next day, they found drug paraphernalia, a couple of half-empty bags of cocaine and a half-empty one-nickel bag of heroin. In 1976 that was enough to suggest the man was not only unstable but overtly criminal.

In the next six years, Dartley took jobs outside the country. By 1980 he was considered one of the two or three best hitmen in the world. So far, he had always gotten his man. So far, he was known to no police force or security agency in the world, not even to Interpol. His strategy was always the same: he moved into the area, usually as an affluent tourist or scholar. He planned his move. He executed his victim. He got out. He did not ever entertain the possibility of being caught and he never was. Never.

There was a catch. Dartley was not fool enough to take every offer that was waved in his face. His price by 1981, moreover, was one million dollars. The intended victim had to be certifiable scum—that, or in some way connected with the Communist takeover of the western world. To Richard Dartley, alias Savage, there was little distinction between the two.

On that score Dartley made no apology. True, he never talked politics to his Washington friends. Still, he was known to hate what passed for liberal philosophy in the United States. When Khrushchev told the world that Russia would someday bury America, Dartley took him at his word. His quarrel was not with the Russians or with the liberal intention of keeping people working in decent jobs. It was the very nature of Communist ideology, which aimed to bend the world to fit its will.

In Dartley's childhood, Washington had been flooded with Eastern European refugees, victims of the Communist takeover. Many of these people were Ukrainian, Polish, Lithuanian, Czech aristocracy; 90 percent of them were Catholics.

In 1959, the local liberals seemed to be relieved that a group of anachronistic landowners had been deposed by a more progressive group, namely the Communists. The liberal press' disdain for Ukranian Catholic aristocracy did not seem to extend to the British or Dutch aristocracy, who could buy and sell the Slavic titles ten times over. Somehow they had bought the fantasy that Britain was by definition an enlightened nation.

While all this ideological hullabaloo was going on, Dartley was in his mid-teens. In those years he tended to be in love with a particular blond, blue-eyed Lithuanian former countess named Dana. All he knew about politics in those years was that Dana had one hell of a pair and a terrific muff. She seemed to agree. As long as her "Dick Dick" wore a rubber, or came in her mouth, Dana was ready, willing and able. Dartley tended to believe her stories about the mass executions and the deportation of the educated classes to work camps in Siberia. Even though she was a great fuck, he could tell she blocked her real feelings. It ate him up, the sorrow of the girl. The week after she told him she loved him more than anyone she had ever met, she committed suicide. Pills. Nothing dramatic. Just plain death.

Dartley couldn't put the pieces together. He walked around in a daze for months. He blamed himself. He couldn't understand how the political activities in a person's childhood could destroy their souls. Then he read Solzhenitsyn's *The Gulag Archipelago*. He read what the Soviets do to people who don't happen to agree with them. He began to hate the Communists more than he had ever hated or feared the Devil. He carried his hatred to Nam. He saw the absolute cruelty of the Viet Cong. More than once the liberals at home, the rich kids, canonized the Communists. They said the Cong were patriots in a war the Americans could not understand. Apparently they had not bothered to read Marx or Lenin. They did not understand that the pretense of civil war is one of the classic Communist tricks in its methodical take-over of any given society.

All during Nam, Dartley had been confused by the American ambivalence in the face of the enemy. He had never understood the ongoing national guilt trip about bombing Hiroshima when Japan would have been willing to stick razor blades into the eyes of every man, woman and child in these United States. He didn't understand why his country didn't bomb Moscow or Peking with a full-scale megaton nuclear bomb and avoid another hundred Vietnams. No one supported that brand of thinking. Maybe it was the death of civilians that scared the do-gooders. The fact that civilians were civilians and he was a soldier always seemed to him to be accidental. Who wasn't an unwilling victim of war? On the subject of women and children, those classic innocents, Dartley had frequently noticed that a lot of slant-eyed kids and their gorgeous slant-eyed big sisters seemed to be carrying live grenades in their market bags just in case an unwary American soldier within throwing distance stopped to light a Marlboro or tie his shoelace.

Finally it all became clear to him. He would pick off the biggies one by one. He was no crusader. He expected to be paid. He wasn't going to trade his life for theirs. He would be expensive, too. He would reward himself for standing alone. He accepted no contracts predicated on domestic unhappiness, such as marital infidelity. There had to be more; the intended target had to be a man or woman whose outsize ego was wreaking havoc in the lives of too many people. Beyond that, he looked for a tie-in with what he considered the Communist cancer. He decided early on he could never accept the job of killing an American. He would never have accepted the job of killing either of the Kennedys or Dr. Martin Luther King. To what end? To further complicate things? No, the older he got, the more Dartley realized he was after bigger game. He was after the source.

Now he was thirty-seven, at the top of his form. His body and his mind had caught up with each other. He didn't flinch anymore. He could roll with the punches. According to the wisdom of the East, the mother of martial arts, the fighter who could absorb the enemy's blows had a better chance of successfully attacking and destroying him. Once the enemy had expended his strength, before he had time to summon spent energies, he could be caught off guard. Dartley knew all these natural laws instinctively. He trusted his instinct more than what he had learned from his experience under fire. His instinct was his inspiration.

At thirty-seven, he still didn't have a place of his own. He could sometimes be found at his Uncle Charley's farm in a studio apartment over what had once been a horse barn. At the farm he read literature on every conceivable kind of weapon. He practiced long hours in the fields shooting at targets. He learned much about custom-made firearms from his older relative.

Dartley needed more than guns. His most valuable resource was his information broker, Herbert "The Viscount" Malleson. Malleson was a naturalized American, a graduate of Oxford and the Harvard Law School. He had computerized facts about every government on earth. He also had an ongoing file on most of the leading political figures, legitimate or otherwise, in United Nations countries. Dartley used Malleson to research his "hits." Sometimes he bought the information to use as blackmail. The Viscount had other talents, too. He was a whiz at unique travel arrangements. He knew when a helicopter was faster than a jet and where a riverboat made more sense than a Mercedes. To the outside world of Washington, Malleson was an award-winning historian who wrote brilliant best-sellers on the great crimes of the nineteenth and twentieth centuries, both American and European. His book on the real identity of Jack the Ripper was generally considered the best book on that subject. His book on the Gloria Vanderbilt custody case became the basis for a successful film. Malleson had also written the definitive biographies of Josef Stalin and of Huey Long, the assassinated governor-dictator of Louisiana. He was an expert on the British aristocracy's infatuation with the Nazis during the 1930's. He also knew where to find the best women anywhere.

Sylvia Marton, 29, sometime Yugoslavian movie star, was Dartley's best friend of the opposite sex. Usually when he wanted to get laid, he had a long list of possibilities and he made the most of them. Which is not to say he was looking to unburden his soul to every call girl who wanted to talk. Marton, who'd seen several divorces, was a different story. She had a first-rate brain and a bank account that afforded her an international life. Unlike most people anywhere, she had friends in Rio, Johannesburg, Athens, Tel Aviv, Beirut, Leningrad, Istanbul, Cairo, Warsaw and Key Biscayne, all of them in high places. She was known as a blue-eyed blond Sophia Loren. If she wasn't on the top ten box-office list, she was still considered an asset to anybody's film and anybody's bed. Dartley did not monopolize her private life nor she his, but they ran into each other more often than not. They both enjoyed life in the fast lane. They both knew they were not the marrying kind. She helped him whenever she could, in any way she could. Sylvia was a crack shot and a good getaway driver. Sometimes when Dartley thought of her, his eyes misted over. Sometimes she seemed like the other half of his mind.

Chapter Five

Greenmountain Lodge, the South's most fashionable resort, occupied over a thousand acres just west of the Shenandoah Valley of northern Virginia. It was built at the turn of the century by descendants of the old plantation society, who were making money for the first time since the Civil War. The main building was a replica of the Lavaliere Plantation in Natchez, Mississippi. The house was a white-columned, white-brick Grecian Revival structure that looked more like the Parthenon than a country inn. The exterior was misleading; the insides were furnished with splendid antiques from every manor house in the Old South, at least those homes that General Sherman had not burned to cinders or the white trash tenant farmers had not looted of every stick of furniture.

The adjoining hotel buildings by themselves covered five acres of grounds. They were white clapboard, multistoried rambling affairs without discernible architectural form. Porches, balconies and gables seemed stuck on at whim. For most of the year, beginning in early spring, the grounds were a profusion of blooms: banks of rhododendrons and azaleas, Judas trees, roses run rampant, lilacs that seemed to blossom all year long, cherry blossoms, crabapple. Single bushes seemed the size of railroad cars; the fruit trees in blossom suggested low-lying clouds, white and pink, with mists of lavender. The grounds gave Greenmountain Lodge the quality of a Camelot or Brigadoon, a mystical place from another time.

At a greater distance from the main buildings were well-stocked fishing ponds and riding trails. Farther still were the expertly designed meadows and moors for grouse and pheasant shoots. Still farther were the forests where the most ambitious guests shot deer and elk and occasionally an unplanned bear or rattlesnake. "There's no telling what lurks in the woods around Greenmountain Lodge" was a familiar saying of the country people who worked there or who supplied them with their fresh produce and poultry.

Most of the guests at the Greenmountain Lodge were, as one might expect, southerners in late middle age. The women's voices were light; a lilting, studied laughter was commonplace. "The voices of birds" was how many described the effect. In the South it was inconceivable that a lady, even in 1983, would deliberately make harsh or unpleasant sounds. At night the couples dressed for languid dinners with a long list of southern specialties from spoon bread to Smithfield ham served paper thin in finger rolls. After dinner, the house orchestra in white tie played sentimental favorites in leisurely tempo. Toward midnight, when most of the senior citizens had gone to bed, the orchestra ripped into fast-paced resort renditions of Benny Goodman and Glenn Miller, and for a few minutes the veterans of World War Two and their wives relived their youth as they chose to remember it. During the day, the wives generally promenaded around the azalea garden and visited the greenhouses to see the world-famous orchid collection. The more adventurous women, particularly those who had grown up in better social circles, rode horseback through the carefully planned and clearly marked mountain trails. Afterward, they went to the spa for their massage.

The men, for the most part, spent their daylight hours playing serious poker or shooting game. The Lodge kept its woodlands carefully stocked with game birds that were bred for them at neighboring farms. Rare was the weekend visitor who in season did not return to Savannah, Memphis or Spring Hill without a brace of pheasant. The Greenmountain staff took special pride in cleaning and flash-freezing all wild game shot on the property. For a reasonable fee in the deer-hunting season, a taxidermist from Charlottesville would transform the dead deer into a splendid mounted trophy with almost undetectable glass eyes; the staff butcher, equally obliging, cut the carcass into venison steaks and chops to take home for all the underprivileged friends and relatives who had never tasted deer.

The three German industrialists arrived separately on April 23, a Saturday. Von Kelsing had been in New York the previous week visiting old friends from the Reich. He bought an 1893 Danish Krag Jorgensen rifle from the collection of an old friend named Gunther Guttenberg. The two men had attended the same gymnasium in Düsseldorf. Both were at Heidelberg when the Fuhrer invaded Czechoslovakia. Later, both worked for Heinrich Himmler taking inventory of Bergen Belsen and Auschwitz, a task they had both regarded as distasteful but necessary. The Kraf Jorgensen rifle was long and sleek, 1330 mm. Its most remarkable feature lay in the pattern of the magazine, which loaded laterally under the bolt through a hinged trapdoor. A definite collector's item. Von Kelsing planned to display it on the wall of his underground shooting gallery next to his uncle's Kar.

While von Kelsing was in New York he did not contact Richard Dartley. His instincts told him he was being watched.

Willi Reiser flew directly from Frankfurt. He was, as always, by himself. He did not understand why he had to come to West Virginia for a meeting, and he did not share von Kelsing's paranoia about being watched. "If they can hear what we say to one another in Germany, what is to stop them from following us to West Virginia?" he remarked almost every time he spoke with von Kelsing in the week before they left home. "And by the way, Werner, who is this 'they' you keep talking about?"

The assumption of all three men was that if someone was watching them, it was a spy from the Turkish underground, most likely one of Ali Ozker's goon squad. Von Kelsing felt fairly secure from the possibility of assassination by Ozker. The Turk had already retaliated for the attempt on his life. The truth was simple. If Ozker killed any of the German businessmen, he risked wrecking the NATO agreement with the men; the Moscow center would not tolerate a loss of what amounted to free research and development.

Bruno Schmidt arrived with Ilse de Brock; they registered as "Mr. and Mrs. Schmidt." Both wore simple gold wedding rings as a social precaution. The agreement between them was that, except for a poker game, Ilse could join the three men at any public indoor gathering. She was at no time to go near them when they were outdoors, unless they specifically invited her to do so.

The first night, they all gathered in the dining room, a bright yellow room with glossy white woodwork. Hundred-year-old Waterford crystal chandeliers from Irish manor houses shimmered like diamonds above the diners' heads. The Germans sat at a large, round, candlelit table discussing their respective journeys. Under the table, unseen by the others, Ilse occasionally placed her hand on Bruno Schmidt's crotch. Schmidt reciprocated, again without attracting the attention of the other two men. Ilse's evening dress, a wraparound black crêpe, had a convenient slit up the middle. "So far, a good beginning," she thought to herself.

As he surveyed his fellow diners, von Kelsing grew increasingly agitated. Where was Richard Dartley? Surely not here. There was no sign of any man who could successfully assassinate a Turkish mob boss. The men eating dinner were mostly elderly gentlemen with unsteady hands. Their younger counterparts, men in their fifties, were portly, used to several rounds of drinks before and after dinner.

On Monday morning the black-haired Washingtonian drove from D.C. to Alexandria using the beltway. Then he took U.S. 50 out of Alexandria going west toward Clarksburg and Parkersburg. His car was, by choice, a silver gray Chevrolet, a 1979 Camaro. His clothing was also unexceptional— a gray flannel businessman's suit, white shirt and navy blue silk tie. His horn-rimmed glasses were non-prescription glass.

The first three hours of his trip were without incident. Once he reached Parkersburg, the flat swampland around Washington completely disappeared, the landscape grew craggier. He was already past the low-lying mountains separating Virginia and West Virginia. The accents of the townspeople in the sparsely populated hamlets began to take on a mountain twang. All things considered, the air bothered him. It was an enveloping gray mist, much too humid for spring. He preferred clear air. Crystal clear. He liked to see details. He liked to see the road in front of him. On this particular Monday morning, he was so close to rage that it took every ounce of his concentration just to drive his car. So far, he had succeeded in keeping his hands from shaking. He was not used to losing control. He liked things planned, step by step, in advance. Chaos was not his forte. Neither were barbarians. What had happened just before he left Washington, D.C., made him wonder about the future of the Republic.

He had swung over onto M Street in Georgetown to phone the Greenmountain Lodge. He found a pay phone inside a diner. The Silver Diner was a leftover from pre-gentrification days when truckers used M Street as a main route into downtown Washington's K Street market. From the pay phone he had a clear view of the parking lot. He didn't know why he felt he had to keep an eye on the parking lot, but he did. It was 10:00 A.M. on a Monday morning. Why should there be any problems? He called the Greenmountain Lodge and asked for Werner von Kelsing. The German's phone rang six times without an answer.

"I'm sorry, sir. Mr. von Kelsing is not in his room. Would you like to leave a message?" said the hotel operator.

"How about Reiser and Schmidt?"

"I beg your pardon, sir."

"Reiser and Schmidt. They were supposed to be with him."

"Let me check, sir."

From the pay phone inside the diner he watched as a gang of black youths in T-shirts and sneakers prowled the parking lot kicking tires. "Why are niggers always looking for attention?" he asked himself. He knew the conventional liberal answer to his question, but it wasn't his answer. He didn't like black kids. He particularly didn't like liberals.

Two of the black kids were trying his car door. Good luck, he thought, confident they'd never get in.

"Hello, operator?"

He heard a click and then a dial tone. He checked his Rolex. It was ten ten. He had at least four more hours of driving until he reached the Greenmountain Lodge.

The two black youths were serious about his car door. One of them had inserted a length of wire into his lock; he was methodically twisting it. The dark-haired man realized he had left a small gym bag on the floor of the backseat. Then, for the first time, dumbfounded, he noticed the security guard.

A coffee-colored man in a guard's uniform was standing on the steps of the Silver Diner. He was watching the youths trying to open the door of the Camaro. His arms were folded over his broad gut; his eyes were half closed. He had seen it all, from Nam to Reagan, and he no longer cared. That morning, as a precaution against the city, he had taken a double dose of Valium.

He had no reason to think the boys were trying

to break into any car but their own; any other assumption would mean he had been brainwashed to think like a white man.

"You need some help, brother?" the guard asked one of the youths.

Just then, like magic, the car door opened.

"No, that's okay, brother. We got it!" the youth called back, grinning. He was missing a front tooth; his expression was macabre, like a carnival reveler in Rio.

Then suddenly his jubilant expression changed. A look of shock came over his face. His eyes widened. In terror he looked down at his hand. The last two joints of his middle finger were missing. The white circle of exposed bone was rapidly drowning in dark red fluid. The severed vein was spurting blood. His hand was wet and sticky. He was unable to comprehend what had happened. In disbelief he began to shake his head. There had been no sound, no warning. What had happened? Was the car's door handle rigged with a straight razor? His friends still had not noticed the boy's catastrophe.

"Say brother, what you waitin' for?"

The boy looked behind him in a frenzy and saw what looked like a tiny dog turd lying in the parking lot.

"Look! Look!" he sobbed. He held up his bloody stump of a finger for his friends to see. His sobbing accelerated into a terrible wail.

The door to the silver gray Camaro slammed shut.

The youth whirled around as the car's doors locked with a click and the car backed out onto M Street. Inside the car, the dark-haired man pushed a button hidden under the dashboard. When the half-asleep security guard squinted to jot down the number on the car's license plate, the license plate was nowhere to be seen. In point of fact, the plate, with its chrome casing, lay facedown on the rear bumper of the car. The man had spent almost sixty thousand dollars and three months of his time having the most ordinary-looking car he could find overhauled and rebuilt. Its windows were now a bulletproof composite of plastic and glass. The seats and carpeting had been removed and layers of armoring laid in. Then the seats and carpeting had been replaced. By the time the vehicle was ready for him to drive again, the car had gained seven hundred pounds; externally, nothing showed. As soon as he was out of sight of the Silver Diner, the dark-haired man again pushed the button under the dashboard and the license plate righted itself.

At the Silver Diner the black teenager had lost control. His mouth was twitching, his eyes glazed over as he continued to scream. He still could not comprehend why he had been singled out: What had been so valuable in the backseat of the man's car that he had to suffer mutilation? The security guard was on the phone with the capital police.

"Thas right," he said. "The man, he drive off in these boys' car. Thas right. He come out the diner. I was standin' right there watchin' the lot, mindin' my own business like I always do. This man he takes this pistol, yeah, a twenty-two. With this silencer.... I knows 'bout silencers. I had trainin'. Thas right, it was a twenny-two silencer."

An hour southwest of Parkersburg, the dark-haired man was beginning to see the humor of it all. A smile played along the corners of his normally hard line of a mouth as he recalled his perfect hit. The black kid had been lucky. If he'd moved his hand, he might have lost his thumb; then he would really have had something to yell about.

At an Exxon station on U.S. 911 he called the Greenmountain Lodge a second time.

"Give me Werner von Kelsing, please."

"I'm sorry, sir," replied the same operator as before. "Mr. von Kelsing is not in his room."

"Do you know where he is?"

"Who shall I say is calling?"

"I'm calling for Dartley."

"Oh, Mr. Dartley, Mr. von Kelsing said to tell you he was out shooting pheasant in South Meadow."

"I didn't say I was Dartley. I said I was calling for Dartley."

"Oh."

He hung up the phone, climbed back into his Camaro and started driving south again. This wasn't going to be an easy job, he thought. Von Kelsing and his two kraut friends sounded scatter-brained. Businessmen sons of inventor fathers. He'd seen it too many times. While the sons drone on about advertising promotional schemes and tax shelters, the basic product is taken for granted. What do pheasants have to do with laser satellites? Herbert "The Viscount" Malleson, his information broker, had given him the lowdown on von Kelsing–Schmidt. The consensus among West German politicians was that Werner von Kelsing was living in a previous, defeated age. With romantics like von Kelsing, it was agreed, bravado often overtook reality. The dark-haired man knew he had to be careful.

In the South Meadow, a mile from the main complex of the Greenmountain Lodge, the three German visitors with rented English setters in tow tracked on the hard ground, their hunting rifles angled at their sides. Clumps of onion grass sprouted in the glare of the fierce spring sun. Flecks of yellow grain, corn, and millet and sunflower seeds lay scattered about on the ground. Von Kelsing was furious. Why was there not a single feeding station for the birds? Why did visiting hunters have to be subjected to such sloppiness? South Meadow, as far as he was concerned, resembled a barnyard. The birdseed wrecked the illusion of wilderness. "Wait," he remarked to Bruno, "when we see them, the birds will probably still have their price tags on them."

The three men carried their Schuetzen rifles, the ultimate in offhand target rifles, collector's items first popular in the early stages of the caplock era. The Schuetzens had elaborately sculpted walnut stocks with curly brass inlays and a back shooting hammer. The sight was unique: a steel post with a fine bead protected by protective wings.

Von Kelsing could not wait till the English setter flushed the first ring-necked bird out of the underlying bramble bushes. For him the thrill of the kill was almost sexual.

Mr. Weber, the Greenmountain Lodge manager, had assured him that "Winter and summer, we guarantee pheasants at South Meadow. We have three thousand a month trucked in from our pheasant farm in Sperryville." Hearing that, von Kelsing groaned aloud. What had happened to the idea of sport?

In Suite 406 at the Greenmountain Lodge, Ilse de Brock was rummaging as rapidly as she could through every scrap of Werner von Kelsing's clothing, toiletries and personal papers. From a third-floor hall window she had watched the three friends leave the hotel, rifles in hand, and head for South Meadow. She knew she had no time to lose. Any one of them might have forgotten a favorite pair of sunglasses and return to his quarters. Von Kelsing was continually forgetting his sunscreen. Bruno could be back in a half-hour's time. Unbeknownst to his two friends, Herr Schmidt did not care for hunting. Like an unhappy wife, he was always coming down with a migraine or twisting an ankle, anything to avoid stalking "barnyard animals," as he called the game birds and wild boar his two friends loved to shoot. Ilse could not chance being caught in von Kelsing's room. She would be immediately fired. Worse, her snooping would cast suspicion on her entire relationship with Bruno Schmidt. She would be thoroughly investigated. At some point witnesses—her landlady, a waitress, a theater usher—would step forward and connect her with too many casual acquaintances of Russian or East German background. At the very least, von Kelsing would demand to know how she had entered his room without a key. After all, how could an ordinary secretary pick a lock?

On top of von Kelsing's dresser she found a scrap of paper, a corner of an envelope. Von Kelsing had scribbled "3:00, South Meadow." So that was it. They were going to meet someone in the South Meadow. It was already a quarter to three. She had to think quickly. Perhaps she could find something of Bruno's he'd left behind in their room, something he might have wanted with him on a pheasant shoot, a gunsight perhaps, or a handkerchief, or his antihistamine. Anything to give her an excuse to break all the rules and run into the South Meadow. She'd look like a hysterical hausfrau, perhaps, but if there was really to be a fourth man in the meadow, she'd get a look at him. Perhaps there would even be time for a few surreptitious photographs.

The new straw sunbasket she'd picked up from the "street vendor" in Manhattan was her best concealed camera yet. The carryall was royal blue with the double handle of a beach bag. Black-eyed Susans with orange and yellow straw petals had been woven onto its surface. The effect was deliberately crude, as if Mexican villagers with no particular skill had done the weaving in their spare time. The bag was, of course, deliberately deceptive. In the bottom side fold of the bag, half hidden in shadow, one particular black-eyed Susan had had a black hole carefully cut out of its "eye"; in the false bottom of the bag a shutter release was connected by a concealed wire to a pressure spot under the left handle. By pointing the bag and squeezing the plastic welt under the handle, Ilse could photograph any man, woman or child within a hundred yards. The Center had planned every detail. Before she left the States, she would leave the bag in the checkroom of a certain Italian restaurant in midtown Manhattan. Both the developed pictures and the negatives would be mailed to her in Düsseldorf. She would pass the pertinent ones on to Greta Polansky. It was one way of avoiding customs inspectors and airport metal detectors. Once she had the photographs in her possession, she would mail them to Rogoff. The Moscow Center files would point the way to the next step, if there was to be one.

Ilse's concentration was broken by the loud ringing of von Kelsing's phone. Odd. He always instructed the front desk to take his phone messages when he was out of the room. The phone rang a second time. Its shrill sound cut through her like an electric buzz saw. Her instincts told her she had little time to lose. She quickly went through von Kelsing's bureau crawers, expecting a third ring. There was none. The silence was ominous; to Ilse that meant only one thing: someone had been checking, someone like her, someone who would probably personally visit von Kelsing's room.

She raced through his bureau. In the fourth drawer, under his skiing sweaters, she found two American sex magazines; one called *Come* featured pictures of men and women having sex. The women were young blondes with enormous breasts; the men, also blond, had great penises that seemed like columns of flesh connecting them with their subservient partners. To Ilse, the phographs looked like Nazi propaganda for the Aryan race. The other magazine was called *American Warrior*. There were numerous articles in it about mercenary soldiers, mostly American, mostly blond, fighting Communist insurgents in Africa and Central America. *American Warrior* also featured hundreds of ads for the most advanced developments in small arms.

She thought she heard footsteps coming down the hall. In Greenmountain Lodge, despite the heavy carpeting, the floorboards creaked. "This is just an old southern house," the bellboy explained when she had remarked, "I'm surprised the floors creak in such an expensive hotel." She had wanted to add, "In Germany our floors do not creak," but she had checked her tongue. She was in West Virginia for one reason alone, to glean whatever information she could about the meeting there.

She dove under the canopied double bed. Its flounces reached all the way to the carpet. If the intruder did not check under the bed, she would be safe. If, however, he did check, and if he discovered her, and if he was a stranger, she would pretend she was the natural occupant of the room and hope to scare him off.

She heard a sound familiar to her, that of a lock being picked. Then she heard the door to the room open and shut. Ilse held her breath, terrified the carpet lint would cause her to sneeze. From her hiding place she heard drawers opening and closing, the same drawers she had just examined. She knew from the direction of the sounds that the intruder was examining von Kelsing's hand luggage. His passport was stuffed in a side pocket of his shaving case. His passport photo was a good likeness. Ilse figured out that the man was probably "Savage." He was checking for evidence that the man or men he was supposed to meet in South Meadow were really who they said they were.

She heard the intruder's footsteps coming closer to the bed. He would undoubtedly check the bedside table. Nothing there but a few loose American dollar bills and some change, about twenty dollars in all. Could this man be a petty crook? she thought to herself. The bellboy perhaps? From under the bed, all she was able to see was a few inches of pale gray-green carpet. As the intruder came closer, she noticed his shoes, plain cordovan pumps, highly polished, without any adornment. Except for their color they could have been standard-issue military shoes. They were well worn and well cared for. She could see that the soles had been replaced; the expected nicks and cuts of ordinary wear had been buffed, sanded, dyed, redyed and polished like fine antique furniture. A fine diagonal line where the new leather sole met the stub of the old one was clear to her from her vantage point.

Then Ilse noticed something odd: his shoelaces did not match. One was round, exactly the color of his shoes, a deep blood red. The other shoelace was a cheaper-looking flat lace, a dark mud brown, probably a replacement for one that had snapped. The man was too precise to make a knot in the broken shoelace and too cheap to replace both laces. He had probably come from the city, she imagined, but what city? New York? Washington? Philadelphia?

Then, for no apparent reason, the intruder picked up the phone, listened for a telltale click that did not come, and hung up. Edging closer, she saw his trousers, a herringbone gunmetal gray gabardine. His fingers were lean and tanned, with knotted joints and spatulate tips. A palmist had once told her that spatulate or splayed fingertips where the ends widen are a sign of people with great executive power. According to the palmist, the great administrators of history, Cardinal Richlieu, Oliver Cromwell, Peter the Great, all had spatulate fingertips. Over the years Ilse had concluded that the palmist was generally correct. Andropov at the Moscow center had hands like that. So did Bruno Schmidt. They were the only two men she knew with hands like that, two of the most successful men in the world. And now there was a third. The intruder in Suite 406. She wished she could see his face. She imagined that it was lean and muscular, too. Hands were usually related to faces. She didn't dare move closer to the edge of the flounce; she knew she'd give herself away.

Then, unexpectedly, he was gone. She heard the door click shut. She waited another full minute to make sure he was really gone. If he was, in fact, the reason being the three o'clock meeting in South Meadow, she had only a few minutes to spare. Ilse decided to chance it; she stuck her head out from under the flounce on the canopy bed and looked around. There was no one in the room. She checked her watch: 2:50. Then she quickly checked von Kelsing's bedside table to see if the intruder had taken the twenty dollars in change.

Nothing had been touched. She checked the hand luggage. His passport was still in the side pocket. What had the intruder been looking for?

Then it struck her. The fool intruder had picked up von Kelsing's receiver with his bare hands. Undoubtedly, he had left fingerprints. Finally she would have information for the Moscow Center. Her superior there, Serge Rogoff, would be pleased, so pleased.

Deep in South Meadow, the English setters had finally found their natural quarry nesting in a blackberry patch. With a loud squawk and a flurry of rustled pinfeathers, the pheasants lifted off their nests in a blur and arose into the gray sky.

Dogs barking, the Germans took aim with their Schuetzen target rifles. In a loud whisper von Kelsing issued his command. "Sh-h-h, this one is mine. Keep away!" He cocked the firing pin, lifted the sight to his right eye, squinted and took aim. At the split second he increased his index finger's pressure on the trigger, he saw the bird's head separate from its body and spin off into the air. He was dumbstruck. There had been no sound, no warning. Nothing. The headless bird fell to the ground like a dead weight, its stump of a neck glistening with wet black blood. As the setters moved in to retrieve it, von Kelsing whirled around to accuse whichever friend had betrayed him.

His two companions were staring at each other with befuddled amazement. Von Kelsing was skeptical and angry. Were these two clowns playing a joke on him after all these years? "Werner," Willi Reiser blurted out to the would-be marksman, "what kind of a silencer have you invented? We heard nothing. Not even a click."

"Neither did I," fumed von Kelsing, peering beyond the men to scrutinize every bush and rock within sight. He saw nothing. Could there possibly be an interloper in the South Meadow? Hardly likely: the trees were too young, too narrow, to hide another gunman. What boulders there were were granite rocks, none as high as three feet, none able to conceal anyone but a small child.

It couldn't have been Bruno, could it? "Always consider the least likely suspect," his father had once advised him in a labor dispute at the firm.

"The mildest employee can often be the hidden Communist." No, not Bruno. Never an agitator, never a joker, Bruno had never been much of a shot either, even in the war when his life depended on his knowing something about guns. Von Kelsing was absolutely mystified. Perhaps a concealed dwarf, a refugee from a circus, had taken aim at the bird. He dismissed the thought, thinking he must surely be mad.

Once more, with the lead setter foraying into the bramble bushes, a second bird driven from its nest repeated the familiar pattern of flight. This time, before taking aim, von Kelsing looked behind him over his right shoulder. His two friends carried their uncocked guns at their sides, waiting for him to shoot. How quick could they possibly be? he thought. Once more he brought the gunsight to his right eye and drew a bead on the game bird. It was a male, a ring-necked ruffled grouse. Von Kelsing could already taste its gamey flavor cooked with another American delicacy, freshly made cranberry sauce, a favorite of his. This time there would be no mistake. This time his aim was perfect. He cocked the firing pin and pulled the trigger.

Again, a puff of smoke, a blast of noise, the smell of powder; again the bird's head separated from its body. A perfect hit. Reiser and Schmidt applauded with rare enthusiasm.

"See, Werner, you did it!"

Except that von Kelsing knew better. There had been too brief a second's difference between his pulling of the trigger and the disintegration of the bird's head. That wasn't all. He himself was using pellets. They were incapable of shattering a bird's head. Whatever had hit the pheasant had to have been using high explosive bullets. But where was the other gun? And where was the gunman?

"Von Kelsing." The voice came from behind him.

The industrialist spun around. He knew the voice was neither Reiser's nor Schmidt's. His two companions were, in fact, frozen in their tracks. The voice without a face was bouncing off trees and rocks in every direction. Von Kelsing looked hard at the trees on the edges of the hunting ground. Nothing moved.

"I am von Kelsing," he called out in English. "Come forward, whoever you are." There was a long silence.

"Who could it be?" asked a puzzled Reiser.

"Come forward," von Kelsing repeated in the best English he could muster. "You will suffer no harm whatsoever."

While the men waited for a response, several pheasants rose into the air. This time the birds kept their heads intact. The disembodied voice stayed where it was. Then came a deep laughter, a mocking laughter bouncing off the surfaces of rocks and trees in all directions. Then, without warning, von Kelsing heard the loud sound of snapping twigs in a thicket ten yards in front of him. He whirled around in time to see two more of the small birds rise up to meet the splattering of their own heads. Again without the sound or smell of weaponry. The disembodied laughter rose higher in pitch. Von Kelsing finally found himself out of control, screaming, "Stop! Stop!" Then he heard the high-pitched screech of Bruno Schmidt sounding as if he'd just been bitten by a mamba. Reflexively von Kelsing moved to whirl around a second time; he found to his amazement that he was unable to turn. Another human being, rock hard, straight as a steel girder, stood fast against him. The man was a wall of muscle. Von Kelsing felt the stranger's breath against the back of his neck. A hot breath. Then he spoke. The voice was an American voice, an eastern voice, hard and cynical.

"What's your problem, von Kelsing? I made it on time, didn't I?"

"Wha—" stammered the industrialist.

"I just needed to see how you guys operate."

Aghast, von Kelsing took a step forward so he could turn around and face this arrogant hireling. But the man stayed with him whichever way he turned. Before he could stop him, the man's arms were around him, arms like cast iron. He could feel the hard wall of the man's stomach against the small of his back. He could feel the man's pelvic muscles too, and his long, straight cock pressing against the back of his ass. Then the man knelt into the backs of von Kelsing's knees, collapsing him to the ground. The German was in a state of shock. Who was this madman? He looked up to see what looked like a country squire. The man, evidently a gentleman to look at him, wore beige jodhpurs of the finest suede. His vest, also suede, was silver gray, and his color-coordinated tweed riding coat was a houndstooth plaid in pale browns and tans fitted at the waist. The man wore a white silk ascot tucked in a lavender oxford cloth button-down shirt. His face was hidden in the shadow of a slightly oversize Irish tweed country hat. To further his anonymity, he wore small, round dark glasses with wire rims in the style of the thirties.

"I am also wearing a gun holster," he said, declining to model that particular feature of his wardrobe. "It's a new model with a silencer. I'm testing it for the manufacturer. I trust these men are Reiser and Schmidt."

"Who are you?" von Kelsing gasped at the man. "What is the meaning of this outrage?"

"The outrage? I couldn't tell you," replied the man. "You're the one who called the meeting."

"Are you Dartley?" asked von Kelsing.

"Dartley sent me," replied the stranger. "You can call me Savage."

"Yes," said von Kelsing, already weary of the man he had been expecting.

"My talent with firearms should be obvious to you," said the man who called himself Savage.

"But where were you?" asked von Kelsing.

"Hidden in that bramble bush," replied the man, pointing to a thickness of half-green shrubbery. "This outfit is perfect camouflage. You kept looking behind the trees."

"Ja," replied von Kelsing curtly. He noticed that Mr. Savage had shoelaces that did not match.

Odd, he thought, for someone with a reputation for being a perfectionist.

"By the way," commented Savage, "before we get down to business, I think you should know one thing."

"What is that?" replied von Kelsing. He had resumed his imperial Teutonic air. He was not used to being bested by a paid assassin.

"Your phone is being tapped and your room is too easy to enter. It took me less than a minute with a nail file and a credit card."

"Gut Gott," groaned Reiser.

"And one other thing," continued the man in tweeds, "some broad who wears Chanel Number Nineteen is hiding under your bed."

"Chanel Number Nineteen?" asked von Kelsing with a cold eye, looking at Schmidt. "What is that?"

"Don't look at me, Werner," replied Bruno Schmidt in German. "I never heard of that perfume. There are many wealthy women in this hotel."

"How do you know Chanel Number Nineteen?" von Kelsing asked the man.

"Believe me, I know," replied the man. His gravelly voice had an authoritarian tone for one who had not yet reached middle age. He was thinking of a certain whore in Tangiers with dark brown nipples almost an inch long. For some reason she had discovered Chanel Number 19, which the Paris conglomerate sold along with its more famous Chanel Number 5. The perfumes in question were common enough stuff for any man with a big bank account, especially a man who'd been invited into more than a few beds. Women were suckers for it, perfume, that is.

In Suite 406 at Greenmountain Lodge, Ilse was in a state of shock. Twice she had dusted von Kelsing's receiver with the fingerprint powder. She intended to photograph the fingerprints. Except there were no fingerprints. None. That was impossible, she reasoned. The man had not been wearing gloves. She had seen his hands. She had seen his fingers. They looked like perfectly normal fingers. Where were the fingerprints? None of this made sense to her. Could he have possibly removed his fingerprints with acid? Who was this man? It was already three thirty. She had no time left; the meeting in South Meadow might be a simple matter of passing an envelope. Still, she wondered if she should try again for fingerprints. Perhaps the intruder had held the receiver with only the tips of his thumb and middle finger. Three thirty-five. There was no time. She had no choice but to get to South Meadow with her royal blue straw bag before the meeting broke up. If she could not get decent fingerprints of the man called Savage, she could at least get his photograph.

Cleaning up took longer than she expected. It always did. In order to get fingerprints, a great amount of powder was needed. For her cleanup procedures, she worked too fast. She should have first completely removed the powder. Instead, the chamois smeared the residue. Now she would have to wait until the muck dried. If she used a wet hand towel from von Kelsing's bathroom he'd notice the smears right away. He might even notice that the hand towel was missing. She became increasingly upset. Then it struck her, how absurd she was being. The hotel chambermaid could just as easily have spilled the wrong kind of cleaning powder on von Kelsing's bedside table. One of them could have easily forgotten to replace a hand towel in the bathroom. What had Ilse to worry about? Men never notice details anyway.

"Gentlemen, let's get down to business," ordered the man with the round dark eyeglasses. The man called Savage. He kept his face down, as much in shadow as he could manage, and he kept his distance.

"All you need to know is that I work for Dartley," he said.

"Why can't Dartley do this job himself?" questioned von Kelsing, peering at the stranger's face for telltale clues to his identity. The English setters barked impatiently. Reiser let go of their leashes and allowed them to wander freely about. The dogs were too well trained. They stayed within throwing distance, and whining, hoping for a great chase through the open fields, a chase that was never to be.

"Dartley is the final authority," said the stranger. "I do the work. That's all you need to know. If you have any problems with this arrangement, talk to Dartley."

"How do we talk to Dartley?" asked von Kelsing.

"The same way you did the first time," answered the new man. "Call Mr. Whitney at his service. He'll get back to you. That's how the game is played."

The stranger knew the Germans would never connect him to Dartley. He had a special attachment that disguised his voice when he spoke to prospective clients. He had to be careful. He operated on the principle that no one had any business knowing who he was. He gave Dartley's service number to no one. It was registered under the name of Whitney, his mother's maiden name. As far as the phone service itself was concerned, Mr. Dartley could have been his business partner, his uncle, his brother-in-law, his valet; in these times, even his live-in lover. He kept the relationship between Dartley and Whitney deliberately vague, as deliberately vague as the connection between Dartley and Savage. It was all deliberately vague for a reason: it was a matter of life and death.

"What are you waiting for?" asked the stranger. "I've demonstrated both my shooting skills and my ability to remain anonymous. What more do you want?"

Von Kelsing cleared his throat.

"Mr. Savage, you realize this is a very delicate situation—"

"And what's more," the brash American cut in, "I'm on time. Ain't that the best yet?"

Von Kelsing appeared to look shocked. The meeting in South Meadow had so far been one series of shocks. His ice blue eyes opened wide. He seemed to be saying, "Can we not be civil; must we always be dealing with barbarians?"

Dartley caught the inference. "Look, Mr. von Kelsing, let's be frank. You've made your big bucks on NATO giveaways. Thanks to you and your pals, we've already got enough Triton missiles to blow up the planet five times over, and they're paying you to make more. For all I know, you're a paranoid schizophrenic. You'll hire me to kill your chief engineer and then you'll hire some jerk to blow me away so I don't talk to the gossip columnists. I have to be careful, Mr. von Kell. I don't take jobs from guys with serious mental problems. I have to protect my principal investment. That just happens to be me. You dig?"

"What liberal publications do you read, young man?" sputtered von Kelsing.

Dartley didn't answer the question. He'd had enough of this old fogey with his implicit demand for good breeding and proper form.

"Von Kelsing, you're sixty-two. Your sperm count is low; your blood pressure one thirty-five, much too high. Take it easy and lay off the salt or you might have a stroke."

"Werner, why are we here?" asked Bruno Schmidt.

"Just one minute," snapped Dartley. "I'll get to you and your secretary."

"My secretary? What about my secretary? Where is she? Ilse? What are you saying?" Schmidt was in no mood to joke, if that's what the stranger was doing.

Dartley turned on von Kelsing. The industrialist could not see the younger man's eyes through his little dark glasses, but he knew they were peering into him.

"You were Heinrich Himmler's personal secretary from 1943 to 1945," Dartley began.

"That's not true!" shouted von Kelsing. He had personally destroyed all of Himmler's records pertaining to him during the final month of the war. He had not even been cited at Nuremberg. There was no proof of anything.

"You personally supervised the Jewish slave labor forces at I. M. Farben and at von Kelsing–Schmidt," continued Dartley. "In the last year of the war, it was you who supervised the brothels for the S.S. in Düsseldorf, in Mainz, in Frankfurt, in Cologne. I wonder what any press, liberal or conservative, would have to say if they knew your prurient interests."

Von Kelsing looked at the stranger and said nothing. He knew full well that because of the nature of his father's company, the Americans had protected him. He was too useful to them. Nonetheless, there had always been rumors that photographs of him in his S.S. uniform were carefully filed in Washington. He had nothing to gain by arguing with this lowlife hood.

"You have no proof," said von Kelsing quietly with all the dignity he was able to muster under the circumstances.

"There are many witnesses," replied Dartley in

a tone so quiet it mocked the man he was speaking to.

"Jews," said von Kelsing, rising to the bait.

"Yes, Jews," answered Dartley. "Mostly professional people. Doctors. University professors. Scientists in the U.S. and Canada. There is a file on you."

"I was for the Jews," sputtered von Kelsing. "I was always for the Jews. I never believed in the Final Solution. I personally told the Fuhrer he was making a mistake. There is nothing wrong with creating a labor force, you see. You liberal American fools. You know nothing of what it takes to control one's destiny."

"And your wife, Mitzi, is addicted to morphine, or did I make that up, too?" said Dartley, smiling.

"This man is a sadist," said Bruno Schmidt.

Von Kelsing's eyes widened. "Who do you think you are talking to?" he asked Dartley.

By now Dartley had begun to focus on the other two men.

"You, Reiser," he said, looking at the man with that name. "You were also S.S. You fathered three children in the program to produce der Fuhrer's master race."

"I have no children," coughed Reiser, ashen-faced. Forty years with his closest friends, and neither von Kelsing nor Schmidt had ever been privy to details as intimate as these.

"There are records for everything," announced the stranger. "You cannot father a child in a Nazi program and expect there will be no records. The Nazis were the perfect bureaucrats."

"I have no children," repeated the older man with the war-scarred face.

"You are considered one of the ten richest men in Western Europe," continued Dartley. "Most of your fortune comes from producing drugs that have sapped a whole population of its vitality."

"What is he talking about?" asked von Kelsing, incredulous.

"I did not create tranquilzier abuse," answered Reiser.

"It comes with the territory, doesn't it?" replied the American. "During the war you were Hitler's personal pharmacist, weren't you? You supplied him with megadoses of any drug his doctors asked for."

"That's not true," insisted Reiser.

"And what about your private vices?" asked Dartley.

Reiser paled. "I have no private vices. None."

"Only little boys aged ten, eleven, twelve—dark-eyed boys with olive skin and black hair at the Hotel Metternich in Hamburg."

"Oh Willi," groaned von Kelsing.

"Werner, I don't know what he's talking about," gasped Reiser in a *Hochdeutsch* whisper. The bachelor was still considered a definite marital catch in the social circles of the Ruhr Valley.

"This man is trying to destroy our morale," shouted Bruno Schmidt.

"And now you, Herr Schmidt," intoned Dartley

the Grand Inquisitor as he honed in on his principle quarry of the day. "What do you know about Ilse de Brock?"

"Nothing," answered the German, terrified of the information he was about to receive.

"There are reliable witnesses who claim she is working for the KGB."

With this, the three older men could not believe what they had heard. The stranger had established his authority with information that each man, according to his own ability to admit the facts of his own life to himself, could decide about. But Ilse in the KGB! The Germans began to laugh at the absurdity of the American's remark.

"There are over five thousand KGB agents and their subordinates working in German industry. Over a hundred work at von Kelsing–Schmidt. There are KGB agents and informers in your strictest security clearance areas. Ilse de Brock, one of the most successful, was born Ilse Panovski in Kiev in 1946. Her uncle was at the Moscow Center, which is the name of KGB headquarters in Moscow. Her mother and father were killed at Stalingrad. She is a dedicated Communist party member. She has contacts all over the Ruhr Valley who act as couriers. These people get her mail and photographs in and out of Moscow."

"What photographs?" scoffed Schmidt.

"It has been surmised that you and she are lovers," continued Dartley, ignoring Schmidt's question. "You should know that she was trained at Verhonoye, the Soviet camp for sexual agents, in the early sixties. Somehow it was hoped that she could have a go at Jack Kennedy. Again, that's just a conjecture, but we do know he had heard of her by the time he died; he had expressed an interest in meeting her. He thought she was Polish, of course, just as you did."

Schmidt was pale. His knees began to shake.

"This is ridiculous," he said.

"Photographs of every piece of paper that go in and out of your office, Herr Schmidt, regularly turn up in Moscow. You see, there are double agents as well as agents, and there are defectors from both positions. Certain things are known," explained Dartley. "There is a good possibility that the Soviets are copying every diagram in your laser research."

"That is impossible," scoffed Schmidt.

"Then if everything this man says is such a lie, Bruno," asked von Kelsing, "what is Ilse de Brock doing with us here in West Virginia? We agreed it was to be only the three of us."

"I insisted she come," said Schmidt. His voice was suddenly harsh, almost inaudible.

"No, that is not true, Bruno," said von Kelsing. "We both know it was she who insisted."

"That is not true, she is just a girl," repeated Schmidt.

"Why is your phone bugged?" Dartley asked von Kelsing.

"Bugged? What is 'bugged'?"

"Tapped. The Greenmountain Lodge is too close to Washington, D.C., you see. Too many men with too many secrets think it's the perfect place for a private meeting," explained Dartley. "Undoubtedly, if you personally speak to every guest registered at the hotel or with every unskilled worker hired since you made your reservation last month, you will probably find a certain new person here, probably some guy who looks old and hard of hearing, probably a soft-spoken 'Polish' refugee, a devout Catholic who wishes only to be left alone as much as possible to commune with nature and with his God. Get the picture, folks? Believe me, Ilse de Brock knows about this meeting. She can smell a plot clear across the Atlantic. The bottom line is, she probably wants to photograph the man you've all come to meet." And with that, Dartley bowed deeply, a courtly gesture from another age. The gesture was ironic; he meant it that way.

The three Germans were silent. Finally von Kelsing spoke one word.

"Conjecture," he responded to the sartorially elegant man in front of him as if he were a particularly virulent form of leprosy, an American strain hitherto undetected. Yet, in his heart of hearts, he knew that everything the stranger, this man Savage, had told him about himself was absolutely true. The thought that somewhere, in Washington D.C. or, God forbid, the Kremlin, an information broker, even a computer, held data on his past chilled him. He wished he could take his rifle and shoot this man Savage in the head and be done with it. No, he'd have to be mad, Savage wasn't the source of his information. There were others who knew far more. What about them? Perhaps if he could strike a rapport with the American, he could discover the sources of his information? Who was waiting until the proper moment to blackmail the three of them? To von Kelsing, the idea of blackmail was the image of an iron fist closing around his throat. He knew that for him blackmail would not mean simple monthly payments in an unmarked envelope. No, he and von Kelsing–Schmidt would be completely controlled by outside political interests who wanted control of the arms race. It was that simple. The last thing he worried about was a crazed former S.S. officer, bent on revenge for years of isolation and misery.

"Who am I supposed to shoot?" It was the American. Who else?

"Don't you already know?" asked von Kelsing, laughing at his own joke. "His name is Ali Ozker."

"Ali Ozker?" replied Dartley. "I'm afraid I don't know him."

"That's a relief," laughed von Kelsing. "I thought you could read minds."

"Is Ali Ozker a Turk?"

"*The* Turk. What you'd call the Turkish Godfather. He's funneling literally tons of opium into West Germany. And that's not all; he's backed by the Soviets."

"How do you know this?" asked Dartley.

"I have contacts in German intelligence. I have contacts in NATO," replied von Kelsing. "Believe me, Ali Ozker is the Turkish Al Capone, except that he's not dealing in bootleg liquor. His biggest stock in trade is pure heroin from the Caucasus. He has dealers all over West Germany. I know. One of his dealers was an ex-employee of mine named Demirel. He was the *first* man I hired to kill Ozker. He was returned to me in an American refrigerator cut up into several pieces. I had ordered the refrigerator from the American PX in Vogelweh as a Christmas present for my wife."

"What is the connection between the dead man and the American refrigerator?" asked Dartley.

"I don't know," answered von Kelsing. "The only people who knew about both Demirel and my wife's refrigerator were Reiser and Schmidt here, and I hardly think—"

"Why should we kill Demirel?" interjected Reiser, suddenly vocal.

Von Kelsing ignored him. "No, it makes no sense to me. It terrified me. I sank into a depression from Christmas until the middle of February. Nothing made sense to me. Nothing."

"The only person who probably knew about both the order for the refrigerator and the dead man Demirel was Ilse de Brock," said Dartley.

"But I did not tell Ilse anything," insisted Bruno Schmidt. "How could she know about Demirel? I could not even remember his name myself."

"If Ozker is really in the hire of the Soviets," explained Dartley, "then the KGB would relay all pertinent information about von Kelsing–Schmidt back to Ilse. It makes sense to me."

"I don't know. I don't know," chanted a dazed Schmidt.

"I cannot tell you that much about Ozker," continued von Kelsing, "except that he has investment properties in both Istanbul and London; he presumably spends a great deal of time in both places. He seems to fly in and out of West Germany all the time. He has what he calls pharmaceutical businesses in Munich and Frankfurt. Actually, Frankfurt is the branch office."

"Ozker makes these terrible copycat medicines," groaned Reiser. "There is no point in spending millions of deutsche marks on research when this pirate comes and steals everything."

"Does he have family?" asked Dartley.

"Family? I'm not sure. I've heard he has small children. I've also heard he has a grown son in medical school. I don't know which version is true."

"What medical school?" asked the American.

"I don't know," replied von Kelsing. "The Federal Republic has a very fine medical school in the university at Munich. You need not be afraid to become ill in West Germany, Herr Savage," said von Kelsing with no sense of the irony implicit in what he was saying.

"I hope I never get sick," joked the assassin-for-hire.

"One other thing," added von Kelsing. "We know that Ozker spends a great deal of time in Bulgaria, in Sofia, at the Hotel Vitosha–New Otani.

This is where Demirel went to kill him. At least, he sent his own gunman there."

With that, von Kelsing sighed deeply and looked very woebegone. "You see, Mr. Savage, my wife is very ill because of what is happening to our country. It is one and the same. We have many layoffs, many absentees, many behavioral problems because of the narcotics. The West German police spend many millions upon millions of deutsche marks to correct the drug problem. The problem only gets worse. Some agents are murdered. Others are compromised, bought off. Confiscated heroin disappears from the back rooms of police stations."

The industrialist looked sadder still. The English setters had stopped barking. They sat on their haunches with young, impatient eyes looking for a signal to run off into the bramble bushes. The dogs were well trained. Their strain at having to sit still took the form of long whining yawns. Every time they opened their black-gummed mouths, high-pitched sounds like squeaking hinges emanated from them. The men ignored the dogs. The pheasant hunt was on the verge of becoming another kind of sport altogether.

"You see, Mr. Savage," continued von Kelsing, "in December, when I saw what the drugs had done to my wife, I decided to take action. What was a Turk to me? This half-educated heap of arrogance, Demirel, you see, owed me a favor. We both had sons—once. We both knew that something had to be done about the breakdown of everything. When I first came home on Christmas Eve after the midnight mass and my wife opened her gift, the American refrigerator, my friend Demirel was inside, his genitals stuffed in his mouth, the severed head, did I tell you this, I knew I had no choice, I would do anything to get rid of Ozker as soon as possible. But I was confused and depressed. I did not know where to turn. Finally, on my own, without consulting my friends, I asked the advice of several American military men, army men from NATO, men who understood the need for assassination in order to save many many lives...."

Dartley was anxious to end the interview. He did not want to be observed by anyone. The Greenmountain Lodge, however distant from the twin citadels of American power, New York and Washington, D.C., was not distant enough. Someone within the hotel was monitoring von Kelsing's phone.

"What is your deadline?" he asked.

"Deadline?" responded von Kelsing. "As soon as possible."

"I have to find the exact moment. You realize this won't be in the middle of the Sahara," added Dartley. "I have to figure out how to kill Ozker and save my own skin at the same time, you understand? I have no intention of spending the rest of my life in a European jail."

Von Kelsing eyed him coldly. "That would not be likely, my friend. You saw what happened to my last gunman. Ozker has many bodyguards. You would undoubtedly be carved up into many pieces before you would end up in court."

Dartley listened to the industrialist's bottom-line description of the real world. Von Kelsing's voice had a subconscious killer tone to it. Something in him wished his paid assassin dead. He undoubtedly did not want witnesses to the death of his soul. Dartley had heard these tones of ambivalence before in men who were passing from the innocence of the civilized to the corruption of the powerful. But he never let the hostility of a prospective employer get in his way. He chalked it up to human nature. Hatred didn't bother him as long as he knew how to assemble and fire a gun. He wasn't in the business of killing to satisfy his own psychological needs. His political beliefs aside, he was in it for the money, and he cost plenty.

Now it was Dartley's turn to lay down the botom line.

"I'm not sure you can afford me," he said.

"I can afford anyone," answered von Kelsing. "Besides, there are three of us with bank accounts. What do you want?"

"Dartley doesn't bargain," replied Dartley. "It's a flat fee. I want half of it in advance and the other half when the job is completed."

"How much?"

"Dartley has a Swiss bank account. I don't begin till I get the go-ahead from him."

"How much?"

"A million bucks."

"A million bucks? A million *dollars*? Are you insane?"

"You heard me."

"Out of the question."

Bruno Scmidt began to laugh. Reiser blinked; he didn't say anything. Von Kelsing seemed to grow rigid with a cold rage. Dartley was in no way intimidated; he'd been here before.

"Dartley figures if top Hollywood stars are getting paid five million plus a percentage for every fucking movie, top assassins can charge a fucking million," Dartley explained. "What movie star ever put his life on the line to stop a heroin dealer who must be costing West Germany multimillions of deutsche marks every quarter?"

Von Kelsing was outraged. To this imperial Prussian, gunmen were evidently in the same category as tree surgeons.

"Your price is out of line with the going rate," he said.

Dartley guffawed like a neighing horse. "Listen, mister," he said, "by the time I've finished paying for forged documents, custom-made weapons, my transportation, my cover, not to mention several changes of socks, I may have already blown a couple hundred thousand bucks."

"A million dollars is out of the question," repeated von Kelsing.

"That's more than I had in mind," pleaded Reiser in German in the tones of a woman at a department-store sale.

"Take it or leave it," said the gunman, buttoning

his jacket and getting ready to leave. "I think Dartley wants me to meet an Arab sheik. Seems like a well-placed Saudi family has too many greedy sons."

"You don't quite understand," said von Kelsing. "I can find a hitman in Düsseldorf for ten thousand deutsche marks, around five thousand dollars, so—"

"Fine," replied Dartley. "Hope he doesn't come back in a refrigerator, too. Well, it's been nice seeing you. I always enjoy getting jerked off once in a while, a little S. and M. provides the cheap thrills we're all looking for, right?"

With that, the American in English tweeds tipped the visor of his Irish rain hat and started back for the Greenmountain Lodge.

"Wait!" called out von Kelsing.

The man stopped.

"Wait, Mr. Savage. Wait. I must admit you are correct. I am asking you to kill one of the most destructive men in Europe. Yes, you are correct. How much did you say you needed in advance?"

There was a long silence. Dartley still had not turned around.

"How much did you say you needed in advance, Mr. Savage?"

Another long pause. Von Kelsing answered his own question.

"Five hundred thousand dollars. Good. I will phone my Swiss bank. The three of us will find a way to pay you the money."

Savage turned around. Von Kelsing expected to

see him grinning. "All the peasants want is money" was one of his favorite expressions. Dartley was grim. The hollows in his cheeks held black shadows.

"And five hundred thousand more when I kill the bastard. Agreed?"

"Agreed," chimed in von Kelsing and Schmidt, followed by Reiser's echo.

"Otherwise, I come after you," added Dartley.

"I beg your pardon?" said von Kelsing.

"You heard me," said the American. "If you don't pay me the rest of the money when I'm through, you'll get a bullet in the head. Agreed?"

Von Kelsing rose to his full height, as the sons of Prussian generals learned to do practically at birth.

"You can inform Mr. Dartley I am a man of my word."

Among the three friends, the price was three hundred and thirty-three thousand apiece.

In that moment von Kelsing decided to keep his own counsel. He decided that the five hundred thousand advance was enough. For another ten thousand he could hire a gunman to shoot Mr. Savage in the head as soon as he finished with Ali Ozker. Savage would hardly be expecting an assassin of his own.

For Reiser and Schmidt a million dollars meant nothing. They would have their accountants juggle the books, pad legitimate business expenses and somehow make the million disappear. In any case, the money would never come from their own bank accounts. They had not gotten to be million-aires by spending large sums of money on luxury items like assassinations. No, a million dollars put Dartley in the same category as Ali Ozker, yet another exploiter of other men's honest toil.

"Another thing, Mr. Savage," continued von Kelsing. "When will I know when and where you plan to eliminate Ali Ozker?"

Dartley answered, "You won't. One morning, probably in early summer, you will pick up the morning paper and read that the prominent Middle Eastern tycoon, Ali Ozker, met with a sudden death. Perhaps it will look like an accident. Perhaps it will look like the work of a fanatic. Perhaps an innocent bystander will be blamed. Do you see?"

"What if it says that he died of a heart attack?" asked Willi Reiser, his setter straining on its leash.

"Don't worry, if it says 'heart attack' your intelligence sources will tell you that it was a journalistic cover-up; although, believe me, if you want a heart attack, there are ways to make it look like a heart attack."

"What do you mean?" asked von Kelsing, intrigued.

"Can't give away trade secrets," replied the American, "but I'm sure that Mr. Schmidt's best Girl Friday could tell you a thing or two. The KGB has a special school for murder á la naturel."

At this point Herr Schmidt could take no more of this half-civilized American's unnecessary jabs.

"I won't stand for these implications," the munitions manufacturer boomed. "Fraulein de Brock is being maligned. In years past these accusations would be reason enough for a duel!"

As the older man's voice reached the unnatural crescendo of a man unaccustomed to anger, Ilse de Brock herself raced into view. She was holding tightly onto her navy blue straw bag ornamented with the yellow and orange straw flowers. She was almost a comic sight. In her free hand she held aloft Schmidt's bottle of digitalis pills for his sluggish middle-aged heart.

"Herr Schmidt! Herr Schmidt!" she shouted in German. "Excuse me for interrupting you, but you left your heart pills behind."

"Speak of the devil," commented the American dressed in tweeds.

"This is my secretary, Fraulein de Brock. Ilse, this is Mr. Savage."

So this is the famous Mr. Savage, she thought as she smiled shyly. Her left hand worked the trigger under the handle of her bag. She pointed the end of the bag at the stranger. She hoped the sharp glare of the April sun would pierce the opaque surface of his dark glasses. She wanted as many pictures of him as she could get away with.

She looked down at his shoes. Sure enough, they were the exact ones she had seen from under von Kelsing's bed.

"But I already brought my digitalis," replied Schmidt, holding up a pharmaceutical bottle identical to the one Ilse de Brock held in her hand.

"How is that possible? Did you bring two bottles to America?"

"No, I only remember bringing one bottle," replied Schmidt.

"That is strange," countered de Brock, feigning ignorance. "I don't understand."

Then, as if on cue, her face brightened. "Oh Bruno, how can you ever forgive me? Please, please excuse me, gentlemen, for interrupting your pheasant hunt. I was so afraid Herr Schmidt would forget his digitalis, I had the pharmacist make up a second bottle identical to the first just in case he ran out of his medicine. I had completely forgotten. I am such a fool."

Bowing backward like a Japanese housewife, she made her apologies. All the while, the black-eyed Susan with the hole in the middle was aimed directly at Dartley/Savage.

The man was no amateur. In a flash he grabbed her purse.

The woman shrieked, "What are you doing? Give that back! Bruno!"

Von Kelsing hardly had time to appraise the situation and issue the command he assumed was expected of him before Dartley dumped the contents of the bag on the ground.

"Here, here!" at least three people cried in unison.

He ripped the bag apart, exposing the camera. At the sight of it Ilse de Brock screamed as if she had been stabbed in the heart.

"You'll have to excuse the lady," the stranger said. "Seems like someone planted a camera in her purse. You've probably been taking portrait shots of me without realizing what you were doing. I guess it's just one of those things."

"That's impossible!" Ilse shouted when she had recovered her state of mind. She pleaded with Bruno Schmidt. "Bruno, what is this man doing to me? Why did he plant that camera in my bag?"

Dartley was now smelling her. He announced to von Kelsing, "That's the perfume that was under your bed. Chanel Number Nineteen."

Von Kelsing was too busy inspecting the camera to notice. He was trying to open the case.

Dartley stopped him. "Don't do that. You'll expose the film. Don't worry. Have it properly developed. I'm sure you'll find some interesting pictures, properly focused and expertly framed. There's nothing accidental about the photography here." He held up the purse for all to see. "See the little round hole in the middle of the straw flower," Dartley said. "That's where the shutter was. Right behind there. The trigger's here under the handle. All she had to do was point the bag in the right direction, right there, and squeeze the handle. Here, Schmidt, you try it."

Ilse reversed her tactics. She grew very still and spoke in a cool, barely controlled whisper. "This man must be working for someone who wishes to destroy von Kelsing–Schmidt," she said. Then she turned to Dartley and peered at him so intently she made him believe she could see right through his dark glasses. "Sir, you have made a mistake. I am only the secretary to Herr Schmidt. I know nothing about photography." Her luminous green eyes had another message, one of mankind's oldest: "Fuck me and I'll do anything you want." Dartley, unfortunately for Ilse de Brock, never found available sex that hard to come by. Usually he was the better half of the bargain.

"It's been real nice meeting you, Fraulein de Brock," was his simple response, a response that infuriated her. He could see that somewhere, way back in her youth, she'd learned the meaning of rigid discipline. She was a professional at disguising her true intent.

Schmidt took her by the arm to lead her away. Ilse, however, did not want to abandon South Meadow so soon. She walked backward, facing her accuser, stunned. Schmidt, holding her arm, was almost dragging her back to the Greenmountain Lodge. Finally, realizing she could not possibly control her access to the information conveyed in the South Meadow, she turned around and obediently went with her employer. It was over. She had been exposed.

"What is going on here?" asked Reiser in a tight, controlled voice. "Who is that woman really working for?"

"What difference does it make?" replied von Kelsing. "She is clearly the enemy."

Dartley asked, "Will you take care of it or shall I?"

"Take care of what?" asked Reiser.

"The secretary," replied von Kelsing, impatient with his colleague. Reiser seemed to have evolved a personal style out of naivete. In truth, he was the shrewdest of the three. He disliked public scenes and emotionalism of any kind.

"We must get rid of her before she does more damage to us," was his only remark.

"I will take care of her," said von Kelsing. "I will take care of her. And now, Mr. Savage, where do we go from here?"

"Like I said," said Dartley. "When I hear from Dartley that you've deposited half a million in his Swiss bank account—here's the bank, the banker's name, the number..." Here he paused and handed von Kelsing a small card with the information on it "...I will begin my assignment. No matter what happens, I will have Ozker dead by the Fourth of July. You see, I'm a sucker for small-town brass bands and 'God Bless America.'"

Von Kelsing peered at the card. Without looking up, he said, "I see. And, Mr. Savage, how will we be able to contact you?"

"I'll call you every week at noon your time. Tuesdays. I've got your private number."

"I mean, how will we be able to reach you in case there's been a change of plans?"

"Change of plans?" queried Dartley.

"Yes, what if I find out that Ali Ozker died in his sleep. Would you not want to be notified?"

"Don't worry," said Dartley, "if Ozker dies in his sleep, the sandman in question will be yours truly. All you have to do in that case is deposit the other half-million in Dartley's bank account."

Von Kelsing looked at Savage and grunted assent. He hated this man, hated this hireling so appropriately named. He hated the invisible Dartley, too, because he had sent the man called Savage. He especially hated Savage's manner and his impeccable English tweeds. More than anything, he hated his mastery of firearms. He could not stop the film in his mind, the ongoing sight of pheasants' heads splattering in midair. It was a nightmare loop. The pheasants' heads became land mines planted in his own brain. One by one, piece by piece, chunks of his Teutonic concentration splattered into gray vomit that strangled his thought processes. He needed sleep. He needed to unwind. He knew it was repressed anger. He knew he felt run over by this stranger. But what could he do? He had never heard of this man Savage before; why was Dartley turning over the job to him? He had sought out the world's number-one assassin. He wanted the best. He also wanted his own self-respect. The gun was part of von Kelsing's self-image. He needed to know he was a crack shot. Were not firearms *his* profession? Who was this Savage? Whom was he trying to impress?

But, of course, that wasn't it. It was the money. It was always the money. One million dollars was absurd. The sum unsettled him. Von Kelsing felt like a little boy again, a naive child. He had not wanted to admit to Savage that (a) he didn't know the price of a good assassin, and (b) the price that Dartley asked was more than he could afford.

Mitzi would have laughed at the whole situation. She would have called it black comedy. She always chortled with glee when her husband got cheated by hotels and restaurants. It restored her sense of perspective. But von Kelsing, quite to the contrary, had never seen the humor in being overcharged. He regularly pored over hotel bills, carefully considering each charge, checking it against his own records, adding his own totals. Wherever he went, he carried a pocket calculator with him.

Once, an Italian financier worth hundreds of millions in real estate had told him he'd never be really rich if he worried about pfennigs. "Oh?" he had replied, affronted. "That's because I can't afford to arbitrarily gouge tenants like you. I am a manufacturer."

"Yes, a manufacturer of firearms," the Italian had continued. "You basically gouge the human race!"

And at that, von Kelsing had launched into a tirade against Italians and why they were too weak to be a first-rate military power. "You are all effeminate artists," he had said. "What could you possibly know about weaponry?"

Von Kelsing himself was well aware of Italian weaponry, especially the Beretta Model 92 and 92S, the Revelli machine gun and the Breda modello 28 aircraft gun, but he shrewdly guessed that the Italian, typically, would know next to nothing about his own country's firearms. His patriotism would consist of over-emotionalized generalizations.

"Too weak to be a military power?" the Italian had replied with a mocking laugh. "Tell me kraut, tell me about the kraut military power. After two world wars, a hundred million dead, tell me about the Schnitzle Empire."

Von Kelsing, then 60, had flung his body onto the smaller man; he intended to gouge out the runt's eyes. He could feel his fingers, with a vengeance all their own, clamp onto the man's eye sockets. He was preparing himself to pop the eyeballs out of their sockets and then pull them loose from the skein of bloodied muscles and nerves.

He had done it twice before, in the war, both times with American boys who thought they were John Wayne. Both boys blond and blue-eyed. Probably German-Americans. Von Kelsing had seen it in the way they moved. They were imitating the movies. Because of their conditioning by the popular American culture that did not believe in evil, they hungered for face-to-face combat, man against man, with gymnasium wrestling skills, adolescent muscles, and bayonets. They clearly were not prepared for horror, for the irrationality of it all, the eye gougings, the castrations, the disembowelings, the faces hanging off exposed skulls, human brains splattered like bird shit on the faces of the advancing army or the retreating one.

Those dear, high-spirited American boys.... He remembered the power he had felt each time, tearing out their eyes as they screamed in unspeakable terror. Mercifully he had sunk his bayonet in their taut young stomachs, popping the skin and stirring the soft mess of entrails underneath. None of this sickened him. To the contrary, he had been intoxicated with his own power. It was more than the love of winning a fight. It was more than mere survival. Luckily for the Italian financier who had insulted the Fatherland, the man had bodyguards. They saved him from the man from Düsseldorf.

In that late afternoon, walking back to Greenmountain Lodge with Reiser, both of them silent, von Kelsing felt certain his decision about the final payment had been correct. Dartley would get half a million, not a penny more. As it was, each of the triumvirate would have to cough up almost a hundred seventy thousand apiece. That was enough to pay for twenty executions. The more he thought about outwitting the arrogant American, the broader the smile on his face grew.

"What is so funny, Werner?" Reiser asked.

"Nothing," said von Kelsing, laughing out loud. "I was just thinking how much I love to have the best of both worlds."

"What do you mean?"

"Don't worry, Willi, we will never pay one million dollars for this gunman. I have figured out a way so that when we have paid him a half million, that will be it."

"What do you mean, Werner?"

"What do you think I mean? No gunman is worth one million dollars." He paused. "Besides, Willi, what is the point of always knowing that somewhere out there, there is the man who knows you financed a major political assassination?"

"Ozker is a major political assassination?"

"Are you a fool?"

The two men were almost in hearing distance of the formal gardens. The manicured green shrubbery sat at the foot of the slope that led up to Greenmountain Lodge. The man called Savage had completely disappeared; von Kelsing had no way of guessing where he was. Knowing him, he might be behind the six-foot hedge listening to every word.

Von Kelsing's voice was almost inaudible. He spoke directly in Reiser's ear. "I am planning to hire a man to track down Savage and eliminate him the minute we know that Ozker is dead. This man will know nothing of the plot to kill Ozker. He will only know he is to eliminate a dangerous criminal."

"But Werner, we do not even know where this Savage will kill Ozker or when. It could be tomorrow. It could be the end of June."

"Don't worry, Willi. I will know. I will know."

But von Kelsing did not know. He could not wait to return to Düsseldorf. There he would summon what he called his "intelligence group," mostly contacts in the German police and the American military. But first, he had unfinished business in the United States. First, there was a sacrificial lamb that must be led to slaughter. Why? Because the lamb was not a lamb. She was a wolf in everything but name.

Chapter Six

In Suite 406, the half-removed fingerprint powder was still smeared on the surface of von Kelsing's walnut end table. When von Kelsing saw it, he knew that Savage had told the truth about Ilse de Brock. Von Kelsing experienced a mounting rage. It didn't make any difference if she wanted any one person's fingerprints or if she was just snooping around. Her sloppiness had added insult to her greater crime—she had intruded on his private terrain. Confronting this fact, von Kelsing felt emotionally drained. He had been violated—raped, really—by a low-level employee. She had deliberately insinuated herself into the sacrosanct gathering of three old comrades. That was bad enough. The deeper truth was blood-curdling. Her intention had been to spy on them so that someone else, an outside agency, the KGB perhaps, could eventually bring them down. Ilse de Brock was a Mata Hari, a mistress of deceit, an agent of death.

A psychiatrist, the one time he had gone to one, had told von Kelsing he was paranoid.

"I come to you for marriage counseling and you tell me I am paranoid?" In the Third Reich psychiatrists were killed for saying less than that.

"Herr von Kelsing," the doctor had replied, "your world is full of demons that do not exist. The devil in question is a product of your own overactive imagination."

"If that is true," von Kelsing had replied, "then I owe everything I am to the devils inside my mind. I have no intention of giving them up. They help me to kill the devils outside my mind." That was his way of telling the psychiatrist to go to hell.

Von Kelsing had a plan that rose full-bloom out of his rage. With the .38 Schmidt kept under his pillow, he would shoot the secretary, place the gun in her hand and call it suicide. He grabbed the phone and dialed Schmidt. It rang six times before the other man answered it.

"Ja?"

"I'm coming down. Open the door when I knock."

"But Werner, we...I am taking a bath."

Perfect, thought Werner von Kelsing, as a new variation of his plan arose in his head.

"I will come anyway. I have to talk with you." He put down the receiver, laughing out loud at the perversity of his thoughts. "The Superpowers think they can enslave a German and a Prussian at that, do they?"

If von Kelsing had known whom Ilse was really working for, he would have given the Savage another mission. Then again, why quibble? She could be working for Ozker. They had both taken part, to a greater or lesser extent, in Demirel's arrival in the American refrigerator. Even if she had done no more than inform a third party, who had himself informed Ozker, Ilse had still been involved in a plot to destroy him.

For sentimental reasons more than anything else, Bruno Schmidt had always shaved with a straight razor. It reminded him of his childhood on his grandfather's Bavarian estate. His grandfather had always maintained that the new safety razors could not compare with a well-honed straight razor, especially one made by Wilkinson, the British swordsmiths. Their steel was incomparable. All that sharpening required was a leather strap. Schmidt was proud of his grandfather's straight razor. It traveled with him wherever he went. When not being used it sat in a magnificent sterling silver case with the big initial S in the old script engraved on it.

Von Kelsing knew exactly where that case would be, sitting squarely on top of Schmidt's bureau, a proud trophy of an older and more important time.

He knocked on Schmidt's door. Predictably, it was open.

"Come in, we are taking a bath," called Schmidt from an inner space in a voice that echoed off the hard tile walls.

Von Kelsing took a step inside. "Hello, Bruno!" he called back, but not before he heard Ilse's

familiar giggle. It was her most annoying man-
nerism. She did it only when drunk on schnapps.

"Werner, you can't come in here," said Schmidt,
laughing. Schmidt had obviously been drinking, too.

So that was it. The two of them were planning
to ignore the appalling incident in South Meadow.
In another week, they would be telling the whole
story at a Düsseldorf cocktail party. With a mouth
half full of curried shrimp pâté, Ilse would be
recounting how when she was in America out
taking a walk, this American in dark glasses grabbed
her purse, emptied the contents, which included
her camera (of course, she always carried her
camera with her when she was traveling), and
accused her of being a KGB agent. Nothing would
be mentioned about the camera's being kept in a
special compartment; nothing would be said about
the daisy with the hole in the middle. The purse
would be long gone, so why bother to support the
opposite side of the argument?

"When are you planning to return?" von Kelsing
shouted out.

"Return? Ilse and I may stay here and have
some fun!" Schmidt shouted back.

The monogrammed case was exactly where he
knew it would be. When he opened it, it didn't
make a sound. Not a creak. Bruno Schmidt was the
perfect country squire. He kept everything well-
oiled—his guns, his cars, even the lid to his shaving
case. Von Kelsing lifted the razor out of its case. Its
long, straight edge caught the light like a mirror.
He unfolded it and stuck it carefully into his back

pocket, its handle jutting out at an angle just where he could reach it. When he walked into the bathroom, the two lovers were chin deep in suds.

"Do you usually watch other people taking a bath?" Schmidt laughed.

"Don't worry, he can't see anything." Ilse giggled. Von Kelsing laughed too. He really wanted to bellow, "You dare to pretend you were not spying on me! You dare to laugh, you traitor!"

"Werner, why don't you join us?" Ilse laughed.

"I will join you if Bruno will leave the bath," von Kelsing answered.

"Werner, I have seen you naked," Schmidt replied, shocked at what appeared to be his friend's display of prudishness. Germans, like their Scandinavian cousins, were not known for squeamishness in the face of nudity.

"Bruno, I have a surprise for you," von Kelsing said.

"A surprise? What kind of a surprise?"

"First, you have to go into the bedroom."

"But how long do I have to wait?"

"Just for a minute."

"Do you promise?"

"I promise."

Ilse giggled again. Von Kelsing was sure of it now: the two of them had come back to their hotel suite and swallowed pills, probably Quaaludes. The industrialist and his secretary were clinging to the fantasy that nothing of import had happened in the South Meadow. They reminded him of the many films portraying doomed Nazis at the end of the war.

Reveling, the Nazis drank champagne and smoked opium as the Allied bombers thundered in the distance.

By now Bruno Schmidt was out of the tub, great clouds of soap bubbles falling off his slippery bulk onto the white tile floor. He resembled a porpoise out of its proper element, gasping for breath on dry land. Von Kelsing, his back pocket with the straight razor out of sight, handed his friend a large Turkish bath towel. Schmidt wrapped it around him like a Roman senator and left the bathroom with the words, "This better be good."

Looking at Ilse, von Kelsing realized with a jolt that the bond between this spy and his longtime friend was as profound as the eternal mystery of man and woman. She had seduced Schmidt, knowing the man's vulnerability, knowing how completely he would surrender to her. All the while she had known exactly what she was doing. He wondered how much classified information from von Kelsing–Schmidt had ended up on her employer's desk, her real employer, that is. Whom was she working for? he asked himself. I. M. Farben? Heckler-Koch? The East Germans? The KGB? He wondered if she was part of a U.S. surveillance team keeping watch over German industry. Sometimes von Kelsing asked himself why the Americans had been so lenient with the Germans after World War II. Why the financial investment? Was their ultimate plan to steal Germany's technological genius? Was von Kelsing–Schmidt being set up only to be pillaged?

Von Kelsing closed the bathroom door behind

him and pushed in the lock. Although there was panic in Ilse's eyes, her mouth at all times retained its toothpaste-ad smile.

"Don't you want to take a bath with Bruno and me?" she asked coquettishly. Her sentence was interspersed with deep gulps of air. Why was this man in her bathroom now? Was he using her embarrassment at South Meadow as a pretext to seduce her? His crotch seemed to be bulging with sexual excitement. Yes, that was it. Why be paranoid? Men only wanted one thing.

"I have come to see you," von Kelsing said, stating the obvious. He could see the expectation in her eyes. He loosened his tie and undid the top button of his shirt. Ilse stared in fascination as he stripped, leaving his clothes in a pile by the side of the tub. He let down his trousers carefully so that the straight razor in his back pocket would not clang on the tile floor. In any case, she was clearly mesmerized by the thick protuberance under his shorts.

"Ooh," she commented. "I'm so glad you're here."

When he let down his shorts and revealed his stout pole, she was relieved.

"We are going to surprise Bruno," von Kelsing said.

"Yes, I cannot wait to surprise him," she echoed, thinking what a superior lover Werner would be to Bruno the Blimp. Werner the Warrior: yes, even in his mid-sixties, von Kelsing was rock hard, with the smooth, hairless body of a classical marble statue. She watched in fascination as he undid his shoelaces and took off his shoes, letting them drop to the floor with a thud. His balls seemed so big, much bigger than Bruno's. What a wonderful man, she thought, what a courageous man. The KGB would love him. How tragic he had the misfortune to be born into capitalistic depravity. So much extravagant wealth, all of it derived from the backbreaking labor of the proletariat.

"What is the surprise?' It was Bruno thumping on the door.

"Give me two minutes!" von Kelsing called out. He looked into Ilse's green eyes with a leer. "In two minutes, I promise you, you will be in heaven."

"I know, I know," she replied, mesmerized by this Aryan god of war standing by the side of the tub. Without another word, he climbed in, lowered himself into the warm, soapy water and pulled her straight onto him, impaling her on his cock. He sucked onto her mouth voraciously like a starving man. His desire alone brought her to an immediate pitch of sexual fever. "Ja, Ja," she sighed. She was orgasmic almost immediately. She did not notice as he reached down over the side of the tub, fumbled for his pants, found the angled handle of Schmidt's straight razor and held it behind his back waiting for the exact moment to strike.

"Are you ready yet?" called Bruno on the other side of the door.

"Another minute!" cried von Kelsing, pumping furiously. Ilse's vaginal flesh sucked tightly onto his swollen cock. Christ, she was so much better than Mitzi! What a waste. She was coming now. He pressed his hand behind her back to support her, to prevent her from leaning too far back. He did not want her neck under water. His timing had to be perfect. He did not want his sperm in her vaginal cavity when the autopsy was performed.

"Aaagh! Aaagh!" Her orgasm was low, guttural, consuming. Now was the time. With a single motion, he withdrew from her, knelt on her chest and pressed her head back into the water. The element of surprise was lethal enough. At this moment she was doubly intoxicated and he was intent on holding her under until her lungs filled with water. Nor was drowning the only murder weapon. The straight razor itched in his hand. He pressed his strong broad knees onto her sternum as he took one hand and then the other and cut deeply into each wrist, carving a straight line across. Then he pulled each wrist down into the warm water. He knew the invisible lines he had drawn would begin to widen into broad bands of liquid red. A pink cloud already swirled in the soapy water over her submerged neck. He pinned her down for another long moment until finally she went limp. Then he let go, dropping the straight razor into the reddening water. He quickly climbed out of the tub, his erection hotter than ever. He wanted to pump his meat right then and there. He had never been so aroused. He was beside himself with lust, but he couldn't chance it. He quickly grabbed his clothes away from the tub, relieved that they were still relatively dry. With a big Turkish towel, he washed himself off at the white marble sink.

"What is going on?" Bruno screamed at the door. "Werner, open this door!"

"Thirty seconds!" bellowed von Kelsing.

Then, out of the corner of his eye he saw a scene out of a horror movie. Ilse had not drowned! She had raised her head up out of the water and was trying to speak. A gargle sound and a strange hissing issued from her anguished mouth. No words came. It was too late. She could not raise her hands. She did not even try. The water in the tub was now dark with blood. Her face and shoulders were paper white, a tinge of purple around her lips. Within a minute, by the time he was dressed, Ilse had surrendered to a welcome sleep. Her cadaverous face was peaceful. She was almost smiling. As for von Kelsing, he had seen death so many times it was like being with an old friend.

Von Kelsing threw the towel into the tub. At the bathroom door he spoke to Schmidt. "Bruno, I have your surprise, but you must go sit on the bed."

"Werner, I don't understand."

"Bruno, go sit on the bed."

Von Kelsing unlocked the door, opened it and walked into the bedroom. He shut the door behind him. Bruno Schmidt, as directed, was sitting on the edge of his bed wrapped in a towel.

"Where is Ilse?"

"Ilse's in the tub. Listen to me, Bruno. Your life is in danger."

"What? Werner, what do you mean? Ilse!"

"Leave Ilse alone! You see, Bruno, you will be accused of a terrible crime. They will try to destroy you, and only I will be able to help you."

Schmidt went white. "What crime? Werner, I haven't done anything."

"Bruno, listen to me. You are a very wealthy man. Many women have pursued you. All have failed. All the while it seems you were romancing your secretary."

"That's nobody's business!" wailed Bruno Schmidt.

"She persisted in getting you to agree to marry her," said von Kelsing.

"That's not true!" cried Schmidt.

"Yes," continued von Kelsing, "she pursued you here to West Virginia, hoping to force your hand, begging you to marry her!"

"No, no," insisted Schmidt. "Ilse never mentioned marriage. Never once. Never. Why do you keep saying this?"

Von Kelsing laid his hand on his friend's shoulder. "Shut up and listen to me, Bruno. I want to tell you your surprise." Von Kelsing spoke in a whisper now. His tone was one Schmidt had never heard before. It frightened him. "Ilse said if you didn't marry her, she'd kill herself. She said she wanted to tell the world about the two of you. But you refused her, didn't you? You said you were an old man and she was just after your money, didn't you?"

To each of these accusations, Bruno Schmidt kept muttering, "Nein, nein, Werner, nein." He was wild-eyed with fright. What surprise could von Kelsing possibly have in mind? And then von Kelsing said it, told him the surprise. Schmidt was at first so distracted that he didn't hear it.

"What?" he asked. He couldn't possibly have heard what he thought he heard. Von Kelsing repeated what he had told him.

"Yes, Bruno, she killed herself all because of you. She committed suicide in the time-honored way. She—"

Schmidt bolted into the bathroom, saw his Ilse white and lifeless in a sea of blood, screamed, "No! No!" and jumped into the tub to revive her. He refused to believe so much life, so much beauty, so much joy had disappeared in the short time since he had been with her. His face distorted with rage, he turned to von Kelsing.

"You did this!"

"I?" von Kelsing asked. "What was my motivation? I hardly knew her. I was never alone with her, not even once until today. You, you on the other hand, you've been involved with her for years. I imagine you had all sorts of inappropriate passion and terrible scenes."

"No scenes! No scenes!" cried Bruno Schmidt. "You did this! I will tell the police you did this!"

"No, Bruno, you will stick to my story. She committed suicide for the reasons I told you."

Schmidt's face was livid. "Suicide? My Ilse? Suicide?"

Now von Kelsing spoke with his terrible whisper

again. "Bruno, Ilse was an agent, an agent of what I do not know, but she was here to spy on us."

Bruno Schmidt was sobbing now. Inconsolable. His face buried in the dead Ilse. He had no desire to hear anything von Kelsing said.

"Ilse de Brock was responsible for Cemal Demirel being delivered to my house in that American refrigerator," von Kesling went on. "Who knows what her connection to the narcotics traffic is or was." He paused. Schmidt's sobbing was loud; he was sucking in great gulps of air. "It would be embarrassing, Bruno, would it not, if *Das Stern* were to connect you to a secret agent?"

Schmidt seemed to stop sobbing. There was a long silence. Then he straightened up in the tub. "Yes, Werner, of course you are right. She killed herself." His voice was flat, without emotion. "It was the camera in her bag, wasn't it? We tried to pretend it was a mistake."

"She was in my room today, Bruno. She tried to take fingerprints."

"Yes, of course, Werner."

"Wash yourself off, Bruno. We must call the police."

"First call Willi. We must tell Willi."

The police were southern men. They understood about women. They listened sympathetically to three sober German industrialists talk about a hysterical secretary. They had seen it all before.

There were problems, of course. No one could figure out how she managed to slit her wrists and drown at the same time, but the sergeant said he had seen that before, too.

No one disputed him.

The lack of a suicide note was the other thing. "I've rarely seen anyone commit suicide without leaving a note," said the sergeant. "This must be one of those times," said von Kelsing. "I think she called my associate, Mr. Schmidt."

"Why would she call me?" said Schmidt. "We were both using the same room."

"I was just trying to be polite about the situation, Bruno," explained von Kelsing.

"This is not a polite situation, Mr. von Kelsing," commented the sergeant. "I'm afraid you're too much of a gentleman for West Virginia."

"I feel personally responsible," replied von Kelsing.

"Oh? How are you personally responsible?" asked the law enforcer.

"You see, Sergeant, it was I who agreed to let Fraulein de Brock come along. We had come to do some good shooting. There was no need for a secretary, but she prevailed upon my associate. At the time I had no idea that she was obsessed with him. Nothing she said indicated her state of desperation. Still, I feel personally responsible."

"No, no, no, Mr. von Kelsing," objected the sergeant. "You go along. I just wish America had more men as 'personally responsible' as you."

When he finally collapsed on his bed, von Kelsing found his imagination was fixed on his lovemaking with Ilse de Brock. Never had a woman been so anxious for him to make love to her. With his .

hand on his organ, he worked his cock flesh up and down over his throbbing core and thought of how her cunt had felt as he entered her. In his mind he relived her giggle as she took him up to the hilt and made little moans and sighs. She had seemed overjoyed to have him fuck her. How wonderful she seemed, now that she was dead. How easy to make love to her now. In his fantasy there was no need for a straight razor as before. True, on some perverse level, he had enjoyed killing her. He had even enjoyed the fantasy and the reality of her sneaking into his bedroom and lying under his bed. Now that she was dead he could experience the love in her, the love that he knew was fueling her deep desire to see him and Bruno and Willi dead.

"Here's to you, Ilse my love," he sighed as a white arc of come coursed out of him. All things considered, he shook with one of the strongest orgasms of his life.

Chapter Seven

There were unforeseen complications.

When he returned to his hotel room after the

meeting at South Meadow, Dartley knew at once that his room had been searched. He had his own methods of detecting the invisible hands of strangers. He always carried carefully composed letters-in-progress, letters written to fictitious generals and ambassadors that usually referred to erroneous incidents such as "the president's apparent heart attack." There were also fictitious letters from chiefs of staff typed on forged stationery, which in the case of Greenmountain Lodge spoke of the secret meeting there between the vice-president and the prime minister of France, both expertly disguised and expertly guarded. Dartley routinely kept his letters-in-progress to the generals and ambassadors in his bedside table; he put the more provocative letters from the chiefs of staff under his underwear in his top bureau drawer. In both cases, the top letter was laid on top of a second letter at a precise angle with an exact amount of the underlying letter exposed. It was always the same exposure. It was something he had rehearsed at home. When he returned to his hotel room, he knew instantly if anyone had read the letters. He had another trick. Before leaving his hotel room for dinner or a meeting, he painted a thin, invisible seal of clear nail polish along a couple of inches of the seam on the side of his suitcases. There was no way the suitcase could be opened without breaking the seal. By the same token, if by chance the perpetrator noticed the broken seal, there was usually neither time nor ingenuity enough for the typical room snoop to figure out how to restore it. In his almost ten years of special assignments, Dartley had never once had his room searched in a hotel room in the States. Still, out of habit, especially when he was lining up a job, he took his usual precautions. At Greenmountain Lodge his room had definitely been searched. The letters had been inaccurately replaced. The seals on three separate suitcases were broken.

It got worse. In the lobby, as he was checking out, he ran into a squad of detectives and police investigating Ilse's death. They wanted to know who he was and why he was checking out at midnight. He presented his phony "Paul Savage" ID and credit cards; explained that he had come to Greenmountain Lodge for a business meeting; that he had intended to stay overnight but his uncle had taken sick in Washington. He had no choice but to return home as quickly as possible. Since, at this point, no one suspected murder in the death of Ilse de Brock, the police let him go.

While all this was going on, Dartley had the strangest feeling he was being watched. He restrained himself, accusing himself of free-floating anxiety and paranoia.

Then, in the parking lot, the situation suddenly went from worse to wacko. Dartley knew immediately that someone with sophisticated tools had tried to open his front door and had failed. He knew because the burglar or agent's hand had slipped, causing an inch-long scratch on the silver gray finish directly under the lock. He wasted no time in tossing the suitcases into the backseat and driving off.

He used the back roads, roads which were unfamiliar to him. Sooner or late he figured he'd see signs to U.S. 119 or to Interstate 81, the main road to Harrisburg. Twice he pulled over to the side of the road, turned off his lights and waited to see if he was being followed. Twice, within ten minutes, a slowly moving cranberry-colored Mercedes with a Washington license plate advanced slowly past him. After the second time he saw the Mercedes, he circled back past Greenmountain Lodge and headed for a motel he knew about. The Colonial Inn Motel. A generation before, his parents had often gone there during the season of the Hunt Club balls and Sunday brunches when Greenmountain Lodge was overbooked.

Eventually Dartley found the Colonial Inn Motel. One old Ford was in the potholed parking lot. Otherwise, the place stank. It was the original "No-tell Motel"; even the hookers had found better places. The paint peeled off the clapboard in great white sheets.

Using the name "Sam Booth," he got his room, a room facing away from "the highway." He explained to the proprietors, an elderly couple dressed for bed at nine thirty, that he didn't like the sound of traffic, especially in the country. He explained that, twice before, he'd had his cars, two different cars, both brand-new, stolen from motel parking lots. The proprietor, who was hard of hearing, said if it would make Mr. Booth feel better, he could park his car on the back lawn right under his bedroom window. The ground was still frozen. It didn't make any difference to him.

Dartley took the man's suggestion. He parked the car, leaving his suitcases inside. After locking the car, he went around to his room, locked the door, turned out the lights and kept watch over the backyard. The Chevy's chrome shone in the light of miniature floodlights attached to the back corners of the motel.

Dartley didn't have long to wait. After twenty minutes he saw a bland-looking bespectacled man of about 35 wearing a London Fog. He was peering into Dartley's car. He was trying to jimmy the lock. This time Dartley was ready. He had already opened his window six inches and pushed up the aluminum storm window. He lifted his .38 with its attached sight out of its shoulder holster, fastened the silencer onto the end of it and took aim at the exact center between the man's eyes. The man in the London Fog must have been psychic. At the precise moment Dartley pulled the trigger, the man looked up into the barrel of the gun. He had the innocent eyes of a little boy caught stealing cookies. The muffled retort of the blast was almost inaudible. By contrast, the sound of the bullet crashing through the man's skull seemed deafening, but Dartley decided this was his imagination. Again he accused himself of paranoia. Again he checked himself.

The man in the London Fog fell silently to the ground by the side of the car. Dartley waited for the second man. There had to be two. Agents always traveled in teams. Dartley did not move from his position at the window. He waited for what felt like the better part of an hour. It was actually fifteen minutes.

He heard the sound of a car door slamming on the other side of the motel. A second man, this one older and thickset, appeared. When he saw the first man lying on the ground, he immediately looked up at the dark row of windows on the back of the motel and instinctively reached for the bulge under his overcoat. This time Dartley did not use the sight on his .38. His first shot missed the man's vital organs; the man was able to wrest his own weapon out of its holster. Dartley continued to fire his weapon. He was determined to kill the second man before he fired his gun. More than anything he feared the sound of gunfire. He did not want to risk waking other guests who were in all probability sleeping lightly, some of them with open windows. He fired his .38 repeatedly until the remaining seven bullets were spent. Some of them must have hit their mark. The man in question never had a chance to pull the trigger on his gun. Dartley immediately closed his window, left his room and went around back to his car. Picking up the first corpse by the seat of his pants, he managed to wedge the dead weight into his backseat, an almost impossible task, given his three suitcases. He left the bags in the back of his car. He did not want to attract attention moving them at two in the morning.

His luck held. Exactly at two, the miniature floodlights in the yard went out.

Dartley opened the trunk of his car. With super-human effort—the effects of fear, really—he lifted the second man by his belt and shirt collar and half-dragged, half-pulled him toward the rear of his car. Again he felt he was being watched, but he decided there was nothing he could do but continue.

The corpse must have weighed two hundred and fifty pounds. Getting it into the trunk of his car was no easy feat. In a panic, he worked feverishly, imagining insomniacs in the motel were staring out their windows. He hoped that the Chevy would serve as an effective screen for his macabre task. Before closing the trunk on the heavyset corpse, Dartley rifled the dead man's pockets. He removed his car keys, a notebook, some change and personal ID. There was no wallet. The man was Leontid Makarovna from the Soviet embassy. Just as he had suspected.

Dartley cursed himself for his spur-of-the-moment killings. He knew better. The police could be on top of him in a minute. He had to leave immediately. First, though, he had to check out the Mercedes in the front parking lot.

Sneaking up against the side wall of the motel, he rounded the corner expecting to see the Highway Patrol rummaging through the glove compartment of the Mercedes. There was no one. The car shone like a dark red cranberry under the dim light of the spring moon. Within two minutes he had searched the glove compartment and taken the car's registration.

There was a camera on the front seat, a Hasselblad. He took that too. He half-expected to find the collected works of Karl Marx, in Russian, stacked neatly under the front seat; but all he could find was a half-eaten four-ounce package of Planters Peanuts and an AAA map of Virginia, West Virginia and Maryland. He left the map on the front seat. His brain racing, he quietly closed the Mercedes' doors, scrambled back to his Chevrolet, made sure the trunk and back doors were locked and drove quietly but defiantly back out onto the narrow country road.

It was 2:30 A.M. His reflexes had gone haywire. He expected to see a flashing red light at any minute or, worse, a Russian corpse looming up behind him to strangle him. He found it almost impossible to believe that he, of all people, had acted so foolishly. He felt sure he would be found out and punished. His Uncle Charles Woodgate had once said that he trod the fine line between madness and genius. "You take too many risks for an assassin," was his uncle's warning. Still, Dartley knew if he could not sometimes throw caution to the winds, he would rather be dead. Danger was an intoxicant to him. Perhaps it was more than that. Perhaps it was his only god.

He deliberately chose the back roads, narrow lanes of black asphalt that clung to the shape of the earth with its continual billows and depressions. Every now and then the woods would open up into cleared acreage; dirt farmers grew corn there during the summer months. Now the fields were stark and raw, the naked furrows desolate in the moonlight.

He had to get rid of the bodies. But where? A dry river bed? Boys would find them. An open field? The rotting flesh would attract the buzzards. The buzzards in turn would attract the curious farmer who would be preparing his fields for spring plowing.

About thirty-five minutes from the motel, he noticed something. A roped-off dirt road leading into the black woods. A faded wooden sign, barely legible, stood by the entrance. It said "Jefferson Limestone Quarry." Tacked to that sign was a bleached-out notice of something. Dartley slowed his car. He found he could not read the notice from the road. He got out of the car to observe it more closely. It was no use. Too many years of slashing rain and harsh summer sun had completely erased whatever message had been there. As far as he could make out, the dirt road leading to the quarry was mottled with at least fifteen years of weed growth. But now, in the late spring, the weeds were scrubby; no young saplings yet grew in the roadbed; its well-worn depressions were thick with limestone chips.

Dartley backed his car up, maneuvered it around the chain that blocked the entrance to the road and drove it up a torturous path that coursed through the hills. After he had gone about half a mile, he saw the black shape of an abandoned shack. It, too, bore the title "Jefferson Limestone Quarry." Not ten yards away was the abandoned quarry filled with water, probably fed by an underground spring. Its surface shone like a black mirror in the moonlight.

Dartley searched for something heavy and metallic. A rusted crane by the edge of the quarry was at least fifteen feet high. It was too big to move. He noticed an old wood-burning stove. It sat outside the door to the shack; a decade of rust had eaten away its once impenetrable black iron surface. He could not move it. Then he saw several lengths of cast-iron pipe six inches in diameter. He guessed that, before the owners had abandoned the quarry to the pitiless spring, they had attempted to pump out the excess water. Perhaps the rate of flow had overwhelmed the capacity of the pumps; perhaps the owner had died; perhaps the limestone had given out. Who knew? Ruins were commonplace in the West Virginia hills. The population began heading west almost since the first day that people had settled there.

In the trunk of his car Dartley always kept a fifty-foot length of strong rope for towing, if nothing else. Usually he was the one who had to be towed when he got stranded in the snowbanks on his Uncle Charley's farm. Charles Woodgate had never paved anything but the front driveway; he didn't want teenagers joyriding through his fields and upsetting what livestock there was, not to mention the invasion of his own privacy.

Dartley wrestled the bodies of the Russians out

of their hiding places and undressed them, folding their clothing and packing it in his trunk. He intended to burn the clothing later. Naked, the two men were both ghostly white, hairless and overweight without being actually fat. They looked odd to him. Despite the constant remarks that European visitors to Washington made about fat Americans, it was the Europeans who had always seemed fat to Dartley. He liked to think of American men as lean, tough and hairy-chested like himself.

To keep his wits, he allowed himself to daydream on the superiority of his own kind as he threaded several lengths of iron pipe with the towing rope, about eight feet in all, leaving about twenty feet of it at either end. He looped the section of rope closest to the pipes around the neck of each corpse, nooselike. He then coiled another eight feet or so around the torso and legs before threading the final ten feet back through the loops, tying it in a knot. The final step of this strange twentieth-century funeral was not as difficult as he thought. By alternately pulling and kicking the bodies toward the edge of the quarry and rolling the iron pipes with his feet, he was able, within the space of five minutes, to push the Russians into the black depths. The splash was minimal. Within seconds the corpses disappeared as if they had never existed.

Still, Dartley knew he was not in the clear. He was still several hours from his bed in Frederick. He quickly checked the ground to see if any scattered clothes were lying about. The ground was clean. He closed the trunk and climbed back into his car to leave the quarry area as quickly as possible.

To his horror, when he turned on the ignition and the dashboard panel lighted up, he saw that his hands were smeared with dark, clotted blood. In a flash he was out of the car, at the quarry's edge, washing off his hands in the murderous pool.

"Grrr."

On reflex, he turned to see a killer dog, red eyes blazing, fangs bared, lunge out of the woods. The whole length of his black body hurtled above the ground like a heat-seeking missile. Dartley reached into his shoulder holster for his .38, took aim and fired directly into the face of the beast.

The fanged monster leapt at him.

Click! The gun was empty. Of course. He had used every fucking bullet at the Colonial Inn Motel.

Dartley's mind was electrified with visions of the dog, probably rabid, sinking its ferocious mouth into his neck. On instinct, he swerved to one side as the animal sailed in his direction. The dog careered into the black waters of Jefferson Quarry with a *kerplunk.* The next sound he heard was his own nervous laugh. Without hesitation he made for his car. His headlights were still on, the motor still running. He wanted to be down the limestone driveway and back out onto the country roads before the fanged predator managed to find a foothold on the edge of the limestone pit. That's when he realized he had a human visitor and a distinctly unfriendly one.

From the edge of the woods a waist-high flashlight shone into his face. Its all-knowing white eye reminded Dartley of a police state where searchlights in the black night were also accompanied by killer dogs.

"What do you want, city boy?"

"Who's that?" cried Dartley, envisioning a man in a trenchcoat.

The man was around 65. He was ravaged-looking, with black hollows in his sunken cheeks and slits for eyes. He held a Springfield M1903.

"I was taking a piss," Dartley said.

"You want me to blow your pecker off, city boy?"

The fanged beast was still thrashing around in the quarry.

"No, sir," said Dartley as quietly as possible.

"Don't you know private property when you see it, city boy?" said the man. "You city people think you can take anything, don't you?"

"No, sir."

The man bent down to help the dog out of the water. As fierce as the mountain man looked, Dartley could tell he was old. He knew he could have strangled him.

"Here, McGill. Here McGill," the old man said to the dog.

McGill. The scene suddenly took on domestic dimensions.

"This used to be a working quarry," the old man

said. "My father's business. His father's business. We supplied limestone for the buildings up in Washington. The Lincoln Memorial. The Jefferson Memorial. The Washington Monument. 'Dead men.' That's what my mother used to say. 'We're living for dead men.' Here, McGill."

McGill climbed out of the water a sopping mess. This time he looked like a real dog, somewhere between a shepherd and a Doberman.

"That's okay, McGill. They paid us nothing," the man continued. "On top of that, they sent my daddy to war, the last six months of World War One. That's the last we saw of him. I was born on Armistice Day. Then came the second war. I was trying to help my mother run the place, but they sent me too. By the time I got back, she'd had a shock and they'd foreclosed. Seems there weren't enough monuments built during the war. The man who took over, the black man, he din' know nothin'. He ruined it."

There was a pause.

"I smell blood," the man said suddenly.

McGill was rigid, his black snout pointing over the quarry.

"Don't move," said the mountain man. "Do you smell it?"

"Blood?" asked Dartley, hoping that the man did not fancy himself a psychic.

"There's blood on the water."

"I don't smell blood," answered Dartley. He was telling the truth—a strange kind of truth, to be sure, considering what he knew. McGill, fully out of the water, was shaking the water off his black fur. In the glare of the old man's flashlight the water shimmered like sparkledust. The old man peered out over the deep with squinted eyes as if he were listening for the sound of the dead. The dog pointed his tail and lifted his foreleg. He was ready to plunge into the pond once more to look for the mangled, bloody flesh he could surely smell.

"Do you see anything?" asked Dartley. He half expected the cold white foot of a dead Russian to break the black surface of the pond.

"Where you from, city boy?" asked the old man.

"Washington D.C. I'm on my way back from Greenmountain Lodge." Dartley paused. He knew his story had gaping holes. "I had a fight with my wife. She says I don't make enough money. She says I'm just a hick. My father was a Missouri dirt farmer; my mother divorced him and came to D.C. as a secretary. I worked my way up through the public schools. I thought if I drove through the back woods I'd have time to think." Perfect. He knew the old man would eat it up.

"Up to what?" said the old man, still peering out over the blood-smelling pond.

"What do you mean?" asked Dartley.

"You worked your way up to what?"

"Oh. I work for the . . . the FBI," he lied again. "I'm a special agent. I'm not allowed to say what I do."

"Do you kill people—for the FBI, I mean?" asked the old man, looking grim.

Dartley looked at the man. "You know, mister, Joe McCarthy wasn't all wrong, no matter what you've heard. The woods are still filled with Communists. They'd like to destroy the American way of life."

The old man turned to Dartley. His face looked tired. The corners of his mouth held deep grooves. Still, his eyes, like the dog's, were hard and menacing. "Maybe someone *should* destroy the American way of life," he said.

Their eyes held each other for a long moment. Dartley could not deny the man his point of view; the old man knew it. Dartley was a city slicker trapped in the mountains with the overwhelming knowledge of another man's pain. The moment of truth was as unexpected as the whole series of events that night.

"I don't know what or who you pushed into the quarry," the old man said. "I just know the iron pipes that were here have been dragged over the edge."

"I told you I came up here to take a piss," said Dartley.

"You weren't the first. You won't be the last," the old man said. "Now get out of here before I begin to wonder how much of a reward I'd get for turning you in."

Dartley walked backward toward his car. The old man still aimed the gun directly at his gut. His flashlight still shone straight in his eyes. When he reached his silver gray Chevy, he quickly turned, opened the door, climbed inside and, in one continuous motion, slammed the car door shut, turned on the ignition and floored the accelerator. With hallucinations of himself being shot in the back of the head with his corpse being dumped in the quarry pond and himself floating downward boggle-eyed into an underwater den of rotting Russian flesh, Dartley managed to reach the back country road alive.

Four hours later Dartley pulled up in front of a plain-looking church in downtown Washington. St. Matthew's Cathedral. It didn't look like a cathedral at all. With its flat gray stone front, it looked more like a museum.

The seven o'clock mass was beginning. Tardy worshipers, mostly D.C. bureaucrats of both sexes, slipped through the tall red doors. Dartley was not a Catholic. He didn't even believe in God. But every now and then, after a difficult assignment, especially when he had just killed someone, he would slip into a cathedral and light a candle.

The ritual was always the same. He did not pray. He watched the flickering flames and he grew silent. For a moment he let the surrounding dark envelop him, just until his heart stopped racing. Then he would leave the cathedral without any further concessions to a belief in anything besides the here and now. He had never told anyone about this ritual of his; he had never brought anyone with him. On this particular day, April 25, he got into his car once more and drove straightaway to Frederick, finally convinced that no one was watching him.

On his Uncle Charles Woodgate's farm outside of Frederick, Richard Dartley drove his silver gray Chevrolet Camaro into the old horse barn and locked the doors. In the first stall on his left was a control panel button. The floor opened; a hydraulic lift appeared. Dartley drove the car onto the lift and by remote control he activated his descent into a basement. Underground, a large workshop was equipped with the latest machinery for working with wood, glass and metals. He carefully measured and cut and placed masking tape on the car's glass and chrome surfaces. He covered the wheels with dark green plastic sheeting, the same as that used in garbage bags. Then he filled a spray gun with black car enamel and began to repaint the surface of the car, spraying the silver gray surface with broad strokes. He knew it would take two or three coats, probably three, to do the job properly. After the last coat of paint had dried, he would have to work with a single-edged razor blade scraping minute splotches of paint off the chrome and glass. He sighed as he worked, periodically stopping to listen for possible noises either in the barn itself or outside. All he needed now was for truant teenagers posing as rebels-without-causes to break into the barn for a night's sleep. In another era they might have been innocent runaways. Now, in the greater Washington, D.C., area, the most unobtrusive person might be the son or daughter of a leading government official or even a double agent working for a foreign power. If they happened to stumble upon the hidden workroom, all it would take after the inevitable reconciliation with the parents was an offhand remark about what they had seen in the Frederick barn. Sooner or later the Woodgate farm would be investigated. In the City of Secrets, people were crazy to know everything about closed doors and hidden passageways.

Dartley finished the first coat. Then he went upstairs for air. He used the back staircase; it led to a private office Charles Woodgate had constructed onto the back of the barn. Ostensibly the office held record books necessary for the raising of racehorses. In point of fact, Dartley kept his own records here, all written in his private code.

It was here at 10:00 P.M. the following Thursday that his Swiss banker, M. Jouet, was scheduled to call to inform him whether a half million dollars had been deposited in his name.

Chapter Eight

The Moscow Center at Number 2 Dzerzhinski Square at the top end of Karl Marx Prospekt is the center for the KGB, the Communist secret police. It is a huge stone complex of office blocks that are mausoleumlike in their gray, compact bulk. Inside, unsurprisingly, its institutional corridors are painted in beige shellac; its overhead fluorescent lights cast a familiar pallor on all who enter there. Under the lights, visitors' faces predictably resemble those of corpses, a not altogether inappropriate image, considering the interrogation rooms in back. In those airless cells, not every suspect who sits down to face the KGB survives his night of questioning. Political dissidents, Jews, Mongolians, ethnic Germans, alienated poets, ballet dancers who unsuccessfully attempted to defect to the West—those are the members of the heroic, vaunted "proletariat" who must be brought forward to discuss their possible sins. The basic activity of questioning suspects, of torturing the silent ones, like the Soviet assassination squad Smersh, is not demonstrably different from the same activity under the Nazis or under Franco in his midcentury Spain. Except that to the committed Communist, Franco considered Spain an end in itself. To the Fascist there is no overriding principle except agreement from everyone on every conceivable issue. To the Communist, Russia is not the end result—it is one step in a progression of steps leading to a one-world state. True, the anarchist being ridiculed and knocked senseless by uniformed guards in a damp underground cell might not appreciate the philosophical distinction between dictator and king. To him or her, the torture feels pretty much the same.

Upstairs, it was different. At least it looked different. On the fourth floor, the Office of the European Division had antique oriental carpets laid over gray-green carpeting. In the outer office there was a sideboard from a nineteenth-century country estate. It was dark and heavy and richly adorned with carvings of acanthus leaves. On top were stacked copies of *Pravda*, Moscow's leading newspaper, the official mouthpiece for the Communist party. Rogoff's buxom receptionist, Sergeant Gudonov, wore a gray wool police uniform, her dark blond hair pulled straight back from her flushed and pockmarked skin. In the inner office, mahogany wainscoting from the old Ulanov mansion, wall-to-wall geometric carpeting from Bloomingdale's in New York, plus a white-marble-slab-topped desk from Milan offered a glimpse of a KGB in transition.

Serge Rogoff, the head of the European Division, a 45-year-old red-headed Slav with a bulbous nose and a permanent blush of dark freckled skin, sat pondering the cable from the D.C. embassy. It read, "Ilse de Brock found dead in Schmidt's bathtub, throat and wrists slashed. Verdict: suicide. Schmidt, von Kelsing, Reiser met with man called Savage."

It was from Vassilov. He had signed on at the Lodge as a yard man the day Ilse notified them of the meeting in West Virginia. They probably discovered her camera, Rogoff thought. He experienced a groundswell of rage. That slut, he thought. She let the sex go to her head. She forgot her primary reason for being there. Goddamn the bitch.

Then he remembered their six months together. New York, 1968. They had both been assigned to the Russian delegation. Ilse had been issued a forged West German passport and driving license. Her orders were clear. She was to be known as Ilse Wagner; her task was to fall in love with as many members of the American delegation as she could manage. It was the season of Vietnam. The Vietcong needed all the help it could get. Defense information was at a premium. Somehow the word must have gotten out on her. Between the delegates who were religiously married and the faintly bisexual ones who had no trouble refusing her sex, Ilse found herself at a standstill. As far as the American delegation went, she actually had trouble getting laid. Rogoff, her superior, got her special permission from the Center to take a six-month vacation from her stock in trade—to spend that time learning the English language. That gave the two of them just enough time to fall in love. After four months he was sure he wanted to marry her, Permission was denied. Ilse was recalled to Moscow to be reevaluated. Rogoff did not see her again for another ten years. By that time Ilse was working at von Kelsing–Schmidt and doing very well at it.

He remembered her capacity for sex. She was emotionally unable to disassociate herself from the men she slept with. The Center thought she was

one of the best sexual spies it had, but Rogoff
knew better. He remembered her threats to jump
off the Brooklyn Bridge if they sent her back to
Moscow. Ah ha, he thought, maybe she did kill
herself. Maybe she fell in love with Bruno Schmidt.
He found himself cursing her ineptitude. When
his receptionist, Sergeant Gudonov, went down to
the cafeteria for lunch, he found himself alone
with the girl he remembered in 1968. He put his
head down on his desk and wept.

By the time Sergeant Gudonov returned from
her midday meal, Rogoff had finished mourning.
Ilse was dead. He didn't care how she died. He
knew only one thing: he needed a replacement for
her. He needed more information on the three
German industrialists. It occurred to him that von
Kelsing might be a better source of information
than Schmidt; now that his wife was ill he might
be looking for female companionship, a woman to
talk to, someone to commiserate with.

There was something else. During lunch Rogoff
received a second report from Washington, D.C.
The two embassy attachés, Makarovna and Chaliapin, had abandoned their car at the Colonial Inn
Motel. Or someone had forced them to abandon
it. There had been no sign of the man called
Savage, although someone corresponding to his
age and basic physiognomy called "Sam Booth"
had checked in at the same motel the night the
Russians had disappeared. A spot-check on Booth
had turned up nothing.

His car, a silver gray Chevrolet Camaro like

Savage's, had a completely different number on the license plate. A check on the license plate led to a Nathan Jefferson on Fourteenth Place, S.E. Mr. Jefferson was black; he owned a McDonald's franchise in Anacostia. He had no police record and no connection with a government agency. The license plate was evidently forged. The Mercedes had been rifled for registration papers. Makarovna's Hasseblad camera on the front seat was missing, although several rolls of film he had shot earlier in the day were found in the top drawer of the bureau in his room at the Greenmountain Lodge. The same was true of their D.C. apartments. Makarovna lived in Bethesda, Chaliapin in Rockville. Makarovna's wife, although hysterical in the face of his disappearance, did not recall that her husband had received any threatening phone calls or letters.

This man Savage. Was he, in fact, a savage? Was he a black radical? Rogoff gave orders for Vassilov to be interrogated as quickly as possible. He needed a precise description of the man Savage. What kind of a car did he drive? What did he put down as his home address in the hotel registry?

Six hours later, Rogoff had his answer, or at least part of an answer.

Vassilov had checked the man Savage's automobile. From the outside it looked completely unremarkable. A silver gray two-door Chevrolet. Vassilov had assumed it was a rented car. His first surprise was that none of his training and none of his tools empowered him to jimmy the lock. He then tried to cut a hole in the glass. It turned out to be bulletproof, two layers of the stuff sandwiching a specially treated plastic. The window was impenetrable. He was stymied. If he cut a hole in the roof, presuming the steel could be cut open, he would risk Savage's knowing he was under investigation. Still, he had something to go on: the license plate. When he copied down the number, 7432 LPA, he noticed that the chrome frame for the plate had an odd construction, almost as if it was made to be slid in and out on a moment's notice. Loosening the bolt, he discovered a second license plate on the reverse side of the first one. That number bore no relation to the first: 149 HKZ. He wondered whether there were other license plates for this particular car—there were—and if tracking them down proved fruitless, which it probably would, there was still one overriding fact about this silver gray Chevrolet the man called Savage had overlooked. There were only two or three body shops in the United States—three at the absolute maximum—and only two on the east coast, that had any expertise at transforming cars into armored vehicles. Armoring cars was a new craft, commensurate with the rise of terrorism in the mid-seventies. Arab oil sheiks in particular were avid purchasers of bulletproof Mercedes and Cadillac limousines. In James Bond fashion, these sleekly styled neo-tanks were capable of almost anything short of giving birth.

Savage had made another big mistake, Vassilov concluded. He failed to realize that few cars undergoing the armoring process would be silver gray Chevrolets. The car, once he located the body shop, would not be that difficult to trace. It was a 1980 model. How many silver gray Camaros had bulletproof glass? It would not be too difficult, once the body shop had been located, to place a night watchman or a cleaning woman to go through the files at three in the morning. Since the armoring work was not illegal, there was no possible reason to consider the files as privileged information. An armored limousine, particularly for a wealthy Saudi, was something to be expected. It was part of the package.

Dartley had always been one step ahead of the game. Part of the deal when he ordered his rebuilt Chevy was that no record of his order was to be kept in the company files. He did not know why exactly. He had an innate paranoia about being traced. Spencer Siddons, the founder and president of Camelot Armoring, the company in question, struck a deal with Dartley. No records of Dartley would be kept in the regular company files. Siddons kept a duplicate file in case of a possible IRS audit or a special FBI investigation. That file was locked away in the subbasement of his house behind a couple of packing cases of his children's discarded textbooks. That file would be opened only to the FBI, presuming they could find it. If Dartley could not accept that arrangement, he would have to take his business elsewhere. Siddons could only guarantee Dartley that information about his car would not be accessible to office thieves or to enemies who might deliberately ransack the office searching for information.

Dartley accepted. He had no choice. Having a car rebuilt was not like having a special rifle made. A body shop was, in many ways, a public service. An automobile was the common birthright of every American. What could possibly be considered secret about a car?

A week later, with Rogoff's go-ahead, Vassilov had the names of two body shops on the East Coast. Frankie's, on Washington Street in Newark, was the first. It rebuilt and armored cars, usually on a confidential basis, for private detectives, insurance claims investigators, and chiefs of police in small towns all over New Jersey, New York and New England. Vassilov arrived with a fake FBI card and a photo of a silver gray 1980 Camaro almost exactly like the one in the Greenmountain Lodge parking lot. The owner, a black man of about 60, sweated good will. Vassilov told him they'd caught the owner of the car in the photo, a suspected Communist. According to Vassilov, the man admitted that Frankie's had done the work on his car. The FBI wanted to know what name the man in custody had given Frankie's, whether he paid his bill with a check from an American bank, whether he referred any of his friends to Frankie's. Clarence Johnson, the owner, furiously wiped the sweat from his ebony forehead, insisted he'd never seen the Chevrolet before and said he'd be willing to take a lie-detector test. "No, sir, Mr. MacLean," he said to Vassilov, "I fought at Iwo

Jima. I don't have no truck with no Communists. I've read about what they do to Jewish people over there. I have no illusions about what they'd do to me." Vassilov reluctantly decided that Johnson was telling the truth. Without offering any further explanation, he left.

Dixie Auto Parts in Chestertown, Maryland, on Maryland's Eastern Shore was another matter. From the outside it looked like a southern auto-parts dealership, which in a sense it was. Soda machines dispensed Dr. Pepper and White Rock orange soda. The owner's desk was littered with unpaid bills, receipts, auto parts catalogues. Empty cardboard cartons that had once held mufflers and seat covers lay scattered about. The owner, a rawboned part-time oyster fisherman named McKenzie James, greeted Vassilov in a studied "good ol' boy" manner. The friendliness was broad, aggressive and without nuance.

"Hi y'all, what kin ah do fer ya?" he said, bounding forward like a retriever.

After Vassilov had presented his FBI ID, Mr. James adjusted his presentation of self. The glad smile withered, the eyes with the crinkle lines suddenly looked gray and cold. The southern accent disappeared.

"What do you want, Mr. Bouvier?"

Vassilov repeated what Rogoff had told him— that the small-town auto-parts store was the front for a vast underground workroom where James and almost fifty skilled workers bulletproofed limousines for political dignitaries with high visibility—members of the Cabinet, presidents of labor unions, ambassadors to politically volatile countries. All of these rebuilt automobiles had been given the green light by various federal agencies. Dixie Auto Parts was the front for the armoring of the most official government cars. According to Rogoff, Washington wanted to keep security jobs separate from Detroit. For one thing, it wanted skilled specialists to do the armoring work. As for late, the Detroit products seemed as though they were being slapped together by half-trained baboons. McKenzie James had a reputation for cracking the whip. Rogoff claimed that James occasionally did work for professional gunmen. The Mafia had used him more than once.

"Listen to me, Mr. James," Vassilov said. "The Bureau knows you occasionally fill orders for the mob."

James paled. He said nothing in response. He focused his eyes on the tip of Vassilov's nose and kept it there. Clearly, if he did nothing else that day, he intended to survive the official visitor without incurring damage to himself or to anyone else.

"Right now," Vassilov continued, producing the photograph he had shown Clarence Johnson, "the owner of the car I'm showing you, his real name is Martin Spilliers, is wanted for murdering the owner of a filling station in Columbus, Georgia. All we know about him is that he went around bragging that you'd armored his car for nothing. If you don't tell us everything you know about Martin

Spilliers, I can't guarantee your contract with the government will be renewed." Vassilov then traded on a piece of information that Rogoff had given him.

"After all, Mr. James, your great and good friend of the Nixon Administration is no longer in a position to help you." The man in question, a Nixon Cabinet member, had had a stroke that left him mute and unable to move the left side of his body. This time McKenzie James looked at Vassilov so intently that both his eyes and mouth seemed to be drawn with a thin purple line.

"I don't know what you're talking about," McKenzie James replied. "That fucking Chevrolet didn't come out of this shop. I don't care what that cocksucker says. He probably did it himself. He probably glued plastic to the windows and stuck aluminum foil on the inside of the car doors and called it armoring."

"Think carefully, Mr. James. Are you sure you haven't seen Mr. Spilliers before? I can only tell you that if you persist in denying you know the man, you will end up in court as a witness. You see, Mr. James, we have proof this car was here."

"What proof?"

"They wouldn't tell me. They said it was privileged information. They said to make sure you knew what could happen to you if you don't cooperate."

"Who's they?"

"The Bureau."

"Who's the Bureau?"

"The Federal Bureau of Investigation."

"Who in the Bureau?"

"How long do you wish to continue playing games, Mr. James?"

James put his hands on his hips. It was a belligerent stance.

"I don't know who you are, but I have friends in the Bureau. I never heard of you, Bouvier."

Vassilov laughed. "Do you know how many agents there are in the FBI?" He himself did not know the exact number; he guessed that the owner of Dixie Auto Parts didn't either. Vassilov was still guessing. It was his only hope to locate the sharpshooter in tweeds and dark glasses who had somehow been responsible for the death of Ilse de Brock. Somewhere, the mystery man that she had perhaps eavesdropped on at the wrong moment would himself slip up. Vassilov decided to give it one more try. He returned the fixed stare of McKenzie James with his own, fully aware from past experience that his black eyes unsettled the most resolute Nordic face.

"Mr. James," he continued, "the Bureau has three workers in your pool of forty-nine skilled artisans who are paid informers. We know that this silver gray Chevrolet came out of your shop. Perhaps you'd care to take another look." He casually held up the photograph a second time. McKenzie James reached out, grabbed it and tore it up.

"I don't know who you are," he muttered, "and I don't know what you want, but you ain't with the

Bureau. They don't got field agents with furrin' accents, as we say in Chestertown."

Vassilov looked at him hard.

"There are furrin' accents all over Washington, Mr. James. Some of them even belong to the good guys."

Vassilov figured that that would throw him off the track. He couldn't risk being picked up on the Beltway on his way back to Washington.

"I will be back tomorrow, Mr. James," he said, "and when you see me again, I will not be alone."

James just looked at his visitor, his arms folded across his chest.

"Right."

Vassilov twice flooded his Volvo, trying to drive as quickly as he could without gettting arrested or a ticket for speeding. He felt like a fool. Either McKenzie James was covering up a gigantic lie or he really did know nothing about the silver gray Camaro. Vassilov decided to pursue two courses of action. One, he could continue making the rounds of auto shops that did armoring. Two, he would, with Rogoff's permission, dispatch one of the American contacts to go to Chestertown, get a job at Washington College there, probably on the maintenance crew, and as soon as possible make friends with some guy who worked at Dixie Auto Parts. He would be given a list of the employees there. Sooner or later the KGB American would be expected to find out from his new buddy whether Dixie Auto Parts ever armored "regular cars." If asked to explain what he meant, the agent was to say that his cousin, who was connected to the Jersey mob, had had an armored car that didn't look like an armored car. It was just a regular 1980 silvery gray Camaro. He was to say he couldn't remember where his cousin had had the work done, but he thought it was someplace on the Eastern Shore. Sooner or later, Vassilov figured, the truth, if there was any in this case, would come out. By that time, other clues to the identity of the man in tweeds would undoubtedly surface. If he was committed to murdering KGB agents, here or in Germany, those murders, whether successful or not, would undoubtedly furnish fresh clues to the stranger's identity. Sooner or later, someone with a KGB affiliation would spot the silver gray car. Sooner or later, the car would be followed and the man's place of residence or work found out. After that, it was a simple matter of breaking into his desk and finding out everything there was to know.

At the Moscow Center, Serge Rogoff could not get Ilse de Brock out of his mind. He found it impossible to believe that Bruno Schmidt had killed her in a fit of passion. In the first place, in all of his sixty-two years, Schmidt had done nothing passionate. Even in the war he had been phlegmatic. His ex-wives had independently labeled him a bore. To be sure, he had his flaws. He overate, especially desserts. He fell asleep at concerts and he was virulently anti-Semitic. He was fully in agreement with the Third Reich on their extermination policies. For all this, he had never been passionate about anything but food and drink. Ilse, for her part, had been too smart and too well trained to arouse murderous passion in a man who was her principal connection to vital technological information to the Soviet. There was more. The report from Greta Polansky, the "cleaning woman," had come in. She couldn't understand it, either. Ilse was fond of Schmidt, and she enjoyed her sex with him. For this reason she always told Polansky she was grateful she could enjoy her work. She was in no way dependent on Schmidt. There was no obsession, no hurt if he looked at another woman. If Schmidt had suddenly died, she would have been eager to find out about her new assignment. She had always wanted to live in Washington or Los Angeles.

Rogoff concluded that Greta Polansky's report was probably accurate. Ilse had often asked to be sent to the United States. The report, to be expected, opened old wounds. He had to wonder about the gaps. If Bruno Schmidt was not Ilse's principal obsession, who was? Himself? Greta Polansky? Ilse had once told him that she considered bisexuality perfectly normal and that when men became wearisome to her, as she suspected they would, she intended to try women. At the time, he had guessed that she was reading Colette. He did not believe that she meant what she said. If she had been a closet bisexual, all the more reason why she would have been able to keep Bruno Schmidt in perspective. All the more reason why there would have been no real passion at Greenmountain Lodge. That is, unless Bruno Schmidt knew something of the vital information Rogoff was looking for.

Rogoff racked his brain. Could there have been a connection between Ilse's murder and the man called Savage? He kept reviewing the scenario in his mind, searching for a clue. The three industrialists meet with the man called Savage. That same day, Ilse is brutally murdered in her bath. Had Savage murdered her? Why? What had she seen? What had she overheard? Did the industrialists realize that Ilse was working for the KGB? Had Ilse uncovered NATO directives aimed at destroying Soviet technology? Did the industrial West hold a secret weapon the Presidium know nothing about?

Rogoff was the grandson of Siberian illiterates. He had worked his way up in the KGB. He began as a 14-year-old. His uncle had been an army colonel and close friend of Lavrenti Beria, head of the KGB. Beria got him a job cleaning SKS carbines at the army rifle range fifteen miles north of Moscow. For the farm boy, the rifles had been a revelation. Daily, as he rubbed and oiled the one-piece wooden stocks of the SKS's, he meditated on the inventors and the craftsmen who had developed the rifles. The Soviet Union had progressed from a dung heap of diseased peasants to the most fearsome power in the history of the human race—because suddenly, at the turn of the present century, the average man had access to superior weaponry. As a result, he was no longer the average man, he was a force to be reckoned with.

Rogoff resolved to avenge the death of Ilse de Brock. In her name the Revolution must go forward. He was determined to find out what was going on in Düsseldorf. Already he found himself hatching plots to flush out the three German industrialists from the thicket of their own secrecy. If in the end he discovered nothing by using the conventional methods at his disposal, i.e., the dispatching of secret agents to von Kelsing–Schmidt, he would be forced to try other means. He would consider using a terrorist organization as a front. The scenario would be a familiar one. One of the three industrialists would be captured, tortured and held for ransom. The necessary information would be extracted. The industrialist would be shot in the back of the head. The terrorist organization would suffer recriminations. The Soviet infiltrator-advisor would then conveniently disappear.

For the moment, however, Rogoff decided on a simpler strategy: to augment the number of KGB agents within the von Kelsing–Schmidt organization. The first one who came to mind was a brilliant psychologist, a half-German, half-Russian Jew named Marlena Kupitsky. She was also a sexual operative. Now that Werner von Kelsing's wife, Mitzi, was being hospitalized for severe morphine addiction, he might need a more comforting personal relationship. One of the last things Ilse had suggested was that another sexual operative could probably move in on von Kelsing himself with great success. After all, it was von Kelsing and not Bruno Schmidt who took charge of daily operations and who made the decisions with respect to the laser satellite program.

"Get me the file on Marlena Kupitsky," Serge Rogoff said to his aide, Sergeant Gudonov. "I think it's time Dr. Kupitsky took a long vacation, preferably in Düsseldorf. The steel mills and the munitions factories there can be so invigorating. The workers there have so many personal problems. It could be so challenging, especially for a young psychologist." He chuckled to himself. Sometimes the humor of it all was too much to resist, even in the inner sanctum of the KGB.

Chapter Nine

Dartley waited a week before the phone call from Switzerland came. His banker, M. Jouet, a man he had never met face to face, said yes, the half million dollars in deutsche marks had been deposited in his account. Dartley smiled, thanked him and hung up.

He was ready to begin. The paint job on the Camaro was done. He had waxed and polished the car twice. He had replaced the forged license plates with new ones; he had the registration papers and driver's licenses to match each one. There were several forgers in the D.C. area adept at producing passports and birth certificates for a fee. Usually they obtained the blank documents from paid sources at the government printing offices, the Department of Records, the Department of Motor Vehicles.

It wasn't difficult. The city boasted the world's largest "upper middle class," a phrase which applied to people with multiple cars, a second home, prep schools, face-lifts and European travel. This privileged class had money left over for designer clothes, psychiatrists and art collections. The lowly bureaucratic clerk, by contrast. was usually someone with a public high school education who had at first been elated just to be living and working in Washington, D.C. Gradually this person began to be aware that he or she would not arrive at middle age as a Cabinet member. It was unlikely that he or she would even see the inside of an embassy. And as he or she watched the parade of lawyers and lobbyists making hundreds of thousands of dollars a year for doing what seemed to be nothing— after all, anyone could smile and shake hands—a decided hostility began to grow. After all, weren't they themselves so much brighter, so much more promising in every way than a Jimmy Carter, a Jerry Ford, a Ronnie Reagan? The very thought of these clowns, and it was commonly agreed they were clowns, was reason enough to begin accepting payments under the table from whoever needed anything. Their safety valve was the amount paid for services rendered. They did not give away blank documents for nothing. A blank passport was five hundred, at least. If a fellow worker wanted to sell them, at cost, for sixty-three cents or in some cases actually give them away, that was his funeral.

For four days straight until it rained, Dartley had practiced shooting. He always bought the latest weapons and tried them out. He was spending a lot of time with an Alpha I belt-action rifle. At first glance it was unexceptional, but with the addition of a 4X scope and a web sling, the test gun still only weighed six pounds fourteen ounces. He shot whatever he could see, mostly burnt-out light bulbs from fifty yards. He had his favorite guns, too. His collection of "antiques," as he called them.

His favorite was an Austrian pistol, the M03, officially known as the Mannlicher Selbstladepistole Modell 03. Its design dated to 1896. Its external appearance was not unlike the Mauser C96. It had a double-pressure trigger rather like that of a military rifle and could be fitted with a stock. It was a pistol made for long-range shooting. The M03 had never seen military service. Dartley liked to kill birds with it; he didn't care what kind. The activity of farm animals;—birds, rats, even dogs and cats—was to him insignificant compared to the human drama in which he considered himself a leading player.

Another favorite antique was the Parker-Hale 82, a sniping rifle. The one-piece body screwed onto a heavy hammered barrel. The foresight was fitted onto a dovetail base at the muzzle and the actual bore at the muzzle was recessed to prevent damage to the rifling. The trigger mechanism was a separate self-contained assembly located by axis pins in the body. The single-stage trigger was adjustable for pull, backlash and creep. One of its useful military features was that the safety was silent in operation. Both Canada and Australia had supposedly adopted the Parker-Hale as a sniping rifle in both world wars; there were rumors that other armies had taken it. Confidants in Madrid told him the Republicans had had ten thousand of them in the Spanish Civil War. The silent safety had been the big attraction—great for zapping village priests between the eyes as they propounded on the Divine Right of Church and King, great for blasting scalps off schoolteachers who indoctrinated young Spanish minds about the evils of Karl Marx and Lenin.

Dartley, who officially had no ideology of his own, had one principle: never kill an anti-Communist. He hated Communists. He particularly hated people who said they were Communists and weren't, like the rich students in Milan, the radical Catholic priests in Nicaragua or the Jewish Socialists in New York. These people said they were Communists to shock their audience. The great enemy to them was always the same: the white working class, the middle class, the upper-middle-class American pigs in polyester pantsuits. Ordinary people whose creed was hard work. They believed in volunteerism; fixing up the neighborhood; using the stock market and the voting booth and going south to retire. It was to these "Fascists" that the self-described "Communists" ceaselessly ranted and raved. The Communists ridiculed the Fascists for their fatness, their thinness, their Muzak and their children's bubble-gum rock. They condemned their Tammany Hall politicians and their goon-squad police. They spat at them for maintaining jails and armies. If anyone dared criticize the Russian slave state, he was told that Russia and Communism were two different things and one should not confuse the two.

Dartley had used the Parker-Hale 82 sniping rifle once—professionally, that is—to kill an American Communist. It had been his greatest personal triumph. The man in question was Osgood "Ozzie" van Courtland, a onetime Harvard instructor. Van Courtland had taken his hatred of red-baiting Sen. Joseph McCarthy to a fever pitch. Van Courtland was the scion of unlimited New England wealth. As a journalist for a leading Socialist magazine, he had first coined the term "McCarthyism" as a synonym for hysterical red-baiting. No one had argued with him. In the years between 1950 and 1954, the anti-Communist obsession of the beefy, alcoholic senator from Wisconsin, a child of the dirt farm and the Depression, began to overrule all regard for the truth. Americans in growing numbers watched McCarthy with mounting alarm. Even anti-Communists began to turn against him. Years later, as upper-class autobiographies of failed sons and homosexual malcontents began to trickle down from the publishing houses in a steady flow, it was apparent that there *had* been many men, mostly rich, mostly infatuated with the social hierarchy and rituals of an earlier, predominantly Anglo-Saxon, society who *had* been Communists. These n'er-do-wells were connected by blood and shared philosophies to British cousins who were couriers, double agents, informers, anything they could think of to sell out the Empire that had denied them whatever meaning it was they were looking for.

In his writings, Ozzie van Courtland began to label the entire era "the McCarthy era," thereby excusing the army of press lords and military leaders who had paved the senator's way to power. He began to label the senator a "debauched peasant," an "alcoholic Irishman," and in so many words assigned the "source of the problem" to the Roman Catholic Church.

Then Van Courtland went too far for a certain Texas oil baron whose wife had been a Wisconsin McCarthy and a distant cousin of the senator. In 1976, van Courtland's biography of the senator came out. It was called *Senator Satan*. Chapter 1 contained five pages of attack on the senator's family. To anyone else, the McCarthys were survivors of the first rank. To van Courtland they were the worst element in the nation. The fact that they were hard-working, educated landowners, albeit on a small scale, made no difference. The oil baron's wife had heard about the book in the most unfortunate way. The paragraph describing her family was widely quoted in the leading book reviews. Van Courtland, like his great friend the writer Gore Vidal, had a knack for unforgettable epigrams. The oil baron's wife tried unsuccessfully to kill herself. Two days later the oil baron made a phone call to Richard Dartley.

Within the fortnight, Dartley found himself with his Parker-Hale sniper rifle on the small stone bridge, Bow Bridge, over the small lake in New York's Central Park. It was four o'clock in the morning. A call boy, blond and beautiful and all of seventeen, was rowing across the lake.

The call boy, one of the more successful in Manhattan that year, was the great-nephew of a leading southern governor. Dartley had paid him five thousand dollars in cash to approach van Courtland as he was eating his customary steak and salad in the back room at P. J. Clarke's. P. J. Clarke's was a super-straight singles bar for young professional New Yorkers. Van Courtland, three times divorced, was to all appearances a bachelor rogue with an eye and an appetite for female flesh. The oil baron knew differently. Van Courtland had left too many tracks, especially in Europe, where he assumed no one knew who he was. The blond boy had specific directions. On their second night together, he was to add a pill Dartley had given him to Van Courtland's after-dinner coffee. When van Courtland became groggy, the boy was to suggest a change of air. He was to take him to the boat house by the larger of the two lakes in Central Park.

Normally at 4:00 A.M., the boat house was closed. This particular night an attendant waited. He was not really an attendant. He too had been bribed and given the proper uniform and forged ID. If any policeman asked, he was to say it was a new policy; the Department of Parks was assigning a night guard to the boathouse. By careful prearrangement the blond boy and van Courtland were to arrive precisely at 4:16 A.M. when no policeman would be patrolling the vicinity. Once van Courtland and the boy were out on the lake on this moonless night, the boat house attendant would disappear.

He did. Everything was exactly on schedule. Dartley waited on the bridge, his rifle under his trench coat in a specially designed sleeve. The silencer was in another sleeve. In 1976 it was the only rifle he owned.

As Dartley waited, the dark bulk of the two men rowed toward the bridge. Dartley removed first the rifle and then the silencer from his sleeves. He fitted the silencer onto the rifle barrel, took aim and fired twice, first at the larger shape and then at the smaller one. Both times he aimed straight at their heads. Both times he scored. The scene on the lake was eerie, what he could make of it. Beforehand, he had visualized both bodies slumping sideways, rolling off the edge of the low-slung wooden rowboat and floating facedown in the lake. It didn't happen that way. Only the oars floated away silently into the lake like matchsticks in a toilet bowl. The corpses stayed in the boat like dead weights; they remained motionless, a compounding of shadows. Dartley felt nothing more than the excitement of a small boy who has broken into an amusement park after hours with a BB gun to shoot at whatever targets, moving or otherwise, he can find. The gun did not even sound like a gun. The only sound was a hollow snap; the darkness swallowed it up.

Then panic struck. In his mind's eye he expected searchlights at either end of the bridge, with police dogs in great howling packs lunging and hissing at him with razor fangs. He could almost hear the sirens blasting his eardrums with their high-decibel wail.

It was nothing like that. Only the continuing silence in the black night where everyone was anonymous until dawn. He ran toward Central Park West, avoiding the footpaths whenever possible. He was almost shocked that he was not pursued. Once he arrived at the western boundary of the park, he slowed his gait and walked to the subway station at Seventy-second and Broadway. He took a downtown express to Penn Station. He had already purchased his return ticket to Washington; as luck would have it, the train, the last Metroliner from Boston, was half an hour late. With sweat pouring down his legs, he stood in the waiting room, terrified that some small boy who regularly read his father's *Soldier of Fortune* would recognize the outline of a rifle and a silencer protruding through his coat. Nobody came. Not even newsboys hawking a special edition of the *Times* with three-inch-high headlines screaming *Dead Bodies in Central Park*. He arrived at Union Station without a gun sticking in his ribs. Two days later, the Washington *Post* carried the story of the famous journalist found dead in a rowing accident in Central Park. There was no mention whatsoever of his young companion. No mention of the gaping hole in his face. The Texas oilman had no doubt paid for a cover-up. Somebody had. Dartley didn't ask.

After that, he had been more careful about killing people out in the open. He researched his victims more carefully. He unearthed as many specific details as he could about their personal habits and schedules. He became an expert in poisons and concealed weapons. He exterminated his victims only when he could catch them alone. In time, he developed more sophisticated ways of killing people. As much as he loved firing a gun, he found it necessary to develop methods of killing that went undetected, at least for a time. His problem was that after a killing he had to make a clean getaway. He couldn't afford a gun battle with the police, especially in a foreign country. He couldn't afford to be known by the secret police anywhere. In short, he could not afford to be seen as the assassin. Once he became known as a professional killer, he'd be the first one they'd track down whenever any penny-ante dictator got himself shot in the head.

Still, there was something in him, a wild quality he found impossible to understand. He enjoyed killing the same way some men wallowed in sex. But it was more than the killing itself. He loved the chase, the strategy, the careful planning of details that would culminate in the death of a big shot. As far as he was concerned, they were all self-inflated bullies, braggarts who loved to control the lives of little men: soldiers, hitmen, guerrilla fighters, tenant farmers, drug couriers.

Finally, when Dartley faced the truth of himself, he knew that the deepest level of his being had something to do with his murdering a world-famous journalist from a bridge in Central Park, primal behavior he repeated when he shot the two KGB agents behind the Colonial Inn Motel. His greatest love was playing Russian roulette with death. Danger in its purest form intoxicated him. If, somewhere in the back of his brain, he didn't relish the possibility of taking chances with his own life, he never would have been able to shoot another human being. He did not understand the death-infatuated killer in himself. He had never read a book on the subject. From certain television documentaries he had seen about hardened criminals, he guessed that psychiatrists would call him amoral. He had never wept for a corpse. To him it was as the movie said—The Big Sleep. Death, like old age, loomed over everyone; it ridiculed the most noble men, reducing them to faded memories. To kill was to gain a small measure of control. In some ways he thought himself the noblest form of humanity. He was an agent of control for men who did not allow themselves to be victims of other men. As far as his killing went, he saw himself as a man who fought back, not against his victims—most of them had no previous knowledge of him—but against death itself.

Finally, he knew one thing about himself: he enjoyed parading his talents for death under the nose of a crowd, knowing he'd manage to escape getting caught.

For that reason, he admired Lee Harvey Oswald—up to a point. In the first place, he gave Oswald the benefit of the doubt. J.F.K., with all the guilt of first-generation wealth and with all the radical ideas about workers' salaries that guilty rich kids seemed to carry around, was probably a closet Communist. Kennedy had always voted against the rich. To hell with Kennedy. Where Dartley parted company with Oswald was Oswald's naivete about shooting a president. Any fool would know that the same people who hired him would hire a second assassin to kill the first. Given the stakes, they'd probably hire a third gun to get rid of the second. Dartley never argued the conspiracy theory one way or the other. To him, it was a foregone conclusion that nobody outside of a state mental hospital would kill an American president unless he was offered a great deal of money. When John Hinckley tried to shoot Ronald Reagan, supposedly for the love of Jodie "Taxi Driver" Foster, Dartley just smirked. To Dartley, the assassin of assassins, it was impossible to believe that a man would kill for the love of a celebrity he'd never met. Absolutely impossible.

Chapter Ten

Herbert "The Viscount" Malleson, Dartley's information broker, was tall and chiseled in the English way with fine hands and a high-bridged aquiline nose, the kind most commonly found on ancient Egyptian royalty. His coloring was anything but Egyptian. He was chalk white, with large, heavy-lidded blue eyes, eyes so light they seemed more like the pale blue-white color of perfect diamonds. His Oxford accent was perfectly in accord with his eyes. It seemed a trifle overdone; yet, with his strangely pitched voice—high, hard, almost flinty—one would hardly have expected the color of the earth. Malleson's ground of being, however, had nothing to do with the earth. His strength seemed to emanate from the upper reaches of his brain.

Malleson was the world's expert in geography; he had been publicly retired as an undersecretary of state so that he could privately advise the president. He knew all the peccadilloes of all the heads of state—from their hidden physical flaws, off-the-record health problems, to sexual preferences and emotional patterns. In the case of those with fatal illnesses, he could prognosticate their loss of vital energies to the month. He even knew which world leaders could be compromised with what are euphemistically called "underage maidens." His basement held an IBM computer that gave him immediate printouts of a given region's political personalities, size of standing armies, gross national product, weather predictions, the going rates for the best hotels and where a gentleman might purchase a good bottle of wine. Dartley regularly paid Malleson 10 percent of his fee; for that 10 percent, Malleson offered Dartley the latest and most precise information on every subject he needed to know about. On more than one occasion, it was information and not guns that saved Dartley's hide.

Malleson lived on O Street in Georgetown in an antebellum mansion on top of a hill, one of the handful of private estates in what had originally been a separate town five miles from the Capitol itself. The whitewash had long faded on the red brick facade; the wrought iron, imported from Lyons, France, almost two hundred years before, was the oldest in the city. Parts of the railing girding the entrance seemed eaten away by time and rust—although, under Malleson's care, all architectural details had been restored to perfection, or what passed for it. Inside, the house was a symphony in beige and white; carpets swept along before the visitor on magnificently rebuilt floors; flawlessly replastered walls shone with a muted lacquer the color of fresh Devon cream. Crystal chandeliers hanging with flat globs of chiseled sunlight in the Williamsburg style cast refracted dazzle in all directions at once. The mansion was a paean to The Enlightenment. Each room, measured in mathematics conforming to the classical golden mean, was a hymn to an ordered universe. The color delighted the eye; the furniture, mostly well-preserved antiques from Versailles, were the best pieces of a kingly age before the peasantry had destroyed the perfect hierarchy of Natural Man.

"Ozker's a pig," said Malleson, giving Dartley the information he had asked for. "He's got pigsties all over the place. Ankara. Istanbul. London. Munich. Zurich. He's been to Moscow a lot; stays in the Kremlin. How do you like them apples?"

"Where do I kill him?" asked Dartley.

"I don't know. Let's see what's on his schedule for the next two months."

Dartley fixed on the older man with his hungry eyes, the gray-green eyes of an Arctic wolf.

In Malleson's basement, unlike the upper floors, there was no distraction. The cement walls held only maps. The light came from industrial fixtures. The chairs and tables were functional pieces, mostly old oak office furniture from the forties. Malleson had been given two days to gather information on Ozker. He knew much about the self-made Turkish millionaire.

"He's an animal when it comes to women."

"What does that mean?" asked Dartley. "He fucks 'em from behind?"

"It means you can use a gorgeous chick, if I've got the phrase correct; and I know you can find one to lure him back to her apartment for at least half an hour, if that's what you want to do. He usually falls asleep for fifteen minutes after he fucks."

"What about his bodyguards?" asked Dartley.

"That's a major obstacle. You'll have to figure out how to separate the two forces. By the way, Ozker carries a Browning 9mm. automatic in a shoulder holster."

"What about drugs?"

"You mean, does he take them?"

"No, the krauts told me he's a drug trafficker," said Dartley.

"It's better than that, or worse, depending on whose side you're on."

"Vy"—Dartley's nickname for the so-called Viscount—"I'm not here to play games."

"The Kremlin, specifically the KGB, gives Ozker a safe haven in Sofia, Bulgaria. Otherwise they protect his German operations in any way they can. It's true, they're doing everything they can to undermine West Germany. It used to be atom-bomb information; I guess it still is; but now they know a country can fall to pieces without a shot being fired. All it takes is a high enough percentage of the so-called thinking class to stop thinking. The next thing you know, the so-called working class has stopped working."

"Is Ozker an addict himself?"

"Only of women, money, power. He likes a good drink. Heroin doesn't seem to be a problem, except that he's pushing it on everybody else."

"Does he drive?"

"There's always a chauffeur."

"*There's* a possibility," Dartley said.

"Do you want to know his schedule for the next two months?"

By now Dartley's brain was already working overtime.

Malleson pushed several buttons on the console.

"He has a son graduating from medical school at the beginning of June. His name is Stefan Ozker."

"Stefan? Really?"

"He changed his name. His mother was a Turk, too. Fatma Abady. Let's see... June 9, 1981."

"Where?"

"Please, Dickie, I'm getting to that.... University of Munich. An 'A' student."

"No doubt he's an expert on drugs. He'll make a good doctor."

"Dickie, wait.... Stefan Ozker. He's doing his internship in Luzern, starting right away."

"Do you think the father will be there?" Dartley asked.

"Where? Luzern?"

"The medical-school graduation in Munich, dummy."

The pupils of Malleson's blue eyes narrowed. "Dickie, give me another day."

*   *   *

A day was all Malleson needed. Like a leading gossip columnist, which was not a bad description, he had contacts all over the world. Those contacts knew Malleson was good for a lot of money if they produced the information he wanted.

Within twelve hours after Dartley left him, a Malleson contact—a Turk living in Germany, Meral Fredericks, thirty-five, the widow of a half-German weapons broker—sauntered into the Goethe Gasthaus on Kaiserstrasse near the University of Munich medical school. Spying a slight young man with burning black eyes wearing a white medical jacket, she asked in Turkish, "Did you get my message?" The young man looked up. He was stunned by the beauty and celebrity of the woman.

"You are Meral?"

She smiled knowingly, aware of her physical impact. Five foot ten with a mane of dark red hair, large, slanted green eyes and the full lips of a true Caucasian, her skin was Mediterranean gold, her breasts almost overflowing her low-cut green cashmere sweater dress; she was the perfect undercover agent. When he caught sight of her full figure, Stefan Ozker's mouth almost dropped to his chin. He had become too used to death and disease. He had forgotten that the "real world" had its spectacular pleasures. He could not believe this lioness was taking him to lunch.

"You don't remember me, I suppose," she said, lying through her teeth. "I think I was twelve when my grandmother took me to visit your grandmother. You were just learning to talk. You were the sexiest little pasha I'd ever seen. I think when I saw you I got wet, if you know what I mean; but I'm sorry, this kind of talk must disgust you, Stefan. I sound like a hooker, don't I?"

"Oh, no, no, no," the young man protested. "I'm just sorry I don't remember you."

"Well, that's all right. You're still sexy," she said.

"Are you wet now?" he teased, testing the proverbial waters of sex. He hadn't had a woman in three months.

It was then that Meral's eyes filled with tears. "It's all my fault for waiting so long. The last time I went back to Istanbul, my grandmother was dying and I wasn't paying any attention to what she was saying. She kept telling me, 'Soroya's grandson, the little Abdul,' I think that's what they used to call you, Stefan...."

He winced at the childhood name he hated so much. It reminded him of his childhood, about which he felt much the same way.

"'The little Abdul is a young doctor in Germany. You must go see him, he will take care of you,'" Meral continued. "I kept telling her I wasn't sick. Then, as I told my late husband who was also a graduate of Munich, one day I was looking through the lists of graduates to see the Turkish names—sometimes I see people I know—and there you were. So I said, 'I know, I can't go to the graduation, but I can at least take the boy to lunch....' Excuse me, 'the man.' You are certainly a man, aren't you, I can at least take you to lunch. We can at least be friends, can't we?" By now Meral was slavering. Under the table she pressed against him, took his hand and rubbed it on her inner thigh.

"Excuse me," she said. "I get carried away by handsome men. I have missed my true calling. I should have been a whore."

"You're the most attractive woman I've ever met," he announced, taking her hand and rubbing it up and down over the erection that sat trapped in his pants.

An hour later they were in her hotel room fucking their brains out. He was tit-fucking her. It was impossible for any normal young man to look at her perfect breasts with their smooth channel and not want to put his throbbing cock there. She pressed her bronzed mammary globes together, smothering his organ in warm flesh. He rode her like a jockey astride a great mare, shouting, "I love you! I love you! I love you!" until he finally burst into orgasm. He shook for what seemed like a minute; the spasm in his loins emptied his body of its stored-up tension. Afterward, he lay cradled in her arms. She stroked his fine black hair.

"My poor baby," she cooed. "If only your grandmother had lived to see you graduate."

"This is better," he said, smiling.

"Don't worry," she said. "I will be your family. There is no reason why you have to go through life alone, without a mother and a father."

"My mother's coming to see me graduate," he said.

"Oh," she exclaimed, "I'm sorry. I thought your

grandmother raised you. My grandmother told me you were an orphan. She kept saying, 'That poor boy, he has no mother and father.'"

"No, no, no," he corrected her. "My mother and father both worked. My grandmother raised me."

"And you still have a mother? She must be very proud of you."

"She is."

"What did your father do?"

"No, he's still alive. Import-export. He's actually done pretty well."

"I'm sorry," she said. "I don't mean to be a crepe hanger." She stroked the side of his face. "Do your parents still live in Istanbul?"

"No, no, they've been divorced since I was two. Maybe that's why your grandmother thought I didn't have parents. My mother was a singer."

"So, she's coming to your graduation?"

"Yes."

"She'll be so proud."

"My father's coming, too. He's coming on the second. He's staying for a week."

"Oh good," she said as casually as she could manage. This was the information she had come for; her heart was racing.

"He has some businesses here," the young man continued.

Meral shifted her weight to her other side and caressed his leg with hers. Her skin felt like satin. At least, that's what she'd always been told.

"Your father has a house in Munich?" she asked.

"No, he doesn't like houses. He stays at his hotel."

"His hotel?" she repeated. "He owns the hotel?"

"No," the young man said. "He just owns some stock in it."

"Well, tell me," Meral laughed. "I'll stay there. You can be my doctor; your father can be my landlord."

"If he met you, he'd take you," the young man said.

"Import-export? Forget it," she said. "Doctors are what turn me on." She nibbled on his lower lip. "I'll bet it's the best hotel in Munich. I can't imagine a Turk not having the best. Just like I'll bet you'll make a great surgeon."

"Wrong on both counts," he said. "My father's hotel has twenty-one rooms. It's called the Munich Sofia; you wouldn't want to stay there; it's really a reconverted flophouse on Beethoven Allee. It's for all his Turkish friends. The staff speaks Turkish and generally looks the other way. And as for myself, I plan to be a psychiatrist. I figure I've grown up with so many crazy people, starting with my mother and father, that I have an inside track on the so-called human condition."

Meral Fredericks smiled, having gotten the information she wanted. Yes, Herr Ozker would make an appearance on June 2, the Saturday before the graduation; he would stay for a week. Her efforts meant three thousand deutsche marks in addition to a good fuck. Good, not great, but at least the dark-eyed young man could get it up and keep it up. It was more than she could normally hope for with the middle-aged establishment types she usually went out with. She took Stefan's hand and ran his fingers up and down her labia until she was wet again.

"Eat me out, you animal," she whispered.

Three days later, Dartley had worked out his strategy of death. The spider and the web. He knew exactly how he would capture Ozker and kill him. The assassination would be in full view of the public, in full view of the KGB. Dartley almost danced with joy. His first step: Camelot Armoring, New Haven, Connecticut.

The president of Camelot Armoring was an engineer out of Dearborn, Michigan. He was Spencer Siddons, age 38. He was the driving force behind the latest vehicles against terrorism, electronically sophisticated armored cars. Fitted with special metals, plastics and fabrics, the body could withstand an armored assault. Even the car's gun ports were standard equipment. Hidden behind the door armrests, they were not detectable from the outside. For the Central American dictator and the Saudi oilman at the mercy of marauding bandits, the Camelot label was considered a smart investment. Begun in 1980, a year later Camelot—with a staff of fifty in an abandoned Marlin Firearms factory near I-95—produced six cars a month. The usual armored car took up to three months. This was Dartley's second order.

"Dart, I can't do a car in three weeks," Spencer

Siddons stated plainly. Dartley looked at his old buddy. They had been in Nam together; they had stuck by each other when most of the so-called educated public called them goons or worse. Under orders, they'd machine-gunned three villages, discovered they'd massacred mostly women and children. Their best buddy stuck his M16 in his mouth after a gook whore cut off his cock with a single-edge razor blade. He pulled the trigger before anyone could get to him. Siddons himself had lost his right leg; during his hospitalization he got interested in improving his prosthesis. That led somehow to improving cars. At first he made cars for paralytics and amputees. Then it occurred to him that a market existed for armored cars: terrorists the world over were wreaking havoc for well-heeled businessmen.

"Spence, you owe me," Dartley said quietly. True enough, Dartley had saved his friend's life in Nam, stanching the flow of blood in a leg artery that stuck out of his stump like a vein in a pot roast. That wasn't what he was talking about. "Spence, the Arab guy."

Dartley has class, the son of a bitch, thought Siddons. Too much class to mention saving his life in Nam. He owed Dartley because, six months before, a certain Saudi sheik had reneged on the payment for three gold Cadillacs, each with an oil-slick device and a smoke-screen system. Each car cost about seventy-five thousand, complete. Siddons had called Dartley in a panic, saying he needed the money to cover his payroll costs and what should he do?

Through an Arab friend, Dartley had gotten notes to the sheik—notes written in Arabic which said that, if he didn't pay Camelot the money, he would kill the sheik's sons one by one and finally would kill the sheik himself. The sheik had seven sons between the ages of two and twenty-seven by three different wives. Each son was better guarded than the next. The note in question was signed "The Wild Beast." The sheik ignored Dartley's note.

Using Malleson, Dartley tracked down the first three sons. Two were in London; one was in New York. His instinct was to use a sniper rifle with a silencer. He soon realized that, given the wealth of the Arab family, he would become the object of an intense police manhunt. He used the rifle only on the first son, killing him on a ski slope in the French Alps. The top of the young man's head went flying through the air like a chunk of sod on a golf course.

The second one, aged 24, was a graduate student at Oxford. Dartley, dressed like a Fleet Street banker, jabbed him with the tip of his umbrella as he was coming through Customs. "So sorry," he said, and disappeared. Dartley had pricked the boy right in the small of his back. Three days later the boy came down with a sudden fever and died. Dartley had, of course, put poison on the umbrella tip. It was a trick he had learned from the KGB.

The third son, 22, by a different wife than the

first two, lived a highly bisexual life in Paris. Dartley followed him to the Orphee Baths, paraded his splendidly masculine body in front of the boy and lured him into a small rented room upstairs. No bodyguards allowed, of course. He immediately slit his throat and disappeared down the drainpipe to a prearranged escape route. The day of the funeral of the third son, Camelot Armoring received payment in full. The gold Cadillacs were shipped out to Arabia on the next boat.

"Okay," replied Siddons. "Three weeks. What do you want?"

"A Mercedes 600," Dartley replied. "The black limousine. I want the regular job; I want all the available options, and then I've got more after that."

The "regular job" meant the Camelot workers took a regular Mercedes 600 and stripped it down. Seats and carpeting were removed; layers of armoring metals were laid in. The car gained a thousand pounds. The Mercedes 600 plus the cost of the basic armoring was $105,800. The optional features included a dual ram bumper ($700) to crash through roadblocks; and the oil-slick system ($825) and the smoke-screen device ($600) to dissuade pursuers from their pursuit. Dartley also wanted the remote starter and the bomb scan ($1250), in case someone put a bomb under the hood; a siren/intercom system ($1000); an electrical device that charged the vehicle with up to

70,000 volts ($925); and a system that fired tear gas from all four corners of the craft ($1300).

Dartley, as he had warned Siddons, wanted more.

"First, I want a chauffeur's window of bullet-proof glass between the front and back seats," Dartley said.

"I think the Mercedes Six Hundred has that if you want it."

"It has shatterproof glass, not bulletproof."

"Okay," said Siddons, "we'll get you bulletproof. Next."

"I want a driver control button that can lock the back doors so that they can't be opened by anyone in the backseat."

"No problem."

"Two more things," Dartley said. "First, I want a compartment under the front seat where a full-grown man the size of myself can hide. The compartment has to have sliding doors, like accordion pleats, so if a person wanted to hide under the front seat, he wouldn't have to climb around doors."

"Right. Jesus, Dart, what are you going to do with this car?"

"Wait. There's more. I want the roof over the backseat to slide back at the touch of a button."

"Wouldn't want them to asphyxiate back there, would we?" joked Siddons.

"And I want a grille over the roof opening, Spence, a grille that's part of the roof itself so it can't be pushed out."

"It sounds like you're turning the backseat into a cage."

"Could be, Spence, could be," mused Dartley, not about to discuss the details of his car with anyone, not even Siddons.

"What else?" asked the armorer from Connecticut.

"The car is to be sent to Harold C. Mount, the Hotel Köblenz, Munich, West Germany. It must be delivered by June first at the latest."

"I'll drive it to the docks myself. We use Baltimore these days. It's cheaper. I'll have a man go with it; he can drive it to Munich himself."

"Just as long as it gets there, Spence."

"We do this all the time. No problem. With you we start today. Immediately."

Dartley smiled. Nothing like a good friend, he thought, in this cold and heartless world.

The same day. Chestertown, Maryland. Rubinek, Vassilov's replacement, felt like the ass of all time. He was proceeding on his case as if the car surgeons who had altered the silver gray Camaro were planning to overthrow the western world.

Did the fucking car have to be top secret?

That afternoon at three o'clock, as he was heading for the library on the main campus at Washington College, he noticed a group of students, mostly male, milling around what looked like a long, black hearse. On the other side of the non-glare tinted glass, an Arab in full regalia sat behind the steering wheel glowering at the students. He was clearly waiting for his boss. The employer in question, a Saudi prince, was inside the main administration building with his son, talking to the head of the political science department about a low grade. In their enthusiasm for the car, the students sounded like 8-year-old boys.

"This car is supposed to be armored like a tank! Faisal told me."

"It's got a thousand pounds of steel plate inside the doors. Plus he said they got rifles over the doors in secret compartments."

"Oh wow."

Rubinek, intrigued, circled the car. He inspected it as closely as he dared. The driver was undoubtedly armed and, without question, high-strung.

Something caught his eye: a small metal label affixed to the rear bumper. A piece of tissue-thin chrome about the size and shape of a collar stay except that its ends were squared off. In minuscule printing, the label read, "Camelot Armoring, New Haven, Connecticut."

How could the Moscow Center have missed Camelot Armoring? The black Cadillac limousine was the most splendid car of its type he had ever seen. It gleamed like the finest onyx. Rubinek wondered about its secret powers, known to no one but the sheik and his driver. He immediately called Vassilov to tell him his good news.

"Then go to New Haven, why the fuss?" Vassilov's contact at the Washington embassy instructed him.

Vassilov felt like a fool. "I don't know what I'm looking for," he insisted.

"See if any order there has anything to do with

Germany, especially von Kelsing–Schmidt, Schiller Pharmaceuticals—Are you writing all this down?"

"I have all the suggestions."

"Also I have new information."

"What's that?"

"The Germans I mentioned. Werner von Kelsing. Bruno Schmidt. Willi Reiser. It seems they tried to eliminate one of our Bulgarian affiliates awhile back."

"Belgian affiliates?" Vassilov had little patience with Soviet double-talk.

"Yes, the affiliate's name is Ali Ozker. He works out of Sofia. Luzern. Zurich. Munich. Actually, any connection between these car places, body shops, as you call them, and any of those cities would be appreciated."

"Comrade," Vassilov said, "I think you're jumping the gun."

"Am I? It's very odd, don't you think, that three of the leading Western industrialists should travel to West Virginia to meet a man who calls himself Mr. Savage, a man who drives a small Chevrolet with trick license plates and bulletproof glass."

"What are you getting at?" Vassilov asked.

"We think they've hired themselves a professional assassin."

They were interrupted. A high-pitched voice from the phone company ordered them to deposit twenty-five more cents or risk extermination. Vassilov deposited the coin. He was free to speak for another five minutes. He had only one further question for his contact in D.C.

"What difference does one two-bit Turk mean to the Center?"

"I don't know. I only know what they tell me. Those are my orders. The Moscow Center says that nothing must happen to Ali Ozker."

That very day at the Moscow Center, Rogoff had just been issued orders from the Presidium. The orders had apparently come from Andropov himself. Strange that the premier should concern himself with a gangster, he thought. Even Rogoff—not then, anyway—did not understand the true importance of Ali Ozker.

Still, he had to ask himself the obvious question. Was drug trafficking in Germany all that important to the Soviets? Surely other Turks could replace the infamous but relatively unimportant Ozker. Surely the acquisition of crucial technological knowledge was more important in the long run. Why destroy an enemy who can provide a valuable service? Rogoff's orders were to protect the life of Ali Ozker at the risk of losing his job. He was not told why.

In the heart of the Kremlin, the architect of "Operation P" peered through the tiny window of his study. His private suite was on the top floor of a turret. The suite was only three small rooms—a study, a living room, a bedroom. As soon as he had been named premier he had requested this inner sanctum, this holy of holies at the center of twentieth-century Russia.

The rooms were dark but carefully decorated. The original paneled oak had not been touched. The plaster walls above the wood had been carefully lacquered in a color the designer called "aubergine." To the premier, whose grandfather, a country schoolteacher, had maintained a small garden, the walls were simply "eggplant," nothing more. An odd color for a wall, but to him the color said everything. It went with the black leather furniture and the oriental rugs. It went with the black-and-white engravings of Lenin and Trotsky and the other mythical heroes of the first days of the Revolution. It was the color of tragedy.

His illustrious and not-so-illustrious predecessors Brezhnev and Kruschev had asked for and received country villas north of the city with flower gardens bordered by formal boxwood hedges. In the winter the hedges had to be wrapped in straw and burlap to protect them from the severe Moscow winter. The villas of his illustrious predecessors had been filled with furniture from Marks and Spencer, Bloomingdale's, Neiman Marcus; nothing from the state-owned GUM.

They, like other Soviet leaders, had from time to time spoken about the "Russian earth" as the key to their personal strength and to the identity of the nation as a whole. To Andropov, the soil was the key to Soviet agriculture, nothing more. Agriculture reminded him of the past, the pre-revolutionary past at that, with its multitudes of illiterate serfs. His great-grandparents, all eight of them, had been born serfs. To Andropov, the past was past. To him, the future of the Soviet peoples lay in their cities. It was in the cities where the brain, above all, was paramount. After all, what was the Revolution but a series of related ideas that had issued from the brains of a few inspired leaders? Because of his understanding of history and the true source of progress, Andropov fled into the Kremlin and not away from it when crisis struck. To him the Kremlin was the holy place, the touchstone to inspiration. His apartment in the Kremlin was where he went to meditate and to plot his strategy, which is always the same: the overthrow of the West in any way possible.

May 14. London. Ali Ozker and four body-guards tour Savile Row, London's street for masculine fashion. Ozker has decided that for his son Stefan's medical-school graduation he will dress as an English yachtsman. A double-breasted navy blue blazer with brass buttons and a white carnation, white flannels, white shoes, white starched collar and a straw boater—its band beribboned with the colors of Magdalen College, Oxford.

"Veddy British," he remarked more than once, inordinately proud of his ability to mimic the different accents of a language he had only begun studying five years before. It was his intention to make his son proud. He had no intention of attending the graduation looking like a tired businessman. He could just see those other fathers: exhausted, overweight, their virility wrecked by too many cigarettes, too much alcohol, too much restaurant food. They would wear navy pin-striped suits and gray hair. Ozker, by contrast, had his dark hair professionally retouched every two weeks when he had it cut. He'd also had his jowls removed by the best plastic surgeon in Brazil. He recognized that he was not a naturally handsome man, but he hoped that by the time he was 55 or 60, he could will good looks the same way he had willed wealth and power. Like most successful self-made men, he knew that nothing was impossible. What the mind dreamed of, Man could accomplish.

Ozker had had two uncomfortable communiqués that week. Both were from Moscow Center. He rarely, if ever, received information directly from Moscow. Usually he had received news through Cemel Demirel and his associates in Düsseldorf. Or from Ilse de Brock. Now, she too had come to a bloody end—in West Virginia, of all places. That had been the first piece of information. He received the news of her death in a panic. What was he to do now? He needed information about the people he was dealing with. His panic only served to anticipate the second message. A waiter delivered it to him at Claridge's, where he was staying. The waiter, a so-called white (non-Communist) Russian emigré about 70 years old, had committed it to memory. The message was "A man called Savage, an American, met with von Kelsing, Schmidt, Reiser three hours before Ilse de Brock's death. He is suspected in the disappearance of two Soviet agents. He is having an armored Mercedes 600 delivered to Munich. Your new contact at von Kelsing–Schmidt is Dr. Marlena Kupitsky."

Chapter Eleven

The Mercedes arrived on schedule, just as Siddons said it would. At Dartley's expense he'd sent along a Camelot employee as driver, watchdog and general all-round car polisher and mechanic from Cherbourg to Munich.

Dartley and Siddons had worked both ends against the middle to obtain the necessary papers. Whenever palms had to be greased, they were greased with the most expensive spread. Using the theory that government officials are no different from headwaiters, official papers were speeded along.

By June 1, Eddie Sevcik, an apprentice mechanic, had delivered the car in Munich to one Harold C. Mount, as Dartley had requested.

Dartley thanked him and wished him well on his flight home. He test-drove the car through the streets of Munich. Heads turned. Even to the Germans, the armored car had an air of authority. It seemed heavier, blacker and, with its tinted windows, somehow more sinister than one might expect.

The Hotel Köblenz had an underground parking garage for more than a hundred cars.

Except for a change of plans in Paris, Dartley's flight to Düsseldorf was uneventful. Customs was no problem. After all, it was peacetime. He was obviously what he appeared to be, a prosperous American, Harold C. Mount by name. His passport said he was a writer, but he was clearly what the Americans liked to call "old money." He seemed entirely too relaxed, too blasé about the world in general to be taken for a self-made man. No, Mr. Mount was clearly out of another era, when things were not so serious. He was, as the historians like to say, "between the wars."

He checked in at the Hotel Köblenz after first inspecting the subterranean garage. It seemed like a World War II bunker with its massive walls and pillars of raw concrete.

"What do you write about, Mr. Mount?" the hotel manager asked him, after inspecting his passport.

"Travel mostly. Foreign countries. I'm a free-lance journalist," adding quickly, "Actually, I spend about half of my time managing my family's stock portfolio."

"I see," replied the manager, satisfied that Mr. Mount was not another one of "those dreadful American hippies." In the late sixties and early seventies, the American counterculture had repelled the West German establishment as much as it had attracted their children. In short, the manager, Herr Ludwig, had no need for romantics who slipped out without paying their bills. Herr Mount, to gain the man's goodwill, had paid his bill a week in advance, in cash. Herr Ludwig seemed pleased. Nothing greased the wheels of international diplomacy like dollars and cents.

The next morning, at 10:00 A.M., Dartley, carrying a small suitcase, was first in line at the Victoria Sporting Goods shop on Dachauer Strasse. He purchased a wet suit, a diving lung, goggles, flippers—everything one would need for a scuba-diving expedition. He told the salesman he was planning to search for the lost continent of Atlantis off the coast of Bimini. On the salesman's advice he bought some shark repellent. "You never know when you meet a shark," cautioned the German.

By noon he had purchased his clothing for his return trip to the United States, a preppy outfit for one Leighton Ledyard of Grosse Pointe. Breton red sailing pants, dirty bucks, white oxford-cloth shirt, blue blazer with brass buttons, white cotton sailing hat and dark glasses. In a secret compartment of his suitcase was his passport and wallet with credit cards for Leighton Ledyard. Plus the bronzer. He intended to leave looking healthier than when he arrived.

His return passport listed him as a 40-year-old lawyer. The passport photo showed him grinning, all teeth, with a dark tan. This was a man who unquestionably enjoyed the sporting life.

When she got Dartley's call, Sylvia Marton, the "blond Sophia Loren" was filming *Rebel in the Rain* in the Australian outback. Even though he had said it was a matter of life and death, Dartley waited for twenty long minutes while they finished shooting her scene. She had been riding a horse on camera, galloping after her lover, the commander of the British garrison in 1784, the year of the story. Her fragile white lace dress had been drenched for the scene with buckets of imported spring water. Her pale nipples stood out prominently through the wet gauze of the dress as she spoke with him.

"Woody, what's wrong?"

Sylvia had always called him "Woody" for Richard Woodgate, his former name. It was her way of owning him all for herself. He, for his part, played the same game with her. He called her "Clarabel," after the old-time Howdy Doody clown.

The two of them had spent their lives on the run, always unavailable for long-term commitment. "My work is my life" was their constant refrain. They were two of a kind. Each canceled the other out. Neither would budge an inch. "In the end," they promised themselves, "when we are old, we will live together in the south of France."

"Are you coning to Australia, Woody?"

"Clarabel, I hope so. Listen, babe, I'd really like to be with you fucking the bejesus out of you, but this is a matter of life and death. I'm calling from Munich. Who do you know who can help me?"

"Help you, Woody? What kind of help?"

"I need a gorgeous woman in her twenties. She has to be willing to fuck, be able to fire a gun and be loyal to the death. I'll pay her a thousand dollars a day."

"I'll do it," said Sylvia.

"We start tomorrow," replied Dartley.

"Fuck," said Sylvia Marton, inserting her middle finger into her vaginal cave. Just talking to him was driving her crazy. She wished that her best friend in Munich were not exactly what Dartley was looking for. She knew they'd end up fucking. The one thing she did not care to know was exactly when he was fucking. She would always claim she didn't care, but she cared. She tried one last time:

"I could say I was sick and had to see my gynecologist in Munich. You could examine me, Doctor. I have a problem. I'm not sure I'm orgasmic anymore. You might have to conduct a series of tests. Of course I could only stay a day or two. This is a very expensive movie. It is supposed to take place in the rainy season and we're in the middle of a drought."

Sylvia could feel herself coming. She imagined her finger was Woody's cock. The fantasy made her warm all over.

"Who is the girl?" Dartley wasn't kidding.

"Bobo Noll," she replied, in between silent gasps. "Malleson has her number and address. She lives near Old City Hall."

"And?"

"She's twenty-seven, five-ten, a former Miss Germany, a model, an honors graduate of the

Sorbonne. She did graduate work in psychology. She's just starting her practice."

"What kind of practice?"

"Don't be facetious."

"Can she shoot?" Dartley asked.

"It was her sport in school. The rifle team. Sometimes I think she's working for the CIA or the KGB, but who knows?"

"Clarabel, what do you mean, who knows?"

It was too late. Her orgasm had begun. He realized he'd heard those sounds before.

"Clarabel, for God's sake, get a good grip on yourself," he joked.

Even in her orgasm, Sylvia Marton was crying silently. Why Bobo Noll and not her? The price of international stardom was almost more than she could bear.

Bobo Noll was closer to six feet. After five years of analysis, she had a lion's mane of tawny blond hair and wore leather suits to match. For those rare occasions when she wanted to look like a lady, she kept a chestful of pearls and a closetful of basic black cocktail dresses. In her growing up, she'd met most of the European royals. Her grandmother had been the illegitimate daughter of the Duke of Saxony, and Bobo looked the part. Under her sensual lips and her overly made-up sooty eyes was the bone structure of an old-line aristocrat. The girl was made of steel.

She was also made of flesh. Within an hour of their meeting, she and Dartley were in bed together,

her long golden legs wrapped around his ass. She was tight and warm and easy to satisfy.

"I love dangerous men," she said when they were finished.

"You're pretty dangerous yourself," he said.

"I'm just a pussycat."

"I don't know about the cat part, but the pussy is pretty good."

"Pretty good?"

"The best."

"My wish is your command," she replied.

"For a thousand dollars a day, I would hope so," he said.

She kissed him on the small of his neck, pressed her perfect body up against his, looked deep into his eyes and whispered, "And to think you could be dead tomorrow."

"I love dangerous women," he said, and decided it was time to get serious. "Get dressed," he ordered her. "It's time to get to work."

Chapter Twelve

The Ozker family was together again for the first time in twenty years. Ali Ozker had walked out on his wife Fatma in 1961, when their little boy was 3. He had married her a month before she delivered the child, at the insistence of her father, who liked to think of himself as a devout Muslim. Abdul Abady, the father, had created the heroin trade in Istanbul in the 1920s. In the disarray following the breakup of the Ottoman Empire in 1919–1920, Abady was singularly aware of the possibilities inherent in growing heroin poppies on his father's estate in Anatolia. At the time he thought of heroin as a fashionable and innocent escape for the wealthy. In no way did he envision the heroin culture of the postwar world or the bloodshed it would bring about. Nonetheless, the man became a tyrant in the Turkish underworld. Abady was finally gunned down in 1961 when his little grandson Abdul was 3. By then, the old man's daughter Fatma had turned into a fat shrew with a wart on her nose.

Twenty years later, when the family reconvened in Munich for little Abdul's, now Stefan's, graduation from medical school, the fat shrew had lost her excess weight, gone to a gym, seen a couple of plastic surgeons, and was considered a great beauty "of a certain age." Actually, she was only 42 and looked at least ten years younger. Ali, her former husband, having left his second family in London, pursued Fatma. By then Fatma was separated from her fourth husband, Anthony Exton, a well-known English lord. She was known as Lady Exton. Very well known. With his money and her beauty, Ali Ozker and Lady Exton were a natural for the gossip columns. They frequented the best restaurants in Munich: Aubergine, Tantris, Der Königshof, Le Gourmet, Walterspiel. They were, as the expression goes, an item.

Richard Dartley of Frederick, Maryland, and Washington, D.C., followed the rekindled Ozker relationship with more than a little interest. It was not to Dartley's advantage to have Ozker walled off from the possibility of Bobo Noll's making an inroad. Dartley needed her. Turkish was not his strong suit. Dartley had a specific hand to play and he held just so many cards, nothing more. He had to be careful.

Friday night at midnight was zero hour. Bobo had to be in the picture by Thursday. She had to deliver the message from the American mob, or there would be no assassination. Dartley decided there was no time like the present to make his move. First, he instructed Bobo to call up the various gossip columnists in Düsseldorf, the same ones who had reported on Ali Ozker and his first wife Fatma, now "Lady Exton." Bobo's routine was to be as follows: "Hello, this is Bobo Noll, I don't understand—Bobo Noll; surely you know me. I was with the Saudi family. Anyway, that's not important. What I called to tell you was it's not true about Ali Ozker and his wife. In the first place, the woman is not English. No, she is Turkish.... No, Turkish.... No, on both sides. She is not half French. Both parents were Turkish. Her father was Abdul Abady, the heroin gangster. You check it out, the father was murdered in

1961. Abdul Abady. In the second place, Ali Ozker and I are lovers. Normally I would say nothing about my private life, but I cannot allow these lies to be printed."

Since everything about Fraulein Noll, except for the part about her and Ali Ozker being lovers, turned out to be absolutely true, the gossip columnists took her word for it that that bit of information was valid, too.

Dartley didn't stop there. While Bobo was still on the phone with the various columnists, messengers were delivering 8×10 glossies of Bobo in evening gowns and swimsuits from what she called "my starlet days." She had promised the press, moreover, that she and Ali had a date at Aubergine on Friday night. If the papers wanted to send a photographer, neither she nor Ozker would object.

Bobo spoke to five columnists this way. Her glossies intrigued them as much as her voice. Was she a star? What kind of a star? Had she once had another name? Four of the columnists in question had the temerity to call Ozker. They asked to speak to his secretary. As it turned out, there was no secretary, only bodyguards. Bobo Noll? Ozker said he'd never heard of her. By the second call, however, he'd not only heard of her, he'd gotten her glossies and a note saying she would telephone at five o'clock.

The woman called on schedule.

"When can I see you?" he asked.

"I have made reservations for us Friday night at

Aubergine," she responded in her distinctly husky voice.

"I can't. I've got an appointment with my wife."

"Fatma Exton is not your wife."

"Our son is graduating from medical school on Saturday morning."

"Listen to me carefully, Mr. Ozker," she said. "I will pick you up in my Mercedes. This is a fabulous car. You will not believe it when you see it. It can do anything including spread tear gas. If you and I can make a deal, the car is yours to keep."

At the other end of the line, there was a distinct pause.

"What kind of a deal?" asked Ozker.

"Maybe you have never heard of Franco Gennaro," she said. "The Gennaro family is the number-one family in the United States. If you will make a deal to meet with a deputy of Franco Gennaro and agree to supply the family with your heroin, I will give you the Mercedes. It is what is called an armored limousine. All the Arab sheiks have them these days. It cost one hundred and twenty thousand American dollars."

There was another pause.

"Miss Noll, I must inform you that my phone is probably tapped. Many of my visitors turn out to be wired for sound. I must inspect my visitors. That will include you when we meet Friday night. And it goes without saying that I know nothing about heroin or organized crime, especially organized crime in the United States. However, I will be more than happy to discuss your business deal with you, whatever it is; and if you insist, take a ride in your Mercedes. I must tell you that from everything you have told me, you sound like a fascinating human being."

"Did you get my pictures?"

"Why do you think I'm willing to go out with you?"

"There's just one more thing," she said. "If we make the deal, you get the car, but not the chauffeur. The chauffeur is all mine."

Ozker laughed lecherously. "I'll bet your chauffeur does more than drive your car for you."

"Oh no, my darling," Bobo said. "He is unfortunately gay. Beautiful and gay. He is a part-time housekeeper for me. You see, I am really a little girl. Sometimes I need looking after."

"I'll keep that in mind," answered the Turk, again with a lecherous laugh to make sure she understood his intentions. All things considered, Ozker was looking forward to Friday night. Lady Exton would be no problem. Besides, she was getting uppity; it was time to put her in her place. Ozker had no use for grandes dames, especially menopausal ones. He much preferred broads. Didn't every successful man?

On the south side of the city, Richard Dartley also was making plans for Friday night. He called Lady Exton and said he was a reporter for *The New York Times*. He was in Munich on vacation, he said. He couldn't help noticing her name in the columns. Seeing as how she was one of the world's most beautiful women, he'd secured an okay from his editor in New York to do a cover story on her for the Sunday magazine. It was to be entitled, "The New Woman: Lady Exton—An Aristocrat at the Crossroads."

"But, darling, what crossroads am I at?" she had asked over the phone.

"Basically, I would like to explore with you just how far in the direction of men you see yourself going," he had responded.

"But, darling," she had joked, "I always go in the direction of men. What other direction is there?"

He went to her hotel suite, camera and tape recorder in hand.

Now Richard Dartley, for the record, did not give the impression of being a matinee idol. He was not pretty. He did not turn heads the way pretty men are likely to. His face was not even particularly strong in the patriarchal sense. He did not suggest absolute authority. Young women looking for fathers did not cozy up to him. Dartley was a rawboned kind of a guy, almost homely, even horse-faced, with a jaw that was too long and gray-blue eyes that were definitely cold. He was too gaunt. If anything—even though the people who met him were not consciously afraid of him— the man definitely inspired fear. These qualities played in his favor that particular Wednesday afternoon.

Fatma Lady Exton had always fallen for fearsome men. This little-known fact was the main reason her present marriage was a disaster. Lord Exton was a beautiful fop, perfectly heterosexual and even monogamous; still, he looked like a fashion plate, always said the right thing, was unfailingly polite, considerate, never forgot birthdays or anniversaries. Tony Exton was what most women claimed they were looking for. But most women were saddled with dumb brutes, uncultivated, beer-swilling slobs. Fatma Exton, having had her share of movie stars, had in her early forties returned to her roots, sexually speaking, that is. Her hunger, like Dartley's own, was for dangerous situations. In her case, she craved dangerous men, men who lived on the edge, men who expected the women with them to share the danger. She lusted for racing-car drivers and soldiers of fortune. She liked African dictators, too. Her several interracial affairs with some of the world's most powerful black leaders had caused a furor in the drawing rooms of Mayfair and Kensington. Her adultery almost ended her marriage, but Tony Exton was not so much forgiving as he was civilized.

Dartley sensed that he and Fatma Exton were two of a kind. This being so, he also knew that if he did not presume he could have her and make his move, she would begin to find him irritating. Women like her wanted to be ravished as soon as possible.

Her appearance made it easier for him. Very easy. She wore her short, jet-black hair in ringlets; they framed her perfect oval face with an abandon not normally found in an upper-class woman. Only her flawless ivory skin, her finely arched brows and her bright gray eyes bespoke the perfect grooming and the deliberately stress-free life that belongs only to the truly rich, those free spirits who have inherited a huge amount of money and who do not have to work. Still, Lady Exton's body, under its stiff floor-length caftan of gold, black and silver brocade, was a mystery to the American. She seemed full-chested, but he couldn't be sure. As for the rest of her—her legs, her hips, her ass, her tummy—he could tell nothing. It was definitely time to make his move. He took her as a starving man might take a loaf of freshly baked bread. Without asking her permission or even giving her warning, his mouth was inside hers, hungrily exploring her, his hands groping to unbutton her stiff outer garment. He could smell her right through the brocade. It was driving him crazy.

"Wait a minute," Fatma announced. "You take off your clothes. I'll take off mine."

She seemed to merely unbutton a button or unhook a hook somewhere, and her stiff caftan fell to the floor. When the two strangers first saw each other naked, their response was the same: "Oh my God." Dartley, all grit and muscle and hair, was the kind of animal she had never had. Even Ali Ozker, the super-ape, as some people called him, tended to gorge himself at meals and had reached middle age with a broad midsection. Dartley by contrast, was clearly a sexual athlete. The man was born to fuck. He had never seen any woman quite like Lady Exton. One look at her, and he was marble hard. Five-four, short-waisted, all tits and ass with perfectly shaped arms and legs, her most prominent feature, her center of gravity, was her twat. She must have had oriental blood: her pubic hair was straight black and glistening. Black beaver. More than anything, he wanted to be inside her hot hole, her legs wrapped around the small of his back as he pumped her full of American cock.

There was nothing delicate about Dartley and the way he made love. He came quickly and he came with passion. If he came too quickly, he figured he could always come again, and he did just that, three and four times a night. Otherwise, he kept things moving with his fingers, his knees, his well-practiced mouth. Fatma's clitoris, also well practiced, responded to the tip of his tongue by glistening pink and hard. The perfect pearl. Fatma Lady Exton, the royalty part, may have been as phony as a three-dollar bill, but every moan from her full-blooming lips was real. She practically sucked his cock into her with her vaginal lips. Dartley bore down on her, rode her, rocked her.

"Yes, yes!" she cried. She was so glad she had agreed to be interviewed by *The New York Times*. This American, he was better than Ali, she decided, really he was. He was even better than the Africans. Those powerful men made her feel delectable, desirable, a precious item in an expensive store; but with this stranger, she felt like a woman. "Yes, yes!" she cried out again, happy to be alive.

The door to the bedroom crashed down. Before she realized what was happening, blinding lights flashed, one after the other. Then the men, two of them, were gone.

"Who was that?" she screamed.

"I don't know, I don't know!" shouted Dartley at his orgasmic peak. He paid no attention to anything around him. His organ swelled; he came; he shot his load, convulsed outward from his groin and collapsed on top of her.

"They were photographers," she said, dumbstruck. "They had cameras. I saw them."

"The lights?" he asked, pretending he hadn't noticed. "Who sent them?" he asked. "Your husband?"

"Which husband?" she asked. "Ali Ozker? Why would he send photographers?"

"Security," Dartley said. "In case you wanted more money from him."

"More money?" she exclaimed. "I got no money from Ali; I got all my money from my father."

"Maybe he'd send the pictures to your present husband to destroy your marriage to Lord Exton, to force you to return to him because he is still blindly in love with you."

"A wonderful theory." Fatma laughed. "A wonderful theory. Blind with love every twenty years."

"Maybe your Lord Exton sent the photographers," Dartley said.

"Perhaps. Perhaps. Although Tony hardly seems to care what I do. Besides, how would he know you were here?"

"I'm sure he's been watching the house."

"But how would they get inside?" she asked.

"Oh my dear," Dartley said, warming up to her once more, "they got in the way they always get in, through the door, through the ceiling, through the floor. For all we know, they were hiding in the closet."

"Yes, yes," she said, "I see."—not seeing at all.

Dartley had paid the photographers five hundred dollars apiece. The photos were to clearly show that the woman was Fatma Lady Exton. The man's face was not to show at all. All Ali Ozker had to see when he got the photographs anonymously delivered two hours later was that the great love of his life, the newly renovated Fatma Abady was out screwing a man with physical attributes that made him, Ali, look like an overweight Buddha. The idea was to make him so disgusted with Lady Fatma that he would eagerly, passionately await his rendezvous with Bobo Noll.

As for the Crime Minister and his Goddess of Twat—his private nickname for her—he managed to calm the lady down. He assured Fatma that she was in good hands, that she was the most desirable woman he had ever met, that he wanted to know the story of her life, every single detail, and that finally they must return to her bed and make love at least once more. That was fine with her. Because of the rude interruption, she had not yet come. Dartley seemed very disturbed about that state of affairs. He wanted to do everything he could to make her come. Everything.

All in all, Dartley figured, Why not have a little fun? It was still only Wednesday. He had enough time. The Mercedes was in the garage of his hotel. He had all day Thursday to find the man who looked like him, the man he had not yet seen or met, the man he intended to kill by Thursday night.

Chapter Thirteen

Thursday. Dartley needed to find a homosexual male who looked like him. He needed to find that person Thursday night at the very latest. His first stop was a uniform supply house, Hassler's, on Bayerstrasse. The preponderance of items seemed to be uniforms for nurses and hospital orderlies. Dartley wanted a chauffeur's uniform for himself—two of them, to be exact. The clerk, a small woman with dyed red hair, put him straight. In a language they could both understand, a combination of English and German, she explained to Dartley that what he really wanted was a basic black suit—an inexpensive suit would do fine—to be worn with a simple white shirt, a black tie and a special chauffeur's hat. She would be happy to sell him the chauffeur's hat. Otherwise, Hassler's had long since decided that even if a few chauffeurs still existed here and there since the war, elaborate uniforms were considered in questionable taste in a democratic republic. Didn't he agree? Dartley explained that he was an American driving for an American, and that Americans did not care for elaborate uniforms, either. The whole transaction was a stage play of forced charm.

Since he had a larger-than-average head for a man his height, he bought a cap for himself in an 8¼ hat size and a second cap in a 7½ "for a friend of mine," he explained. He bought several sizes of white shirts. His own collar size was 15½, a little narrow for a man his height. He also bought shirts with 16 and 16½ collars. The red-headed salesclerk seemed puzzled, but she could tell her American customer was determined. Odd behavior for a chauffeur, she thought. Or was *behavior* the right word? It was more like an attitude. She couldn't quite define it. He seemed too hard for a mere chauffeur.

Next, Dartley went to a shoe store and bought two pairs of plain black shoes in his size. He also purchased a bottle of black shoe dye.

He brought the clothing he had purchased back to his hotel room and deposited it in his closet.

Leaving his hotel once more, his next step was a chemist on Goethestrasse. Malleson had given him the name. The chemist was right out of central casting. Tufts of white hair encircled his bald head. The man had the oversize nose and the undershot jaw of a cartoon mad scientist. He knew why Dartley had come.

"I am expensive," he said.

"You know what I need," replied Dartley.

The chemist (his name was Herr Maier, but his name was of little importance to Dartley since he did not intend to make friends with the man) stepped into his laboratory in the rear of his store. A minute later he returned with a small wooden box. Inside, each in its own compartment, each wrapped in cotton, were four ampoules. They seemed identical to amyl nitrite ampoules, favored by homosexuals in their lovemaking. A whiff of amyl nitrite was said to enhance the orgasm. The deadly look-alikes were filled with prussic acid. One whiff was guaranteed to cause a heart attack within five minutes.

The cardboard box, like the clothing, was deposited in Dartley's closet in his room at the Hotel Köblenz.

At the cocktail hour on Thursday, Dartley went out looking for the man he could bring home. He figured that picking up a man would not be impossible. More important was his being able to find someone who looked like him. He wasn't sure how easy this would be. Dartley was at most one-eighth German. He had a great-grandmother whose maiden name was Rybeck. He had never been told he looked German. He seemed leaner and more muscular than the typical German male of the 80's. By their late thirties, most German males, like their midwestern American cousins, seemed hale and hearty, robust specimens, to say the least. Still, Dartley figured that the Anglo-Saxons and the Germans were really of the same basic stock, and that among the gays especially there would be a high percentage of men like him who were fanatics about keeping fit and trim. Malleson had suggested the Wildschwein, a leather bar off Hofgartenstrasse.

"You really should go to Hamburg," he told Dartley, "if you want whips and chains and the most masculine of men, so to speak." Laughing at the absurdity of his definitions, he had further explained that Düsseldorf was known for having some of the wealthiest and best-dressed men in Germany. "Their masculinity is more a matter of being chairman of the board and driving a Silver Cloud than of walking around in skintight jeans and displaying a hairy chest."

Hamburg was too far. Dartley had neither the time nor the patience to try and convince a man in Hamburg to return to Düsseldorf with him; and lugging a corpse back, particularly in August, was out of the question.

The particular leather bar Mallenson had recommended, "Wildschwein," "the Wild Boar," had a whole collection of stocky, overly muscular men with puffy red faces and closely cropped orange blond hair. They wore blue-tinted aviator glasses and black leather vests over their weight-lifter bodies. Their clean-shaven chest muscles seemed to be molded out of flesh-colored plastic. Another

type, well covered in denim, was the tall ecto-
morph with an earring in the left ear and, again,
the closely cropped hair—this time, jet black. Some
of these seemed to carry bunches of keys on one
side or the other. The keys signaled their sado-
masochistic preferences. Depending on whether
they wore their keys on their right or left sides,
they signaled to interested parties whether they
preferred to give pain or to receive it.

Dartley was not sure how to present himself for
the occasion. He bought a pair of too-tight jeans
and pushed up his testicles into the crotch so that
he'd look as fully packed as possible for someone
who happened to get off staring at crotches. A
brand-new black leather jacket to be worn only
once seemed too extravagant. Instead he wore a
black T-shirt—again, much too small, so that about
an inch of his hard, hairy stomach showed. In a
religious goods store near the cathedral, he found
a silver-plated Saint Christopher's medal on a chain.
That bit of glinting metal on his muscular neck
was, by homosexual standards, the ultimate in
kink. What else did he need? His body, for men
into men's bodies, said it all. Sinewy, hairy arms
and a hard ass. It was all in the way one dressed.
He greased his hair back away from his face in as
close an approximation to a fifties ducktail as was
possible. Sexier still, Dartley's crowning effort, he
thought, was the way he used a mascara pencil,
also purchased from the five-and-dime. He smudged
a deep five o'clock shadow over his day-old beard.
By the time he completed the effect, his beard

looked blue-black. His final touch was to draw a fine black line under each eye. He did not smudge the line. On his rugged he-man's face he wanted the deliberate suggestion of decadence, just the right touch of perverted femininity, the kind of masterstroke that would make another man look and say, "No, it can't be"; or for the man who was looking for a companion to take a second look and say to himself that the man with the black line looked interesting—Who could he possibly be?

In the Wildschwein, there was more than one back room. There was more than one bar. There were rooms upstairs and in the basement. There was even a basement under the basement. There were even cubicles, it seemed, for "taking a little rest," no doubt with the best friend of one's choice. There was a room-size sauna in the basement where naked men groped for one another in the half-light. There was also an infamous room known as "the urinal," where naked men lay on the floor as others urinated and defecated on them: "piss'n' shit," as the vernacular put it.

Once inside, Dartley was having his problems seeing men's faces. The light was bad and he felt embarrassed staring at activities that were naturally repugnant to him. Still, he persisted. He had to find his double.

In the subbasement, he found what he was looking for. In the torture room, where the truest devotees of S-M gathered for their rituals, the "masters" or "dominators," as they were called, outfitted in black leather harnesses and masks, waited with whips and chains to punish those men who wished to be punished. Those unfortunates— or fortunates, depending on one's point of view— were called, naturally enough, "the slaves." The masters, the spiritual descendants of the Marquis de Sade, were delighted to find an outlet for their temperaments. Better to punish a willing slave, they reasoned, than to torture an unwilling victim in the outside world.

Dartley noticed that some of the men got off on costumes. He saw S-M versions of the SS, of American army officers, of the local police; there was even one Ku Klux Klan member dressed in a long white robe with its familiar hood. It was almost comical. The men in question, however, were deadly serious. Just from their appearance, it was clear they were deeply into private mythologies of power and domination carried over from childhoods whose patterns of random or sustained violence was anybody's guess.

Dartley could not make out faces. The men wore black leather masks over their eyes and noses. Who could they be? he wondered. Why the anonymity? He had always thought that most homosexuals were weak. The ones he had always noticed in America seemed to be mostly hospital orderlies and record-store clerks, boyish men with limp wrists and snippish remarks. Their humor had always seemed bitchy and predictable. Why not? Homosexuals were victim souls, were they not? He was well into his thirties before he found out that a certain percentage of men in power were homosexuals, too. They were of a different sort from the relatively harmless, good-natured boy-men who were so often the object of ridicule and discrimination. His uncle Charley Woodgate had clued him in on the bank presidents and brain surgeons whose sexual pleasure came from beating other men.

"I would think the victims would be the ones who would enjoy beating others, as a kind of revenge on their fathers," Dartley had said.

"Some do," said the uncle. "Who can predict? Sexual behavior is a complete mystery. The real-life victims are often victims by choice. Their sexual behavior is no different. They prefer to be victims in bed. The ones who have chosen to be masters of the business world often prefer to play the same role in bed. Or it can be the other way around. People can use the bed to take revenge on their circumstances. Who can predict? Is the subconscious really the deeper layer of the personality? Is the id the underlying truth, or are these things just rooms, separate rooms, no larger, no more important, than any other room?"

The next thing Dartley saw made his eyes pop. In the smallest room in the house, deep in the subbasement, he found, without intending to, the "fist-fucking" room. He had heard of fist-fucking before, but he had never seen it. To his knowledge, fist-fucking began in New York in the mid-seventies; for all he knew, it had always been around. He was told these things by Malleson. Malleson had presumably seen these things himself or had asked someone who had. Malleson told him that fist-fucking had begun with heterosexuals. A certain per-centage of women, less than 5 percent, were constantly looking for a bigger cock because, according to the theory, they needed to be filled up with someone else's power; some of these women had begun to take men's hands, and then their fists, into their vaginal canals. Before long, the fists became the whole arm up to the elbow. Some men had pretty big forearms, and for some of these women, the bigger the better. The same vaginal muscles that opened wide enough to permit an infant's head to pass through could, with patience and discipline, be trained to admit the arm of the brawniest male. For the women interested in sheer size, cocks were beginning to lose their age-old appeal.

Then the other side of the argument, often called reality, began to rear its predictably ugly head. Some women experienced tearing of their vaginal walls. For others, infections set in. When the practice of fist-fucking passed into the gay community, that alone was enough to make the straights think twice.

With the gays, the practice spread to leather bars around the world. Since the anal canal had never been intended for fists, much less forearms, the practice constituted such a health hazard that in San Francisco an emergency medical team maintained an all-night weekend clinic to sew up the recipients of other men's fists. Still, the practice continued to grow. For those men who craved the attention of other men to the point of wanting to be physically invaded, nothing else would satisfy. For those other men who enjoyed touching the insides of a member of their own sex, they craved being the counterpart companion to the perversion.

In the subbasement of the *Wildschwein*, Dartley could hardly believe what he saw. There were two men in the dimly lighted space. There was no furniture except for a medical examining table. Both men were naked, but they were in shadow; at first Dartley could not make out their faces.

The young man on the examining table was lying in a fetal position on his side, with one leg lifted up, his erection prominent. The other man, a tall, sinewy man with excessive body hair, had his arm in the younger man's rectum; it was more than that—he had his arm practically buried in the other man. It was buried in his anal canal all the way up to the elbow. The younger man, using a lubricant from a tube, had greased his cock; with his right hand he was jerking himself off. With his left hand, he had reached out for the older man's cock, which was large and throbbing, with a purple knob on the end. Dartley felt fear in the pit of his stomach. The event he was witnessing sickened him and fascinated him at the same time. On some perverse level he identified with the fist-fucker. He felt as if it were he who was invading the younger man. However perverted the act seemed—that of two men with an overpowering appetite for each other and a need to publicly express their perversion—still, he felt the intimacy between them.

"Poppycock, no pun intended," Malleson would have said in his superior British way. "They're perverts, Richie. They don't know what they want; the truth is, they just want to be different." Good old Malleson. His unorthodox views on just about everything unorthodox at least afforded Dartley the chance to laugh. He saw the humorous side of all the modern sacred cows, from Eastern religions to the jet set. According to Malleson, the whole world was mad; the more he could demystify the madness with precise, exact information, the happier he became.

On the medical examination table, the young man now was moaning; his frenzied masturbation had begun to take effect. Finally, mercifully, his rigid little prick released its arc of seminal fluid and almost immediately began to droop. The older man, with his free hand, then placed his erection in the younger man's mouth. Dartley wanted to say, "Excuse me, I must be going," but he found himself rooted to the spot. How was it, he kept wondering, that he remained there watching? Why was the door open? Why did they allow him to watch? For all the publicness of the act, why was it that the owners of the leather bar kept it hidden in the subbasement? Were the owners of the Wildschwein afraid to allow fist-fucking upstairs? Was the practice too perverted even for Germany?

Often in his killing, Dartley thought that maybe he was perverted, too. Whenever he shot a man, certainly a KGB agent, he imagined the bullet tearing through the flesh of the man. To Dartley, that flesh was always pink flesh, vaginal flesh, cunt flesh, cunt lips. He could not help himself: to him the kill was always sexual. Always. Always a turn-on. It was his deepest, dirtiest secret. In his own way he was perverted and he knew it. He was the same as what he saw in the subbasement. How could he judge? In a different way, he had also fist-fucked; and what he did was worse, he thought, because when he killed a man, he imagined the bullet hitting the soul, splattering its tiny light until there was no more light, no more soul, only the beginning of darkness and the eventual decay of the flesh. That's the way it had always been; whereas the fist-fucker brought pleasure to the pathetic boy who needed it, Dartley brought no pleasure—he only put out the light.

The men in front of him knew he was there; they seemed to take his presence for granted. They did not look up. The younger one was speaking in German. He sounded like a woman. His tones were sweet and full of intended love.

Dartley knew he was face to face with something sacred—not about the men in front of him; he was smarter than that—but something sacred about himself. He did not understand what, exactly.

A tear rolled down his cheek. He did not understand why. Sometimes he thought he did not understand the slightest thing about himself except that he could get a job done. Still, he knew that he was not the worst of his breed. If he sometimes shot people in the head, the Communists were worse. They routinely crushed genitals, enslaved women and children, made political prisoners sleep in water, put red-hot iron bars up men's anal canals, let lice and vermin collect in overcrowded jails where everyone went slowly mad. He had read Solzhenitsyn, read *The Gulag Archipelago, The First Circle, The Cancer Ward* many times over. He believed that if he killed too many people too often, somewhere out there, there was a meaning or something like a meaning. He was almost sure of it.

Groaning, and thrashing about, the older man, the fist-fucker with the sinewy body, ejaculated in the younger man's mouth. Sperm dripped from the corner of the boy's lips. It was then that Dartley understood at last why he had been standing there.

For fifteen minutes, without knowing it, he had been watching himself in the older man. Because of his natural revulsion to the act, he had not recognized himself at first. When the man finally raised his head and looked straight into Dartley's eyes with hunger and bottomless appetite, it was then that he knew he was looking at himself.

There were subtle differences. The color of the eyes was not the same. Dartley's were gray; they were cold eyes without pity. The homosexual's eyes were black, suffering eyes, eyes without light. There were other physical differences as well. The other man's body was more animal, his muscles more pronounced, his body hair coarse and black on the whitest possible skin. To Dartley, the man seemed primal and obscene. Yet, for all the differences, he was more like Dartley than any man Dartley had ever seen. Although the other man's face had more prominent cheekbones and a more defined jawline, and the grooves in his face were more like furrows, their facial planes were decidedly similar.

Dartley did not for a moment underestimate why he was there. He held the gaze of the other man. He knew that the other man would see himself in him; that fact alone would hold the other man's attention. They were too much alike. It was immediately clear to both of them that they had a common destiny.

Dartley also knew that the other man could in no way suspect how seriously Dartley interpreted that destiny.

"Come with me," said Dartley. He repeated his request.

The other man did not drop his gaze. Who was this creature standing in the doorway staring back at him? Were they twins? No, definitely not twins. There were differences, differences that must be explored.

The other man spoke English.

"Do you want me?" he asked with a thick Teutonic accent.

"Come to my place," said Dartley.

"Not here?" the other man asked.

"Come with me," repeated Dartley, never for a minute dropping his gaze.

The young man on the medical examining table looked up with a pained expression. In the light his face was that of an angelic child; large blue eyes—too large for a grown man—with an unlined face, a little boy's snub nose and a rosebud mouth, sweet and pursed, perverse in its apparent innocence. He was 27. He looked closer to 13.

When the boy-man saw the mutual infatuation of the two older men, a look of horror came over his boyish face. The older man seemed locked into an intimacy far more intense than that he had just felt. They were, in some way, horrible for him to see.

"Nein!" he cried. "Nein!" Then he spoke excitedly in German to the older man, begging him to stay with him. "Papa, papa." he cried to the man who was neither blood relation nor in any sense paternal. With no regard for his feelings, the man who had just fist-fucked him was now putting on his clothes; black leather pants, black leather boots, a black leather vest. The garments were studded with stainless steel fasteners. His hat was like a railroad engineer's, except that they usually wore denim and his was, predictably, black leather with the omnipresent studs. Other than the clothing mentioned, he wore many necklaces and bracelets fashioned out of brass and stainless steel, most of them hung with Nazi war medals, the Iron Cross being the most prominent.

As the two older men left the basement, the boy-man said nothing. His eyes were filled with unfathomable pain. He could do nothing to pre-

vent the love of his life from walking out on him.
But that had been their agreement. Their deal.
For almost ten years they would meet once a week
at the Wildschwein. The older man would fist-
fuck him; he would suck the older man off; there
would be no privacy; anyone could watch. The boy
could say what he wanted, but he must not expect
a single kiss or caress in return. He was not to
whine or complain when the older man left him
for someone else, whether his leavetaking was for
an hour, a day, or the rest of his life. That was the
agreement. "Take it or leave it" was the bottom
line. He took it. How much longer he could take
it, he did not know.

For the next hour he lay on the examining table
without moving. When the next man arrived, a fat
blond man of about 40 with dark glasses and a
broader-than-average, mushroom-shaped cock, the
boy-man let him do whatever he wanted. The
younger man showed no enthusiasm. He could
not even get an erection. The blond man became
enraged. He began to hit the younger man. Still
the boy-man made no effort to defend himself.
His greatest desire was to be beaten into unconsciousness and finally to be beaten to death, where
he would have no more responsibility to be strong.
He could not be strong. He would never be strong.

This time, however, he was not killed. The
owner of the Wildschwein happened to be making
the rounds, inspecting the premises. From the top
of the subbasement stairs he could actually hear
the blond man beating on the boy. The owner

stopped the man, screaming, "Are you blind? Can't you see there is something wrong with this boy?"

The owner was a Turkish immigrant. He could not afford a scandal. As it was, he spent half his profits in payoffs to various policemen and politicians.

"Get dressed," he said to the boy. "You need some air."

"Is that what I need?" asked the boy dumbly.

"You would be better off if you would get angry," said the Turk.

"Angry?" the boy asked as if the question were rhetorical.

"Don't you understand that it is not normal to want to be punished?" said the Turk in concerned tones. He often said he ran the leather bar because he was cognizant of the facts of life; but the truth was, he was concerned with outcast men and broken lives. Being a good Turk, he knew how to turn a profit; being a man who had suffered discrimination, he had little patience for the self-destruction of others.

"But I'm no good," wailed the boy-man.

"Who told you you're no good?" asked the Turk, furious that another human being could have so little grasp on life.

"I've always been no good. I never should have been born."

With that, the Turk socked the boy. "You! Your whole breed!" he snarled. "You've forgotten what's out there! You've forgotten what they do to you if you don't fight back! I despise you! I despise all that you represent! Now get out of here!"

Then the Turk left him. The boy-man felt better. How could he argue with the owner's argument? The Turk was right. He was right to punish him. He had perfectly described the boy's affliction. Perfectly.

Dartley walked hand in hand with the German back to his hotel. They did not speak. Each was anxious to be alone with the other, to reveal himself to the other each in his own unique way.

When they reached the Hotel Köblenz, the bellman, a graduate student in German literature, looked hard at Dartley with an expression of shock. That's allright, old boy, thought Dartley. This is my last night here. By tomorrow night I'll have my million bucks and you'll still be stuck here behind your fucking desk disapproving of everything you don't understand. Then he smiled benignly at the bellman, as if to say, "You asshole; you are nothing to me but a troublesome servant."

Once they had reached Dartley's room and closed the door, the man fell upon Dartley with all the passion of a lover who's been separated from the beloved by famine or war. Dartley, for his part, felt like laughing in the man's face, but he didn't dare. He needed the man; he was crucial to his strategy. If he lost him, he would fail.

"Kiss me," murmured the man.

Dartley thought to himself, Okay, I'll kiss him.

I'll lead him on. But that's all I'll do. Here goes nothing.

As he kissed the man, open-mouthed, the man ground his pelvis into Dartley's. With each passing second he could feel the man's cock expand and grow more rigid. His hands were kneading Dartley's ass as he forced his tongue into his mouth. Dartley kept saying to himself; I cannot believe this is happening to me. This is the fourth dimension. My face has been turned inside out. I'm kissing myself. Myself is kissing me. It's the ultimate in masturbation. Why are straight men so afraid of homosexuals? There's nothing to it. It's like having a piece of veal in your mouth, except that it's called a tongue and it's attached to somebody else.

In the middle of his internal dialogue, Dartley realized that Germany's favorite fist-fucker had not washed his hands. Enough. It was time to get back to work before a pair of dirty hands tried to open him up.

"I'm perverted," he announced quietly.

"Oh, no, no, no," the other man reassured him.

"No, you don't understand," said Dartley. "I have this special perversion."

"Special perversion?"

"Yes," answered Dartley. "A special perversion. I want you to fist-fuck me like you fist-fucked the blond boy, but not here."

"Not here?"

"No," continued Dartley, "that is my perversion. I have to have all my sex in my Mercedes."

With an unexpected blurt, the other man

guffawed. His pronounced horselaugh annoyed Dartley. He did not like to be made fun of, especially when he was lying.

"What is so funny?" he asked self-righteously. "My car is a masterpiece."

The man continued to laugh at him. "A Mercedes!" He chuckled. "Das ist stupid!"

"Listen," said Dartley, grabbing the man by the shoulders and affecting as intense a stare as he could, terrified that he himself would break into laughter at the greater stupidity, that this power-lusting idiot should trust him. What did he take Dartley for, a garage mechanic?

"Listen, Dartley explained, "when I was very young, my parents were never home. My father was an international banker; my mother always went with him. She was terrified that if she stayed home, my father would fuck every piece of tail between Baltimore and Burma. Me, I always stayed home with the servants, the maid, the cook, the chauffeur. To my parents they were perfect employees; but the truth was, they hated the rich. In their own quarters—don't worry, I listened through the furnace gratings—they spoke endlessly of Marx and Lenin and world revolution. They couldn't clean the silver without bending it out of shape, but they were all set to scour and polish the entire earth."

"What does this have to do with you?" asked the man. Of course he already knew what Dartley was going to say. He had heard variations on the story many times before.

"Yes, it was the chauffeur," said Dartley, seeing by the look in the man's eyes that he understood. "I was three and four and five; he used to take me into my father's garage to the front seat of my father's Mercedes. You see, no one but he ever went into the garage. My parents always waited in front of the house. Only this man, this chauffeur... He was like you, so strong, so muscular, so covered with black hair like you; his eyes were black, too, black like yours, black like the night; there was no light in him, only force, like you. He was the one who wanted to scour the world, to murder the priests, he said. 'Kill the whores,' he said. 'Murder the president. Kill the rich.' He took me to the garage, to the Mercedes. He undressed me there. The front seat was so soft. Glove leather. Black. Then he would take down my underpants and kiss me all over. Maybe I was a substitute for cunt."

"No, little boys are special all by themselves," interrupted the hairy man.

"He stripped me of all my clothes," Dartley continued. "He put his tongue, his lips, his breath all over me. I was so little. And then—Did I tell you the door was locked? Yes, the door was locked— then he let down his pants.... He never stripped, he just unbuttoned the bottom of his shirt and let down his pants. His bush was so black, so black like yours; and his cock... I swear to God, his cock was as big as your arm; when I saw your arm, I knew it was his cock, my chauffeur's cock. He used to enter me, fuck me; I was so small, I could not take him. I must have been seven or eight before I could take him, take all of him."

And then Dartley let out a sob. He did not think it sounded convincing, but the hairy man did not seem to notice. His crotch seemed very full. He was rubbing himself along his bulge.

"The chauffeur was the only one who came close to me," Dartley went on, teary and sad, "the only one who risked everything to be close. He could have lost his job. He could have been arrested. He could have been ruined for life."

"Where is he now?" asked the other man.

"I don't know. I don't know," moaned Dartley. "He left when I was ten or eleven. He just left. He never said good-bye. He never wrote. He never came back. No one came back. No one. He was just like you."

The other man's eyes were glowing. "Where is your Mercedes?"

"In the garage downstairs," said Dartley.

"Let's go."

"Wait," said Dartley. "Wait." With that, he flung open his closet door and took out the chauffeur's uniform. "This is for you," said Dartley, showing it to the other man. The man grinned. He unbuttoned the top button of his black leather pants and proceeded to wrest them around his engorged organ. Dartley, sick of seeing the man's enormous cock, turned his back.

"What's wrong?" asked the other man. "Is there something wrong with my cock?"

"No, no!" cried Dartley. "It's so magnificent,

your cock. I'm saving it for downstairs, that's all.
For downstairs."

The fist-fucker's chauffeur's uniform was a size
too small. Still, he looked more than presentable.
As a matter of fact, Dartley concluded that he
looked as though he'd been hired on the spot and
handed a former chauffeur's uniform to wear
until he bought his own. Dartley decided that the
black boots with the studs looked fine. A little too
cowboy-Western for Düsseldorf, but flair never
hurt. Ali Ozker would have appreciated the man's
flair. The boots were appropriate to the situation.
Dartley found a white dress shirt that fit his new
acquaintance; the black tie was no problem. The
smaller of the chauffeur's caps seemed to fit the
man's head exactly, as Dartley thought it would.
Dartley himself wore a white oxford-cloth button-
down shirt over his black T-shirt.

"Why did you do that?" asked the German.

"I'm a little cold," answered Dartley.

"I cannot wait to fuck you," proclaimed the
other man.

"I cannot wait either," replied Dartley, hoping
that his hotel room had not been bugged by the
KGB, the CIA or *The National Enquirer*. The sex
part didn't matter. It was the other part. The
unspoken part. Dartley was playing with fire.

As they were leaving, Dartley remembered the
ampoules on the closet shelf.

"What's that?" asked the German.

"Amyl nitrite," Dartley responded. "It's the best
there is. It comes from Saigon."

The German seemed impressed. "I could try it," he said.

On the elevator going down to the garage was an overweight middle-aged woman in a gray silk suit. She carried a lapdog in her right hand. A Shih Tzu. As she talked animatedly to the little dog, whose name was Schotzie, she kept looking up at the two men. It was clear to both of them that she found them extremely attractive.

She's looking for a fuck, thought Dartley.

After the elevator reached Level B of the parking garage she followed them both down the concrete corridor that connected the elevator to the garage.

Dartley had had it. Abruptly turning around, he confronted her. "Don't follow me or you'll be sorry."

At that, the woman's jaw dropped. She lost her grip on Schotzie the Shih Tzu. Luckily, she'd put the little pooch on a leash that was securely wrapped around her girth. After Dartley's rebuke, she stood paralyzed, afraid to move. The men continued until they reached the parking garage itself.

In the dark the Mercedes 600 looked as black and slinky as a hearse. Dartley had carefully parked it in the corner of the underground chamber, as far from any entrance as he could. The limousine sat in deep shadow under a concrete overhang.

"Welcome to my car," Dartley said as he reached for his keys. The German grinned and adjusted his cap.

"My Mercedes," he remarked, petting the roof of the car in jest.

Dartley grinned and looked around. The dog woman had disappeared. The two men were alone. How much longer they would be alone, he did not know. The garage seemed full, but who could tell? Doctors on call might rush out in the middle of the night. Unhappy wives might decide to go for a drive.

Dartley unlocked the front door to the Mercedes. "Get in," he said to the man dressed as the chauffeur. Grinning, the German homosexual climbed into the front seat of the Mercedes. The smell of fresh glove-leather upholstering bespoke rare luxury, as did the fruitwood burl of the dashboard. In the precarious space between the concrete wall of the garage and the enameled steel of the luxury car, Dartley squeezed in on the far side. Opening the door on the driver's side as wide as he dared, he wedged himself into the front seat.

"I should have gotten in first," he remarked. He was absolutely right. What was he doing? Terror lay like a malignant turmor in his gut. Why hadn't he gotten in first? Was he trying to wreck the car? He seemed to be losing touch with basic strategy. The German, who was used to fearful men, snuggled up to Dartley and began to affectionately suck his neck. My God, Dartley thought, how much longer can I play this charade?

"I'll show you the dashboard later," he announced

to the other man. "First I must show you the fucking place."

"The fucking place?" repeated the German, not quite sure what Dartley meant.

"Ja, the fucking place." With that, Dartley turned on the ignition and locked the doors. The German fidgeted. "Wait," cautioned Dartley.

Dartley pressed one of the key buttons that Camelot Armoring had built into his car. Behind the men's feet, under the front seat, the wall to the hidden compartment separated in the middle. Each section slid back on either side like a louvered folding door into compacted accordion pleats. The hidden compartment, while it utilized the space under the front seat, was constructed separately, a fully enclosed metal compartment. Like the vegetable drawer of a refrigerator, it hung below the floor of the Mercedes by about four inches. Needless to say, although its insides had been upholstered with soft nylon carpeting, it was never meant to contain human beings. At least Camelot Armoring had not constructed the compartment either for fucking or for corpses.

"Get in," Dartley said to the other man in as seductive a voice as he could manage.

"Get inside there?" the man asked. "When you were a little boy, your chauffeur, he lie under the front seat of your car like this?"

"I'm not finished," Dartley said. "There are more surprises."

"More surprises?"

"This is a very special car, more special than you

can begin to imagine," Dartley said. He had to be careful. His tone was too insinuating; it suggested too many double meanings. His single intention was to get the man under the seat and into the hidden compartment. He checked to make sure his ampoules were still in his coat pocket. They were.

"All right," commented the German, crouching down. "But I think I am too tall for this compartment."

"Don't worry," answered Dartley, again improvising, again hedging his bets. "You cannot look until I tell you to, but my backseat is a bedroom out of the Arabian Nights. I call this my secret entrance to the Cave of Paradise."

"Couldn't we use the back doors?" the German said.

"It would be no fun to use the back doors. We would lose the mood. We would lose the mystery. We would lose ourselves." Dartley reached out to caress the man's ear. It was the least he could do, he thought, considering what his intentions were.

The German was now wedged inside the hidden compartment under the front seat. His assessment had been correct. The space was too short. He had to double up a little bit.

"This space is too small," he complained.

Dartley was looking for ways to keep the man's attention. He unbuckled his belt and unzipped his fly. Then he lowered his underpants. By now he was kneeling on the floor of the front seat. He could see through the car windows out into the parking garage. No one was around. Not a soul. The dog lady had not returned.

"You have a wonderful cock," observed the German, reaching out to caress Dartley's genitals.

Dartley knew he had to move fast. The man would begin to wonder why he was not sexually aroused.

"Here, try this," he said, casually removing an ampoule from the box in his pocket. The so-called amyl nitrite. The very best.

"We should wait until orgasm," said the man.

"Wait till you try this; you have to try it," insisted Dartley. "I have three more for later."

He put all of his energy, all of his training, all of his brains into acting as nonchalantly as possible. He casually broke the ampoule under the German's nose. The man breathed deeply with great satisfaction. "Nothing is happening," he said after a moment.

"Oh, don't worry, something is happening," said Dartley. "You don't know it's happening, but it's happening."

The German unbuckled his pants buckle and stuck his hand down his pants. He had less than ten minutes to go. Dartley was determined to press his luck.

"Has something happened yet?" Dartley asked.

"Nothing has happened," repeated the German. "I don't feel nothing." He was now fondling his cock and balls. "I love my cock," he said fondly. "I am so lucky. God gave me a huge cock."

"Let me try again," suggested Dartley, reaching

into his pocket for a second ampoule. "Here," he said without skipping a beat, breaking the second ampoule under the German's nose. "Maybe this will work."

"What? What are you doing now?" the man said.

"Maybe something was wrong with the first ampoule."

"The second is no good either," said the German. "I feel nothing."

Dartley affected a look of great anguish. "He must have cheated me."

"Who cheated you?" asked the German.

"The pharmacist. He charged me twenty-five deutsche marks apiece."

"Apiece?" exclaimed the German, shocked at what seemed like an extravagant amount of money. "Twenty-five deutsche marks? That is too much money. Especially when there is nothing in them but colored water." The German laughed. "Come kiss my cock," he said. Dartley snuggled down in the floor of the front seat, facing the German.

"Wait," Dartley said. "You're supposed to seduce me."

"Seduce you?"

"Yes, I am a little boy, Mr. Lawrence."

"Mr. Lawrence? Who is Mr. Lawrence?"

"'Mr. Lawrence' was the name of my father's chauffeur." answered Dartley as coyly as possible.

"My real name is Wolfgang," said the German, approaching real intimacy for the first time all night. "Americans think Wolfgang is a funny name."

"I don't think Wolfgage is funny," replied Dartley. "I think it's beautiful. Like Mozart."

"Ja," said the German. "Mein mutter, my mother, she loved Mozart, except my name is not Mozart, my name is Gross, Wolfgang Gross. Americans tell me 'Gross' is funny, too. I guess I was never meant to live in America." With that, he kissed Dartley once more on the mouth, a tender kiss, the kiss of a mother for her babe, a good-night kiss. Wolfgang seemed quieter now, as if he were truly alone with a special friend.

"We are hidden from the world," he said. "I love to be hidden with you."

"I love to be hidden with you too," echoed Dartley, looking into his own face.

"What do you do...for a living I mean?" asked the German. "When you are not being a pervert." He laughed at his own joke.

"I'm an international assassin," replied Dartley.

Herr Wolfgang Gross thought Dartley's remark was the funniest thing he had ever heard. He laughed so hard he bumped his head on the roof of the compartment.

"Ow!" He laughed again. "An international assassin! You are so funny. What is your real name?"

"Richard Dartley," the Crime Minister replied.

"Richard Dartley? Such an ordinary name for a pervert." The German laughed again. Then he grabbed Dartley for one of his prolonged kisses. How long, O Lord, how long? prayed Dartley, giving in to the stranger's muscular tongue. The man's hands were fondling Dartley now. The same hands that had fucked the blond boy. The same hands that had not washed. All of a sudden, Dartley felt overwhelmed with the disorder of the man lying next to him. His lack of hygiene seemed like a deliberate shattering of all rules of ordinary decency. To Dartley, the German, because of his inherent carelessness, was becoming a principle of unreason. He was becoming chaos itself. He was becoming darkness. He was the antichrist. As he stared into the eyes of his companion-beast, Dartley forced himself to maintain a look of utter compassion and understanding.

"What do you really do?" asked Wolfgang Gross.

"I teach English," replied Dartley. "High-school English—the gymnasium," referring to the German name for high school.

"That's what I thought," replied the man. "You look like an English teacher. I teach biology myself."

"What kind of biology?"

"Regular biology—in the gymnasium, too. Biology one-oh-one. We...how do you say...we dissect frogs. We look at amoebae and paramecia under the microscope. A life of high adventure, but you already know this. You already know everything about me. You and I have come together through some principle of destiny, and somehow I know that we will never be apart."

"Never," Dartley assured him. "I shall never forget you."

It happened sooner than the pharmacist had

predicted: four and a half minutes from the first ampoule.

Wolfgang Gross had lowered his pants to his knees. His erection was throbbing. His main concern was Dartley's complete surrender to him.

"Richard, let me fist-fuck you," he begged.

"In a minute, Wolfgang," Dartley kept saying. "In a minute. I have to get used to the idea."

"But I thought you wanted me to be the chauffeur when you were a little boy. No?"

"But you don't know how excited I am."

"You are?" said Wolfgang.

"You are a very exciting man," Dartley explained, stalling for time.

"No, you only say that because you are a pervert," Wolfgang said. "I want you to see me, the real me. I want you to feel me, feel me deep inside you. I want my hand to reach up and touch your heart, to touch you from the inside."

Those were Wolfgang Gross's final words. With no warning, he clutched his heart, squealed once like a dog who's been kicked, gasped for air, wanted to speak, could no longer form words. Before he went unconscious, he looked at Dartley with intense eyes filled with pain and pleading. Dartley looked back at the man with equal concern. Death had never been trivial to him and he did not want to appear unconcerned. He wanted Herr Gross to know how deeply he cared—up to a point. Then, mercifully, the German's eyes went dead. They were still open, but the pupils, pitch-black night, had opened wide. The man's face was frozen in an expression of absolute surprise.

"Thank God," said Dartley, quickly zippering his fly and buckling his pants. He performed the same service for the corpse under the front seat. Poor guy, he thought, amused at the irony of it all. "He never knew he died for his country. It's your fault for looking like me," he muttered. "Maybe it's God's fault. Maybe it's just one of those things."

He had trouble zippering Herr Gross's fly. In death as in life, his erection was prominent. "Jesus Christ!" muttered Dartley as he pressed down on the dorsal surface of the man's cock. "All I need is to get the fucking zipper caught on his fucking cock and I'll mess up the job." Finally, after a long minute he managed to get the zipper zippered, the belt buckled and the pleated doors under the front seat closed. His alter ego was now in place. The hardest part of his preliminary work was done. There must be a God, he thought. Someone is looking out for me.

Making sure all the doors of the Mercedes were locked, he got out this time on the right side. He could not believe the greeting committee. The dog lady, Shih Tzu in hand, was standing in the exit door. "Where is your chauffeur?" she asked Dartley.

"He was drunk," he answered. "I sent him to his girl friend's. She can worry about him."

"I did not see him leave," replied the woman.

"He left through the garage," answered Dartley.

"Oh?" said the woman. "I did not see him leave."

"He left immediately," answered Dartley.

"Oh?" said the woman.

Dartley was becoming annoyed. "Lady," he said, "I don't know if you want to have sex with my chauffeur or if you're some kind of a car thief, but my Mercedes here has an alarm system. If you go near that car, I will know about it and have the police here immediately."

The dog lady's eyes, which had opened wide at the word *sex*, had changed expression when she heard *thief*; now they were little slits of hatred.

"American!" she hissed.

"We won the war, lady," replied Dartley as nonchalantly as he could manage.

The woman had been pushed to the limit. Forgetting she was holding a live animal, with an explosion of rage she began to hit Dartley with the dog, striking him wherever she could, as if the dog were a blunt instrument. The dog yelped and squealed and then stopped making noises altogether. The lady had broken its neck. Still, she used the dog as an weapon until Dartley, whose arms were longer than hers, held her at arm's length. It was only then that she noticed that her beloved Schotzie was no longer with her. Her scream was terrible.

"You have killed Schotzie!" she raged. "You have killed him! You broke his neck! You have killed Schotzie!" She continued to scream in both English and German, gray tears of wet mascara coursing down her cheeks. She was wailing at such a pitch that the humanistic streak in Dartley wanted to comfort her, to put his arms around her and say, "There, there." But he knew better.

He raced up the stairs to the lobby of the Köblenz, called the manager and explained what had happened with the woman.

"That's Mrs. Buckius," the manager said. "She's under psychiatric care. That's the third dog she's killed that way."

"I'm just afraid she's some kind of a car thief," Dartley explained. "I had left an envelope in my glove compartment. She was hanging around the garage. She wouldn't leave. She was asking me questions about my car. It made me very nervous."

When the manager arrived with a policeman, it was just as Dartley said. He found Mrs. Buckius trying to break into the Mercedes. The car alarm was ringing full-blast.

"The chauffeur, he is in the car," she kept saying.

Dartley explained to the policeman what had happened.

The dog woman kept insisting that Dartley had locked the chauffeur in the car and killed the Shih Tzu. Dartley explained that he'd entered the garage with an old friend who was dressed in black. The woman had mistaken the friend for a chauffeur. She had seemed inordinately interested in the man, he explained—inordinately interested. Dartley had gone to his car because he had left a letter from a common friend on the front seat. He retrieved the letter and gave it to his friend, who presumably left and went home. The whole time

Mrs. Buckius was standing around trying to cause trouble.

"The chauffeur, he is in the car," insisted Mrs. Buckius, her eyes now red from incessant weeping.

"Could you please open the car?" the policeman asked Dartley. "We will settle the question now."

Without saying another word, Dartley opened the car. "See, there is no one here."

The policeman seemed eager to inspect everything.

"Sir, I will not tolerate this invasion of my privacy," Dartley exclaimed. "You can see there is no one here."

"But this car, it is magnificent," said the policeman, examining the dashboard, more complicated than any dashboard he had ever seen. It had buttons and dials that were incomprehensible to him. "I have never seen a car like this," said the policeman, climbing onto the front seat.

"Officer!" Dartley said. "I would appreciate it if you stayed out of my car."

"I am an officer. I can do what I please."

Dartley, standing at the car's open door, took the policeman by the shoulder and pulled him back. "Officer, I would appreciate it if you would terminate this matter of Mrs. Buckius and the dog."

"All right," said the officer, pushing buttons, testing dials, in no sense understanding that he was inside an armored car.

"Ah ha! What is this?" he exclaimed as he was climbing back out of the front seat. He had seen a piece of a broken ampoule.

"What is what?" asked Dartley. "This? Amyl nitrite."

"Amyl nitrite?" queried the policeman. "Amyl nitrite is for sex. You have sex in your car?"

"What's it to you?" replied Dartley, annoyed.

"Amyl nitrite. This is a drug."

"It's not against the law," said Dartley.

"The chauffeur, he is in the car," continued Mrs. Buckius, talking to the manager of the Köblenz as if he alone could solve her problems.

"Take that woman upstairs," said the policeman to the hotel manager. "Take her to the lobby. I will be right there."

"But the chauffeur, he is in the car. I know he is in the car," continued Mrs. Buckius as she was being led to the exit corridor.

The policeman and Dartley were now alone in the parking garage.

"Was this chauffeur a man who buys drugs from you?"

"Buy drugs from me?" repeated Dartley. "What kind of drugs are you talking about?"

"I don't know what kind of drugs," answered the policeman. "Maybe you tell me what kind of drugs."

Dartley looked at him with a blank look. His internal dialogue, on the other hand, was violently at odds with his external mien. His brain was screaming, "Get this Nazi off my back!"

"Perhaps I will return with other policemen," replied the officer. "We will have the authority to make a thorough search of your Mercedes. If you are a drug dealer, we will find particles of heroin or cocaine or whatever it is you deal in under the carpet, under the seat, who knows?"

By now Dartley was sweating.

"Do you want to make a deal?" he asked.

"A deal?" said the policeman.

"I can't afford to be arrested," said Dartley, "not now. I'm just breaking even."

"I might be interested," replied the policeman. "I like your car. I would like to drive a car like this." He stroked the chrome strip. "I would really like this car."

"You know, it's not so easy," said Dartley.

"What's not so easy?"

"I get dealers who charge me high prices for bad drugs, you know—coke that's been mixed with flour or sugar, and I pay top dollar. My customers come after me with a knife. I mean, I even paid ten dollars an ampoule for amyl nitrite. See."

Dartley took a third ampoule from his pocket. "Looks perfectly good, doesn't it?" Then, without warning, he broke the ampoule and stuck it under the policeman's nose. "See? Nothing. Nothing at all."

The policeman grabbed Dartley's hand and held the ampoule under his nose.

"Ja," he remarked. "Nothing."

"I got rooked," said Dartley.

"Rooked?" echoed the German, not understanding the word.

"Rooked," repeated Dartley. "You try to do a

good job and somebody cheats you or tries to. Rooked. I'll tell you what..."

"Ja?"

"Let's go upstairs. Let me take you to dinner. We can talk."

"No, I can't. I'm on duty," replied the policeman.

"Can we meet at eleven-thirty, then? I'll bring some stuff."

"What stuff?" asked the policeman.

"I don't know. Whatever you want. Coke. Heroin. Grass. Hash. LSD What do you want?"

"Heroin," replied the cop, his blue eyes gleaming.

Dartley knew the eyes were gleaming with an official gleam. The man was hoping for a drug bust. Somewhere behind his stolid Teutonic exterior, he was running the Hollywood version of his life. He'd be a hero in Düsseldorf; they'd eventually make a movie of his early career; his mother could brag to the neighbors that her son was an international celebrity.

"Where do I meet you?" the German asked.

"The lobby upstairs. Eleven-thirty tonight."

"Are the drugs in your room?" the policeman asked.

"Oh God, no," said Dartley. "That's all I need. I don't know where they come from. I have my own contact, a Turk. If you want, I can introduce you before I leave Germany so you can buy from him directly yourself."

The policeman laughed. "Doesn't it bother you that I'm a policeman and that I'm willing to break the law?"

"The law doesn't make any sense," Dartley replied. "Drugs are a recreational necessity these days. Everbody takes drugs. Everybody *I* know, at least. It's like Prohibition in America. The Volstead Act. Prohibition was the law. The law ended up causing more crime that it was worth—everybody drank. It's the same with drugs today. The way I look at it, you're one smart cop."

Six minutes. Six minutes at most, he thought. I've got to get upstairs so the guy can have his heart attack alone.

"Listen," Dartley said. "I hate to break up this meeting, but I've really got to take a shit. Toiletten, bitte."

"Ah," said the cop, smiling. "Good. Good. Ja. I see you in the lobby at eleven-thirty. You bring the drugs."

"You bring the money," countered Dartley.

As they walked toward the exit door, they shook hands and smiled.

Dartley made like a jackrabbit for the stairs.

Within three minutes he was back in his room. The phone ran almost immediately. It was the manager; he assured Dartley that Mrs. Buckius had been taken to the psychiatric ward of the nearest hospital.

"For observation. Just for a couple of days. There seems to be something wrong with her."

"I'm glad somebody took action," said Dartley. "Thank you very much for being so sensitive to the problem. You're doing a magnificent job."

"Danke schoen," replied the manager.

Dartley hung up. He walked into the bathroom and took off his clothes. The first thing he wanted to do was brush his teeth and gargle, to get the taste of Wolfgang Gross out of his mouth. The slimy wretch, he thought, shuddering at the memory of the man. Aaagh! This is freedom in the West, he thought, fist-fucking and drug dealing. No wonder the peasants become Communists. Then he addressed the dead man in his mind. "Herr Gross, never you mind, you done good by your death. You done good, Herr Gross."

The toothpaste tasted like peppermint. A good clean taste. It was about time. He was hungry for a Wiener schnitzel crisply fried with a big wedge of lemon, and some German potato salad with dill and sour cream. Life has so many small luxuries, he thought as he climbed into a hot shower, grateful for the rush of heat on his tense muscles. The green soap smelled of pine needles. He would have spätlese wine with his dinner, he decided. Afterward, he would get an early sleep. He had to be up early in the morning. Very early. Like 3:00 A.M. He had so much to do before the end of the following day. So much.

Dartley hurried to finish his shower. He still had to get dressed. By the time he got downstairs to the lobby, there would be commotion everywhere. He would probably be asked some questions, but who could say?

As usual, his instincts were correct. The lobby was jammed with police. In the distance, the wail of a hospital ambulance could be heard. It seems there had been a terrible accident. The young policeman who had come to investigate Mrs. Buckius' complaint was in the process of leaving the hotel. He was, as a point of reference, passing through the revolving door when, it seems, he had a heart attack.

"It's absolutely unbelievable," remarked the hotel manager to Dartley. "He was so young."

"These things happen," said Dartley.

"It wasn't clear if he got caught in the doors and panicked. I don't know."

"I don't know either," said Dartley.

"Of course you don't know, my good man," said the manager. "You've been through too much tonight, as it is. I want you to have dinner on the house in our restaurant. Please have a wonderful meal."

"Do you have Weiner schnitzel?" asked Dartley.

"But of course," replied the manager. "Of course."

"Don't I have to answer any questions?"

"Questions about what?"

"Well, I did meet the policeman who died. I thought maybe someone would want to know if he seemed sick when I met him."

The manager put his arm around Dartley. "Herr Mount," he said. "Please. Do not trouble yourself. These things are the will of God. There is nothing you can do except accept them."

"Yes, you're right," replied Dartley. "I guess there is no justice anywhere."

"Ah, who knows, Mr. Dartley," said the manager, leading him into the dining room. "Tomorrow it could happen to you or to me. One minute you could be driving your car, the next minute..."

"I know. I know," answered Dartley. "You don't have to tell me. You don't have to tell me. There are unseen forces that make fools of the best of us."

"Ja, ja," affirmed the manager, shaking his head with reverence at the thought of Dartley's noble sentiment. Having paid homage to the underlying irrationality of death, he felt better. He was now ready to get on with his life. "I may join you later for coffee, Herr Mount."

"You do that, my friend, you do that," replied Dartley.

"Or an after-dinner drink. You do drink, Herr Mount?"

"Sure I drink. I do everything," said Dartley. He laughed. It was a joke. Why not laugh? Just as the poem said, he had miles to go before he slept. Miles.

Chapter Fourteen

At Camelot Armoring in New Haven, Connecticut, Vassilov found the information he'd been looking for.

Within a week on the job, he'd befriended a garrulous welder, a heavy drinker named Kris Lindquist. Lindquist was, as one might expect, divorced from a first wife and separated from a second. Leading him to a local watering hole late at night after four or five hours of overtime was no struggle. Over vodka, Vassilov did his usual anti-Communist bit, railed on about how the Soviets were going to take over the world if Americans didn't do the right thing and blast them to oblivion.

By the third night he knew that no matter what he said by way of sex, religion, or politics, Lindquist was in another movie. The welder had long, insistent messages about the dog-eat-dog world out there, most of which made no sense. The messages were carried over from childhood traumas. "It's hell out there" was his favorite and recurring statement. Vassilov waited and listened. Before long he realized that every time he, Vassilov made his own statement about the world, Lindquist would in so many words tell him he didn't know what he was talking about. He would then offer a verbal list of data as proof to the contrary of whatever Vassilov's position was. Much of his proof seemed obscure; it was anecdotal and frequently sounded like half-digested history. "Roosevelt gave away East Berlin to the dirty bums. Nobody listened to Hoover. He would never have surrendered half the country to the bleeding hearts. When my father came home from the Bataan Death March, you better believe he called up Walter Reuther."

On their fourth evening out together, in the

middle of a Lindquist monologue about the absurdity of Social Security, Vassilove casually said, "That's very interesting. I guess it's like the cars we do."

"What do you mean?" asked Lindquist, red-nosed and bleary-eyed.

"I mean that all the armored cars go to Europeans and Arabs. Americans can't afford them—we're giving all our money to taxes and Social Security."

Lindguist was indignant. "The most expensive car we did all year was ordered by an American. We just finished it before you came. It's on its way to Munich now. A friend of mine, Eddie Sevcik, is driving the car from Cherbourg to Munich."

"You just proved my point," said Vassilov. "It's being delivered to Germany. The guy who ordered it is obviously not a real American."

"What do you mean, 'real American'? Real Americans are all over the world investing real American money in real American businesses. Hell, we built Germany up from scratch. It'd be nowhere without real Americans."

"A point well taken," replied the cagey Vassilov, "but why was the car the most expensive?"

"I'm talking about the black Mercedes 600. I thought it was here when you arrived. My friend told me who owned it. I never heard of him. Richard Dar—Let's see....Richard 'Dar' something. Richard Darton. Something like that. Siddons said he was a great American. I think they were in Nam together. Siddons said he was one tough hombre. Don't ask me what he does."

"What so was so unusual about it?" asked Vassilov.

"Everything. The guy wanted everything done, and he wanted it all done in two weeks. Unreal. The killer was the sun roof. He had this grille put in that covered the whole roof so you couldn't pull it out. I guess he didn't want people climbing down into the backseat and killing the passengers. Then he had this compartment big enough for a person to hide in put under the front seat. We figured it was a hiding place for an extra armed guard or even for the owner himself—You know, his double sits in the backseat sipping champagne; and the whole time, our man in Havana is hiding in a secret compartment. Pretty clever, huh? And the fuck's an American."

"Richard Darton? Never heard of him."

"Yeah, well, I *saw* him," said Lindquist. "He drives up in this Chevy Camaro. Turns out that's been armored, too."

"Gray Chevy?"

"I think it was black. Could have been gray. Yeah, I think I heard someone say he must have painted it himself, it looked better gray. I can tell you one thing, black it looked like shit. Now, him, I wouldna minded looking like him."

"The guy?"

"Yeah, he looked like Lee Marvin used to look. Tough guy with a killer's face."

"Lee Marvin?"

"You know what I mean. He looks like the marines used to look—rawboned, with these slit eyes and high cheekbones and this tough-guy voice. Yeah, that could have been me," continued Lindquist. "I could have been a killer, too, except I fucked myself up with women and booze."

"What would you have done if you hadn't been a welder?" asked Vassilov.

"Listen, Vassi," said Lindquist. "Once I fucked this movie star. Her name was Barbara O'Brien. She was under contract to MGM or one of those. Every time we fucked, she begged me to let her get me an agent."

"So why didn't you?" asked Vassilov.

"Why didn't I? 'Cause at the time I was supposed to be married and my wife got pregnant every time I looked at her. There was no way, I mean no way, I woulda left my family to be a movie star. Of course, now what difference does it make? I ain't fucking no movie stars anymore. I heard Barbara O'Brien has this dancing school somewhere in Ohio or Indiana or one of those; and, what the hell, I look like shit. Come on, Vassi, have another beer; you're getting sober on me."

By midnight Vassilov had gotten the information to Rogoff at the Moscow Center via the embassy in Washington, D.C.

Before six o'clock the following morning, Greta Polansky had broken into von Kelsing's files. It took her three-quarters of an hour. Finally, under "Miscellaneous Office Expenses," she found the name "Richard Dartley. Savage. Greenmountain Lodge," plus a Maryland phone number with the name "Whitney" written after it. There was a second paper stapled to the first. A "M. Jouet," a Swiss bank and a phone number that turned out to be a Swiss number, plus what was clearly an account number. Again the name "Dartley" appeared.

By noon, the KGB agent in Munich had already spoken to Ali Ozker. Did Ozker know anything about Richard Dartley? No. Savage? No. Greenmountain Lodge? A black Mercedes? He was expecting to be picked up in one and brought to a clandestine meeting at the Doppler Electronics plant across the Wittelsbach Bridge. The meeting was ostensibly with France Gennaro, a New York crime boss. The agent informed Ozker that the car and probably the girl he mentioned, Bobo Noll, were connected with Richard Dartley. As with Demirel they had every reason to think that Dartley was being paid by the three industrialists.

"Do you want me to kill him?" Ozker asked.

"Oh, no. We have a better plan. We will entrap him. We will be staked out at the Doppler Electronics plant. It is our opinion that he has been paid to kill, paid by the von Kelsing people. It seems likely that the Mercedes will take you to Dartley himself at the Doppler plant."

Ali Ozker made a fist. "How do I know you won't scare him off?"

"Mr. Ozker," said the KGB agent, "this Dartley could just as easily shoot you in the head. If you think you're going to saunter into Doppler Electronics and start shooting, you're crazy. He could be hiding there. This man is clever. The man who introduces himself as Dartley may not be Dartley after all."

Ozker paused. "Well, what does Dartley look like?" he asked.

"We don't know. We can't seem to find a file on him. We plan to have our people, ten of them, disguised as night watchmen and janitors, cleaning ladies and the like. We're also investigating the owners of the Doppler plant to see what their connection with von Kelsing–Schmidt is."

"And the German police?"

"We've got to be careful. We have already subjected the production manager of Doppler to sexual blackmail. A year ago we wanted to buy so-called technological secrets from him. He refused. Within six months we had photographs of him with two women, one black, in bed. The president of the company is a devout Lutheran in a very Catholic city. He has made a habit of hiring other Lutherans; he has made it clear he expects them to be above reproach. He will not tolerate sloppy behavior. So you see, we now have our technological information and no one is the wiser. Tonight the manager will let us in before the end of the working day. Dartley will probably have been hiding there for a day or two. Who knows? We would assume he's an expert. It seems that he's been paid half a million dollars already."

Ozker coughed and turned pale. Now his imagination began to run away with him. "And you say you want me to walk into the factory? How could I possibly do that? Perhaps I should get my double to walk into the factory."

The KGB agent said nothing. He had been instructed to tell Ozker to wait for further instruction if the Turk offered any resistance to the plan.

A half hour later Ali Ozker sat in the English Garden waiting for his contact. It was Agent Karpov. He was in direct contact with Rogoff at the Moscow Center.

"Comrade Ozker," he began, "you are directly ordered by the Center to follow all directions. You are in line for a very important request. We cannot afford to lose you. You will be issued a bullet-proof vest if it will make you feel better."

"I already have my bulletproof clothing. I already have my bodyguards. Imagine how you would feel, Agent Karpov, if a paid assassin was out there in the dark waiting for you. I do not understand how it is there is no record of this man, no record of when he came into the country."

"Herr Ozker," the agent replied, "it is Munich in June. Surely you are joking. It is greatly to our advantage and to yours that this man will be tricking you into meeting him at a specific place. He is clearly some kind of stunt man, an assassin-performer. We are dealing with a Jack the Ripper. This man has a deep-seated need to tempt fate. He would never be content to lie in wait for you behind closed blinds. You are lucky we can flush him out."

Ali Ozker had not forgotten Agent Karpov's earlier remark. "You said I am in line for an important request. What are you trying to say to me?"

"I do not know the full details."

"The full details of what?"

"All I can tell you is that, since Andropov, you are considered the Center's most important middleman. At some time in the future, you will be contacted by the people responsible for this decision."

"What decision? I do not know what you are saying."

Karpov was empowered to say only what would keep Ozker alert. Beyond that, even he had sketchy facts. As an organization, the KGB was not immune to the ancient and immutable laws of power. According to those laws, colonies and satellites must operate with partial information and limited facts; otherwise, knowing everything, they would be empowered to replace the central power at its source.

"All I can tell you is that the Agency plans to move against certain world powers in a more direct way. In exchange for making it possible for you to operate your heroin empire out of Bulgaria with impunity, the Center will expect you to protect those agents who will need food, shelter, ammunition, and safe passage into and out of the country. You will be compensated for your trouble."

"Nothing you are telling me is specific, Agent Karpov."

"I told you. I do not know the specifics. I have simply been instructed to let you know that the Center has great need of you. And to remind you that if you intend to continue to use Bulgaria as your base of operations, you will have great need of us." The agent smiled, flicked his Galloise, and took a sip of Chateau Rothschild '78 out of a silver flask he normally stored in his attaché case. "Ours is a symbiotic relationship, Comrade Ozker."

Through his sunglasses, Ozker stared. He had never liked being indebted to anyone, least of all to the Soviet Union. He had presumed, naively, that the effect of his heroin distribution on the German morale and character was enough to gain him Soviet support. Now he realized what a rube he was. A country boy. He smiled, smiled at his stupidity. Did he really think he could outwit the KGB! What a dunce! He had been in bed with the devil since his first day at the Hotel Vitosha-New Otani.

So Ozker decided to trust the KGB. He had to laugh at himself. It was like trusting a king cobra. On the other hand, if they had wanted him dead, he would have been shot or poisoned years before. His bodyguards would have been on the Moscow Center payroll. He would have been driven into an empty wheat field in any number of countries, hit on the head with a shovel, his body dumped into an eight-foot-deep freshly dug grave and immediately covered up and planted over. The death and disapearance of one's enemies were interrelated phenomena with which he was not unfamiliar. For anyone familiar with them, they were easy to achieve. The ocean was as bottomless as the earth itself. Fire could reduce any human being to ashes in a matter of minutes. The same machines that could reduce a thousand-pound steer to hamburger meat in a couple of hours could grind human flesh and bones into a pulpy residue. There was never any excuse for bodies being left in the street. Murderers who made it possible for their victims to be taken to the coroners were clearly begging to be caught. That's what bothered Ozker most about himself: his self-destructiveness.

Cemel Demirel was a case in point. If he had simply buried Demirel and his idiotic gunman in a block of cement somewhere deep in a Bulgarian forest, von Kelsing and his cohorts would not have pursued him with the same vehemence. But now, because of his egomaniacal pride that all of his wives and several mistresses had repeatedly warned him about, he had to deal with a half-million-dollar assassin. He could not believe his stupidity or his fate. He had been ordered to play along with a professional killer—he, Ali Ozker, shipping magnate, real-estate czar, a sultan in everything but name.

Who then was this Bobo Noll? Clearly a pawn of the killer, clearly another cocksucking Western whore. The Russian women who sucked cock were at least at the service of a socialistic state, and the women of Istanbul really enjoyed it. Western women were just cheap sluts after money. He had never met one who wasn't.

* * *

"Raoul?" the bodyguard made Ozker look like a midget.

"What is it, boss?"

"What is the time?"

"Seven, boss."

"I'm supposed to meet that whore at ten. I'd like to fuck her here and get it over with."

"Do you want me to call her, boss?"

"I'll fuck her in the backseat of that car if I have to. She says she's giving me the car."

"Yes, boss."

"Is there a car I don't already have?"

"No, boss."

"Gennaro will be waiting, she says. Dartley will be waiting. Everybody's waiting for Ali Ozker." He grabbed his bodyguard by his tie. The giant shook with fear. In his heart and mind he was still 4 years old. Ozker was simply a stand-in for his father. Day after day Raoul worked out in the gym. The larger his muscles got, the more afraid he was of tough little men. He began to think that the men with the biggest heads were the men who rule. His head, after all, was tiny compared to his father's. His mother had once told him that people with the biggest heads made the best generals. Everywhere Raoul went, he stared at the size of men's heads. With the short, stocky Ali Ozker, he found the biggest head of all. In Ozker's presence he felt both humiliated and elated at being in his service. In other words, he felt entirely at home.

"Raoul, you will stay with me, right by my side, all evening."

"Whatever you say, boss."

"This will be a particularly dangerous evening. I can feel it. You must keep your eyes open at all times."

"I would not do anything else, boss."

"I feel like I'm being set up."

The bodyguard said nothing. He did not dare to reassure his boss. Once he had tried that. Ozker had flown into a rage. "Never patronize me!" he had screamed. "Never! Do you understand!"

If, on the other hand, he agreed with the older man's outbursts, he was accused of being a toady.

"Tomorrow my son Stefan graduates from medical school."

"Yes, boss."

"He is the only decent thing about me. I had no influence on him, of course, praise Allah, but at least I can say I paid for his medical school education."

"That is a wonderful thing, boss."

"Of course he did inherit my ambition, my drive, my hunger to be somebody. When I die he will inherit my money. He will be rich as well as respectable. My son, you see, will have riches of the soul. He will help other people and he will never have to fear for his life. Isn't that remarkable; I will be able to say I am the father of such a man. Me, the gangster, the killer."

At the word 'killer,' Raoul looked wide-eyed.

"Don't be so surprised, Mr. Muscles. That's exactly what I am. It was either that or be owned by the Germans and the Americans. If I went back to

Turkey, I would be owned by the Greeks and the Jews. Nobody owns Ozker." Then he leaned into Raoul and whispered his secret: "We have nothing to worry about. The KGB will be looking out for us tonight."

Chapter Fifteen

The Wittelsbach Bridge over Munich's Isar River was rarely used. Named after the royal dynasty that ruled the Duchy of Bavaria from 1180 until 1918, the bridge was a nineteenth-century architectural experiment. The art-loving Wittelsbachs were directly responsible for the grandiose look of Munich's old sections. Importing Italian architects, they built their vast winter palace, the Schloss Nymphenburg, in the center of the city. The Italians were responsible for the Renaissance flair of Munich's public buildings and parks dating from that period. King Ludwig I had heard of a certain Italian architect, Ruggerio Di Salvo, who had presented plans for a 100 percent iron bridge over the River Po in Florence. The city council there had rejected it, ruling that an iron roadway would require too much maintenance. Another Wittelsbach,

Leopold I, saw the Di Salvo plans and wanted the bridge for the Isar. The king was particularly attracted to the elaborate wrought iron panels that functioned as guard rails for pedestrians. He asked Di Salvo to substitute copper for iron in fashioning the panels. He felt, rightly, that the Venetian green patina of oxidized copper was the perfect common ground between the new technology and more traditional concepts of beauty. Copper reminded him of iris and eucalyptus leaves, and he asked that they be incorporated into the design of the panels.

The bridge was completed in 1874. It was a two-lane bridge, smaller than it looked; it connected Leipzigerstrasse north of the famed English Garden. It was probably just as well that in succeeding years the city moved south. From the very first day, bridge traffic sounded like thunder. The iron panels in the roadway rumbled; it seemed as though it would be only a matter of minutes before the entire structure came crashing down. In succeeding years there were continual problems. The city council forbade the use of the bridge as a bus or truck route. And the Florentines had been correct—the maintenance was astronomical. Corrosion was a constant threat. Still, the Wittelsbach Bridge was pretty to look at; most architecture buffs felt it was only a matter of time before the landmarks commission ruled it off limits to vehicular traffic. In the mean time, there were grand homes and a few businesses on the east side of the bridge, and the bridge provided a convenient shortcut.

In the twentieth century the bridge's greatest claim to fame was that at one point during the darkest days of the Second World War, it was the only bridge in Munich still functioning. To the predominantly Catholic people of the city, the Wittelsbach Bridge became a symbol of their own strength. What had seemed flimsy and ornate became, in a crisis, their avenue to survival. Despite all, the bridge stood—infrequently used, it was true—but a monument nonetheless.

At 4:00 A.M. his alarm rang. Several minutes later, Dartley ventured out into the predawn dressed in his best dark suit, a white dress shirt and a navy blue tie.

"Please call me a cab," he said to the sleepy-eyed desk clerk.

The cab took ten minutes. "Leipzigerstrasse, bitte," he told the cabbie. The driver launched into an animated monologue in German. Dartley tried to tell him he didn't speak German. It did no good whatsoever. The man prattled on. Insane, thought Dartley. They're all insane. Someday they'll rouse themselves. The good people. The hardworking little folk. They'll rouse themselves from their unconsciousness and start slaughtering their masters. Anarchy is their only hope.

He tried to shut off his mind, but he could not. His inner voices were more tyrannical than the driver's. It was a familiar experience for him. On the eve of a job, he normally became grandiose. He made plans for the human race. He concocted global solutions. He experienced himself as a hundred news commentators all talking at the same time. His madness during this time was something he had come to accept. It was all part of the job.

When they arrived at their destination, he paid the driver and tipped him generously. It was four-thirty. He had about an hour till daylight.

Dartley didn't have to look for the Wittelsbach Bridge. Its ornate charm loomed before him in the morning fog like a set for a musical comedy. He found it impossible to associate the bridge either with war or with death. Close up, it was an eerie specter, at once ghostly and skeletal in the summer predawn.

Dartley checked to see if anyone was coming. No one. Four-thirty was the deadest hour of the night. He walked slowly along the pedestrian walkway. Normally it was extremely dangerous, as it was no more than a two-foot-wide metal sidewalk separated from the roadway by its four-inch elevation. At least one person a year had been killed outright by drivers who found it impossible to maneuver a straight line in so narrow a space.

He walked to the exact middle of the bridge. His footsteps bothered him. They were loud, almost as loud as a woman walking in high heels on a wooden floor. When he had bought his black dress pumps, his best shoes with their leather soles and heels, he did not have Wittelsbach Bridge in mind. He again castigated himself for a lack of precise planning. "Good God, Dartley," he said to himself out loud. "Another mistake." He could hear his voice carrying across the darkness. The river Isar, like all water, was a natural transmitter of sound.

Dartley's voice echoed downstream to a spot across the river, two blocks south of the Leipziger-strasse entrance to the bridge where Patrolman Helmut Krueger, 26, was taking a five-minute break. He stood looking at the ongoing blackness of the Isar. In the dark the river looked like an oil slick. Shiny and black and streaked with colored light. Krueger was primarily responsible for checking the block-long, four-stories Doppler Electronics plant. The Wittelsbach Bridge, by contrast, had never been a security problem. What was there to steal? Patrolman Krueger walked across its quarter-mile span twice each evening. Patroling the bridge was never a matter of concern for the bridge itself. The real concern was for would-be suicides. The roadway was no higher than a four-story building; few died upon impact with the river. Most died from drowning. The strange beauty of the Wittels-bach Bridge and its relative isolation from the center of Munich drew the lonely and the unhap-py like a magnet. Underlying the surface of German genius for technology and innovation lay a dark, romantic soul moored in a landscape of Rhine maidens, Black Forests and death. Just earli-er that evening, at 1:30 A.M., Herr Krueger, on his first walk across the bridge, had come upon a pair of young lovers. She was threatening to jump. Her boyfriend did not believe that she would actually do it and he was daring her to go ahead.

When Krueger overheard the boy taunting the girl, he had taken the boy by the shoulders and told him that if anything happened to the girl, he would hold him personally responsible. The boy, hearing this, began to scream obscenities at the policeman. He then burst into tears and ran off. That broke the spell of impending death. Patrolman Krueger patted the girl on the back and advised her to go home and get a good night's sleep. He was an old pro at dealing with would-be suicides. For the past two years his wife had been dropping hints that he should study for an advanced degree in psychology. What was the point of his wasting his obvious intellectual talents on bridge-jumpers?

When Dartley had arrived at the middle of the bridge, he took out of his vest pocket a special tool Spencer Siddons had given him, at his request. It was a cord, no more than ten inches long, fastened at either end to what looked like a short length of broom handle, each about six inches long. What made the cord different was that it was impregnated with and coated with industrial diamond dust. Its purpose: to saw through metal as quickly and as cleanly as possible. His plan was to saw straight through the ornamental ironwork in the middle of the span in two places, the second cut roughly eight feet to the right of the first cut. In effect, he could be creating a panel of his own. By design the cuts would be virtually unnoticeable. With a certain amount of pressure—how much he could only guess at—the panel would snap off at the bottom and give way, falling, crashing into the Isar. He had asked Siddons for a tool that would enable him to saw with the least exertion. He wished to avoid, if at all possible, broad arm and hand movements. Siddons's solution had been ingenious, he thought.

In his first ten minutes on the bridge, Dartley had managed to saw straight through one line of curlicues right down to the base of the railing.

He saw Patrolman Krueger the minute the policeman stepped onto the east end of the bridge. Knowing the officer would question him, he moved, as imperceptibly as possible, eight feet to the left of the cut, all the while pretending to admire the ornamentation. His cutting string, as before, was hidden in his vest pocket. Dartley caressed the pale gray-green ornamentation, running his fingers around the stylized tendrils of flowering plants. Why not? Some art historicans claimed that the ironwork on the Wittlesbach Bridge was the precursor of Art Nouveau.

At first Patrolman Krueger spoke in German.

"Ich bin American. Ich spreche kaum Deutsch," replied Dartley, explaining in his best Berlitz that he didn't speak much German.

"I speak English a little," said Krueger. "Are you satisfactory?"

"Yes," replied Dartley.

"You do not jump bridge?"

"Oh no," he exclaimed when he understood the patrolman's concern. "Oh, no, no, no. I would *never* jump off the bridge. I came here because my great-grandfather, he worked on the bridge."

"You are Wittelsbach?" asked Krueger, instinctively adopting a reverential tone of voice. Could it be that a young prince had returned to usher Munich into a new Golden Age?

"No, no, no," explained Dartley, breaking the spell. "My great-grandfather was Luigi, Luigi..." He searched for an Italian surname. "Pavarotti. He was an ironworker. See"

"Pavarotti the opera singer?" asked Krueger.

"No, no," exclaimed Dartley. "Pavarotti the ironworker."

"Do you know Pavarotti the opera singer?" Kreuger asked.

"No relation," answered Dartley, smiling. "No relation." He paused once more to admire the bridge. "My grandmother always told me if I ever came to Munich, I should see the Wittelsbach Bridge by moonlight. My girl friend said to hell with it. She went back to the hotel."

"What hotel?" asked Patrolman Krueger.

"Hilton," replied Dartley.

"Ja?" asked Krueger.

"Ja," answered Dartley.

"Okay," continued the officer. "You have nice time in Munich. You do not jump, okay?"

"Okay," answered Dartley. "Okay."

He waited for ten minutes after his official interruption had returned to the west side of the Isar.

It was almost 5:00 A.M. Dartley had little more than half an hour left before the sun rose. Eight feet to the right of the first cut, he made a second. This time it took him almost twenty-five minutes. He figured his cutting tool must be growing dull.

At five-thirty the horizon was beginning to glow.

The bridge rumbled. With a start he straightened up and pretended to be enjoying the scenery. A taxi passed. After a moment he continued sawing his second cut. It was like sawing through rock. A milk truck passed. He straightened again. Then he saw two joggers enter the bridge from the west side. Once more he straightened up. Dartley wondered how much time he had before the stream of westbound commuters began their daily trek across the bridge.

Then Dartley realized he had made a serious error. None of his preliminary studies, certainly not the photographs, had prepared him for the four-inch iron base below the copper ornamentation. In the photographs Malleson had shown him, the iron base was nonexistent. He decided to saw horizontally along the bottom of the ironwork until he either finished the job or the police stopped and asked him what he was doing. Curiously, his luck held. In the next twenty minutes he crouched down, his back to the ongoing oncoming traffic, and sawed away. Only once, an early dog-walker with two schnauzers stopped to stare. Dartley looked up, smiled and said, "Guten morgen" with a confident air of authority. The dog-walker, a young blond woman, probably a student, stared back. She had a disapproving look on her face, but she soon gave up trying to read his mind. Besides, her dogs were pulling at her with hurricane force. She concluded that the man was probably a bridge inspector testing for rust.

When Dartley had sawn three-quarters across the bottom of the railing, he felt the entire eight-foot-long panel he had created begin to reverberate. He began to saw on the other side. It was almost six o'clock. No one stopped him. Finally he had sawn through everything but one jade-green stalk of what looked like a stylized tiger lily. He was done. He would not know until one the next morning whether he had failed. His greatest fear was that he would forget where he had sawed. He decided to return later in the day and glue a couple of ordinary bike reflectors to the middle of the section.

He was beset by fears. What if sometime during the day, a Wittelsbach Bridge aficionado happened to walk across the bridge, west to east, with one hand skimming along the rail? The break would be felt and then noticed. The question was, would it be reported to the bridge authorities? Would a welder be called in on an emergency basis to solder the damage? Would wooden scaffolding be erected to create a barricade over the damaged section? Dartley had no way of knowing. In this job, as in every other one, there were manifold uncertainties and the possibility of failure.

The sky was on fire with dawn. It was definitely time to leave the bridge. He put the cord into his pocket once more time and walked west on the bridge back toward the city. The joggers were more frequent now, about one every thirty seconds. Rush hour was beginning. Before he reached the western end of the bridge, the rumbling of cars over the iron railway had become like thunder.

Dartley wished he had spent more time figuring out how he could have shot Ali Ozker in the head with a sniper rifle. His real problem was that he had been unable to figure out a plan of escape. Prussic acid would have been another solution, much cheaper than an armored Mercedes. Fewer margins for error than half-sawn-through ornamental railings on world-famous bridges and corpses left in parked cars.

Am I a crackpot? he thought to himself. Am I some kind of psychotic nut? All I want is to do my job right and not have other gunmen running after me? What's so crazy about that?

As he walked back to the Hotel Köblenz he found that on that particular morning at least, all other things considered, he was glad to be alive.

Chapter Sixteen

Friday, June 8. The actual execution was swift and brutal. After weeks of meticulous planning, Dartley's chutzpah carried it off.

All during the day primal energy rose up in him like desert heat. Like an evangelical minister, he would later claim he had merely been a vehicle for a higher power. The gods had acted through him. The gods or the demons. He had merely been the instrument of fate. The truth was, he loved the energy that flowed in him on the day of an execution.

At noon he called Bobo Noll. The former Miss Germany was on her slant board doing scissor kicks.

"I just want to know," she asked, "will there be gunfire when we get to the other side of the bridge?"

"You don't have to worry about that," Dartley said.

"Will there be guns?"

"Ozker wouldn't risk a gun battle. He's too old and too fat."

"Will there be guns?"

"I want you to sit in the front seat with me," Dartley said.

"Ozker will want me in the backseat next to him," Bobo replied.

"I'll stop the car just before Wittelsbach Bridge. You think of a reason to get in the front seat. Anything. Your money will be in a business envelope on the front seat."

"I don't know," she said.

"Wear a money belt under your dress. As soon as you get in, put the money in your money belt."

"What are you trying to tell me?"

"Do as I say." Dartley's voice was flat.

"A money belt? Okay, I'll wear a money belt."

At teatime, 4:00 P.M., Ali Ozker and Fatma Lady Exton waged a cat-and-dog fight in her dainty satin suite. Ozker held the photo of his ex-wife sucking cock.

"Fatma, you are dragging down the family name."

"Ali, I have enemies."

"Don't worry, after these pictures, I am one of them."

"Did Stefan see them?"

"Poor Stefan. He's been through so much."

"Ali, how do I know you didn't send the photographers?"

"And you told me you had fallen in love with me all over again. What kind of a woman are you?"

"What kind of a man are you? I heard you're a Communist."

"I heard you're a slut."

"Get out of my house! This instant!"

He was glad to leave her again. She had always been a slut; she always would be. Her father before her had been a pig. Compared to Abdul Abady, Ali Ozker was a Christian saint.

Besides, if Bobo Noll looked anything like her photographs, his evening was assured.

During the late afternoon, Dartley checked out the Maximilian Bridge, about a mile down from the Wittelsbach. Under the bridge on its west bank stone stairs were cut into the wall, just as Malleson had said. They led up to Steinsdorf Strasse, within walking distance of the Hotel Köblenz.

At 7:00 P.M., Dartley dressed in a conservative gray flannel suit, ate a light dinner in the Köblenz dining room. Bismarckhering, kartoffein salat, mineralwasser. That was it.

At eight, wearing dark glasses and his trench coat, he walked up to the Wittelsbach Bridge. At the midway point he affixed two strips of bicycle reflector tape next to the cuts he had made the day before. The glittering red-orange surface of the tape would pinpoint the exact spot on the bridge where the railing was weak.

At nine he dressed in his chauffeur's uniform. He packed the cap in a small waterproof duffel bag which he carried with him. The duffel bag also carried a red turtleneck and a pair of pants and shoes. He needed the clothes because under his chauffeur's uniform was his wet suit. To confuse the hotel staff, he wore his trench coat over the whole business.

Downstairs in the garage, no one had touched the Mercedes. Inside, he opened the door to the compartment under the front seat. He pushed the duffel bag in over the body of Wolfgang Gross—whose eyes were still open. It was too late to close them. There were other problems. A faint odor was beginning to be noticeable.

He left the garage without incident. Two blocks from the hotel, he stopped the car, deposited the trenchcoat in a covered trash bin and donned the chauffeur's hat.

At nine-thirty he picked up Bobo Noll. She was wearing a form fitting evening gown of maroon sequins. In the front it was slit to below the navel. Her breasts looked as if they were going to pop out the front of her gown. So far, so good.

At ten he deposited her at Aubergine.

"I'll wait across the street," he said. "I'll be expecting you around one. Remember, by the time we get to the bridge, I want you in the front seat."

"Whatever you say, Mr. Money," she said.

At ten-fifteen, Ali Ozker and four bodyguards arrived at Aubergine.

"Allah be praised," he said when he caught sight of Bobo Noll. Occasional Muslim profanity was his one concession to Turkish culture.

Noll and Ozker sat together at a round table in a corner of the main dining room. The four bodyguards positioned themselves at two small tables in front of the adoring couple. All the men, including Ozker, faced outward looking toward the entrances. In point of fact, except for the aborted attempt by Cemel Demirel, Ozker had never been subjected to an assassination attempt. Still, nothing gave him greater pleasure than the status symbol of bodyguards.

"What is the deal with the New York families and when do I get you alone?" he said to Bobo Noll.

"Afterward."

"After what?" he knew what her answer would be. He just wanted to see how well she lied. As far as he could tell, she was a consummate actor.

"The meeting with Franco Gennaro is at the Doppler Electronics plant at one. It's on the other side of the Wittelsbach Bridge."

"And your chauffeur will take us there in the car you promised me."

"If you make a deal—"

"Why does Gennaro need me?"

"He says your track record is impeccable."

"Does he have a way of getting my heroin into New York?"

"You don't have to worry about that," she said.

"Since when?"

"He'll pick up the heroin in Sofia."

"How much per kilo?"

"That's what you gentlemen have to discuss."

"Eat!"

He found himself dazzled by her green eyes. Still, it was hard to concentrate on her and know that by the end of the evening she might be dead.

The spaghetti sauce had flecks of lamb mixed in with the pork and beef. The tomatoes had been put through a processor that removed their skin and seeds. After a brief minute of sautéing a cast-iron skillet, the waiters, in white tie and spats, spread them over the hot, fresh pasta. Impeccable. The Turkish kingpin was not looking at the food.

"There's a room in back," Ozker announced with wild, hungry eyes. "Nobody's using it tonight. Come on. I know the owner." He didn't; the owner was in the south of France. Ozker, as usual, hedged his bets.

Jesus Christ, thought Bobo Noll, the animal wants to fuck. So what else is new?

Ozker turned to his bodyguards. "As long as I'm in there, don't let anyone go in that door."

Outside, Dartley waited in the Mercedes 600 rehearsing his part for the remainder of the night.

In Moscow, Serge Rogoff waited in his office, reading Lenin's journals for the tenth or eleventh time. He planned to wait through the night until he had definite word that Savage was dead.

At the Doppler Electronics plant, the KGB team had positioned themselves. Without exception, they stood as still as death.

In Düsseldorf, the three industrialists were at a dinner party at Willi Reiser's house. Von Kelsing had brought Marlena Kupitsky. Schmidt had arrived alone. As for Reiser himself, at least four of the male guests seemed too young and too pretty for the older crowd.

All three men seemed depressed. They had not gone hunting in weeks. There had been no word from Savage. Or Dartley. Nothing at all.

In the back room at the Aubergine, unknown by the restaurant management or staff, Ali Ozker had his time-honored way with Bobo Noll. He decided that if she was a murderer's accomplice, she was also great at giving head. She's got to be a pro, he thought. She is too good.

Her behavior was a dead giveaway. No ladylike protests, no feigned shock. The girl had been around.

For him, in the beginning of every relationship, at least, sex had always been a statement of territorial imperative. In the kingdom of darkness, cock was king.

"What time did you say this meeting was?" he asked again.

"One o'clock. My car's outside," she said, looking up.

To her, the sex meant nothing. She might as well be sucking on a lollipop. She could play any game he could. All that mattered to her was the money on the front seat of the Mercedes.

They finished their sex, rejoined the bodyguards in the dining room and went on to rack of unborn lamb. As for alcohol, Ozker took his vodka straight. At his insistence, the bottle sat on the table.

"Is it time yet?" he asked again.

"Almost," she said.

"I'm going to fuck you in the backseat of the car."

She shuddered, thinking about Dartley's insistence that he join her in the front seat.

A half hour later they were out on the street. The armored Mercedes gleamed like black patent leather.

"It's just a fucking limo," Ozker said.

"It's armored," she announced.

"Yeah?"

"There are gunrests above the windows and portholes for shooting out."

"Yeah?"

"A thousand pounds of steel to protect you. Bulletproof glass."

"Yeah? I need something like this. When do I get a demonstration?"

"After the meeting."

Dartley stood by the open back door.

"Hey, we can't put five people back here," Ozker protested.

"The lady can sit in front," Dartley suggested.

"Sit in front? Oh no, she's sitting in the backseat with me. I'm fucking her. That's all she's good for." Ozker was drunk. He knew it and he didn't care. "Put the bodyguards in the front seat," he ordered.

"Four bodyguards can't sit in the front seat," the chauffeur replied. "Maybe the lady would want to sit in the front seat."

"I said I'm fucking the lady!" Ozker screamed.

Dartley did not turn around. He did not want to see the terror in Bobo's eyes. He knew he had to figure out some way to get her out of the backseat before he started on to Wittlesbach Bridge.

"I hear you got a hidden compartment under the front seat!" bellowed Ozker. Dartley, hearing this, did not flinch. No one could possibly open the compartment without knowing exactly which button to push.

Bobo saved him. She pushed Ozker into the

backseat with her breasts, all the while nibbling the back of his neck. The Turk did not resist her.

Two bodyguards sat in the front seat, two in the back.

For the next ten minutes, Dartley drove. Ozker and Bobo made love, in a strange kind of intercourse, she facing the back window, straddling him, neither one looking at the other. Ozker did not seem to care if the bodyguards looked on. Despite his love of the good life, he was in no sense prone to what is called the Bourgeois sensibility.

"We're almost at Wittelsbach Bridge," Dartley said over the loudspeaker. It was his last clue to Bobo to find her way out of the backseat.

Her solution was desperate but effective.

"How come Turks have such tiny cocks?" she asked Ozker as if she were commenting on the weather. She said this while they were still fucking.

"What?" he asked. He could not believe what he had just heard.

"I mean, I don't want to insult you, but I don't know what you're doing. I can't even feel you. I mean, it's ridiculous. I'm sorry. I know how this sounds. I don't want to hurt your feelings, but you're just too small for me. It's like fucking a pencil."

The bodyguards, hearing her, snorted into their hands. They tried to pretend they were coughing, but they were in no sense sophisticated men.

"Get out of here," Ozker began in a hot whisper, "before I kill you."

"Franco Gennaro's not going to like the way you treat me," she replied.

"Fuck Franco Gennaro! The meeting's off! Get out! Get out before I kill you!" Ozker raged.

Dartley pushed the button that opened the back. In a flash, Bobo was off Ozker and out of the car.

"Take me back to the hotel!" Ozker screamed. "Beethoven Allee!"

Ozker looked out the darkened window. The vast emptiness of the night stretched before him on all sides. He felt completely unprotected and completely alone.

"Tell the two in the front to come back here," he ordered. "This is a set up. I can feel it in my bones."

Once more Dartley opened the doors. The two guards in the front seat climbed into the back and the four men surrounded Ozker.

Dartley locked the doors once more. As the Mercedes sped off, Bobo Noll saw the envelope lying in the street. Dartley had let it slip through the crack in the door. Inside was three thousand dollars.

"Thank you, Herr Dartley," she said. "There is a God."

"To my hotel!" Ozker raged.

"This is a one-way street," replied Dartley over the intercom.

"No, it's not!" screamed Ozker. "It's not a one-way street. Turn this car around or I'll shoot. Raoul, stop him! He's taking us across the bridge."

The Turk's mind had snapped. He was hysterical. "Shoot him!"

Raoul took out his Walther P5 and began to fire. The bulletproof windows were impenetrable. The bullets riocheted.

"Open the doors! I'm getting out!" Ozker screamed.

The doors would not budge. They were locked in.

The Mercedes was now on the Wittelsbach Bridge where Officer Krueger was making his first inspection tour of that evening.

Dartley pushed the button that controlled the sunroof. In a matter of seconds, the grille was exposed.

"Help!" screamed Ozker, attempting to dislodge the grille. The animal in him was caged. He was trapped and he did not know why. He never would. His analytic brain had ceased functioning ten minutes before. Now only his will to survive pushed against the constraints of the armored limousine. Together the five burly men wedged themselves against the roof. It was to no avail. Camelot Armoring had done its job.

Officer Krueger heard their cries and turned to see the limousine speed past him. Dartley peered ahead, looking for the bicycle reflector tape. So far he had seen nothing.

He was almost at the midpoint of the bridge. In fact, he was sure of it. Where were the reflectors?

Then, to his horror, he realized why they were invisible. A young couple in love were standing in front of the railing, exactly where he intended to drive. He honked the horn. The couple ignored him. As he turned toward the railing, he honked again. It was too late. As they looked up, the huge black limousine smashed into them, pressing them against the rail. The railing did not budge.

Krueger came running toward the limousine, blowing his police whistle.

Dartley backed up the limo and tried again two feet to the right of where he had aimed before.

This time he floored the accelerator.

In the backseat of the car, Ozker, for the first time aware of Dartley's plan, pounded on the divider window with his pistol—screaming in Turkish. Dartley turned off the intercom. Behind him, in the rear compartment, was a silent movie of human despair.

The Mercedes 600 hit the railing square-on. The panel Dartley had cut out snapped off its one connecting piece and sailed out into the black void above the river, carrying the young lovers with it. Dead, they looked like rag dolls. The limousine followed behind the railing, arcing out into the void and then falling headlong from a height of forty feet. Dartley braced himself for the crash, not knowing if he could possibly survive.

The crash into the Isar did not extinguish the interior lights of the car. In the backseat, the river rushed through the open grille. The men screamed and pushed. They knew that if they screamed loudly enough, help would come. It always had. Finally, like any drowned animals, within the briefest amount of time—no more than two minutes at most—they floated dead in their watery tank. Ozker's head, his eyes wide open, bobbed against the dividing wall.

Dartley was astonished to find himself still alive. He pressed the button that opened the doors to the underwater compartment. They opened without any trouble.

The front compartment was water-free. Still, there was only so much air; he had to work fast. Wolfgang Gross, he soon discovered, was as stiff as a board. No matter. It would be many hours before the car was recovered from the Isar. By then, what could the coroner say if he even bothered to look for another explanation? That the chauffeur, upon hitting the water, had died of sudden fright? Would the German government really care about the death of a heroin exporter and his bodyguards or his chauffeur?

Dartley lifted the body of the dead homosexual with greater effort than he had predicted onto the front seat. There was no sense in trying to reverse the rigor mortis and seat the man in the driver's position. In the next minute and a half, he doffed his outer clothes, stashing them in his watertight duffel bag. Next, he put on the oxygen tank, the goggles, the flippers—all the paraphernalia he would need to swim a mile downstream underwater in the dead of night.

Extricating himself from the car was a matter of opening the front window and waiting until the compartment filled with water before swimming free.

Overhead, Patrolman Krueger had not even called for help. He was still looking down at the river, hypnotized by the lights of the Mercedes. He could still see them gleaming dimly under the waves. He was still hoping that the occupants would swim free. It would be five minutes before he would come to his senses.

It would be dawn before the frogmen arrived, noon until the Mercedes was lifted out of the Isar.

It took Dartley fifteen minutes to swim a mile downstream. He stuck his head above the water once, after ten minutes, to see where he was in relation to the Maximilian Bridge.

Once he arrived at the bridge, he waited in the water for almost an hour until two young men who were discussing politics finally left and went home.

He climbed up the old stone stairway cut into the wall. He removed his wet suit, then hurled the suit and the equipment piece by piece into the black river, where they immediately sank or were carried farther downstream. Upstream he could hear sirens. Many sirens.

He dressed himself in the clothes he had stashed in his waterproof duffel bag. On his way back to the Hotel Köblenz, he disposed of his duffel bag and all unnecessary garments in several covered bins.

He did not plan to sleep that night. It was almost 3:00 A.M. His plane left at dawn.

Chapter Seventeen

June 9. Düsseldorf. Marlena Kupitsky completed her first week as the new staff psychologist at von Kelsing-Schmidt. This time the Moscow Center took no chances. Kupitsky's credentials were first-rate. She had earned her doctorate in clinical psychology from London University and her certificate from the Jung Institute in Zurich. By the time she was 30, she had been analyzed backward and forward by Jungians, Freudians, Adlerians and Sullivanians. She gave each successive analyst a variation on a case history that had nothing to do with her. She was inordinately proud of her control over her fellow psychologists. Not one had ever suspected her true intent. Kupitsky was a committed party member. All her reading in world history had convinced her that when mankind is left to itself, the strong will always dominate the weak. As a Communist, she was determined that mankind not be left to itself.

Within a week of her arrival at von Kelsing, over late lunches and lingering teas, Marlena Kupitsky, with her chiseled features and her ballerina's body, had taken Werner von Kelsing into her confidence, such as it was. She spoke—in perfect German, of course—of her passion for the Fatherland, of her dream of a united Germany and a defeated USSR. With Bruno Schmidt, Ilse de Brock had never said much more than "Bruno, what a big cock you have!" It was the perfect compliment for an over-the-hill industrialist in a country that had known two major defeats in a century. Marlena Kupitsky was smarter than that. She went right to the source. Von Kelsing himself. After she had told him what a big cock he had—standard procedure for sexual operatives—she assured him he would also guide the destiny of the Fatherland. Von Kelsing had been waiting for thirty-five years for someone, preferably a woman, to tell him that. In his heart of hearts he knew he was a leader of his people, but he did not dare say so aloud. Finally, unexpectedly, when he was almost at the end of his tether, when it was almost too late for a political career, the most brilliant woman he had ever known had said it to him within a week of their first meeting. Why, oh why, he wondered, had he let Mitzi drag him down!

Mitzi. Poor Mitzi. His wife was now permanently in Berchtesgaden with round-the-clock nurses and a round-the-clock guard. During her withdrawl from drugs, her mind had snapped. After that she never again mentioned her husband to anyone. Her sole concern was herself. She was 5 years old again, and back in Zurich. She was sitting by the edge of the lake with a box of pastels sketching the trumpeter swans. The lakeside was where she lived now, safe inside her mind where no one could reach her. She was safe from the Germans, safe from the dreaded Hun.

"Oh Marlena, Marlena, how can you love me? I am so old and you are so young." whispered Werner von Kelsing to his new found lover.

"Nonsense, Werner, I may not look it, but I am forty-two and you are only a few years older. What is the harm in that?"

"But, Marlena, I am sixty-two."

"Werner, when I met you I said to myself, 'That man is almost most fifty. He is so strong, so commanding.'"

"Oh, Marlena."

"You will live to be eighty-five. At least. Besides, Werner, you have no choice. The Fatherland needs you. It is time to cast off the American yoke. It is time to root out the Russian disease. Our youth, as before, are infatuated with Communism. It is so horrible, I find it hard even to say the word. Oh, Werner, don't you understand? The people are looking to you for strength."

"Marlena, I'm afraid."

"Of course, you're afraid. We are all afraid. That's why I'm here. Now you have someone with you who will back you up one hundred percent. Someone you can tell everything to."

From then on, whenever he undressed, she gasped at the perfection of his limbs and swooned at the power of the man. Or so she said. In any case, von Kelsing was smitten; that was all that mattered.

Kupitsky, ever attentive, the soul of compassion, asked most of the questions. Von Kelsing did most of the talking, mostly about himself. He did not have to know anything in particular about her. She was, after all, a doctor. As a psychologist, moreover, she was a fountain of wisdom about the human species, exactly what he had always been looking for and never found in a woman.

June 9. Düsseldorf. The television coverage of the mishap in Munich was thorough. Or so it seemed. There was no talk of assassination. In actual fact, the Bonn government was conducting its own investigation. The railing had clearly been cut beforehand. The chauffeur had been dead before he got in the car. Wolfgang Gross was a biology teacher. None of it made sense. The vehicle, moreover, resisted removal from the river bottom. It was too heavy for the cranes. Engineers were working on the problem. The police were ordered to give out no information that would encourage terrorists.

The news coverage spoke of the incident as an accident and of Ozker as a "foreign businessman."

"See, it was an accident. Savage did nothing, nothing at all!" von Kelsing screamed.

"Maybe he set it up!" said Bruno Schmidt.

"Set what up? What? A car drives off a bridge? We don't owe him a single deutsche mark. Nothing."

"Suppose he did it, Werner?"

"I don't believe it."

"He will come after us."

For two days von Kelsing brooded. He would reveal his thoughts to no one, not even to Marlena Kupitsky. On the third day he called assassin number 2.

He had just the man for the job, a young metalworker, a fanatical collector of Nazi memorabilia. The boy's name was Gunther Herrmann. He was 23, with the face of an angry old man. His rage seemed bottomless, but its target was clear; it was directed at any person who directly criticized or in any way cast aspersion on the destiny of West Germany. Von Kelsing had come to know Herrmann because the young worker had begged to meet his employer. It seems that he idolized von Kelsing as a great warrior from a heroic past.

When they finally met, Herrmann pressed for details about "how things were then." He wanted to know exactly how the SS were trained and what they were taught about killing. He had heard that they were experts in the art of assassination. Herrmann particularly wanted to know why the Reich had surrendered in utter despair.

"What do you mean?" von Kelsing had asked, shocked at the question.

"What do I mean?" the boy had replied belligerently. "Half of Germany is under Russian domination. There is a wall in Berlin separating East from West, and you ask me what do I mean?"

"How much would you be willing to do for the Fatherland?" von Kelsing had asked him. He sensed the opportunity was his for the taking.

"I would die for the Fatherland," the boy had answered with shining eyes.

Von Kelsing struck like the serpent he was.

"There is a man...I cannot tell you his name. He is an American. He periodically travels to Germany and steals our technological secrets for the Americans."

Gunther Herrmann, hearing this, turned pale with suppressed rage.

So far, so good.

"Recently," continued von Kelsing, "this man has been responsible for the deaths of some key German scientists. I cannot tell you their names either: my friends in the government have sworn me to secrecy. All I can tell you is that our scientists are dead, and their deaths were reported as due to natural causes. Believe me, the man I am telling you about is an expert in poisons. He is deadly." Von Kelsing cleared his throat and looked very sad. "At some time in the forseeable future, Herr Herrmann, I will need a man such as yourself to undertake to destroy the man I have been telling you about. For the sake of the Fatherland, of course."

"I will do anything you ask, whenever you ask, mein Herr," answered a grateful Gunther Herrmann. The worker had heard about von Kelsing's idiot son Arne, Catholic Marxist, instructor of South American Indians. Herrmann had already fantasized that he could be what von Kelsing had always wanted—a son who was, above all, a German;

a son who would, if need be, give up his life for his father.

"Why do you talk to that boy so much?" Marlena asked him.

"What boy?"

"Gunther is his name."

"How do you know his name?"

"I asked," she said. "I saw him around here. I knew he was important to you. I wanted to know who he is. Did I do something wrong? I am only concerned with one thing, and that is you, mein Werner."

With that, von Kelsing unburdened his soul. "Oh Marlena, you are so young. You know nothing of death. My whole life I have lived with death. The two wars. Friends. Relatives. Dead. My favorite uncle. The same. In the Second War, I too became an agent of death; but not for myself. I promise you. It was always for the Fatherland, for others, always for others."

"Of course, my love," she said, nuzzling him, guiding his hand to her cunt." I know you would only kill for a reason."

"There was a man," he continued, "a criminal, a Turk. He brought narcotics to the Fatherland. Narcotics and organized crime. I twice hired men to seek him out and eliminate him. The first time, my man Demirel was returned to me in several pieces. This happened on Christmas Eve. It's what made Mitzi go berserk. She has never recovered.

She is one of the living dead." A tear spilled out over von Kelsing's eye.

"What about the second man?"

"The second man?"

"You said you hired two men."

"The Turk is dead," von Kelsing replied.

"And what about the boy?"

"The boy?"

"Gunther Herrmann. Where does he fit in?"

"Gunther Herrmann will eliminate the assassin. I want no witnesses. Nobody who knows too much will be allowed to survive."

"Oh Werner, you are so thorough. So German. So Prussian. So wonderful. How can I convince you to run for political office?"

He kissed her tenderly.

"This is what happens," Kupitsky continued. "All the really brilliant men go into business. It's a national tragedy."

Von Kelsing continued kissing her until they began to make love. As they rocked together in the familiar dance of flesh, Marlena Kupitsky realized how much she loathed von Kelsing. She did not know how much more of the Fascist she could take. If Rogoff were not so anxious for information about the von Kelsing-Schmidt industrial complex, she was certain she would have long since given her new lover a dose of prussic acid in an amyl nitrite vial. He would have expired of a respectable heart attack at a respectable age. That way, they would have both been lucky. He would have received his so-called eternal reward, and she would have rid the earth of one less capitalist, a Nazi to boot.

She began to speculate. What would happen if she disobeyed Rogoff and killed the German industrialist in some undetectable way? Would Research & Development at von Kelsing–Schmidt really go down the tubes? What about Bruno Schmidt? Could he not continue running the company by himself? Bruno Schmidt may have been an SS officer, but he was a simpler soul than his best friend. All evidence pointed to his being nonpolitical. Schmidt liked nothing better than schnitzel, schnapps, strudel and sexual intercourse. He was an oral personality. His center of pleasure was his tongue. Even his idea of sexual nirvana involved a mouthful of pussy. After reviewing Ilse de Brock's information on the man, the Moscow Center concluded that Schmidt was basically harmless; he had merely had the good fortune to be born to a successful father. Of the two, von Kelsing had always been the dangerous one.

"Werner, oh Werner, do it again. You're so wonderful. I don't want to ever be apart from you."

Von Kelsing smiled at her sexual hunger. His instincts about Kupitsky had been absolutely correct. She was definitely a woman who appreciated powerful men like him. He congratulated himself: he had been so intelligent to begin this affair with Marlena rather than allow Mitzi to drag him further into despair. He had finally found the perfect partner. Marlena Kupitsky completely accepted him as he was. His political beliefs, which Mitzi called "silly," were a turn-on for the eminent psychologist. Kupitsky was so brilliant. She actually encouraged him to be powerful. She actually recognized his capacity for leadership. Best of all, when it came to the Fatherland, she, like him, was a fanatic of the first order. After three weeks of his Marlena, von Kelsing could not imagine how he had ever managed without her. His life after years of a neurotic, unhappy marriage finally had a smidgen of meaning. He was beginning to experience joy. Joy. The word and the experience had until recently been absent from his life. Now, in the twilight of his middle years, he was beginning to live.

"Oh Werner, do it again!"

There was no doubt about it. Marlena Kupitsky was the doctor of desire. She had healed him. What a saint! What a blessing!

July 10. After a month of waiting, Dartley knew he would never get the money. After eight calls, his Swiss banker, M. Jouet, was beginning to be annoyed.

"I will call you when the money comes, Monsieur Dartley."

"Merci beaucoup, pal."

Dartley called von Kelsing at his office. The secretary informed Herr Savage that Herr von Kelsing was out of the country. Bruno Schmidt's office had evidently been warned, too.

He knew he could get through to Willi Reiser.

Of the three, Reiser was the most interesting. He was both the most secure and the most insecure. In his youth he had been among the most handsome men in Germany. Now he was among the ugliest, his face burn-scarred beyond recognition. The man's capacity for love made him notorious. He was the illegitimate father of three, and the illegitmate lover of countless young men. In short, the man knew life, such as he found it.

"Hello, Herr Savage, what is the problem?" asked Reiser on the transatlantic phone call.

"Mr. Reiser, I must inform you that the rest of the money has not yet been deposited in my Swiss bank account, as agreed upon. Not only that, von Kelsing and Schmidt refuse to pick up the fucking phone."

"I will speak to von Kelsing."

"Tell him if I don't get my money, I will take action. Got that, pal?"

Dartley hung up the phone with the premonition he would soon be traveling to Düsseldorf.

"He will have to take action? Take action, is that what he says? Take action?" commented Werner von Kelsing when Willi Reiser told him of his phone call.

"Werner, remember he said he'd kill you if you didn't pay him what you owed him."

"I don't owe him a thing. He's already been paid half a million for a murder I don't believe he committed in the first place."

"But Werner, he told us in advance it probably wouldn't look like murder."

"Willi, look at it this way. In order to kill me and you and Bruno, three grown men—imagine that—this man Savage would have to spend a small fortune. And he wouldn't make a pfennig off our deaths. He'd be wasting time he could be spending on a paying job; and, what's more, he risks getting caught. It's one thing to kill for a cold-blooded motive. At least then, Willi, the killer's mind remains relatively cool—but to kill out of passion, and he'd definitely be killing us out of passion, that's when killers get caught. Their feelings are so intense, you see, emotion clouds their judgment and impairs their memory. They become maniacs with guns. They leave behind too many clues. The murder becomes a personal vendetta. Subconsciously they want the world to acknowledge the rightness of their cause."

"But Werner," protested Willi Reiser, "we are talking about a business deal. We agreed on another half million."

"I don't want to discuss it!" bellowed von Kelsing.

"But Werner," pleaded the man with the scarred face. "He'll come, I know he'll come. He called me."

"When?"

"This morning. He asked for the money. That's why I'm here. I promised him I would speak to you."

"Willi, sit down. Would you like an acquavit?"

"No, thank you, it's too early in the day."

Von Kelsing's office, newly redecorated, shone with an architectural Nordic purity. The blond wood walls were mostly bleached oak. Great sweeping ribs of the same material arched through the fifteen-foot-high pitched ceiling. They reminded visitors of the frame of a Viking ship, exactly what their Finnish designer intended.

"Willi, there is nothing to worry about," von Kelsing insisted. "These gunmen, these gangsters, they are like kidnappers and hijackers and blackmailers. They are vermin. We cannot allow them to strangle us. They will, you know, if we let them. Willi, you know Marlena, of course. Marlena knows everything we are doing."

"Marlena who?"

"Turn around; I'll introduce you."

"Wha.."

Reiser whirled around to see the blond Marlena dressed in a Karl Lagerfeld recreation of a Chanel dinner suit: beige with black trim. It was severe, sophisticated and expensive, with a touch of the military. It was just like Marlena; it was the latest style. He was frankly surprised that she was there at all. He assumed his meeting with von Kelsing was top-secret. Who was this interloper? Reiser had never met her. He had never even heard of her. She acted as if she were right at home. The redecorated office even matched her suit. Was he imagining things, or had von Kelsing said, "Marlena knows everything we are doing?" Not possible. Not in a million years.

"Marlena Kupitsky, Willi Reiser, the world's

greatest living inventor. Willi invented the tranquilizer. He is the tenth-richest man in West Germany."

"Werner, please..." stammered the inventor in question.

"You two should have much to talk about. You are both healers," continued von Kelsing. "Marlena is our new psychologist. Her doctorate is from the University of London."

Marlena saw the scars of Reiser's face. She realized there was more to the man than his résumé allowed. She had already been briefed by the Moscow Center on the man's personal history and his personal tastes. Before their first meeting, as far as she was concerned, Reiser was a pushover. A genius perhaps, but, like most geniuses, more in touch with his own subsconscious than with the here and now. She realized now that she had not been told about his tenacity. Reiser was not the tenth-richest man in West Germany by accident.

"Marlena knows everything we are doing, does she?" said Reiser unexpectedly, a smile playing around the corners of his mouth. "Tell me, young woman, what exactly do you know?"

What did his smile mean? He was too clever for simple friendliness.

"Know about what?" she asked coyly.

"Don't be such a silly goose, Marlena," broke in von Kelsing. "Tell Willi the truth."

"But it seems so sacred," replied Marlena.

"You can tell me," whispered Reiser.

It was pure cat-and-mouse.

Kupitsky pointed her left toe inward with the calculated pose of a schoolgirl.

"I don't know exactly," she lied. "Something about you hiring an assassin to kill this Turkish gangster. I don't really remember. I am more concerned with everyone's mental well-being here. When it comes to assassinations, I'm just a babe in the woods. The more important issue here is that Herr von Kelsing has a sick wife. Such domestic problems should never be allowed to interfere with the greatness of a man like Herr von Kelsing. So, you see, Herr Reiser, what I really know, if I know anything at all, is the absolute greatness of your friend Werner von Kelsing."

She could see by the expression in Reiser's eyes that she was pushing too hard.

"When I say greatness," she explained, "I mean the man's potential for leadership of the German people. What do you know about that, Herr Reiser, or are you too busy taking vacations in your middle age?"

Reiser studied the woman's flawless skin. Like that of many Slavs, her skin was bronzed like molten gold. Not a pore showed. For good reason, perhaps the oldest in the world, she had a hold on Werner von Kelsing.

"Young woman," he said, peering at her through precariously balanced eyes that had been rearranged by no fewer than three plastic surgeons, "there are things I could tell you about the absolute greatness of men who decided they were absolute rulers. But you are too young, too untried, too full of ideals to understand. I can see it in your magnificent face. You are brilliant and clearly with no personal experience of the tragedy of life. My only question is why you know *anything, anything at all* about the private business of von Kelsing and me."

"Willi, it just slipped out," murmured a suddenly penitent von Kelsing.

"It just slipped out? 'Slipped out'?" repeated Reiser, his indignation growing. "What slipped out, Werner? Your cock? That's what happens when you get old, doesn't it? It gets harder and harder to keep it up. All sorts of things begin to slip. Your hearing, your eyesight, your mental faculties. Mein Gött, have you lost your mind!!!" Reiser clenched his fists and screamed at the top of his voice until his face turned the color of a cooked lobster.

Marlena Kupitsky decided it was time to intervene.

"Herr Reiser, you are clearly distraught. Perhaps you would like..." She caught herself. She didn't dare say the word.

"Like what?" Reiser snapped. "A tranquilizer? Is that what you were going to say? Have you forgotten already, Dr. Kupitsky, that I was the one who invented them?" Then he turned his wrath on von Kelsing. "Ilse de Brock wasn't enough. Now we have this one."

"This one? What do you mean, Willi? She just happens to be here."

"Did you check?"

"Check what?"

"To see if she's KGB."

Marlena Kupitsky paled visibly; fortunately for her, the two men were involved in their own acrimony.

"How would I check to see if she's KGB?" gasped von Kelsing.

"You know perfectly well how you'd check," answered Reiser. He was referring to their CIA sources. They had connections through NATO. Not every KGB agent was known. Hardly. Still, if the name of Marlena Kupitsky had ever figured in a previous investigation of someone, say, of the Russian ambassador; or if she'd ever had a known love affair with an English, American, French or German diplomat, a highly placed government executive or especially a top executive in the aerospace or weapons field, there'd be a dossier on her. And there were always double agents in Moscow itself; if her name was somewhere in somebody's file, they'd eventually find it.

"I hardly think a psychologist trained in London would be working for the KGB," scoffed von Kelsing. He was outraged. She was the best lover he'd ever had. She didn't have a political bone in her body.

During this conversation Marlena Kupitsky grew very still. For good reason. She had a great interest in the occult. One of her pet theories, still scientifically unproven, was that everybody knows everything about everybody else. Her hunch was that every person sends out unconscious signals about who they are and what they want, especially what they are hiding. So she found herself almost frozen with paranoia—thinking that the two industrialists somehow knew who she was. She did know one thing for sure: for whatever reason—the war, his wife's illness, his infidelity—von Kelsing was clearly acting out of guilt. Like the hero of a Sophoclean tragedy, he was trying to bring down the House of Von Kelsing–Schmidt. That's why he had told her about Ozker and the man called Savage. That's why he told her about Gunther Herrmann. He wanted to bring it all crashing down. Of course. It was the classic guilt syndrome. But how and when would it come crashing down? she wondered. And would she, of all people, be caught in the middle? Would the Turkish Mafia retaliate? Would they deduce that after the Demirel incident that von Kelsing had pursued his vendetta? Did not Ozker have lieutenants, affiliates, anxious to teach his assassins a lesson and in turn protect themselves from a common enemy? Of course. How could von Kelsing expect to remain untouched by such powerful enemies once he had provoked them the way he had?

And this business of not paying his gunman the sum agreed upon. Von Kelsing clearly wanted to be punished. It was only a matter of time, she thought, before he brought about his own end.

Von Kelsing was now in tears. Unbelievable for him, he was sitting on the floor, clearly disoriented.

"Willi, you don't understand. I have needs," he whimpered. "You get to reach a point where you've got to have someone to talk to."

"Really?" replied Reiser as coldly as he knew how. "Really, Werner? I thought Bruno and I were the people for you to talk to." Then, turning to Marlena Kupitsky, Reiser said, "Is this what you do for Herr von Kelsing, reduce him to tears? See,

Werner, this is your great Jewish psychology. Sigmund Freud, the great hero of the West. He was out to destroy people like us. Look at you, Werner, you're sitting on the floor." Reiser had never been so angry. Werner von Kelsing was the strongest man he knew. With vehemence, he turned on the well-coiffed blonde who had invaded their lives. "To hell with psychologists! All you want to do is have people feel their feelings. Achievement counts for nothing. Work counts for nothing. The Fatherland counts for nothing!" He was in a rage, "*Kuptisky*, what kind of a name is that?" he shouted.

"My family is Christian," she replied, sensing the anti-Semitic undertone of his question. "My father's people have lived in Germany, Hamburg, for six generations. My mother was a Wagner. She is a second cousin of the composer."

"We should do a computer check on you, Dr. Kupitsky," Reiser remarked. "We'll see how German you really are."

She had lied, of course. She had not a single drop of German blood. I will call their bluff, she thought to herself. Nineteen eighty-four still does not mean the state has a computer bank in every city. Not yet anyway. I do not believe data on me exists. Impossible. The man is just upset. They will discover nothing. Besides, these men are expendable. The only reason they will go unpunished for the death of Ozker is because they provide a free research laboratory for the U.S.S.R. Life can be so rewarding when one is willing to kill; a clever murderer can have it all, as long as he's careful to cover his tracks.

There could be no resolution to the impasse in the executive suite. Even Reiser had to admit that it was not Dr. Kupitsky's fault if von Kelsing had been imprudent enough to confide in her and tell her everything. In the same vein, von Kelsing's mental deterioration could hardly be attributed to the company's blond psychologist. He had survived thirty years of his wife's game-playing and drug addiction. He had survived the ongoing failure of his only child. He had survived the humiliation of his country's defeat and the long struggle out of the postwar rubble.

From time to time it crossed Reiser's mind that perhaps Ilse de Brock had not died by her own hand. Barring a sex-thrill murderer at the Greenmountain Lodge, there were three other possibilities: the man known as Savage, Bruno Schmidt, and von Kelsing himself. Savage was the least likely. He killed only for payment. Besides, if Bruno Schmidt's version of what happened was correct—and von Kelsing had corroborated it—both men had been on the premises while Ilse, behind closed doors, slit her own throat. From casually observing the two men in the weeks that followed, it was clear to Reiser that Schmidt blamed himself for what happened. "Why did I leave her in her bath?" he kept repeating out loud. Von Kelsing, on the other hand, when asked for the lowdown on what really happened, had maintained that he really did not know. His version of the tragic event was that he had gone to Schmidt's suite, assuming he would be there alone. He had assumed that Ilse de Brock, being Schmidt's secretary, had a room of her own and a bath of her own. He insisted he had not known that while he was in the outer room talking with Bruno Schmidt, Ilse was in the bath.

The story had never washed with Reiser. Bruno Schmidt, moreover, had a long history of making excuses for his secretary. His grief at her death was, to say the least, immoderate. In the first few weeks of her death, it was as if a member of his own family had died. As soon as he arrived back in West Germany, Schmidt had escaped to his country retreat near Hinterzarten in the Black Forest and unplugged his phone.

Von Kelsing, on the other hand, at first showed no emotion. He acted as though one of his several thousand employees had met with an unfortunate accident: unfortunate, but no reason for him to unravel. After a couple of weeks, however, a strange phenomenon began to make itself known. Von Kelsing was observed, at least once a day, breaking into high-pitched giggles. His noises sounded like a laughing-gas attack. Shortly thereafter, the reported affair with the new company psychologist, Marlena Kupitsky, began. The company executives, seeing them cuddling in public, were amazed. Some even expressed shock at the specter of the puritanical mogul, usually so disdainful of what he called "Mediterranean peasant behavior," acting like a lovesick adolescent. Von Kelsing had never

fooled around. His idea of an outside sexual partner had always been the highest-priced call girl in
Munich or, better yet, Hamburg. His favorites had
always been sloe-eyed Eurasians, preferably teenagers with high, tight asses and pointed tits. Never
a Ph.D. blonde in her early forties. Unheard of.
Yet, there it was. Then came the prolonged
depressions, the calling in sick, the von Kelsing
servants' reports of the man's loud outbursts of
weeping. Now here he was sitting on the floor of
his office, bleary-eyed. Reiser, for one, was convinced that von Kelsing had had something to do
with Ilse's death. The man's behavior was frankly
bizarre; bizarre was the one word one would have
never associated with Werner von Kelsing.

Reiser, for the first time in his life, was unable
to properly focus his thoughts. He was unwilling
to deal with Werner while the ever-present psychologist Dr. Kupitsky stood guard. Without saying
another word, he turned on his heels and literally
fled the premises. He needed time to think. Von
Kelsing–Schmidt was not the primary concern. He
was strictly Schiller Pharmaceuticals. He didn't
know a Maxim machine gun from a Mauser and
could have cared less. Still, he did care about his
friend. He cared about the man's mental health,
such as it was. He cared about the triumvirate.
Why he cared he did not know. He just knew that
if he could not care about his two best friends,
that he himself would die. He had no other attachments to the world. Everyone else he loved was
gone. Gone or dead or moved away, unknown: the

children he had never seen, the men and women he had slept with and never loved, the civilians he had bombed in the war, the enemy soldiers he had shot, the Jews he had gassed. Gone. Even the latest enemy, Ali Ozker, gone.

The triumvirate. It had a talent for death, those three. Von Kelsing. Reiser. Schmidt. Only they were still alive. Only they. Reiser promised himself that he would not let them go, too. Not they.

Chapter Eighteen

Gunther Herrmann arrived at Dulles International Airport, passport intact. No one was really expecting him. Certainly not the man known as Savage.

Why would anyone have looked at Gunther Herrmann twice? Many Germans visited D.C. all the time. Tourists. Diplomats. Businessmen. Germans, being a particularly prosperous and a singularly handsome people, were welcome everywhere in the United States. Indeed, in many ways, Germans seemed to typify the qualities that Americans most prized in themselves. It was disheartening for many Americans to consider that the two similar peoples had fought each other, not once, but twice in the first half of the twentieth century.

Through von Kelsing's contacts at the Germany Embassy, "Mr. Whitney's" answering-service account had been traced to the farm of a Charles Woodgate in Frederick, Maryland. Little information could be found about Woodgate except that he was an uncle of a man named Paul Savage. Nothing else was known. Von Kelsing's private investigators could find nothing about either the life or the death of the man.

Herrmann's orders were to contact Richard Dartley in the guise of hiring him. Herrmann was instructed to ask for Dartley's gunman, a man named Paul Savage. When Savage showed his face, Herrmann was to shoot him with a .357 Magnum he'd bought in D.C. Once he'd killed Savage, Herrmann was instructed to drop the Magnum in the Potomac River from Chain Bridge in the early A.M. and immediately leave for Frankfurt on the next available plane. He was also instructed to kill Savage in such a way that the body would not be discovered for at least a week. If he was unable to find Savage, he was to contact Dartley, tell him he had been instructed to hand Savage the money in person. If Charles Woodgate got in the way, Herrmann was to kill him too.

Von Kelsing told Herrmann that Woodgate had been a prosecutor at the Nuremberg Trials. This was untrue, but he figured that Herrmann would never check. This was true, too. The young metalworker was so convinced of his destiny, he was almost desperate to find a way to serve the Fatherland. With this assignment, he considered himself among the most privileged men alive.

Herrmann rented a Hertz coupe, took the Belt way to the Frederick exit, and once he arrived in town began asking questions.

He was confused. Richard Dartley and Paul Savage were two men who were hard to track down. Still, it seemed there was one strong lead. It seemed that Charles Woodgate had a nephew. People spoke of him as Richard Woodgate. People remembered him visiting his uncle when he was young. "When who was young?" Herrmann had asked. "The nephew. The nephew was young." Richard Woodgate's father, he discovered, had worked for the government. The father had been murdered in Argentina—Hadn't Mr. Herrmann heard about that?

At the Texaco station, he asked directions to the Woodgate Farm. In his broken English he explained that he was a cousin from Germany. The gas-station manager, a burly southerner with a potbelly, a veteran of the Second World War, expressed surprise that Charley Woodgate had German blood. "My mother, she was half English," lied Herrmann. "We are actually only second cousins, but our mothers, they are close." That seemed to satisfy the southerner, who, being southern, had insatiable curiosity about family relations. Directions handed out, Herrmann headed for the second traffic light. There he would turn left and continue on three miles up Blair Road until he saw a mailbox that read "C. Woodgate."

As for Charles Woodgate, he told Herrmann he knew nothing.

"Pardon me, sir, I am looking for Richard Dartley or Paul Savage."

"I am not sure I know them," Woodgate had replied.

"I have a payment for Mr. Dartley," Herrmann insisted.

"A payment for what?"

"I cannot say. It is a private matter. I have come from Germany for my employers. Mr. Dartley, he do a job for them."

Woodgate was clearly not convinced.

"I'll get a message to Mr. Dartley," he said.

"Where would Mr. Dartley be?" asked the German.

Woodgate smelled trouble. The visitor was too insistent. His rawboned look was another thing. Woodgate had seen it before. The eyes were dead, the features muscle-bound. Woodgate could sense the singular energy emanating from the man, a suppressed energy, something violent in him forcibly held in control by an act of the will. He seemed more like an executioner than a messenger. He threatened to explode at any given time.

Woodgate explained to the German that occasionally Dartley was in touch with some people he knew in Washington. He could leave a message for him. He couldn't guarantee a thing. He was sorry; that was the best he could do.

Herrmann's face froze. He ordered Woodgate to leave a message for Dartley saying he'd meet him at the farm in three days. Woodgate could see the man was confused. The German wasn't sure what he wanted to do. His youth and inexperience were all too evident, for the time being at least.

When the visitor had left the front porch and driven off the property, Woodgate closed and locked the front door as well as the screen door. He shut all the windows in his house. It was 97°, stifling; still, he could not chance being overheard. For all he knew, his visitor could have doubled back on the back road; he might be listening under a window.

Dartley was in his workroom under the old horse barn. Woodgate called his nephew there.

"There's a visitor. A German. He doesn't know whether he's looking for Dartley or Savage. I told him I'd get a message to Dartley."

"What kind of message?"

"He wants Dartley to meet him here in three days. There's something about him, Dickie. I'd say he's a gunman."

"Where is he now?" asked Dartley.

"I don't know. I watched him drive off the property, but I closed all the windows just in case he's under one of them."

"Good."

"Listen, Dickie," continued the older man, "I won't go near the barn. If you hear someone trying to get downstairs, you can be sure it won't be me."

* * *

It was in Frederick two days later, when Gunther Herrmann was screwing Donna McCarron, that he found out about Dartley's secret room under the old horse barn. Dartley, like a fool, had screwed her once himself. Worse, he'd let her fall in love with him. Only then had he decided what he should have known in the first place: that she was dangerous. Donna McCarron was too curious. She was too ready to tell the world everything she knew. In short, she talked too much. Like most country girls infatuated with a man who exudes power...or sophistication—she wasn't sure which —she took Dartley's rejection hard. One minute she hated him because she considered him no better than she; the next minute she would do anything for a reconciliation. Dartley in the very beginning had decided that he must restrict his sexual affairs to women who had never even heard of Frederick, Maryland. Now, unbeknownst to him, Donna MacCarron, a woman scorned, was in predictable fashion staking the place out.

After only one day, she discovered more than she had expected. From behind a pile of brush she watched as Dartley disappeared into the horse barn. She was already well aware that the horse barn contained not a single horse; after an agonizing wait of an hour, she summoned the courage to peek into the barn. She saw nothing. Now she was hooked. She knew she was onto something, but she didn't know what. She hid out, waiting for Dartley to appear. After another hour, she watched in amazement as the floor of the horse barn parted and an hydraulic lift brought Dartley to the surface. Now, insatiably curious to know the secrets of the barn, she waited until he'd gone before she began poking around. She pressed knobs, nails, loose floorboards; she made contact with everything until she finally found the control box. It didn't take long for her to summon the hydraulic lift.

Dartley was no fool. Before Donna McCarron was able to put one foot to the lift, he was there beside her. Her pressing the lift button had triggered an alarm in the Woodgate house. It was Dartley's one precaution against strangers' entering his workroom.

"What do you want?" he had asked.

"You're hiding something," she said.

"It's my workroom," he replied. "Do you want to see it?"

He decided he'd better show it to her rather than have her return later with her uncle, the police chief, and a search warrant. Donna was likely to imagine he was harboring the FBI's Ten Most Wanted criminals or in the process of making his own A-bomb. As it so happened, he had merely been threading the barrel of a Remington Model 700 to receive a silencer. This procedure was against the law, but as a precaution Dartley had locked the gun in his wall safe. Except for the various power tools and cutting machines, the workroom was bare. Donna McCarron was clearly disappointed.

"What do you do down here?" she had asked. "Carve up girls?"

"I like an airtight workroom," he had replied angrily. "I have tools down here that aren't likely to be stolen or borrowed. Dust and rain and bird droppings and little kids and little girls"—he looked hard at her when he said that—"aren't likely to sneak in here and wreck the place. Now, have you seen enough?"

"I know that's not all you do," she said, looking at him with shining eyes like a doe in heat.

If Dartley had thought he could get away with it, he would have strangled her right then and there. The next day he was sorry he had shown her the underground room. He knew that if she was ever in a position to cause trouble for him, she would. It took her five years.

"What do you know about this man Dartley?" Gunther Herrmann asked Donna McCarron.

"Dartley?" she repeated. This wasn't the first time she had heard a stranger refer to Richard Woodgate as Richard Dartley. Sometimes she wondered if Charles Woodgate had two nephews.

"What does Dartley do?" she asked.

"He plays with guns," joked Herrmann. "Just like me."

"All I know is old man Woodgate has one nephew. He's in his late thirties," Donna replied, adding, "He's not in town all that much. He thinks he's God's gift to women, and he works in a workroom in the basement. Maybe Richie has another name, I don't know."

Then the light dawned.

"Wait a minute," she said. "He once told me his mother's name was Dartley. They were supposed to be a famous family; they came over on the Mayflower or something."

"The Mayflower?" asked the German, not understanding the reference.

"The la-dee-da," she replied. He didn't understand that either.

Then she remembered: the summer they first slept together, he'd just found out that he was adopted and that his birth name was Paul Savage.

"Gunther," she whispered, half in love with the danger she was creating, "I just realized. Richard Woodgate and Richard Dartley and Paul Savage are probably all the same man."

"The same man? Ja?"

"Ja," she answered. In that moment she wished Richard Dartley dead. They had not touched in thirteen years. In all that time, she had hated him; longed for him; prayed for his death; prayed for his glory; prayed that no matter what happened, her name would be engraved on his brain.

Within five minutes, Gunther Herrmann was gone from her side. He took his .357 Magnum with him. Then it struck her. How could she have missed the gun? Herrmann had told her he worked for the NATO special forces. "Is that why you're looking for Richard Dartley?" she had asked, not really understanding. Richie was always in Europe; Charley Woodgate had always said as much. She had assumed he worked with NATO, with somebody's special forces. Something like that. But, of course, she knew nothing. It was all guesswork. And now a gunman was after the man she loved.

Donna dialed the Woodgate farm: 553:5263. She hadn't dialed the number in years; she knew it as well as her own birthday.

Dartley answered.

"Richie?"

"Who is this?" he asked.

"Richie, don't hang up. It's me; it's an emergency. This German, his name is Gunther, he's got this gun. I think he's coming out there. It's my fault. I finally figured out you and Richard Dartley and Paul Savage were the same person."

There was a pause. How could there not be?

"Donna?" he asked.

Donna.

He'd said it. He knew her voice. That made thirteen years worth waiting for. Now she knew. He really was in love with her, after all.

"Oh Richie!" she blurted out in tears. "I don't really want you dead. I just thought I did 'cause you never pay any attention to me!"

"When did this man, this Gunther, leave you?" he asked.

"He just left. Five minutes ago. He said he's with some kind of NATO special forces."

"What else did he say?"

"I don't know, Richie. I told him about your workroom in the barn. We fucked. I couldn't help it, I've been so lonely. He was trying to figure out who was Woodgate, who was Dartley, who was

Savage; and I remembered your mother was Dartley. You told me your mother's name was Dartley but your real name was Savage."

"Listen, Donna," Dartley said as slowly and deliberately as possible, "what you know could cause not only my death but the deaths of many women and children. I use those names in my work. I work for a secret agency in the United States Government. I'm not allowed to tell you anything else. I'm not even supposed to say I work for the government. Do you understand?"

"Yes, yes," she replied, eating up every syllable of his that she could—because it was *him* and he was talking to *her*.

"Enemies of the United States who learn my secrets will ultimately cause the deaths of many innocent people."

"Yes, yes," she replied. "Yes."

"Donna, I love you," he lied. "I have to go." With that, he hung up.

Again, Dartley wished there were some way he could eliminate Donna McCarron and dispose of her body, but at the moment he was at a loss. Thinking of Donna, though, he had to laugh. There was absolutely nothing he could do about her except kill her, and he couldn't kill her. He'd have to live with her. Thinking about her would at least serve to keep him on his toes. The very thought of her would serve to remind him that somewhere out there lurked active forces of destruction.

He reached the barn door less than five minutes

before Gunther Herrmann reached his uncle's driveway. By the time Herrmann had parked in front of the barn, Dartley was downstairs waiting for him. For all his instincts about his own survival, he had mixed feelings about Herrmann. The man was so obviously stupid that he hated to kill him. Even Donna McCarron had known enough to stake out the place. Even she had had the brains to wait until he appeared. Not Herr Gunther. He could not wait. The Reich was invincible. He pressed the right button. The alarm in the house went off. Woodgate had been warned in advance and told to stay in the house.

The hydraulic lift appeared. Below it was the well-lit workroom.

"Richard Dartley?" Herrmann called out, his .357 in his right hand.

"Who is it?" Dartley called back.

"Are you Richard Dartley?" shouted the German a second time.

"Come down, come down," called out Dartley as if he were inviting a neighbor down for a beer. Herrmann folded his arms across his chest in such a way that the Magnum was hidden. He stepped into the hydraulic lift; his weight activated its automatic descent.

Halfway down, Dartley stopped it.

Startled, the German, who could see the American without any trouble, looked Dartley straight in the eye. "Are you Richard Dartley?" he asked him a third time.

"Yes, I am," replied Dartley. "Are you Gunther Herrmann?"

The German's eyes widened. He could not believe his ears. How did Dartley know his name? Who was this man?

They were alone, that much was clear. Unbeknownst to the master of the workroom, the visitor had a gun in hand. Why wait?

"I have come with half a million dollars from von Kelsing," the visitor announced, intending to throw Dartley off guard.

"You have the cash?" Dartley asked.

"Yes," replied the German.

"Throw it down," ordered Dartley.

Now was Herrmann's big chance. He uncrossed his arms and pointed the gun at Dartley's head.

He cocked the firing pin.

The moment of truth arrived. Dartley was ready for him.

The world's most notorious assassin had no cute assistant, pearl-handled revolver in hand, hiding in the shadows. In keeping Donna McCarron out of his life, he had at least prevented that. He also had no hidden guns, no electronic circuitry, no special buttons or levers hidden in the floor. Still, he was prepared. He knew exactly what he was doing. Even though it was true he spent most of his career stalking human prey, as the last of the great white hunters, he was still sometimes smart enough to lure a victim into his web. If the gunman's hand was on the trigger of the .357 Magnum, Dartley's was on the power switch. The split second before Gunther Herrmann fired, Dartley put out the lights and ducked. With a burst of sparks and a loud blast, the Magnum fired. Still in the dark, Dartley pressed another button. The elevator shot up to the floor of the barn and in that same instant reversed itself and dropped like a stone to the workroom floor. Gunther Herrman had not weathered the descent; he lay groaning on the floor.

As to what happened next, there were no gimmicks and no surprises. It was simply human communication at its most direct and violent. Without any weapons to speak of, only his strong work boots. Dartley walked over to Gunther Herrmann. He jumped up and down on the man's head as if he were trying to smash a coconut. Mostly he used his heels. He came down hard with all his weight. After smashing his head several times, he kicked in the man's face. Within five minutes, Herrmann's skull was a fibrous mass of bloody pulp.

In a particular cupboard in the back of his workroom, Dartley stored body bags. They were biodegradable. Once buried in the soil, once in contact with moisture from both the surrounding earth and the corpse itself, the bags began to decompose, releasing a chemical that aided in the breakdown of bone and muscle and hair. Six months after burial, virtually nothing remained of either the corpse or the bag.

Less than three hours later, by the time Charley Woodgate shoveled the last spadeful of earth over the grave of Gunther Herrmann, Richard Dartley was over the Atlantic. This time he was lucky. This time he'd found a direct flight to Düsseldorf.

Chapter Nineteen

He'd come in as Anthony Weber from Saint Louis, an alias he'd used several times. The real Anthony Weber, three months older than Dartley, had died in a crib accident when he was two and a half. Dartley had checked the Saint Louis papers. The child had choked on a bottle cap. On his passport application, where it said "occupation," he had written "sales representative." If anyone asked him what company he worked for, he usually answered, "I'm a hardware free-lancer. Right now I'm working for New Britain Hardware. I'm scouting German tools." Dartley had enough of a sustaining interest in gadgets to keep up on the latest developments in hardware. He was usually way ahead of his questioners.

Düsseldorf was grey. It was early August. Like everywhere else, people were on vacation. Still, there were crowds at the airport. The Germans, traditionally a nation of travelers, loved to gather at the airports and watch the planes take off and land. Still, the crowds made Dartley nervous.

Dartley made himself deliberately inconspicuous. He wore a gray gabardine suit, a white shirt, a navy blue tie and a London Fog raincoat. The name "Weber" was perfect. As a German-American in his ancestral homeland, Dartley would be viewed with more warmth than that accorded the average tourist.

Once downtown, Dartley booked a room at the Adler, a small, third-class student hotel on Bahnstrasse. Two streets over was a back alley without a name. Four restaurants backed onto the alley. Garbage trucks were the only real traffic there. To get out, they had to back up. Otherwise, the alley seemed useless. It was too narrow for regular parking; for all practical purposes, it was a cul-de-sac. It ended at the back wall of a medical supply house.

Still, to those who were better informed, the alley could be a fascinating place. It was the home of a gunsmith, a Frenchman who had once collaborated with the Nazis. He was Herr Alphonse Bertin, with the emphasis on the first syllable instead of on the Gallic second. As soon as he had checked into the hotel, Dartley went directly to the nameless alleyway to Herr Bertin.

The entrance to the gunsmith's residence was three steps down. It was a metal door without an identifying name; it seemed more like an exit door. Its peephole was the only reassurance of a human presence within.

Dartley knocked. After a few minutes, a voice on the other side of the door replied, "Ja?"

Dartley answered, "My name is Anthony Weber. Are you Herr Bertin?"

The door opened an inch. "Ja?"

"I need a gun," Dartley said in English, then repeated his request in French and German.

"What kind of a gun?" whispered Bertin in heavily accented English, opening the door still more.

Dartley entered furtively. He did not wish to be overhead discussing guns in the alleyway. As in all large cities, the citizens of Düsseldorf listened attentively to every sound. Inside was a long, dimly lit hallway.

"Follow me," ordered Bertin. In the light, Bertin looked exactly right for his surroundings. He was small and swarthy, a Mediterranean Frenchman from an impoverished background. His face was a dark landscape of shadows and depressions. He held his hands close to his body. When he gesticulated, his movements were constricted and apologetic. He led Dartley past three successive steel doors, each one exactly like the entrance door.

The fourth door was the last of the series. Bertin opened it with one particular key on a key ring that held at least fifty keys. Inside was a small room, about eight feet by six, lined with metal shelves containing metal boxes. In the middle of the room was his work platform with drawers filled with machine parts. The machine on the table was a precision instrument with attachments for cutting, shaping and polishing metal.

"I do everything with metal except smelt steel," said Bertin. "What kind of a gun do you want?"

"There's no time to make one," replied Dartley. "I need your best sniper rifle with a silencer."

"I see," said the gunsmith.

"I will be back for the rifle in the morning," said Dartley.

"Tomorrow morning?" asked Herr Bertin, taken aback.

"That gives you almost a full day to thread the muzzle and remove the serial number. Is there a problem?"

"There are no other specifications?"

"I couldn't afford to bring a gun like that through Customs," Dartley went on. "They'd assume I was coming to kill the Prime Minister. You know how the Germans are—a civilized people. The truth is, I've come to kill boar."

"Boar?"

"You said it, pal. I want a German automatic with a silencer, and I want the serial number removed."

"I can give you a Heckler and Koch V.P. Seventy," said Herr Bertin. "But I don't understand. Why do you need a silencer for killing boar?"

"I don't want to frighten the other boar. You know how pigs are," said Dartley. "You kill one and the rest go crazy." He didn't want to discuss his plans with this freak. He resented any questioning at all.

"And why do you want the serial number removed?" was the man's next question.

"Why do you want to know?" asked Dartley.

"I have responsibilities," replied the onetime Frenchman.

"Responsibilities?" echoed Dartley. "Responsibilities?"

"The police want to know."

"So does Simon Wiesenthal," replied the American.

"Simon Wiesenthal? The Nazi hunter? The Jew?" asked Herr Bertin, ashen at the mention of the name of the man who was still hunting down key Nazi criminals more than a generation after they escaped punishment. "What are you saying?" he rasped in the isolated glow of the one fluorescent light. With his beady black eyes and his underslung jaw he seemed ratlike. Appropriate, Dartley thought.

"There were three thousand French Jews in Lyons whom you put on the express train to Germany. In case you've forgotten."

"That is not true," whined the gunsmith.

Dartley had gotten his information from Malleson, who was stationed in Lyons during the war. Bertin's name had been Vigneau then. With his heavy French accent, he dared not assume a completely German identity after the war. Malleson knew of the name-change from a friend in French intelligence. In a sense, Bertin was correct about his past; it was unlikely that Wiesenthal would track him down. He had been second or third in command. His signature had graced—or disgraced— no deportation orders for Jews. Still, the citizens of Lyons knew of his extreme and vicious anti-Semitism. They knew how many families he had informed on. If he lacked the authority to implement the Nazi death drive, he was nonetheless in his own quiet way a diabolical force.

"Come tomorrow," he said wearily. "A Heckler and Koch V.P. Seventy will cost you two hundred and fifty deutsche marks. A hundred dollars." The price seemed low. Dartley chose not to argue about it. All he wanted was a gun.

Once more the intoxication of danger had overtaken him. In truth, it was more than danger, it was recklessness; he found himself addicted to it. Some psychologists would have likened it to drug addiction. To Dartley it was more like gambling. The possibility of loss was great, almost certain. Intellectually, he knew the day would come, a day as sure as death, when he'd be caught. He never worried about the actual kill. Killing von Kelsing would be easy enough. And Schmidt too, if he didn't hand over the cash immediately. Reiser might be more difficult; somehow Reiser seemed like an essential survivor, with his reliance on his brain rather than on some mystical notion of luck or fate. Dartley couldn't pinpoint it. Perhaps it was the facial scars; the grotesqueness of the man's appearance suggested a man with deeper reasons for hanging on than merely looking good.

The real problem was always the same: getting out without being caught. Even then, escape was not so simple; a thousand young Gunther Herrmanns waited to be asked to pursue and destroy a man such as him. Youth, almost be definition, rejected boundaries, rejected even the suggestion of failure. So it was that the human race restored itself.

Dartley, for the first time, had begun having premonitions of early death. Death by retaliation, no doubt. Logistically it made the most sense. At some point, probably when his reflexes were beginning to lose their automatic elasticity, he would slip up. His mistake might very well be macabre. He might, for instance, forget to load his gun, a situation he would have roared with laughter about not so many years before.

At some point he figured he'd slip and leave a few clues behind. Impossible? "To err is human" said the sage. Dartley increasingly had to psyche himself before killing anyone. The older he got, the more a dark power, once unknown to him, rose up from the innermost rescesses of his brain to take revenge for the deaths he had caused. Reasoning alone would not still the force of that quiet authority that he knew was intent on destroying him. And so, the older he got, the greater became the stakes.

He could easily have killed the gunsmith with the old standbys: the poisoned aspirin, the whiff of prussic acid, the KGB umbrella tip. He was also adept at what is commonly called "the accident in the home," such as hiding until the person, the victim, was alone, then pushing him headfirst down a steep flight of stairs. Once Dartley had had to drop a man—the man was a Pakistani heroin dealer and a devout Muslim—from the top of a minaret, where, at gunpoint, he forced him to write what amounted to a suicide note. After the sun was down and the recorded message in the minaret tower had proclaimed that there was no god but Allah and Mohammed was his prophet, Dartley lifted the man by his legs and neck and tossed him off. The combination of dusk, recorded noise and the faithful being on their knees and facing the ground provided a good cover. Not perfect, but good. By the time the heroin dealer was discovered dead at daybreak, Dartley was aloft in an Air India turbo jet.

A rifle had to be the worst possible way to kill von Kelsing, yet Dartley ached to pull the trigger right in the industrialist's face. His ache became an obsession. Yet, as happened so many times, the day before the prospective death, he was still ignorant of how exactly he would kill him.

In his mind Dartley reviewed the givens. His return passport and his identity papers were in order. For his trip home to Washington, he would be a low-level government accounting clerk, Harold C. Mount of Hyattsville, Maryland. His clothes—a winter-weight black suit and a burgundy Lacoste sports short and a blue porkpie hat—would proclaim to the world that he was a Middle American, of the people and by the people. Still, Dartley was not one for caricatures. If the truth must be known, Harold C. Mount would be an unhappy man. He would drag his feet when he walked, head down; he would have nothing to declare. He would wear thick eyeglasses and sport an overgrown mustache. The Heckler Koch sniper rifle, once used, could be discarded in the Rhine. Dartley seriously considered leaving from Frankfurt: he did not wish to be recognized by the same customs officials who had been so friendly to him when he entered the country. Weighing the balance, he decided to leave in disguise from Düsseldorf; it was more important for him to be out of the country immediately. But if, in fact, he departed from Frankfurt, he risked running into a cordon of West German police carefully checking all American males in their thirties.

Such considerations were mere rationalization. Above all, the danger of being caught was the greatest lure. The danger motivated him and drove him on.

First, the phone calls. Malleson had given him the telephone numbers of all the men. Von Kelsing. Schmidt. Reiser. The home phones. The unlisted phones. The phones in bathrooms and dressing rooms. The phone in the duck blind on Lake Constance. The phone in the locker room at the Heidelberg Club, the phone in von Kelsing's shooting gallery.

"Hello, this is Dr. Karras. I am the American doctor who's been working with Dr. Sauter on Mrs. von Kelsing. Frau von Kelsing. I must speak to Herr von Kelsing. Immediately. You see, his wife... I'm sorry I'm not free to discuss the case."

Von Kelsing's private secretary put her hand over the receiver.

"Herr von Kelsing, this man says he is an American doctor working with Dr. Sauter. He says it's urgent. Something about Frau von Kelsing."

Von Kelsing grew red. "I never authorized an American doctor. Get me Dr. Sauter." He picked up the phone. "Hello. Who is this? Dr. Sauter?"

"This is your friend with the gun, Mr. von Kelsing. I believe we met somewhere in West Virginia. I believe I told you if you didn't pay your debts you'd be sorry you hired me."

There was a pause. There was always a pause when rich men who didn't pay their bills were confronted by their creditors. To Dartley it was the same old story. Some people thought the world owed them a living.

In his office, von Kelsing, alone, experienced the full force of his anger for the first time in his life. Perhaps it had been the truth-telling sessions with Marlena Kupitsky. Gradually he had begun to feel rage. What he had assumed was his anger in the past had been cantankerousness. He had never felt his real anger before, especially his anger at the Americans for stopping him, stopping the Fatherland, destroying der Führer and stealing the best German scientists. The best. Werner von Braun.

And the films...the constant documentaries about the Germans, the German guilt, the "good Germans," the so-called Germans who, believe it or not, had said, they "didn't know" about the concentration camps. After World War One, the French had humiliated the Reich the first time—those slimy French, almost as bad as the Jews.... Worse, worse than the Jews.

Now the Americans, dividing his country, blaming it on the Russians. Goddamn Roosevelt. Von Kelsing would have his revenge, he decided. Something. He didn't know what. Not yet. A bomb to destroy New York. A guided missile that would fly below the radar detection line to destroy Washington, D.C. It would fly low through southern Maryland, up the Chesapeake, up the Potomac, through southwest Washington, through the slums and hovels of the *schwarzers*, right to the Capitol itself. A megaton bomb. Yes, he would destroy the American President, the American Congress, the Pentagon, the CIA. The whole world hated the CIA. It typified the Americans. Bloodsucking hypocrites who robbed and stole in the name of Jesus Christ and the will of the citizens.

A river of rage erupted at the base of von Kelsing's spine and spread like liquid fire up his spinal cord. His brain received the fire. All hope of intelligence vanished. Subtlety was now unknown. His brain was white, his gray matter glowing. Von Kelsing was the avenging God. He was Jehovah. He was the Father. There was no difference, no distinction between the two.

"I will destroy you," he whispered, his voice like lava, like molten rock. "I will destroy you." When he said it, he believed he would. When he hung up, he felt invincible. Nothing would touch him, Nothing ever had.

The next call was to Bruno Schmidt. Dartley thought of Schmidt as a grieving widower. Still, even funeral directors must be paid. Schmidt was sitting at his desk when the phone rang. He had been looking out the window, feeling nothing, thinking of nothing. He would soon be 63. He had never worked, not really. Once it had all been handed to him. Now it had all been taken away. The inner bathroom with the sunken tub had long been locked. He had not been inside it since West Virginia. When he returned from America he had simply locked the door and put it out of his mind.

It. Everything.

When the phone rang, his secretary was out to lunch. She had been gone for over two hours. He no longer cared. He could do all his work by rote in an hour and a half a day. When it came to adding figures and checking reports, he was an automaton. For the rest of the day he usually looked out the window.

The window was all he had.

"Hello?" he said.

"I just called Herr von Kelsing," said the voice. "He hung up on me."

"Who is this?" asked Schmidt, recognizing the American voice. A voice of male authority, rare for the times. "Who is this, General McAdams?" The voice was similar to that of the American general at Vogelweh. The man with the lovely Scottish wife, Jennifer.

"General McAdams, how is your lovely Jennifer?" Schmidt asked in a dead voice.

"This is Mr. Savage. From West Virginia. Von Kelsing won't pay me what he owes me. I told you the price you'd pay, didn't I?"

"Wait!" called back Schmidt. "Perhaps we should have dinner and talk."

"There's nothing to talk about."

"We can always negotiate. Surely—"

"There's nothing to negotiate. We already did that, didn't we?" answered the American. "You owe me half a million dollars, or else."

"What did von Kelsing say?"

"I told you. He hung up on me. Are you going to hang up on me, too?"

"No, no, I never hang up," pleaded Schmidt. "I'm not that kind of a person."

"Do you intend to pay me?" asked Dartley, growing impatient.

"When have I never paid?" replied Schmidt. "I thought von Kelsing paid. He said you didn't do the job. He said it was an accident. He said the driver of the car, the Mercedes, was on drugs." Schmidt ran his thoughts together. He really didn't want to talk about dead Turks. Now was his chance. "Mr. Savage," he blurted out, "tell me the truth. Did you murder my Ilse because she was KGB?"

"I?" asked Dartley, amazed at the question. "Did I kill Ilse de Brock? Oh no you don't, pal. De Brock might have been KGB, but that was her business. I never kill for free. I only kill when I'm paid to kill; and when I'm not paid, I'm just your average good ol' boy, do I make myself clear?"

Bruno Schmidt, now that he had raised the question of Ilse de Brock, was so distracted by memories and demons he could not think clearly. "What?" he asked. "I'm sorry, Herr Savage. I'm sure von Kelsing will arrange everything. You don't have to worry about money." With that, he hung up as if the phone call and their mutual business had naturally terminated.

Now it was Dartley's turn to feel rage. Schmidt's approach had been, "the check is in the mail, you peon. Don't worry, don't you worry about money. It will get there next month or next year. Civilized men don't worry about money. Money will always come. Civilized men always pay their bills. Why would you be so rude as to question us? Didn't we hire you? Weren't you working for us?"

Dartley went to his bed at the Hotel Adler, but he couldn't sleep. His brain was too full of details about the following day. He saw it before him laid out like a movie, one scene following another. He saw it all; the close-ups of his hand, the trigger finger, the Heckler & Koch VP 70. He saw von Kelsing, Reiser, Schmidt. He saw the expressions on their faces when he made his appearance. He heard the dialogue. In imagining these scenes, he made nothing up. It all came to him from somewhere deep within him where there were voices. As for his escape from Germany, he would take everything with him in his satchel: both passports, both sets of papers. He would wear his departure clothes to his day's business. All he had to do afterward was put on the mustache and glasses. As simple as Groucho Marx. Life was just a musical comedy, as every good American knows. That, or a Western. No, this was definitely Groucho Marx. Dartley laughed. The next day was going to be wonderful.

The next morning he hated the alarm clock. It read 5:45A.M. Too much time till he visited Herr Bertin.

Reiser. He'd forgotten to phone Reiser. Now was the time. He'd be home in bed. Clearly, undoubtedly, the three men would have talked the night before.

It was clear to Dartley now. The reasonableness of his present behavior. He had not come to exact revenge. His only reason for being in Germany, really, was to retrieve his money. He was a businessman. He wanted his five hundred thou. Why not? The Mercedes alone had cost him well over a hundred thousand. His travel. Malleson. The passports and identity papers brought the sum-total close to two hundred thousand dollars. Too expensive and too dangerous to settle for half a million. He'd killed two KGB agents, too. The Moscow Center, if it ever figured out who he was, would not forget him. Everyone, it seemed, had debts to be paid. Debts and payments. Such was life. Why fight the obvious?

He dialed Reiser at his home. No answer. He let

it ring fifteen times. Finally, a male voice answered, a younger man.

"Herr Reiser?"

"Nein."

"Wo ist Herr Reiser?" Dartley asked, attempting to speak German.

"Herr Reiser ist nicht hier," answered the young male voice.

"Wo ist Herr Reiser?" Dartley repeated, immediately translating, "Where is Mr. Reiser? Who is this?" Dartley hung up.

Where was Willi Reiser? At Von Kelsing's? At Schmidt's?

As it so happened, Reiser was on vacation. It was, after all, August, and he had worked hard at Schiller Pharmaceuticals. He had met a boy in Hamburg, a Swedish boy, 17, with perfect skin and a wonderful mouth. There was something about boys once they reached 19 or 20, Reiser often said to friends of his own persuasion: "Their mouths sour; it ruins everything." He'd taken the boy to Morocco. The boy had never been south of Bonn. On the way back, if they were still speaking, Reiser intended to surprise him with a trip to Rio. The boy would be able to name-drop for the rest of his life. A truly wonderful present, Reiser thought. He'd bought himself an entirely new wardrobe, all white, with white fedora hats and dark glasses. He frightened so many people with his scarred face. Women, to say the least, were not amused at the sight of him. But to some boys, especially the softer, prettier ones, he was, in his deformity, the ultimate male. Reiser was the monster father they had never quite known. He was preeminently worth traveling with.

At nine-thirty. Dartley checked out of the Adler. At ten he rented a VW van. He told the dealer he'd bring it back the following day.

At eleven-thirty Dartley entered the cul-de-sac off Bahnstrasse. Once again he knocked on the metal door. Once again there was a long moment's pause. Once again came the sound of the voice within.

"Ja?"

"Weber," answered Dartley.

Again, after another long pause, the metal door opened a crack. A black eye peered out. Seeing that the caller was indeed the man called Weber, Herr Bertin opened the door and led him in. The underground corridor seemed labyrinthine to him, almost clandestine; although in fact it was neither. On the other hand, its darkness was oppressive. He longed to get the gun and get out.

The Heckler & Koch VP 70 reminded Dartley of himself. It was dark and tough-looking. It was snub-nosed and efficient. It belonged to the city, to desperate men who worked in the dark. It had none of the beauty of a bolt-action rifle, none of the raw fury of a machine gun. It was just what it was, as deadly as hell.

Like all Heckler & Koch products it was meticulously crafted. The magazine in the butt carried the remarkable number of eighteen rounds.

Bertin, according to Dartley's specifications, had threaded the barrel and removed the serial number.

"Here is the silencer," the former Nazi sympathizer said. He demonstrated to Dartley how the black rubber cylinder screwed onto the end of the barrel.

"How do I carry the gun?" asked Dartley.

"Do you want a violin case?" asked Bertin, half joking.

"No, thanks," said Dartley. "I carry everything in my beach bag here," referring to his navy blue canvas satchel with the initials "P.P.A." on the side. He bought the satchel on sale, already monogrammed. To him the initials stood for "Paid Political Assassin." The monogram was one of his many jokes with himself, one way he had of personalizing a grim vocation. "Humor never hurts," was a Dartley motto.

After a brief demonstration where Bertin fired the pistol into what seemed like a horizontal laundry chute chiseled out of concrete, he let Dartley go. As far as he could make out, the Heckler & Koch was not rigged to explode in his face. He was half expecting Bertin to try to kill him to shut him up about the business in Lyons during the war. If the former Frenchman had made one false move, Dartley was prepared to land a karate chop on the side of his neck. A couple of well-aimed kicks at vital spots would then send Herr Monsieur Bertin-Vigneau into the land of make-believe. Nothing like that happened. The gunsmith let him go. Theirs was definitely a relationship of mutual distrust, but by tradition the professional assassin and the gunsmith are symbiotic creatures. One feeds on the other.

Malleson had given him the route to von Kelsing's chateau outside the city. When he first saw it from the front gates, Dartley had to admit the house made most American mansions look like brick shithouses. It was a palace on the scale of an English country seat like Castle Howard or Blenheim Palace, both of which seem more like vast apartment houses. Von Kelsing's estate was no different. The pink granite building blocks of the main house had been cut into squares so perfect that mortar seemed unnecessary. Too perfect, Dartley thought. It invites the wrecker's ball. Human beings can only stand so much symmetry. Our loathing of geometry must have something to do with the shape and texture of our brains.

His first disguise was easy enough. He had applied three layers of bronzer. The color on his face was deep and rich. Then he had donned the black cassock and the Roman collar of a Catholic priest. To that he added a full black beard and dark glasses. With a Spanish accent, Dartley seemed altogether different from the boastful man in English tweeds who had commanded everyone's attention at South Meadow.

At the front door, in Spanish-accented German he said he was a coworker of Arne von Kelsing; that he had just come from Ecuador and that Arne had told him to stop by and say hello to his parents. "Oh, but Frau von Kelsing is in the mountains and Herr von Kelsing is at the factory," he was told. The servants offered to give him directions.

"No, I prefer to wait," he replied.

"But Herr von Kelsing is not expected home till this evening," the butler protested.

"But Arne told me his father comes home for lunch every day," Dartley insisted. "Perhaps if I called him..."

A phone was brought to him. "No, you call," he said to the English butler, Edwards. "Just say my name is Father Juan di Monti. Tell him I have urgent news about his son's injury."

Edwards gasped. "Injury?"

"I cannot stay," Dartley insisted, waving his hands about like a hysteric. "I must leave within the hour; my own mother is dying in Essen. I only came here because when Arne came out of surgery he begged me to see his father."

By now, the servant—who had obviously once had great affection for the little boy named Arne— was beside himself. He reached his employer and in great burst of emotion relayed everything the stranger had said to him.

"Herr von Kelsing wants to speak to you," said Edwards.

"Hello?" said Dartley into the receiver in his well-disguised voice. "I'm sorry, my German is poor. I would come to see you, Herr von Kelsing; but, you see, I received news that my mother is dying in Essen. She is a church-worker there. I cannot waste time. I merely came to your home because Arne told me you always come home for lunch."

"But I never come home for lunch," sputtered von Kelsing.

"Perhaps when the boy was young..." said Dartley, offering a possible explanation.

"Never!" repeated von Kelsing. "I have always eaten in the executive dining room at von Kelsing–Schmidt."

"Perhaps he imagined it. He was always telling me what he wished had happened in his childhood."

"Arne was given everything," insisted von Kelsing.

"Well then, perhaps it was the drugs," replied the man who called himself Father di Monti.

"Drugs?" repeated von Kelsing. "What do you mean, drugs?"

"His illness."

"What illness?"

"I cannot talk about it on the phone. I must see you in person. Some things are so personal they must be said face-to-face, so that you do not form the wrong impression in your mind."

"I will be right there!" von Kelsing thundered and hung up.

Dartley waited in a room with a bleached oak ceiling and framed tapestries of a medieval unicorn hunt. The tapestries looked bleached out, too. He tried to rehearse his story about Arne. He did not want to overdo the melodrama. At first he had thought to say that Arne was in a land-mine explosion and had lost his legs. Then he thought about saying that the young man had suffered a nervous breakdown. By the time von Kelsing pulled up at the porte cochere and came running in to the antechamber with Marlena Kupitsky behind him, Dartley had concocted the perfect story.

When von Kelsing entered the room, Dartley ambled toward him and embraced him like a long-lost brother he had not seen in sixty years.

"My name is Padre—Father di Monti," he announced. "Arne was my dearest friend."

"Was?" asked von Kelsing. Was this visitor ignorant of proper grammar?

"Dear Herr von Kelsing," the visitor continued, "I regret to inform you that your beloved son, Arne von Kelsing, is dead. He was killed by Communist guerrilla troops. Shot in the back. He lived for a week. He was in excruciating pain. We fed him morphine. It was all we could do."

At the word 'morphine' von Kelsing winced.

"Dead...I don't understand 'dead,'" said Marlena Kupitsky. "The Germany ambassador would have called us from Quito."

"The Germany ambassador was out of the country on vacation."

"The acting ambassador."

"No, when it happened, Arne was still conscious. He begged the chargé d'affaires not to call you until after I'd spoken to you myself. He died only yesterday, you see." With that, for a brief moment the priest seemed to lose control. Marlena reached out to comfort him, but he drew back, intent on keeping his composure. He was successful. It was clear to all present that he cared deeply for Arne von Kelsing.

"You see," the priest repeated, with absolute determination not to break down, "Arne died yesterday. Just yesterday."

Von Kelsing's eyes filled with tears. He took a deep breath and looked like a defeated man. It made no difference, he had already given up.

"If you had seen him before he died," Dartley went on, "you would know that it was just as well. Some things are inevitable." He paused just long enough for the news to sink in. "I cannot stay. I must go to Essen immediately. You see, my mother is dying of cancer. She is a church-worker there. This will be the last time I see her."

Dartley had not figured out exactly how this Ecuadorian priest he was pretending to be would have a mother in Essen, a town to the north of Düsseldorf; luckily, no one pressed him for details. They had other things to think about. Von Kelsing was hanging onto Marlena Kupitsky, sobbing. He had been devastated by the news of his son's death. That the father and son had not gotten on only made the situation worse.

"But his mother. How can I tell her?" von Kelsing said. "What will she do? What will she say? Poor Mitzi. Poor Mitzi. This will destroy her."

"Are you Arne's mother?" Dartley asked of Marlena Kupitsky, knowing she could not possibly be the Mitzi that von Kelsing was talking about.

"Oh no," she exclaimed, "I'm just a psychologist. No, Arne's mother is very sick, very sick." At that moment Dr. Kupitsky felt the absurdity of everything. The industrial West. The revolutionary East. The priest. The chateau. What was the point of anything? Everything ended in death. She felt overwhelmed by absolutes that seemed bigger and more terrible than anything the human species could perpetrate on itself. God seemed the cruelest force in the universe.

As they spoke, Mitzi von Kelsing was indeed past understanding or feelings. She sat in her room in Berchtesgaden looking out at the pine trees. If Arne were really dead, the news of his death would not have affected her. She would not have known who he was. In the same way, the events of the next hour, when she was told of them, would make no impression on her.

For half an hour, Father de Monti regaled the sobbing father with stories of his son's adventures in Ecuador. Kupitsky, who remained skeptical, because she distrusted excessive emotions no matter what their source, stroked her employer, soothing him with "There, there, Werner. We have to go through these things." Then, suddenly, the bearded priest spoke up. Dartley was now ready to play his trump card.

"I just remembered," he said to von Kelsing. "Arne told me to take you to the old smokehouse on the other side of the apple orchard. He said he had left a message there written on the inside wall for you and his mother."

"What are we waiting for?" exclaimed von Kelsing.

"Is the smokehouse still locked? I don't know. Should I ask Edwards? Where did he go?"

"I'm sure it's open," answered Dartley. He had to be careful about pushing his luck. Kupitsky would know something was up. He hadn't counted on her. For all her present sorrow, the woman remained extremely cool.

They left the chauteau without telling the staff where they were going. What was the point of that? They were only going to the old smokehouse. Besides, Father di Monti assured them they'd come right back. It was only a message from Arne.

Von Kelsing was not used to traveling in VW vans.

"To think this was called the postwar miracle," he kept saying.

"The miracle was the bug," countered Marlena, referring to the small Volkswagen Beetle so popular all over the world with the postwar generation.

"You'll have to direct me," said Dartley, lying.

Malleson had shown him an exact plan of the house and grounds. He had sent a surveyor there the week before. The man was ostensibly working for the Federal Republic on some kind of landscape commission. There was some talk of Roman baths on the von Kelsing estate, he had explained. The man said he wanted to make a topographical survey. Could he please see floor plans of the house? He wanted to check how the basement was constructed. Von Kelsing, not questioning, referred him to his architect.

Indeed, there had always been rumors of Roman baths in that general area; that much Malleson knew without too much effort.

The plans were delivered. They were exact. Dartley committed everything to memory. The smokehouse, larger than the American southern-plantation version, was almost as large as a small two-bedroom house. The great houses of Europe had been planned to provide meals for hundreds of guests as well as retainers and men working in the fields. Smoked ham and smoked pork snout were staples.

The smokehouse was constructed of precisely cut fieldstone. Its door was open. A better policy than locking it, von Kelsing had once decided. Besides, thieves had never been a problem on his estate. His security was much too well organized.

"Which wall?" asked the industrialist as he entered the cool, dark space.

"The basement wall, the back wall of the basement, I think," said the dark-complexioned priest. "I've got a flashlight in case there's no electricity down there." He carried his satchel with him. It contained his flashlight and other things.

"It's like a morgue," exclaimed Marlena Kupitsky as she stepped inside.

Inside, the rooms were cool. Great curved metal hooks for the meat stuck out of the stone walls; a huge cast-iron brazier stood in the middle of each room.

"These rooms were for the final flavor," explained von Kelsing. "The real smokehouse is downstairs."

The three of them walked carefully down the

dungeonlike stone stairs to the basement. There, behind a heavy wood door, was a large, dark room still smelling of hickory smoke. There were wooden ramps, now closed off, where the logs had been rolled from the woodshed and from the miniature lumber mill affixed to the back of the stone building.

"But where is the message?" asked von Kelsing.

"Here, take my flashlight," said Dartley, taking an electric torch out of his satchel.

"Come here, Marlena," ordered von Kelsing. "I do not see so well these days. Father di Monti, what do you think? Can you see the message?"

"I'll be right there," called out Dartley. He was fishing in his bag as if he were looking for something more important. He was.

The industrialist and his psychologist walked hesitantly toward the far wall of the basement room. Their flashlight cast its soft glow on the ancient stone walls. The room, ironically, had been an icehouse before it was converted to a smokehouse in the late nineteenth century.

Dartley closed the door behind him and took out the Heckler & Koch VP 70.

"Leave open the door!" called out von Kelsing. "It will be easier to see the message!"

Dartley did not believe in deathbed speeches or the melodrama attendant to execution. He worked for the money and the satisfaction of getting the job done. Personal recognition was not the point.

He turned his pistol on the two figures at the far wall of the room.

"I cannot find the message!" cried von Kelsing, half sobbing.

"Here is the message!" cried an exultant Dartley as he shot the two of them, first von Kelsing and then Marlena Kupitsky. When von Kelsing fell to the ground, he dropped his flashlight. Dartley could not see. It took three shots before he hit Kupitsky. She had tried to hide under some wooden shelves, but the shelves were too close together and too close to the ground. She had only the dark to protect her and nowhere to run. The third bullet found her and so did the fourth. The two of them lay moaning with the uncontrollable agony of the nearly dead. Dartley walked over in the direction of the moans, found the flashlight and shot each one in the temple. A trickle of blood ran down from a small red spot above von Kelsing's eye. He had a rush of blood between his lips. Kupitsky had blood in her eyes. The victims of Dartley's revenge were still. Both were silent. Both were growing cold.

There was a large closet off the basement room, just as Malleson's surveyor had said there was. Once, the closet had held the utensils used in smoking meat. Dartley dragged the bodies into the closet and shut the door. He had brought with him three combination locks because the surveyor had told Malleson the smokehouse had no locks. Dartley padlocked both the closet door and the door to the basement.

Within a minute and a half he was back in his VW van traveling up the gravel road past the great house, von Kelsing's imperial chateau, toward the front gate and guardhouse where he would smile at the boy in uniform. His HK was tucked away nicely in his navy blue satchel.

Bruno Schmidt was next. Dartley had to be careful. When von Kelsing did not return for dinner, his servants would begin making phone calls. In time, in very little time, they would go out searching for him. Dartley's exit plane was scheduled for 4:15 from Düsseldorf. Every minute counted. Every minute was a matter of life and death, mostly his own.

The next phase would be the most exciting. He could feel his adrenalin. It was like Vegas: Could he beat the system? He wasn't sure, but he intended to give it his all.

He parked his car in the employee's lot, explained to the attendant that he was a friend of Bruno Schmidt and wanted to surprise him. Being a priest, and a con man at that, he knew how to make himself believed.

As Father di Monti, Dartley rushed into the office of Bruno Schmidt. "I am Father di Monti," he explained to the secretary. "I have just come from Werner von Kelsing. I must see Herr Schmidt immediately. This is a matter of life and death."

"What is this about?"

"Please, please, there is no time. Herr von Kelsing is still on the autobahn. I have just given him the last rites." Dartley's eyes were filled with pain and brimming with tears. He was sweating. He was desperate.

The secretary believed him. She was very religious. She immediately jumped up and rushed into Bruno Schmidt's office. Dartley followed her. Schmidt, in his usual daze before his window, turned around to face the commotion.

"You must come with me immediately, Herr Schmidt, there is no time."

"What?" he exclaimed.

"I have just given Herr von Kelsing the last rites of the Church!"

Dartley cried. "He asked me to bring you to him. Please, Herr Schmidt, my car is downstairs in the employees' parking garage."

"My car is already outside!" cried Schmidt.

"But, but..." Dartley stammered. "I need to use my car anyway. You may as well go with me!"

"Ja, Ja," rejoined Schmidt, checking to see that he had his wallet and keys. Downstairs on Level C, only three cars away in a Peugeot, a young couple were making out in the front seat. Dartley's brain raced.

"Would you mind sitting in the backseat? he asked Schmidt. "My front seat is wet."

"Wet?" exclaimed Schmidt.

"It was an accident," Dartley explained. "I spilled a Heineken. You will ruin your suit."

To get into the backseat, Schmidt had to first squeeze into the narrow space between the VW van and the Fiat parked next to it.

"Sit on the far side," Dartley suggested. "It will be easier for us to talk."

As Schmidt opened the door to the van and climbed into the backseat, Dartley was well aware that the couple in the Peugeot could see everything above waist level. How could they fail to be curious about the bearded priest in the black cassock?

Dartley took out his VI 70 and whispered to Schmidt, "Herr Schmidt, I want you to know something. I am Herr Savage, the man from West Virginia. I spoke to you on the phone a couple of days ago. Herr Schmidt, I want you to know something, I have just shot and killed Herr von Kelsing. I will shoot you too, if you do not do exactly as I say."

"I will get you your money," rasped a terrified Bruno Schmidt.

"Lie down on the backseat with your head over here next to me."

Schmidt did as he was told. Still, he could not prevent himself from whimpering like a child.

"Down!" ordered Dartley. "Put your head down."

Dartley knelt on one knee on the floor of the garage, his head well below the bottom line of the van's window. As soon as Schmidt was lying down, his legs dangling off the end of the seat, he looked up wide-eyed at Dartley.

"Where do you want me to put my hands?" he asked.

Dartley did not wait for an answer. He shot the man right between his eyes. The HK made a popping sound; it made the couple in the Peugeot sit up and peer out their window. Fron his navy blue satchel Dartley extracted a dark brown blanket. He pushed Schmidt's body onto the floor of the backseat, covered it with the blanket and shut the door. It would be days, if not weeks, before anyone searched the back of the van at the airport parking lot.

Dartley drove immediately out of the parking lot past the staring couple. He drove out past the main complex of von Kelsing-Schmidt, waving hello to the security guard at the front gate. So far, none of the personnel at the plant suspected that an entire era, for whatever it was worth, had come to an irrevocable end.

Once out on the highway, Dartley pulled over to the side at the rest area, removed his beard and cassock, stuffed them into a paper bag and put the paper bag into a public trash receptacle. He had packed a damp towel in a plastic bag for washing the bronzer off his face. Except for his suit jacket, which was folded neatly in the bottom of his small two-suiter, he had worn the clothes he needed under the cassock. The glasses and mustache, which matched the passport photo of Anthony Weber, took five minutes to apply. Soon he was off again. It was almost three o'clock. He had one remaining task before picking up the one-way ticket to Dulles International reserved in the name of Anthony Weber.

The Heckler & Koch VP 70.

There was only one place to get rid of a gun—

deep water, the deeper the better. Where else but the Rhine, the deepest, darkest, the fastest large river in Europe. Fate, like God, seems to smile on those who help themselves, he thought. A pistol dropped into the Rhine would never be retrieved. Its deep waters rushed with a fury unlike any river in the world.

Then it struck him—the hubris of dumping a gun in the Rhine at three in the afternoon with pedestrians in full force, policemen, army personnel and security guards everywhere one looked. Even more apparent was the river traffic, especially the coal scows and oil tankers that seemed nonstop and never-ending. What could he do? He only had a half hour before he had to be at the Düsseldorf airport.

Leaving his jacket and tie under the front seat in the van, and taking his navy blue satchel with the HK 95 hidden inside, Dartley parked the van on a small street off Flingerstrasse near City Hall. He locked the van.

He had to be careful. It would be the irony of ironies if thieves broke in and found Herr Schmidt's body on the floor of the backseat under the brown blanket. He assumed he'd be ticketed. He prayed the van would not be towed. He knew he was much too close to City Hall. The Rhine was three blocks away.

Even at a distance, the river was a powerful presence. As he left his van, Dartley could smell the oil from the passing tankers and the bratwurst from the riverside cafes; he could even smell the water-cooled breeze and the cold pungency of the local beer. Germany, like everywhere else, had its own smells. Strong smells. Acrid. Biting. As Dartley drew closer to the river, his heart sank. The entire waterfront had become gentrified. The old sailors' haunts by the Rhine were now chic outdoor cafes with beautifully dressed men and women sipping choice wines, admiring the hustle and bustle of one of the world's busiest rivers.

Dartley saw that he had but one course of action if he wished to dispose of the HK and make his plane to Dulles. First, he checked to see that his passport, ID and wallet were secure in his buttoned back pocket. Next, he took out his camera from his bag and put it around his neck. Then, like a Kodak-happy American tourist, he began taking pictures both of the Rhine itself and of the river-side cages. By design, he kept backing up toward the river as he went. When he got to the guardrail he sat on it, still snapping away. A policeman—he expected one would show up—approached him to order him off the rail. Dartley grinned at the man, pretending that he, not knowing the language, assumed that the officer was being especially friendly and in no sense enforcing the law. The policeman, to be expected, did not speak English. He growled in a particularly harsh northern dialect. Dartley knew he had to act quickly.

Acting like the complete fool, Dartley feigned great glee at being given the opportunity to photograph a policeman on the job. As the man came closer, he took Dartley by the forearm to force him down. Dartley could see the man peering into his carryall to investigate what contraband he was carrying. Human nature at its most perverse. To his horror, Dartley saw that some of the metal of the HK 95 was glinting through. It did, in fact, look like part of a lethal weapon; but of course that was impossible—how could it be? The policeman, curious, put his hand into the satchel to see what it was.

In that instant Dartley stood up on top of the guardrail with a loud "Hey, hold still, Fritz, I want to get your picture!" In one continuous action he raised the camera to his eye as if he were going to check his focus and took one step backward, pretending that, fool that he was, he'd forgotten he was standing on a guardrail by the side of the Rhine. The last thing he heard before he hit the water was the loud outcry of the cafe patrons who of course had been quietly scrutinizing the little riverside drama.

Underwater, Dartley kept his eyes closed. The river was gray with the waste of an industrial society. He had one intention and he fulfilled it expertly. That single intention was to take the gun and the box of ammunition out of his satchel and let them drop to the bottom of the Rhine. This he achieved. It was all so simple. In a flash the gun was gone. Then the ammunition. Then he let the satchel go. If it sank, fine. If not, who cared?

Dartley had forgotten about his disguise. His Anthony Weber eyeglasses and his fake mustache.

He'd forgotten he was wearing them until the Rhine washed them off his face and carried them out of sight. The cafe owner, a stocky Westphalian, threw the struggling American a rope. The rope was especially reserved for idiots like Dartley. The policeman had a double reaction; he was laughing scornfully and he was furious.

"Where is your satchel?" he asked Dartley through an interpreter.

"Oh my God!" shrieked Dartley. "My father's birthday present! I've lost my father's birthday present!" He checked to see that his back pockets were still buttoned. They were. All he needed now was fifteen minutes in a men's shop for a change of clothing. The policeman had other ideas. He insisted that, according to law, Dartley must be checked out in a local hospital. The Rhine was known to carry twenty-one communicable diseases.

"I'm fine. I'm fine. Tell him I'm fine," Dartley begged the interpreter to explain to the officer. The policeman, young and of an authoritarian bent, had other ideas.

Finally Dartley played his long shot.

"Tell him my father is in an American hospital dying of brain cancer. I came here because my father was born in Düsseldorf; he never had the money to visit it himself. I wanted pictures for him to see before he died." Dartley stopped his narrative to stifle a tear. It was difficult for him to continue. "Now the pictures are all lost. All lost," he sobbed. "The doctors called me this morning. I reserved a seat on the last plane out at four-fifteen. If I have to wait till tomorrow, it may be too late." And with that, Dartley began to weep. He wept for all of them. For Ilse de Brock, for the Russian agents at the Colonial Inn Motel, for Ali Ozker and his bodyguards, for Werner von Kelsing and Bruno Schmidt.

This time his tears were real. The late spring and early summer had been a carnival of blood; he had been the bloodletter nonpareil. In his mind's eye he saw the bodies bathed in blood, those poor human forms, those mother's boys, the women who had been little girls, dead, all dead. He thought of the orphans he had created all through his career, the wives and children he had impoverished, and he wept. Not exactly crocodile tears. He experienced true grief. After all, he was a wellspring of sorrow and a source of death for others. How could not some of the feelings rub off on him? Dartley was relieved to see he was still able to feel for the dead, even if he had summoned up his grief for reasons pertaining only to him and to his own survival.

"This man is a crackpot," he heard someone say. It was an American voice. He realized he'd gone too far.

"My father is dying and I'm late for my plane. I can't go to the hospital to get checked out. There's nothing wrong with me," he protested wearily.

"Let the poor guy go," said the voice. The voice repeated the request in German. The man turned out to be a German-American who'd returned to his homeland and joined the police force in Düsseldorf.

The rest was easy. Dry clothes and a new pair of loafers were easily obtained. When he returned to the VW, which mercifully had not been ticketed or towed, Bruno Schmidt had not arisen from the dead. At the airport Dartley left the car well locked in the airport parking lot, a speck of beige in a sea of automobiles, many of them VW vans also beige. At the TWA desk, he made a joke out of the damp passport and the missing mustache. How could there be a problem? Anthony Weber was clearly as capricious about his looks as any other man. The return flight was uneventful. At Dulles International, he explained that he'd lost his glasses and shaved his mustache. As before, the explanation was unnecessary. No one had questioned him. Why should they? He had nothing to hide and nothing to declare.

On the drive back to Frederick, Dartley felt justified. No matter what, he had not allowed life to make him a victim. Besides, if he had created the dead, he had wept for them, too. He was not inhuman. The deaths he had caused were minuscule compared to the legacy of his own century. A hundred million murdered in the wars of Europe alone. Who knows how many killed in China, in India, in the tribal wars of Africa, in the ongoing conflicts in Latin America?

"I take life as it is," said Dartley to himself. "I don't make up the laws of nature. Along with disease and ignorance, God created Man. His so-called children. He created them, us, with overwhelming greed. Thus, God, by his stupidity, has given rise to the Communist state. Fuck God—He contradicts himself."

Somewhere, Dartley thought there must be another God beyond all the invented gods. Maybe on another planet. Maybe there was no God at all, only the dark, the all-encompassing dark. In either case, he was glad he had killed whomever he had to kill in order to stay alive. Killing was better than being killed, any day.

As he drove into Frederick itself, Dartley thought maybe it was time to give Donna McCarron a call. It had been a while since he'd had a piece of American pussy, ready, willing and able. American girls—the ones who like to fuck, anyway—have fun when they fuck, he thought. That's the difference. American girls have fun. He'd had enough intensity for a while. He needed fun. He needed his mouth full of Donna's cooze. He could smell that girl across Grand Central Terminal if he had to, he thought.

The next morning, the *Post* ran an item about Werner von Kelsing, famed industrialist, found shot to death with his company psychologist. The West German police suspected foul play. The item also mentioned that von Kelsing's partner Bruno Schmidt was missing.

Dartley called Malleson. According to the information broker, nobody in Germany was looking for a mysterious American anyway. The only suspect so far was a missing employee named Gunther Herrmann.

What about Willi Reiser? Dartley had to smile at the thought of him. Later that day, from a pay phone outside The Watergate, he called Reiser's office. He left a message with his secretary. The message read: "I'll give you a week to deposit the five hundred thousand."

Reiser was, of course, immediately hunted down by aides from the German consulate in Tunisia. When they finally located him, he was on the fifth day of his vacation, holed up with his blond boy in what was once euphemistically called the Casbah. The blond boy had been ready to return to Germany on his second day. The news of von Kelsing's death and Schmidt's disappearance came as a reprieve for him.

On the morning of von Kelsing's funeral, car thieves finally broke into the VW van in the Düsseldorf airport parking lot. Schmidt's body had to be immediately cremated.

At the von Kelsing funeral, Mitzi von Kelsing did not seem to know who she was or where she was. Her son, Arne von Kelsing, had been backpacking in the Ecuadorian Andes. He arrived a week later to disclaim his inheritance in the name of Jesus Christ. Later he changed his mind and bought a villa in Palm Beach.

Reiser very definitely got the message Dartley had sent. The afternoon of the von Kelsing funeral, he deposited the half million in Dartley's Swiss account. As Mr. Savage had predicted at South

Meadow, Reiser had no desire whatsoever that the various authorities discover the plot against Ali Ozker. More than anything else, Reiser feared the Turks. He knew that if Ozker's cohorts discovered the source of their compatriot's tragedy, he would be dragged from his offices at Schiller Pharmaceuticals and literally dismembered piece by piece beginning with his most private parts.

The half million arrived. Dartley said thank you to M. Jouet. "Now I can pay my rent," he said.

As he hung up on the Swiss banker, he searched for his address book.

It's time to let by-gones be bygones, he thought. I'm going to call up Donna McCarron and invite her to dinner. She'd probably like Billy Martin's Carriage House.

"Who are you calling?" asked Charles Woodgate.

"You remember Donna McCarron from Frederick?"

"The girl who caused you so much trouble?"

"No, Uncle Charley," Dartley replied. "It's time to forgive and forget and get on with my life."

"Forgive and forget? You?" asked the astonished older man.

Dartley wasn't listening. He already had visions of a particular red-gold bush with its mouth-watering pussy.

"Hello, Donna, this is Richie. I'm sorry to bother you. I know it's late, but I wondered if you were busy tonight."